Pol Trek

Pol Trek

By the name of Polish Republic

By Luiza Dobrzyńska

PAPERBACK ISBN: 979-8-9853307-4-8

EPUB ISBN: 979-8-2011918-3-2

***

WRITTEN BY LUIZA DOBRZYNSKA

PUBLISHED BY ROYAL HAWAIIAN PRESS

COVER ART BY TYRONE ROSHANTHA

TRANSLATED BY SZYMON NOWAK

PUBLISHING ASSISTANCE: DOROTA RESZKE

***

FOR MORE WORKS BY THIS AUTHOR, PLEASE VISIT:

WWW.ROYALHAWAIIANPRESS.COM

***

VERSION NUMBER 1.00

To reinforcement of hearts and
entertainment of minds

Thanks for help in creating the characters and realities for the users of the USS Phoenix portal with nicknames: Q_, Madame Picard, Kanna, Allucard, Arek, Veronika, R'Cer, Spohkh, Dragon, FederacyjneMSZ, biter, Seybr, Elaan

Table of Contents

PROLOGUE

It happened in 2315, not very long ago, and in a galaxy not far away, and no great Empire really had a finger in it, though a few smaller ones got involved in the action over time.

A small and not very rich country on a global scale, Poland, followed the achievements of the Star Armada with genuine interest. There were not many cadets from this country in the Space Academy, because despite their courage and considerable intelligence, they were people so full of fantasy that the best drill specialists broke their teeth on them. Nevertheless, at some point the Poles concluded that they were not inferior to the rest of the United Earth - in fact, although the Earth was united as such, some state entities, as they were now called, still stubbornly defended their separateness. Among other things, it was Poland who did it, and at some point, someone there came up with the idea to build a Constans class star ship, or at least the outdated NXY, at their own cost. The latter solution was chosen, because many military surplus parts could be obtained cheaply for the NXY, and the country by the Vistula River didn't have a high budget.

However, it is always a long way from an idea to a construction, and even more so in Poland. The project, therefore, wandered through various instances, and it seemed that it would get stuck at one of the committees there, when suddenly something unexpected happened. A certain high-ranking politician, driven by a rudimentary sense of duty, after a lavish banquet, instead of home - went to the office of the Council of State and began to stamp overdue papers. Though alcohol was so buzzing in his head that he didn't even know what he was approving, later his ad hoc decisions were largely accepted. Among other things, he put a stamp on the act that allowed the construction of the ship to begin - and the military eagerly took advantage of this, as they were very keen on the prestigious undertaking.

The social assessment of the ship's construction was very different from the beginning. Part of the society even fell into euphoria, claiming that "Poland is not yet lost", since it can afford such gestures. An equally large group expressed doubts as to whether the ship could be built at all, since, as usual, half of the materials would be resold illegally. It was argued that even if the construction was completed, it remained a great question whether it would fly at all and whether it wouldn't be smashed after reaching the warp speed for the first time. There were also those who mistrusted, as well as a very serious number of those who, from the beginning of construction, meticulously drank to every stage and almost every screw that was placed, thus supplying the state budget via the monopoly department. After all, whole Poland followed the construction, and numerous stakeholders took bets on whether the construction would be completed on time and what would go wrong.

The members of the Planet Union, especially a delegation from the planet Pandoria, helped Poles in the implementation of the project. The blue-skinned race of warriors, adorned with distinctive antennae above their foreheads, from the very first contact with Earthlings, felt an inexplicable weakness for the swashbuckling, undisciplined nation of the small country on one of the continents they visited. The delegates from Pandoria willingly brokered the purchase of parts, provided plans, even gave Poland a warp reactor with paralite crystals. To everyone's surprise, this help was also joined by the most advanced members of the Union, Uoltans, a race devoid of emotions and extremely logical. They were most likely to torpedo the project, but it turned out otherwise.

Thus, despite continuous, though temporary difficulties, the construction was completed. The ship was ready at about the appointed time, didn't fall apart, and it looked not too bad. The name 'Hermash', painted in red with white stripes, flaunted in its residential and social part. To tell the truth, initially it was supposed to be called 'Hermashevski', but in the middle of painting the inscription, the company selected in the tender was examined by the prosecutor's office, which proved that the whole event had been rigged - and as a result the painting of the name was discontinued, the manager immediately emigrated and there was no time to make a new tender. The inscription remained as it was, and as a result of the change, it turned out to be asymmetrical in relation to the axis of the functional part of the ship - it gave the impression that the massive central module froze in a malicious half-smile. It, however, didn't bother anyone.

The matter of the crew was much worse. The selected officers collectively sent excuses to avoid flying under any pretext of health, and the captain himself, a few days before the planned take-off, got drunk in a bar. He caused then such a brawl that he was arrested, which, it was widely claimed, was a very skillful move on his part. The only logical solution seemed to be postponement of the take-off of 'Hermash', but it was unthinkable for the army. So, there was organized a real roundup of officers who had anything to do with space flights, and they managed to assemble the command section in an accelerated mode, but unfortunately without a captain.

After long browsing through the files, General Jaruzelski, a distant descendant of another famous general with the same surname, finally found a captain with a starship experience. It was Lilianna Zakrzevska, commanding the ground defense unit. Petite, delicate in appearance, and very slim with a long blonde braid, she looked anything but an air force commander, let alone a starship captain. Nevertheless, of all the senior officers whose candidacy lay on the general's desk, her qualifications were the best, and time was getting on.

Therefore, without playing diplomacy, the general called Captain Zakrzevska and said briefly:

"We urgently need the commander of 'Hermash'. You are a volunteer. Dismissed."

Captain Zakrzevska, brought up in a family with very long military traditions, didn't even think to protest. She saluted and within twenty-four hours was aboard the ship with hand luggage and her favorite ferret, Gizia. Now the pride of Polish technical thought was ready to take off.

I.

There were one hundred and four crew members on board 'Hermash', the vast majority of them complete novices. Most of them were tempted by a space adventure, others signed the contract out of boredom. Only the officers had experienced real, non-simulated space flights, though mostly in-system ones. Captain Zakrzevska found out about it after a very cursory study of the crew's files and looked up in mute terror.

Then she checked the skeleton crew files. It was not much better here, but still: the main medical officer turned out to be a native female Uoltan, Dr. TiShan, a young and inexperienced person, but with training at the Armada Star Academy. Commander Arkadiusz Liljew was appointed the first officer - she knew him personally, he served on a short-range ship, had been dismissed after an argument with the captain. The second officer was Lieutenant Jürgen von Ravensburg, who had participated in an internship in the Merchant Armada (it's something). The head of the scientific section was a certain Andrew Karpiel-Baguette, and his deputy and at the same time the deputy head of security - Uoltan, lieutenant commander ArCer, which proved Armada's interference in the selection of staff. Otherwise, how would have two Uoltans found themselves there? On the other hand, it was even good, as it guaranteed a bit of logic on board.

The head of the navigators was Christopher Mayher. The captain knew him personally, too - a maniacal collector of all kinds of weapons, touchy and capricious, and at the same time perhaps the only real astronaut on board, the one who had gained his skills far from the Sol system, not inside it or in a simulator. In turn, the chief engineer, Lieutenant Charles Mikhalov, had never set foot on board of a starship, except in a shipyard in orbit, during repairs. According to the file, there was no better warp and propulsion engines specialist than him, and he also had the qualifications of an antimatter engineer. However, the short note 'B.A.' in his files, indicated quite a temperament and a tendency to get into various quarrels.

Further study of the files was interrupted by the vigorous pounding on the door, which was probably intended to be a gentle knock.

"Come in!" she screamed.

The door slid open and a young boy with extraordinary dimensions, fair hair and an honest, not very intelligent face stood at the threshold.

"Let me report you," he boomed servicely. "I'm Johnnie Caterpillar, your bootblack, I will be at your ladyship's service."

"Rest," the captain replied automatically. "And rather an orderly, right? That's number one, and the second, not ladyship, but captain. Are you from Zakopane?"

"No, from Poronin, but brought up in Silesia."

"Alright. Now that you're here, come and take a look."

She took the ferret off her shoulder and put it on the table.

"Oh God, weasel," Johnnie rejoiced, coming closer. Gizia sniffed at his hand, then sat up and started washing her fur.

"Not a weasel, but a ferret," Lilianna said sternly. "This is my pet, and remember that she is untouchable. If something happens to her ... God forbid! Is that clear?"

"I swear to God, I'll take care of her like of my own kid."

"Fine ... Now check out the ship and remember to carry communicator everywhere. When I need you, I'll call you."

"Yes, sir! I mean, sir-ma'am!"

Johnnie turned back, vigorously crossed the threshold, hit the crown against the top frame, grunted "Oh God!" and disappeared down the corridor.

"What an orderly they sent me, a Silesian grunt from Giewont, it couldn't be worse," Zakrzevska chuckled silently and returned to studying the files.

They were definitely less funny than her new subordinate. According to a cursory calculation, ninety percent of her new subordinates had never been in fair outer space. Meanwhile, the Star Armada set tough demands - they had to cope without anyone's help, if they wanted to count on 'Hermash' belonging to this formation and thus, all the associated privileges. The captain was quite young, but not stupid or self-righteous. She knew well how difficult the task had been set before her, and wondered how she would be able to accomplish it with such a crew at her disposal.

She returned to the files of both Uoltans. General Jaruzelski didn't like this breed and didn't trust it an inch, so he certainly objected to their presence on board. Star Armada had its way, and what would come of it, time was to show. ArCer's files were quite uniform: wife and son, comprehensive education, many years of experience as the first officer, exemplary service record. Dr. TiShan's file, on the other hand, was like a rowdy novel. Left on Earth as a five-year-old, she grew up in Poland, in a large and cheerful family. Seven years later, she was taken to her home planet despite her opposition - so violent that a psychologist had to be hired to solve the problem. When she turned eighteen, she ran away from home and somehow smuggled herself onto a ship bound for Earth. Having returned to her foster family, she graduated from the Medical Academy in Warsaw and practiced in one of the capital's hospitals. She was known to have very amusing disposition, quite different from the usual Uoltan composure.

After reading this, Lilianna felt she was done and decided to stop reading the files. Anyway, it was high time to go to the bridge. The scheduled take-off time was approaching inexorably.

II.

If Captain Zakrzevska had looked into the engine room now, she would probably have agreed with the previous management of her chief engineer. Lieutenant Mikhalov, who had already boarded the day before, cursed like a sailor and pushed his subordinates around, personally checking each department and threatening with the most terrible consequences if he found just one screw not tight enough. Behind him there was running a joyfully pale brown creature resembling a six-legged raccoon. It was a tame vall, a kind of raccoon from the planet Mordasya, Mikhalov's favorite and the only creature he cared about.

"Boss, when our missus sees this rat, she will be furious," engineer Joseph Stelmach dared to say. "I know the officer from her unit, she's a devil, not a woman."

"You'd better check the plasma cables and don't be smart," was the reply. "For you, it's a captain, not a missus, understood? And if she tells me even one word, I get off at the nearest station and let her screw her with this wreck! This bat can rule the whole ship, but the engine room is my place, and no one will nose into it, not even Supreme Admiral of Armada. What are you looking at, fools?! Go to work, finish the review, or I will break your shanks!"

The team of engineers scattered around the engine room like frightened ants, and Mikhalov took the vall in his arms and tousled its back.

"Yes, my little one, no one here will complain about you," he muttered.

Meanwhile, the last crew members were arriving to the ship - Dr. TiShan, beastly drunk, a few soldiers from security, and the youngest helmsman, ensign Veronika Bumblebee, accompanied by a huge, shaggy dog. Like the captain, she had no one to leave her pet with and decided to discreetly sneak him aboard. Admittedly, in this case, "discreet smuggling" was not an option, because the dog weighed sixty-five kilos and it was difficult to hide it...

Technician Zdzislav Lalevich, commonly known as Dish, the head of the transport, widened his eyes in surprise at the sight of the new crew member and asked:

"And this one, where is it assigned to?"

But then he waved his hand and replied to himself:

"Actually, what the hell ... I'm paid here the same amount, no matter who I teleport."

Veronika smiled at him with a mixture of embarrassment and gratitude, while trying to look much older than her seventeen years.

"Don't tell the captain yet, okay?" she asked. "I couldn't leave Bear; I only have him."

"Sure thing. Our missus will find out too soon, anyway. But easy, baby, she came in here with a ferret on her shoulder, and the chief engineer with a vall. It will not be a ship, but a flying zoo. Anyway, it doesn't bother me." The technician returned the smile and handed Veronika her ID. The girl took it and left the transport hall, jumping, and the sheepdog ran after her, barking happily.

Another signal flashed on the console and Lalevich frowned in dissatisfaction. He didn't expect anyone anymore. Nevertheless, he entered the code, and a young woman with short black hair cut short materialized on the landing. Without getting into unnecessary discussions, she waved her assignment in front of him, took a large bag with hand luggage from the landing, grabbed the ID that was thrown to her and ran out. He checked the list once more and finally found an unchecked crew member - Second Lieutenant Malvina Krencik, Communications Department. She was close to staying on Earth. Now the crew was really complete and Lalevich could calmly sit in the chair of the technician on duty, immersing himself in his favorite book "Adventures of a good soldier Švejk".

Outside the transport hall, there was confusion - the crews were looking for their quarters, bumping into one another and trading barbs. As it turned out, no number on the assignment list corresponded to reality, the quarters were either unmarked at all or mislabeled, and finally it was necessary to call the chief quartermaster, who, furious that his nap had been interrupted, somehow disentangled this jumble. The easiest thing was with married and engaged couples, the hardest with singles who were not entitled to single accommodation. It was known in advance that there would be a reshuffle in the first days of the flight, but the idea was to accommodate everyone at least temporarily. It was possible only after several hours of lamentations, complaints and threats flying in the air like dangerous insects.

'Hermash' was finally ready for its maiden voyage.

III.

At the sight of the Captain Commander ascending the bridge, ArCer raised slightly his slanted eyebrows. It seemed to him that the ground command was kidding. Not only was Captain Mrozik, a tough and experienced man, replaced by the woman, but also by such a woman - she looked like a girl dressed for fun in a replica of her parents' uniform. To make matters worse, on her shoulder sat a lithe, short-legged animal with a flat head and a fluffy tail. ArCer had known for a long time that it was difficult to expect logic from the Earthlings, but the Poles, whom he was just beginning to get to know, knocked spots off everyone else.

He watched some of the crew discreetly. Among them was a young couple who never stopped arguing, a grim engineer talking to himself, a diplomat who ran straight to the kitchen and started cooking. And also, to his greatest displeasure, a Uoltanian doctor. She arrived on board in such a state of intoxication that her deputy, Dr. Jacob Zmiyevski, immediately put her to sleep. It would have been completely incomprehensible if ArCer hadn't known that the doctor had been brought up on Earth, in Poland, so you could expect everything from her. ArCer wasn't happy with the new assignment, but it would have been illogical to protest about it. Command knew what it was doing, assigning him to the repmobile that barely didn't fall apart. It is possible that in time he would have to take command here to save at least part of the crew. This bizarre captain didn't inspire confidence.

Lilianna was not particularly surprised to see the blue-skinned cadet by the comm console. It was foreseeable that the Pandorians, having helped so much, would impose their observer on the Poles, although the captain expected someone more experienced. The girl by the radio looked very young, and the uniform showed that she hadn't even graduated from the Academy yet. So why exactly her? The captain postponed an explanation of the matter until later. She walked steadily to the command chair, sat down on it and ... immediately slipped to the floor.

"It starts nicely," she grunted, standing up and rubbing her bruised buttocks. There was a muffled snort coming from the side of the first mate's position. Arek Liljew, a very cheerful young man, was known for his tendency to laugh and play.

"Don't laugh at someone else's fall," the captain said, and switched on her communicator. "Engine room, send someone to the bridge with a screwdriver. The command seat was not bolted to the base."

"Damn scrubs," there was heard a growl of Mikhalov, who was not very patient with his subordinates. "I'll send someone over there."

"Are the engines ready, by the way?"

"As much as anything can be ready here. It won't be better anyway. Before reaching the warp speed, I advise you to pray and say goodbye."

A mechanic from the engineering section and a black-haired girl in the uniform of the communications department ran onto the bridge at the same time. Without further ado, she drove the Pandorian from her seat and sat down at the console, apparently very pleased with herself. Now everything added up - Malvinka Krencik, called by her colleagues Malva, to whom communication on the ship was subject, according to the records, a person very disciplined and independent, but very bold.

"To what do we owe the honor of seeing you here?" Lilianna asked scathingly.

"I report, Captain, that I said goodbye to my friends, and then the shuttle refused to wait," Malvinka replied cheerfully. She clearly felt no guilt.

"Turn on your console, woman, don't upset me," growled Christopher Mayher from the controls.

"Since when are we on a first-name basis?" Miss Krencik asked rhetorically.

"No arguments on the bridge," the captain cut in, while the young engineering boy was hurriedly tightening the screws that held the command chair to the base. "Please connect me to air traffic control, Lieutenant."

Lieutenant Krencik sat down with an offended expression and called the air traffic control center.

'Hermash' reports readiness to take off," Zakrzevska said, sitting back in the armchair and concluding with satisfaction that this time nothing broke away.

"Ground control here," a loudspeaker screeched. 'Hermash', you have permission to take off. May you have high vacuum."

Christopher Mayher put his hands on the controls, and Mstislav Deadskull did the same in the co-pilot's seat. The captain crossed herself in an old-fashioned way, which caused ArCer's eyebrows to move under his typical Uoltan bangs, and ordered:

"Well, in the name of God. Forward, first stage warp speed."

***

Of course, no one expected that reaching the warp speed for the first time would be uneventful. There were gloomy considerations in the engine room as to whether the ship would fall apart immediately or only in the second minute of flight. Earlier, there was even a proposal to organize a lottery, but the project failed, because it was not known who, to whom and how would have paid in the event of a win. However, as it turned out, no one was prepared for what happened. 'Hermash' fell into turbulence, tumbled so stronly that everyone fell out of their seats, and suddenly, having straightened the trajectory, glided along the introduced course like a mad firework.

"Captain, I'm reporting that we have a 7th degree warp speed and I can't go any lower," Christopher Mayher reported with impeccable diction, while his friend was struggling with the controls, cursing up a storm in an undertone.

"Engine room, why can't we slow down?" Lilianna asked, turning on her communicator.

"The control circuit broke down, ... damn it!" Mikhalov's enraged voice shouted in the loudspeaker. "It will take a while to fix it, but if we don't hit anything, everything should be working in two hours."

"Okay, two hours is two hours ... Can you do it, Mr. Mayher?" the navigator's captain asked.

"Without struggling," assured her unfazed Christopher. "It is enough to strengthen the shields, and we will be fine."

"Engine room, put some more in covers 1."

"We already put, prophylactically before the start, and good, otherwise something would have hit us long ago," Mikhalov growled in response and broke the connection.

'Hermash' was flying forward, showing no tendency to fall into pieces, scattering around the surrounding void, despite the fact that it was only a beefed-up NXY, in addition assembled from parts obtained in various circumstances. Had it been known on Earth that this ship, instead of gently reaching the warp speed, would at once achieve the seventh stage, there would have been a bet of two hundred to one that it would collapse in the first seconds. Meanwhile, it somehow flew and did not even creak. Engineer Mikhalov kept his word - after less than two hours the regulation circuit started working and 'Hermash' gently slowed down to a reasonable speed known as the third-degree warp. At this speed, the ship finally reached a point where it was really on its own, for it was no longer protected by the network of union outposts scattered across this part of the galaxy.

"Point zero," said helmsman Deadskull.

Lilianna got up from her chair and stretched delightfully.

"Arek, you are taking over the bridge, I'm going on my rounds."

"What rounds?" ArCer wanted to ask, but refrained. The captain apparently had her own concept of command, but for now he was only supposed to observe.

Zakrzevska first of all took the elevator to the first deck, where the infirmary was located. Looking there, she saw a large crowd of lamenting crew members, each of whom, judging by the sounds made, was either gravely ill or dying. After squeezing among her people, she found Dr. Zmiyevski, who, with the help of a qualified nurse, Sister Lolita Icant, administered some injections to the patients and gave them comfort.

"What's going on, Jacob?" she asked.

"Space sickness, what else could it be?" the doctor replied. "They're all newbies. They must go through it and they will be like new."

"And where is this Uoltan?"

"She is still sleeping away the goodbye party. She came aboard in such a condition that I could have her liver operated on without anesthesia. Lolita, give me more torecanolium."

"Alright, Jacob, set them up, and in case something bad happens, report it to me. Now I have to eat something."

At the mention of food, half of the waiting people turned even greener, and one of the girls, a junior technician Tekla Watery, galloped over to the sink and vomited in front of the rest.

"Eh, civilians," the captain muttered with palpable contempt. As an air force officer, she could do stunts in a typical fighter without any stomach sensation, or fly at Mach 2 without any additional protection.

She looked in the wall mirror and pulled down her uniform. Uniforms on 'Hermash', although resembling typical Armada uniforms in shape and color, differed from them by the "stand-up collar" decorated with a white eagle on a red background and similar cuffs. Considering that she looked impeccable enough, she headed for the mess.

At a bend of the corridor, she was knocked unexpectedly by a mass of brown fur, which happily ran its tongue over her face and barked deafeningly.

"Oh, gosh," the captain grunted. "Why do the dogs here kiss me?"

Gizia, not at all embarrassed, jumped on the back of the shepherd dog, which seemed to see nothing wrong with serving the ferret as a horse.

"Bear, heel!" Veronica's breathless voice sounded from the end of the corridor. "Forgive me, Captain, he escaped me."

"You both fell off the moon," Lilianna got up, dusted off her uniform and took Gizia from Bear's back. "I would put you in custody, but if I wanted to obey the rules, I would have to send most of the crew there. You, lady, make sure that this bear doesn't eat anyone as a snack, and it will be fine."

"Yes, ma'am!" Veronika stiffened servicely, tapped with her heels and fastened the leash to Bear, which was gaping happily with his mouth. The captain casually patted him on the back and moved on.

After a few minutes she reached the mess, where, at the table in the corner, Johnnie Caterpillar, beaming, was already noshing a third plate of cabbage soup with potatoes. A cook in a white apron, casually thrown over his uniform, was pouring him a fourth in advance. After looking at the "chef", Lilianna was surprised to recognize in him Matias von Braun, assigned to the 'Hermash', specialist in diplomacy and interplanetary law.

"Mr. Matias, what are you doing here as a cook?!" she exclaimed.

"As a cook I cook," von Braun reported cheerfully. So far, there is nobody to negotiate with. For you, a steak, Mrs. Captain, or pasta with bacon?"

"Give me the pasta, just add an extra-large portion of cheese," the captain decided after a little thought.

"It's a good choice." Matias quickly mixed the freeze-dried ingredients in the dish and slipped it into the automatic synthesizer, which in a minute transformed the resulting products into a steaming casserole. He handed the plate to Lilianna, thinking at the same time that if she ate like this on a daily basis, her slight stature was indeed a miracle of nature.

"Enjoy your meal," he said kindly.

IV.

Meanwhile, in the engine room, the chief engineer was furiously picking the so-called Pawries' tube, cursing the shipyard scrubs, while his deputy, second lieutenant Gregory Brzenchyshchykievich, was repairing the damaged console.

"If I got those who assembled it, I would bite their heads off," he muttered furiously. The console resisted all attempts to make friendly contacts with it, so at last he cursed and hit the top of it with a traditional wrench. The device screeched and suddenly all the lights came on.

"Physical violence is illogical," recited a sarcastic voice in Gregory's skull.

"Shut up, SyTar," the engineer muttered. "You have no idea."

Sometimes he was fed up with this undesirable company, although he had come to terms with it a long time ago. He was one of the very few people who had a Uoltan heart implanted, adapted through a special genolocation process. His own structure was also slightly changed so that the organism would not reject the foreign heart - but the matter was bizarre for another reason. Gregory belonged to the Terra First organization, he considered other races to be of inferior species, and along with his heart (which was horrible enough) he had been unconsciously implanted with something that the earthly doctors didn't know about: Uoltan vatra, the essence of the mind of the deceased Uoltan. SyTar, to make matters worse, was an emotionally unstable, mischievous asshole - and his presence had taken its toll on the engineer at times.

Mikhalov crawled out of Pawries's tube, smeared with grease from head to toe, and looked at Gregory checking the console.

"It works?" he asked.

"For now. Because nothing is happening. As soon as the buzz starts, it will get tired and refuse to obey.

"Made in Taiwan," the chief engineer laughed. "Okay, I'm going to take a shower, keep an eye on this pack, which pretends to be a technical team, and call me in case of need."

"Yes, sir," smiled Gregory. He had the impression that he would be comfortable working with the new supervisor. They were quite alike.

Mikhalov took a long, hot shower, changed into a clean uniform and left the bathroom, followed by his inseparable vall. Already behind the door of the hygienic room, they both came across Tekla Watery, who, seeing the six-legged animal, threw herself backwards and screamed so that perhaps three surrounding decks heard her:

"Oh mommy, what is this filth?!"

"First of all, I'm not a mommy, but an engineer," Mikhalov corrected her with dignity. "Secondly, it is a vall and his name is Vuvu. And lastly, I resent a filth! You think you are a wonder? If you want to see a filth, look at the nearest mirror."

For such a compliment, of course, there was nothing for Tekla to do but give the interlocutor a bitter slap. Then she tossed her head back proudly and entered the bathroom. After a while, her indignant scream came from there:

"Something would happen to you, goddamn engineer, if you left the lavatory seat lowered?!"

"What would happen to you if you watched what you sit on, you cow?" Mikhailov shouted back victoriously, then took Vuvu in his arms and headed for his quarters. He hated when someone insulted his beloved pet, and now he was sure he wouldn't like Tekla.

V.

On the bridge, Malvinka Krencik, bored at the communications console like the devil in the belfry, switched the auxiliary line to the private channel, called one of her ex-husbands and got into a happy conversation with him. Second Officer Jürgen frowned in displeasure, but said nothing. As long as First officer was on the bridge, reaction was his task. However, Arek didn't intend to care about discipline, and he did something more interesting - eavesdropping on what happened in different rooms. Due to the rush during assembly, the internal channel was devoid of standard safeguards and after opening it at any point of the ship, you could hear what was said in the engine room, mess, infirmary ... depending on the setting. Arek chose the engine room because, as experience told him, the most interesting usually happened there.

"...why is it all in such a state?" the displeased voice growled from the loudspeaker. "Anything you touch, falls apart. Now these valves ..."

"They are Chinese," murmured the voice of Jolanta Stern, the head of the first shift.

"Chinese valves, Korean screens, computers from Taiwan, and do we have also any red Vietnamese on board?! How does it all stick together?"

"Poles assembled it, so it doesn't fall apart."

"It's good that at least the warp reactor and antimatter hardware were given to us by the Pandorians because I don't know if we would have left orbit in one piece. In addition, that woman on the bridge who pretends to be a captain ..."

"Are you sexist?"

"No, I'm not! But I will not be commanded by someone who pee while sitting."

"I don't know what you will do with it, will you get off and come back to Earth using rocket hitchhiking or on a comet?"

"Well, the matter is lost in advance, but this is the first and the last time."

"Are you a bachelor?"

"I think it's obvious!"

"Well, it's no wonder that you still have some illusions."

Arek, amused, switched the intercept to the mess for security soldiers.

"... Have you seen that Negro, who works in the science department?"

"Seriously? Probably as an experimental monkey. What he is doing here? It's a Polish ship ..."

"A Negro can also be a Pole, no worse than you or me."

"You're raving, man. I have no prejudices, but asphalt should be on a street."

"If the missus hear you, you will be scrubbing the decks with a toothbrush."

"I'm not sca... Oh, Captain, welcome!"

There was a rustle in the loudspeaker as if dozens of chairs had been pushed back.

"Rest," it was the voice of Captain Zakrzevska. "Where's Lieutenant Gvizdak?"

"Somewhere nearby ... I mean ... We don't know exactly, Captain ... I mean, we haven't seen her at all. We are just thinking who should lead us ..."

"If it turns out that she stayed on Earth, then after returning, I will hit this Gvizdak in the ear so much that she will remember it for a whole year. Who is replacing her?"

There was a murmur of uneasy voices, but somehow no one wanted to speak.

"What's wrong with you, has a cat gotten your tounges?!" the captain roared. "Alright, so far you are commanded by Mr. ArCer. He's a Uoltan, but God forbid, you complain about that, understood?!"

"But ... but ... why is a Uoltan here, captain? We can manage ourselves ... A person like him probably tells you to breathe on command ... and for a smile on duty, he will send you to the detention center ..." spoke worried voices.

"And good. You'll need some discipline, you gypsum heads, because what I'm seeing here is a Pornion brothel, not security! What am I saying, in a brothel, there is an order and all the green bitches there go like clockwork ... Learn from them, you wonderful cows!"

There was much more of it, with an unusual flowery, and Jürgen stared at the loudspeaker, unsure whether he should have reacted somehow (for example, turned it off) or not. Arek covered his mouth with his hand to restrain from laughing, and ArCer, who, of course, had heard it all too, raised his eyebrows and shook his head slightly. His grade regarding the situation he found himself in, worsened with each minute. On receiving this assignment, his supervisor had warned him:

"You will find yourself surrounded by people who don't like Uoltans, and who are also very temperamental. It will be difficult for you, but please persevere at your post and not resort to solutions that will be logical, but will put you in the role of a usurper. Now he understood why he had been warned in this way, but for now he didn't take any action.

The light on his console flashed a little red, signifying a break. He decided to leave. There was nothing to do on the bridge anyway. He only stood behind the science officer, breathing down his neck. He was about to take up duties of a security chief ... He didn't know much about it, but he had completed combat training. Now he stepped into a quick-elevator and went to the deck where the security station was located. He passed by the captain in the doorway, nodded at her, then stepped inside.

There was the same commotion in the room as during the captain's entrance.

"Sit down," he ordered. "I'm Commander ArCer, and I am here on the orders of Star Armada HQ. On the captain's orders, I also fulfill duties of a security commander. I'm asking everyone to introduce themselves now."

He thought that this type of behavior would be more acceptable to these people. Everyone presents stood up and said their name. The Uoltan quickly caught the one who had expressed his racist views, but so far hadn't shown it.

"Thank you. Now what our work will look like. Everyone will be divided into four groups. Three-shift work system. If necessary, the group first and second, and third and fourth will come together and work twenty-four hours. Since there isn't much to do for now, the fourth group goes to sleep and will show up here in the morning. The fourth group includes ..." here he listed the names of six security members, and then gave the division into the other two groups. "Group four can go out."

He waited for the soldiers he indicated to leave, then told the other two groups what to do. They were to scan all decks for all possible bombs and wiretaps. Then he ordered all but one man to march away.

"And, you, Mr. Hob," he said to the short, broad-shouldered blonde, "will take a toothbrush and report to engineer Mikhalov to clean Pawries' canals."

The blonde's eyes widened and he whispered only:

"Why?"

"You made it happen yourself. Maybe you will stop feel like expressing your views out loud about the skin color or origin of the other crew members. That's all. March off."

ArCer didn't know that everyone on the bridge was listening to his speech. They were very curious to know what the Uoltan might have come up with. Now they knew, and they exchanged amused remarks in an undertone, and Christopher Mayher, though generally taciturn, said his opinion quite aloud:

"If you give a mouse a cookie, he will always ask for a glass of milk."

"Sie Navigator, Ich bitte dich, so etwas nichts zu sagen," Jürgen admonished him.

"He's right," Malva said rebelliously from her seat. "Why does this pointy-eared man care about what our soldiers talk about, and privately?"

"Why the hell did they get us lumbered with him?" added technician Joseph Watery from the machine room console.

"Everyone burdens with what they can - the headquarters, with the Uoltan, and you, with your wife ..."

"Leave Mrs. Tekla alone. She has the appropriate qualifications and will be helpful during the trip."

"Yeah, and half of this ship will hear your quarrels every night ..."

"I prefer her to cuckold me here than on Earth. It will be closer when I have to hit somebody in the face."

While there was this rather unnatural conversation going on on the bridge, ArCer left the security section and found the black crewman from the science department.

"Are you Polish?" he asked. The man's eyes widened in surprise.

"Yes, but my father is from Africa. Somalia to be exact. My name is Jarek Nbeba."

"So don't let others humiliate you, Ensign," the Uoltan said enigmatically, then headed for the speed-elevator, smiling slightly to himself.

Nbeba looked at him and muttered to himself:

"You will be very surprised ..."

He had his reasons not to say that he was not actually a crew member, but a passenger...

VI.

Johnnie Caterpillar finished his meal, then, pleasantly lazy, he continued his "sightseeing trip", peering wherever he could. He had already seen the department of cartography and data analysis, from which he had been chased off unceremoniously, because he had interrupted strip poker. He entered the engine room, where he got acquainted with the deputy chief engineer - Greg judged from the first sight that this kind-hearted bully was not a threat, but he could be a good friend, and treated him in a friendly manner. Straight from his room, Johnnie went to the research department, and on the way, he came across Andrew Karpiel-Baguette, who was walking carefully, holding onto the wall, with his expression indicating a giant hangover. It was indeed so. Andy had worshiped his departure with his friends for so long, so zealously, and so deeply that he now wished he had been hanged forty-eight hours earlier.

"Hello, officer!" Johnnie roared in the best faith. Andy groaned and gripped the communication panel on the wall, feeling as if his poor head had been about to explode.

"Gosh, boy, be quieter," he muttered, barely moving his lignified tongue. Nevertheless, his accent was clearly audible and pointed to a highlander. "Right away, I will be completely sick. I drank something yesterday ... to be honest, a little too much and fell down. I don't even know how I got here."

"Oh, I understand," Johnnie nodded with understanding, very glad that he had tracked his compatriot from Giewont. "Officer, I have a good medicine for it, which my father gave me for the journey. It's his moonshine, it has seventy percent. I swear to God, such hair of the dog is the best for a hangover. Have a drink, you'll recover, sir."

He handed Karpiel a flat bottle in which something splashed pleasantly. Karpiel took it with a trembling hand and took a big sip. After a while his head grew lighter, his thoughts began to settle in some more reasonable order, and the nightmarish nausea calmed down and ceased to threaten "a violent outburst of emotion," as people in his home research institute used to say.

"Oh boy, your old man is a genius," he said, gasping for breath. "I haven't drunk such a moonshine since my visit to Ukraine ... Thank you, I owe you my life."

"My fun," Johnnie smiled, taking the flask from his hands. "If there was any appropriate place here, I could assemble a moonshine machine. I know the recipe like a prayer."

"I'll let you know when I find a quiet place, and we'll both take care of it," Andy promised him, feeling that he was completely regaining his balance.

He already remembered the whole party, including the dance of the green-skinned girl who had jumped out of the cake, the firework display, and the march with torches to the transmission station, the staff of which, frightened by such an invasion, called the police. He even remembered hazily that after the transfer, some curly blonde shouted at him in the transport hall:

"How could you get on the platform in such a state?!"

And his semiconscious answer:

"Co ... colleagues helped ..."

Teleportation in a drunken state was strictly forbidden, but of course hardly anyone cared about it. This boy from the transport hall also snaped his fingers at the whole matter and simply ordered two privates from the security to transport the completely drunk officer to his cabin. The privates did this, put him on the bed, and even took off his shoes, showing a great deal of understanding for human weaknesses. The question is whether the captain would have been equally understanding.

Suddenly the lithe, short-legged animal flashed down the corridor.

"Oh god, weasel, my missus will beat the shit out of me!" Johnnie screamed at the top of his lungs, and ran after the amused ferret.

"If you chase her, she will run away even faster!" Andy shouted to him, but Johnnie had already disappeared from view, so he waved his hand and went where he was going from the beginning - to the research department. He was to have an extremely unpleasant conversation with Professor Dinosław Trekovsky - the gray eminence of the department. He knew in advance that the man always did what he wished. He was the star of two institutes, a genius, as people said, but Andy strongly suspected that both of these institutes had gotten drunk completely with delight when Trekovsky had been delegated to board the Hermash. Working with him had been like a minefield dance, and there was no reason to believe that it would be any different in space than on Earth.

VII.

When Greg saw the heavily built blonde who stood in front of him armed with a toothbrush, he asked in confusion before he thought:

"Are you a dentist?"

"No. Ensign Hob, at your service," the blond replied in a dejected voice. "Commander ArCer sent me here to clean the Pawries' Channel."

"Excuse me ... what do you need a toothbrush for then?"

"Well, that's what I'm supposed to clean with, as ordered."

"What?!"

"Well, because I said that we don't need a Negro here ... and I also called him asphalt ... And Mr. ArCer wants to wean me off such lousy views."

"Look at him, what a pointy-eared hotshot," the engineer snorted angrily. "Take a normal machine and go into the tunnel with it, and with this brush, just scrub the surface for order. Mr. ArCer will not rule in the engine room, here the orders are given by me or Mr. Mikhalov."

"What will he say to that?"

"Does he need to know? I won't tell him, it's probably clear. Damned cold-blooded logicians, they get on everyone's case, though no one asks them to do it. They should guard their planets ..."

"And vice versa," said the voice of SyTar in his skull, but this time Greg didn't pay attention to him.

Ensign Hob relaxed visibly and even smiled.

"Yes, sir," he said arresthtly, took the automatic mop handed to him and walked with it into Pawries' tunnel, singing happily:

"Poland is not lost yeeet

while the chicken is in the pot!

When the chicken is coooked

each of us will eat one knob."

The engineer Brzenchyshchykievich smiled to himself at this free reworking of the national anthem, and returned to his work in a much better mood.

Meanwhile, Johnnie Caterpillar made efforts to catch up with the playful Gizia, who was zipping happily along the corridors, waving her fluffy tail. Finally, he managed to corner her and grab her by the neck.

"Easy, don't bite," he said gently. "Be a nice weasel ... that is, not a weasel, but a fry or something like that ... You run away, and your mistress will be angry with me."

Gizia climbed onto his shoulder, sat down there, and began washing her face with both paws. She seemed completely unabashed.

The highlander thought for a moment what to do with this crib, then he went in search of the captain. She had been in the security section recently, and now? He asked the encountered patrol, looking for all suspicious devices with handheld scanners, but the only advice he got, would have been very difficult to implement. The one who gave it was furious for some reason and clearly lacked knowledge of human anatomy. Fortunately, shortly afterwards Johnnie came across Veronika, who was just going to the bridge.

"The captain is in the conservatory," the girl said cheerfully and scratched Gizia's head. "He is just scolding our gardener because he forgot to take the seedlings from the Earth."

"Thank you, miss." Johnnie smiled and headed towards the conservatory.

The stocky black man in the uniform of the science section passed him on the way. Johnnie turned around to look at him and, without noticing engineer Mikhalov, bumped into him with all his weight.

"You goddamn elephant, watch your step! Mikhailov yelled, picking himself up from the floor. "Where have you lost your eyes; you baboon kicked in the ass?! You think this is the Gobi Desert?! People walk here, you have to be careful!"

"Officer, I didn't want to, the black guy surprised me ..." Johnnie began to explain, and at that moment he saw Vuvu. "Oh, what is this weirdo? Kitty Kitty ..."

"You must have lost your marbles, it's not a cat," Mikhailov's anger began to wear off when he noticed that the fair-haired, merry-mouthed giant looked at his Vuvu with sympathy and extended his hand to him without fear.

"I know that, Officer, he has a different face and six legs ... but I don't know how to call one like that."

"Vuvu, after sniffing his hand, concluded that this big guy didn't endanger him, and snorted friendly. Gizia, sitting on Johnnie's shoulder, squawked in response and began to twist restlessly.

"Yours?" Michałow asked.

"No, it's our missus' ... I mean Miss Captain. Gosh, I was to find her! I'm sorry, I have to go."

Johnnie galloped towards the conservatory with such haste as if he had been competing in the Velká pardubická steeplechase run.

"You know, Vuvu," Mikhailov said to his favorite. "I think I will be comfortable on this ship. I will definitely not be bored here." Then he moved on.

VIII.

Malvinka Krencik was so bored at the communications console that she finally decided to take a break. She summoned Inga Lausch to her place, then went to the mess. On the way, she almost ran into a man in the uniform of the engineering department, followed by a six-legged creature, merrily jumping.

"Oh gosh, what is it?!" she exclaimed, stopping.

"Vall, a rodent from a very distant planet," the man told her proudly. "I bought it from Savinius Jones, an interstellar dealer, when he visited Earth during his journey. I'm Charles Mikhalov, the chief engineer on this garbage truck. And you miss, who are you?"

With clear pleasure, he looked at the black-haired person with a cheerful demeanor, and in addition pleasing to the eye.

"Malvina Krencik, for friends Malvinka or Malva, to choose from. I manage the communication.

"Well, at the moment you are probably headed elsewhere..."

"It was boring, so I decided to eat something. Wow, he's nice."

She crouched down and rubbed Vuvu's back until he purred happily and finally fell on his back, waving all six paws in the air. Mikhailov smiled with satisfaction. He already had at least two people on board that he wouldn't argue with. It's something, and on top of that this girl, um ... he liked her. And it was a certain sensation, because in general, for him all women, except Jolka Stern, were stupid cows. If not worse.

***

On the bridge, Christopher Mayher handed over the main reins to Mstislav Deadskull. His place in the co-pilot's seat was taken by a young girl with light red hair, and Mayher went down to the mess. He took a portion of the steak and fries and went to his place, for he didn't like to eat in a company larger than two. Previously, when he had been one of the pilots of the USS Rodan, he had been considered the most unsociable guy on board. However, his skills had been valued, and the captain of the sister USS Gojira had even claimed that such a good pilot should have joined the army and flown in some combat squadron.

"Commanders would have turned gray in one day, as if they had such pilots who only obey their own orders," said Captain Zakrzevska when she heard about it, but she was the first to support Mayher's candidacy for the chief navigator of 'Hermash'.

They had known each other since childhood and even made their first long-haul training flight together - for Lilianna, then only a second lieutenant, it was her only such flight.

Chris was just finishing eating when someone knocked on the door. The bell system, of course, didn't work, how could be otherwise?

"Come in!" he exclaimed dissatisfiedly.

Someone kicked the door that didn't seem to open, then swung it open by hand to the accompaniment of colorful curses. Mayher recognized the voice of Captain Zakrzevska and smiled slightly. He didn't know the greater and sassier vixen, and yet she was the only woman he felt at ease with.

"How are you, Chris?" she asked when she finally managed to get in and collapse freely on the sofa. "What's up? Do you still sleep with the Beretta under your pillow?"

"Now with a mazer. You know I like to feel safe."

"I know, and really well ... because it isn't security if you don't have a whole arsenal at hand."

"Exactly ... will you let me decorate the walls with my collection?"

"How did you smuggle it in? It's forbidden. Never mind, don't tell me, I don't want to know. Hang on the walls whatever you want, even a cannon from the cruiser Aurora."

The navigator smiled again at the nonchalant statement. The captain was not famous for blind obedience to regulations, and the soldiers from her unit used to say that although she screamed a lot, if something bad happened, she always took her people's side.

"Is it true you slapped Admiral Cormack?" he asked as he forked the last fry. "The soldiers from your unit said: "Our old ass isn't scared even of the biggest shots; you should have seen her hit in the face the top admiral of Star Armada himself ...""

"It has already spread, huh? The old coot deserves it. Supposedly, he came for an inspection and was decent, and he suddenly felt like pinching the Polish soldier. She's out of his league. He will remember my hand for a long time."

They both laughed. Lilianna, brought up practically in the military unit - her father was an aviation major, and her mother one of the military pilots - had been familiar with the military language from childhood and no curses impressed her. She knew what her soldiers called her among themselves, and was aware that it was simply the female equivalent of the 'Old geezer' epithet, which was bestowed on usually liked commanders. The Polish army had not changed much in this respect since the times of Švejk.

"But they gave you command."

"Because there was no other candidate. Only I had passed an interstellar flight test and somehow no one cared that I was on board as a "bottle washer" and not as a board officer."

Christopher thought with a certain nostalgia about those days. Well, now at least they were serving together again. It was the plus of the whole situation.

IX.

The pleasant conversation about the old days was interrupted by the squeal of her personal communicator.

"What do you want?!" she shouted to the small device.

"Captain, ship course on an asteroid!" Arek's excited voice reported. "I mean, the ship on course's asteroid! I've wanted to say ..."

"I know. I guess. I'll be on the bridge right away. Over and out."

She turned off her communicator, jumped up from the sofa, and ran out. She burst into the first elevator she encountered, moved the start-up lever, and commanded loudly:

"The bridge."

The elevator moved with a creak just to stop right after. The captain tried to start it by hand, then cursed with utmost passion, climbed onto the railing halfway up the elevator, and opened the top hatch. She had a choice - wait for someone to fix the elevator or try to get to the bridge via an alternative route. She chose the latter. She managed to climb up the safety rope to the opening of the ventilation tunnel, and after a long crawl, having broken the grate, she grovelled onto the bridge as a crumpled and dirty victim of fate. Everyone presents, including the composed ArCer, stared at her.

"What?" she grunted, getting up and wiping her face with the sleeve of her uniform, which, by the way, was counterproductive. "That stupid elevator broke down in the middle of the way. What is this asteroid?"

"It's big," Jürgen replied succinctly. "And according to our readings, it's not an asteroid at all, it's a spaceship."

"For sure?"

"Well, unless asteroids are hollow and contain nitronium," Arek cut in, bravely fighting a giggle. He found the view of the captain dirty with grease extremely amusing, but it was not proper to show it openly.

"There's more to it. This asteroid is not flying along a blind course, but in a planned manner," reported ArCer, leaning over the long-range scanner. Somehow, he looked now like the famous Spox from the USS Superprice. He had similar, economical movements and the same manner of speaking, as well as was characterized by the same dignity and self-control. Among others, due to this reason, a large part of the crew had felt a violent reluctance towards him from the beginning.

"Ha!" Captain Zakrzevska wondered, then looked at the helmsmen. "Mr. Deadskull, Miss Bumblebee, interception course. We will examine this quasi-asteroid. Scout composition: me, Mr. Jürgen, Mr. ArCer. Mr. Liljew, you are taking over the bridge. I am going to change into something less dirty, and gentlemen, I'm asking you to prepare universal suits for the three of us. The devil knows what we will encounter there."

"If I may, Captain, you shouldn't go on such a dangerous reconnaissance," ArCer said. "The captain's place is on the ship. The Star Armada regulations have recently been revalued and ..."

"Liar, liar, pants on fire," interrupted the captain. "For now, I'm in charge here. Please stop jawing and report to the transporter."

ArCer's eyebrows twitched, but he controlled himself quickly. If this woman wanted to die, maybe it would be for the best. It would have been safest for the entire crew if he had taken charge.

The captain went down to the third deck through one of the Pewries' emergency tubes (she preferred not to trust the elevator this time), washed quickly, and changed into a clean uniform. She took a moment longer to connect to the engine room and have them check all the elevators, then headed to the transport hall. For the first time she had a chance to see it from the outside, previously she had left it in a hurry and hadn't looked back at the door. It was only now that she saw that it was decorated with a huge inscription "Ferdynand Kiepski Transport

Hall". The shipyard workers must have had a sense of humor - she had already noticed that above the security station there was an inscription "13th Station", and above the dining room - "L is for Love". She suspected that there were many more such inscriptions on the ship and decided to write them all down when she returned from the reconnaissance. Now, she had to explore this peculiar asteroid.

X.

ArCer and Jürgen were waiting in the transfer hall. Both of them had already prepared universal suits - such ones that protected against radiation and other unpleasantness - as well as basic reconnaissance kits.

"Why are you standing like the wives of Lot?" the captain scolded them. "Dress up, now."

She coiled her braid into a makeshift knot so that it could fit under her helmet, and quickly put on her suit. Both men followed her without saying a word, not wanting to expose themselves to further shots.

"Dish, calculate the transport parameters to the interior of this counterfeit asteroid. Keep targeting and be ready for our every call," the captain instructed the technician as she stepped onto the platform.

"Easy, dress, I know my job, they didn't give me the diploma for waving a broadsword," Dish growled, flicking switches on the console.

ArCer barely stopped himself from lifting his eyes skyward (which would have been difficult since he had only the transmission room canopy above him). Not only was the captain here, well, unusual - the entire crew seemed to be worth her.

"Did you give instructions in case you don't come back?" he asked, standing next to Lilianna.

"Don't sorrow for that," she replied sarcastically. "And in that case, I don't advise you to try to take command. Nobody will listen to you."

"I don't want to take command at all."

"It's not about what you want, but what seems logical to you. Logic is not in fashion among Poles, and if the crew came to the conclusion that you wanted to lead, you would be in trouble. Dish, transport!"

The reconnaissance party materialized beneath the surface of the artificial asteroid, which inside, indeed, looked quite peculiar. It was like a maze of tunnels with a lot of scrap metal. Interestingly, the lighting worked there, although they couldn't see its source. Jürgen turned on his scanner, the only one he trusted. It was his personal equipment, not an assigned South Korean trash composed of parts from different manufacturers, but a solid device.

"Captain, I'm recording life signals," he said after a moment. "They are quite peculiar; this configuration is not in the database ... but next to it we also have a clearly Uoltan signature!"

He looked at ArCer, aimed the scanner at him, then back in the previous direction.

"Yes, no doubt," he confirmed. "This is a Uoltan, in very bad physical condition."

Lilianna turned on her communicator.

"Hermash, how do you hear me?" she asked.

"Excellently, Captain," Inga Laush squeaked from the comm console. "I'm reporting that the first mate is molesting me!"

"It doesn't matter. Hit him in the face, and he will stop. Keep targeting the reconnaissance party and don't you dare lose us, is that clear?"

"Yes, ma'am. Mr. Arek, what are you doing ...?"

"Arek, stop or after my return I will send you to wash dishes! Please molest the crew members after hours of duty, understood?!"

"Yes, Captain!" Lilianna turned off her communicator and looked around carefully. Her scanner, though a mere allotment scrap, also picked up life signals. They came from somewhere on the lower decks, where there was a deep well, probably a remnant of some dismantled elevator.

"We're going down," she decided. "I go first."

"Why?" ArCer blurted out.

"Firstly, because I am an experienced mountaineer, and secondly, so that you have something to ask about."

ArCer, resigned, fell silent. He waited for the captain to come down, clinging to the tunnel ledges, and when she was safely on the bottom, he followed her. The last one to descend was Jürgen, who was not a great fan of climbing, but he knew what to do.

On the lower deck, the signals were much stronger, and there was more order there. "Record everything," she instructed the officers, and began to look around carefully.

On the sides of the corridor there were open rooms, interestingly, adapted to humanoids. One of them was a sort of locker full of what appeared to be portions of food. Scanners classified the frozen tissue as organic - vegetable, something between fungus and lichen, rich in nutrients. In another room, the scout noticed something strange - some object that emitted a bioelectric field but, according to the scanner, was not a living thing. It resembled a surreal sculpture made of translucent, multi-colored elements, glowing with point lights, irresistibly reminiscent of controls.

"It would be worth investigating," Jürgen observed. "It doesn't come from any known planet, and it seems to be a mechanical device. Our science department should check it."

"Radiation?"

"Doesn't show."

"Okay, if we can, we'll take this thing to research. For now, let's find this Uoltan and see what beings imprison him or her."

"We don't know if the Uoltan is a prisoner. There are no logical premises to think so," ArCer said calmly, forgetting that he had promised himself not to say anything else.

"Of course. The Uoltan got in here and voluntarily drove themselves to a critical condition. It is a truly logical conclusion." Lilianna snorted contemptuously and moved forward, guided by the ever-stronger signals of life. But when she saw what was emitting, she literally threw herself backwards.

The creatures resembled jellyfish, rather large and solidly built. Their translucent bodies pulsed with changing colors, and it seemed that they could form different organs, depending on their needs. At the sight of the intruders, they froze at first, as did they.

"These grunges are staring at us," Jürgen whispered in horror.

"I'm wondering with what," the captain whispered back.

The beings suddenly moved and merged into one shapeless mass, threateningly bristled with hair-thin protrusions that hadn't been seen before.

"Fascinating, they must be nematocysts with some poison?" ArCer, as usual, approached the matter scientifically.

"I suggest not checking," the captain reached for a mazer.

At the sight of the weapon, the combined creatures retreated as if in panic.

"They know what it is and react like thinking beings. We must not hurt them, the Uoltan said firmly. "They are not in the databases, although they come from this galaxy. Maybe it's a species that is almost extinct ..."

"If they get us, we will be extinct. Don't talk nonsense, ArCer. I'm not going to hurt them, but I want to get your compatriot out of here, and possibly in one piece."

The captain strode forward, raising the mazer menacingly. The creatures parted ways and scattered around. Their reaction did indicate a certain level of intelligence, though it was hard to tell what. In any case, they definitely knew and feared weapons.

"They're in charge here?" Jürgen asked ArCer.

"There's no evidence of that," replied the Uoltan. "This ship was built for humanoids, not for amorphous creatures like these. However, their behavior indicates considerable intelligence, although it is difficult to determine now whether they are social animals or a rational race. Though ..."

Certain markings on the walls and rounded concavities here and there indicated different conclusions. An image began to loom in ArCer's mind, but still indistinct and lacking many elements. The ship was definitely not Earthly or Uoltan. However, the registration of the scanner indicated a nitrogen-oxygen mixture, as well as a large admixture of aliphatic ethereal compounds with a clearly organic structure ... In other words, if it had not been for the suits, they would have been able to breathe freely, but they would have certainly been surrounded by an unbearable stench.

"Here's the computer panel!" Jürgen cried suddenly, peering into one of the side rooms. "I'll see what I can download from it."

"I will take care of transporting the object we found to Hermash," ArCer turned on the communicator and gave several commands to the research section. Then he began to diligently inspect the walls and take samples for research. His suspicions were starting to crystallize.

"Hey, you there! Should I honk at you?!" the captain shout was suddenly heard in the communicators. "Move your wretched asses! I found this Uoltan and he need to be taken out of here right now!"

Both men ran into the dilapidated but still habitable cabin. On what might have been considered a bed, a young boy lay limp, covered in tatters that were hard to identify, but which must once have been the uniform of a Star Armada cadet, for the badge on his chest was still visible. The boy's long hair was matted, and his body thin and dirty. On his skin there were gray-green stains, as if from suckers.

"He's alive, but barely," Lilianna said. "Judging by the readings, he's been unconscious for days. On his skin there is the same substance that the bioscaner recorded in the structure of these creatures in the corridor."

"Does that mean they ...?" Jürgen ran out of breath.

"We don't know what that means, but we're taking him out of here anyway." The captain took out her communicator and tuned it up a bit. "Dish, are you there? Four people for transportation. Get ready. And let the medical team be waiting for us."

ArCer picked up the unconscious boy in his arms. It seemed to him that the kid weighed nothing, and he could hardly resist the urge to take off the gauntlet and touch his temple. He was eager to find out what had happened here, and connecting minds was the easiest way. He had to wait, however.

XI.

"Captain!" Jürgen called from the next room. "Please take a look!" Lilianna left ArCer with the young Uoltan and walked over to him. Jürgen pointed to the floor. There lay the corpses of humanoid creatures in various states of decay, some quite fresh. The captain looked at her officer. His face, visible through the glass of his helmet, was as pale as paper, despite the fact that he bravely tried to remain calm.

"Write down the bearings, Second," she ordered. "At least a few of these bodies will have to be examined. We will find out why they died and how these jellies contributed to it. For now, let's go to ArCer, they'll bring us aboard."

Having materialized on the landing, Captain Zakrzevska immediately became furious, because the ordered medical team had not yet deigned to show up.

"Medical team to the transport hall!" she roared into the communicator. "Is anyone there, damn it?!"

"I gave what was needed," said Dish cautiously, "and to Dr. TiShan herself."

"And what did she say?"

"She said: Get lost, you moron."

"Was she sober?"

"No. It is impossible to live sober."

"Medical team, damn it!!!" the captain screamed a second time.

The hall door slid open and two paramedics with a wheeled cart and a very nervous doctor Zmiyevski marched inside.

"I'm sorry, ma'am, but we've had summons from all over the ship since the morning, and all were fake," he said in a tone of excuse. "That burns me up."

"Is Dr. TiShan in working order?" Lilianna asked sternly, taking off her suit.

"Of course. However, her humor is terrible, because half of her luggage, as it turned out, remained on Earth." The doctor helped ArCer put the unconscious boy on a wheelchair. "Gallop with him to the diagnostics ward."

ArCer took off his suit, folded it meticulously, handed over his gun, and headed for the bridge, where the captain had just scolded the first mate.

"Captain, may I go to the infirmary?" he asked. "I graduated from the Uoltan Academy of Sciences at several faculties, including medical one ... I can be useful in the examination."

The captain, who didn't like being interrupted while scolding someone, glared at him. She hated Uoltans and didn't trust them, but ArCer showed concern for his countryman, which she understood and supported, so she waved her hand and said shortly:

"March off, Commander."

ArCer left the bridge and went to the infirmary, where in the doorway he collided with a young representative of his race, shaky and agitated in a way completely inappropriate for a Uoltan. He held her shoulders.

"I heard you were drunk," he said sternly. "And I think you haven't sobered up so far. You disgrace your planet."

The doctor freed herself from his hands.

"Please leave me alone," she hissed. "You are not my supervisor and I won't explain myself to you."

ArCer smelled alcohol on her, but suddenly realized it was just cologne - an aggressive scent eagerly used by earthly women.

He had no idea what for. He had never smelled anything like that on a Uoltanian woman, and to be honest he didn't like the habit.

"Go to your quarters and rest, I'll take care of the patient," he said disapprovingly.

"Back off at last. Why do you stick it to me?" TiShan glared at him, pushed him away from the door and entered the infirmary, where Dr. Zmiyevski was examining the asteroid boy. She walked over and delicately stroked his matted hair.

"Don't die, SiWok," she whispered.

XII.

Andrew Karpiel-Baguette was amazed at the device that had been brought from the mysterious asteroid. He had no idea which side to examine it from.

"I wouldn't be surprised if it turned out that it was bred, not built," he muttered to himself. A detailed scan showed a multi-polymer structure and, to Andy's relief, no trace of the typical signals of life. He walked around the device. According to the scanners, it contained something like a database of about eight hundred gigabytes. The problem was that although you could scan it at will, it said nothing about how to get this strange device working. So far, Andy simply couldn't do it.

Mikhalov, disheveled and sleepy, burst into the warehouse. An urgent call roused him from his first sleep, which he didn't like very much, but at the sight of what Andy was just examining, he got tongue-tied.

"What's that?" he asked, having found his voice.

"According to all data, it's a computer, although its creators had nothing to do with any known rational race," replied Karpiel. "I managed to establish that it is not alive anyway ... that is, it won't die if you don't feed it in time, and won't bite off someone's hand. Still, I have no idea how to get it running, or even how it works."

Mikhalov walked over to the device and inspected it carefully, trying to control himself not to kick it to see how it would have reacted. He touched the casing. It felt like a hardened ballistic gel. He pressed it a little harder, and then the outer plate suddenly twitched and slid down, revealing rows of round bumps. Mikhalov realized at once that these were sensor buttons that started individual programs. He connected to the bridge and smiled with satisfaction at the hearing of the voice of Malvinka, who had already returned to the comm console.

"Lovely, could you tell the captain that this is undoubtedly a computer?" he said sweetly. "The building material used is multi-polymers, as our egghead says. Reacts to changing pressure. I mean the computer, not Karpiel, anyway the devil knows, he would probably react to something like that, too, although maybe it depends where you would press him. We'll try to get the data from what the hard drive replaces here, but it'll be a child's play compared to decoding it. How have you understood me, over?"

"I've understood it well. Keep working, boys, the captain is not in the best mood."

"As far as I know, she has always been like that."

Michałow turned off the communicator and went back to examining the unusual computer.

Meanwhile, in the outpatient clinic, the medical team was finishing the examination of the young Uoltan. His body seemed very emaciated, although the same substances as on the skin were found in the blood - and no bacteria or viruses. It was very strange.

"He's alive fortunately," Dr. TiShan said, reviewing the results. "Although with such an advanced anemia, it is unusual."

"Could this substance X act as a biostat?" ArCer asked.

TiShan nodded.

"Very likely. But I still don't understand much of it."

"Maybe the humanoid section, brought from the asteroid, will help? Or maybe trying to connect minds? I'd do it myself, but I think you know this boy, so that better be you."

TiShan shook her head, and horror flashed in her eyes. She clearly had a bad experience with this ancient technique, which isn't so weird. Incorrectly made connections could cause the most fatal injuries and lead to disorders that were not easy to treat. ArCer felt his initial dislike of the young doctor fade away. He even thought that he must have misjudged her. She was badly brought up, it is a fact, but still, she probably had grounds for not very normal behavior for a Uoltan.

"I'll lead you," he said softly. "It is not dangerous or unpleasant if the connection is made in the right way."

"You don't understand, I can't ... You do it."

"Alright," he decided that it would be better to postpone the analysis of the doctor's inhibitions until later. "But tell me how do you know him?"

"Yes ... no ... I mean ... I knew him when he was a little boy. I took care of him on planet Uoltan. He's the neighbors son. I was very close to him, but I haven't seen him since ... I left the house."

ArCer reasonably refrained from voicing his opinion on the adolescent girl leaving arbitrarily her family house. He knew from the records that TiShan's parents were not the most caring - it is outrageous that the flesh-and-blood Uoltans had left their child for five years among the people and had not even taken an interest in her during that time? No wonder the girl was irreversibly contaminated.

"Okay, I'll take care of SiWok," he said amicably. "And you do an autopsy on one of those bodies that were sent to the lab. Maybe we'll find out something."

XIII.

"Sir-ma'am, I've been looking long for you ..." Johnnie strode onto the bridge with the ferret on his shoulder, clearly lost and unhappy.

"Corporal, I've been looking for you, and you are here," Arek muttered amused.

Captain Zakrzevska prodded him in the ribs and turned to her orderly in such a tone as if she had been speaking to a child:

"What happened you're looking for me?"

"I can't enter my quarters, the door is stuck," Johnnie replied humbly. "The weasel doesn't want to sit still, but runs around the entire ship. Plus, I don't know how to say it..."

"The nanny didn't wash the diapers, the cat drank the milk, and the doll broke,"[1] said softly and ironically Mstislav Deadskull, who liked to quote great literature.

---

[1] "With Fire and Sword", the line of Mr. Zagloba.

"...I forgot I have a letter for you from the general!" the highlander finished desperately.

The captain sighed slightly and replied gently:

"When they repair the door, you will enter your quarters and give me this letter. Nothing's probably happened, I don't think he's inviting me on a date in it ... in these conditions it would be difficult ... And the next time you look for me, ask the on-board computer."

There was a signal of internal communication on the bridge. On all Star Armada ships it was the sound of the boatswain's whistle, but this one here was like a sound of an old, rusty trumpet.

"Captain, would you please come to the infirmary?" Beautiful contralto TiShan spoke from the loudspeaker. "We have interesting observations, but this is not a long-distance conversation."

"Gee, what did they find out there, uoltan swine flu?" chuckled Malvinka Krencik, who felt as at ease on the bridge as in the hotel and didn't think to change her behavior.

"As far as I know, Fräu Krencik, there are no swines on planet Uoltan," Jürgen pointed out.

"Well, then, flu from another creature ... Some animals live there, after all," Malvinka didn't give up.

"You'd better come back to intercept," the captain said dryly. "Arek, the bridge. I'm going to the infirmary. Oh, ensign Watery, please get someone from the engine room and have him check the door of Johnnie's quarters, as well as the door of the main navigator. They also jam."

She took Gizia from the shoulder of her orderly and left. This time the elevator went down where it needed to be, without any problems. Dr. TiShan was sitting in the infirmary, clearly pale, though she tried to calm down.

"It's good that you came," she said at the sight of the commander. "This case is getting more and more mysterious. What I dissected ... it just looked human. Its brain was at the stage of development of maybe ... a lizard? It seems that these humanoids were just animals, maybe farm ones. And they have a structure similar to Uoltans, copper-based blood and so on."

She rested her head on her hand.

"Mr. ArCer is examining SiWok's memories using the fusion of the selves," she added wearily. "He'll be here soon."

"SiWok? Do you already know the boy's name?"

"I know him from planet Uoltan. This is SiWok, the son of my neighbors. I don't know how he found himself on the asteroid, but Mr. ArCer is trying to find it out."

Doctor Zmiyevski with two padds left the hospital department.

"Hello, Lila," he said, not very consciously. "If you're curious about the state of the security chief and chaplain, they'll both be back on duty tomorrow.

Oh, the missing person was found ... Lieutenant Gvizdak reached the deck?"

"Yes, but she had a strong attack of space sickness ... Father Toadstool too, but they both are feeling better now."

"Father Toadstool? Thaddeus Toadstool, a Redemptorist? So they sent him to us to get him out of the Earth? Man, I knew they'd give us a chaplain, but I didn't think that him. Well, we will have Chinese dance here, let all the saints watch over us."

"And over atheists?"

"Atheists too. If he takes care of them, they will even believe in the god Wicli-Pucli for the sake of peace. Anyway, he isn't important now..."

The captain sat down next to TiShan. Gizia got off her shoulder and climbed onto the desk, where she stood and sniffed the air like a meerkat. The smell of medicines and disinfectants clearly fascinated her. This is how ArCer saw her when he entered the room, and he could hardly refrain from saying something unpleasant. Not only was the captain of the ship parading with this creature on his shoulder, he also brought it to the hospital section! The Uoltan's face was easy to read.

"Don't be in a huff, the ferret is a creature of God and more sympathetic than many people," said Lilianna. "What did you detect with your Uoltan method?"

ArCer controlled himself and walked with dignity to the desk.

"I know everything," he replied. "Or enough, at least."

"SiWok took part in a mandatory internship on a medium-range ship that stumbled upon this asteroid. He joined the away-team. While on the asteroid, they encountered several Clingorgs who tried to kill or capture them. SiWok was shocked with a mazer, the rest managed to escape. They left him on the principle that the life of a few is more important than the life of one. Unfortunately, they didn't get far - the Clingorgs destroyed their ship with a photon torpedo. What happened next is not entirely clear. It seems the creatures we saw got rid of the Clingorgs and kept SiWok as a food reserve. They were feeding on his blood after they had finished all the humanoids on the ship. Before you start throwing thunder at their cruelty, I will also say that they managed to establish a telepathic connection with this boy, and according to his memories, they were very surprised to discover that he was not an animal, but someone intelligent. They went to great lengths to keep him alive and treated him well in their own way."

"Man, what a treatment," muttered the captain and thought deeply. Finally, she got up and straightened to emphasize the importance of her words.

"We're calling a meeting of senior officers. We need to establish a way forward."

She scooped Gizia off the desk and left with a sweeping step.

"Computer, where is the conference room?" she asked in the corridor, remembering that she hadn't located this room yet. The loudspeaker croaked, then screeched and crowed like a dying capon.

"Second deck, section F," he replied, finally in a whisky bass.

"Thank you," Captain Zakrzevska couldn't be surprised anymore. "Switch the channel to general. Attention, this is the captain! Gentlemen Liljew, Mayher, Karpiel, ArCer, Michałow and von Braun, as well as Mrs. TiShan, please come to the conference room! Quickly, ladies and gentlemen!"

On the bridge there was an agitation - with the speed of a machine gun, speculations were said about what was happening, ranging from an attack by the menacing Casulan race to an overload of the power core. Finally, Arek gave command of the bridge to Jürgen and rushed to the conference room.

"One move and we have a wire," Malvinka suggested, looking hopefully at Jürgen. The man, however, shook his head refusingly and with a dignified movement sat down in the command chair. The poorly tightened bolts failed and the second mate found himself on the floor, provoking a collective outburst of laughter on the bridge.

"Polonische Durcheinander," Jürgen said furiously, picking himself up from the floor.

"German insolence," Technician Watery retorted from his console. "You are on the Polish ship, Herr Offizier, and I advise you not to use such terms if you want to live to see your return from this mission. Why did you sign on 'Hermash' at all?"

The rest also looked offended.

"I have Polish citizenship, so I got this assignment," replied Jürgen dryly. "Do you think such a repair is a good job?"

This question remained unanswered, as Lieutenant Krencik suddenly caught some distant, weak signal, the frequency of which seemed familiar to her.

"Be quiet!" she called, boosting the signal in her headphones. She listened for a few minutes, then looked at Jürgen and the rest.

"I think it's the Clingorgs," she said softly. "They're far away, but not far enough for us to be safe."

Jürgen pressed the communicator button.

"Research department, what about the readings from that other computer?" he asked.

There was a buzzing noise in the loudspeaker, then the voice of Dr. Lemow, head of the data processing department, said:

"The data is in Clingorgian, or rather in one of their dialects. The translation will take a while."

"That's what I thought. These jellies have something to do with the Clingorgs. We need to let the captain know, but not yet. Fräu Krencik, please try to track down the enemy ship and determine its probable course."

"I'm proceeding."

Malvinka went to work briskly, singing "Dotted pants" at the same time. Jürgen frowned in displeasure, but preferred not to say anything anymore.

XIV.

"The creatures that we discovered on the asteroid are a highly developed, peaceful race," said ArCer, sitting at an oval conference table (apparently it was not round due to social protests caused by unpleasant historical associations). "At first, they thought SiWok was an animal, like those humanoids from their home planet. Realizing that he was an intelligent being, they tried not to harm him more than necessary. Unfortunately, they didn't have much choice, because the creatures that served them as food suppliers died due to some disease ... The asteroid is flying to a nearby planet, where living organisms have a structure compatible with these creatures. To sum up, they don't pose a threat to us."

"What do the Clingorgs have to do with them?" Arek asked.

ArCer pursed his lips lightly.

"I don't know exactly," he replied after a moment. "The language of these creatures is incompatible with any humanoid dialect. It is impossible to communicate with them because there are no proper measures. I'm afraid we even lack common concepts. One thing, however, seems clear. This group we've met is running away from something, I'll risk saying that from the Clingorgs."

Andrew Karpiel-Baguette scratched his part anxiously.

"That other asteroid computer is undoubtedly Clingorgian," he said. "But that doesn't prove anything."

"It proves, combined with the fact that SiWok's scout came across the Clingorgs."

The captain looked at Christopher Mayher, who, apart from being the main navigator, was also the deputy of the deck armorer. The armorer himself, a Russian from Siberia, Vasyl Anecdotych Zaychik, was currently in the infirmary, though not because of a space disease, but due to ordinary scarlet fever. How and where he contracted it during the era of universal vaccination was a mystery.

"Can we defend ourselves against the Clingorgs?" she asked.

"With what we have? Come on," said Mayher. "Weapons are our Achilles' heel. Apparently, someone from the Star Armada has studied the history of Poland and came to the conclusion that we only need a saber to charge the tanks."

"Also, a white horse or Kasztanka," added Arek.

"We don't have even it here. After the conference I will check the torpedo launchers and the cannons, although according to the technical passports everything works fine, but it's better not to rely on it too indiscriminately."

"Deflectors?" The captain looked at engineer Mikhalov, who was in his seat, making such a face as if he had been swallowing a frog.

"They're pretty good," he replied. "Such middle-class ones. They should withstand a little, as long as the engines don't turn off at the least convenient time."

"What's the opportune time for an interstellar engine to break down?" Matias von Braun wanted to know, but the captain didn't allow him to dwell on the subject.

"Mr. von Braun, you are a specialist in interracial law and such nonsense, please tell me if we have to obey any rules when we encounter a race in conflict with the Clingorgs?" she asked.

"Such a rule, turn tail and run for the hills" Matias replied vividly. "You can be hit in the face from both sides."

There was a collective chuckle in which only ArCer didn't take part.

"Calm down, there's nothing funny about it!" The captain banged her fist on the table. "When the Clingorgs shell us, we'll all laugh in a ram's voice!"

"Why would they shell us and what for would they get here?" Arek wanted to know, but the intercom buzzer sounded as if on request.

"Captain, the Clingorgian unit is approaching us," reported Malvinka Krencik. "It is flying along an intercepting course to the asteroid. Mr. Jürgen went to the science department to check on their computer."

"Anyone wanted to know where the Clingorgs are coming from?" The captain looked at her first mate with a kind of tired sarcasm. "Lieutenant Krencik, please keep tracking these Clingorgs, block our own signals, and see exactly where the asteroid is going."

"And shouldn't I also stick a broom in my ass and sweep on the way?" Malvinka asked matter-of-factly. "Either one or the other, I'm not able to do it at the same time with this equipment. This console is some Russian junk."

"I will take measurements of the asteroid," said Veronika Bumblebee's polite voice in the background.

"That's great," nodded the captain. "Let Ensign Veronica take care of the asteroid, and you of Clingorgs. When you think, you will always come up with something. And when Jürgen comes back, please notify me immediately. You are free for now; we will resume the meeting when something is known."

XV.

Jürgen chased up the science team and got down to work himself, so that soon the record from the Clingorgian database could be read - well, maybe not all, but except for individual words whose meaning was not clear, the rest was decoded satisfactorily.

"Unfortunately, the grammar is terrible, because it is a border dialect, not honest Clingorgian, so the translators couldn't cope, but the merits are clear," he said when at the request of his captain, he showed up in the conference room. "These creatures come from the very core of the galaxy, from a planet that was discovered and conquered by the Clingorgs. As these creatures defended themselves, they were almost completely exterminated, but some of them were left alive, as it turned out that they could serve as a kind of biological weapon in the fight against the Uoltans and Cumulans. They feed on blood rich in copper or a substitute obtained from plants. And these two races just have copper-based blood."

"Every child knows that, go on," the captain urged him.

"On the home planet of these jellyfish there was no food shortage, because there were many unintelligent life forms based on copper, as well as plants rich in this element. They, no matter how you call them, have never encountered intelligent humanoids before and are a peaceful race. Still, on Cumulus or Uoltan they would pose a public threat, especially since they are very difficult to destroy. The Clingorgs succeeded because they simply annihilated the entire planet, admittedly by accident."

"How can you destroy a planet by accident?" Dr. TiShan asked skeptically.

"You can, if you don't know the exact composition of its shell and turn on a device that shouldn't be turned on," explained Jürgen. The Clingorgs initiated a chain reaction, so that of the entire population of these nameless creatures, only the group of artificial asteroids, previously taken to be transported to Clingorg, survived. Along the way, these creatures, as far as we could learn, took possession of the ship, disposed of the Clingorgs, and altered its course. Now they are flying in a smooth glide, according to Ensign Bumblebee, towards a M3 class planet only a few light years away. They will be there faster than a ski jumper at the finish line."

"Oh Malysz, damn it ..." Mikhalov muttered.

"Do we know the parameters of this planet?" the captain asked.

"We know. It is hostile to humanoids, but may be suitable for them. Lots of copper salts in the spectrum."

The captain got up and started pacing the conference room. It was evident that she was thinking hard on what she had heard and on what she had already known.

"Damn. We have to associate the asteroid, the planet and those Clingorgs that are starting to tread on our tail feathers," she said after a moment. "Those Clingorgs didn't come here by accident, well, there are no miracles!"

"You blaspheme, my daughter," said Father Thaddeus Toadstool's voice from the threshold. His charismatic figure appeared in the conference room like a devil out of a box.

"Praised," the captain said automatically, "it's just a figure of speech, Father."

The priest cleared his throat as a sign that he could believe it, but he didn't have to, and changed the subject.

"Where's the deck chapel?"

"I have no idea," Lilianna replied sincerely. "You would have to ask the quartermaster."

"The chapel isn't far from here, Section C," the First Officer said hurriedly. "Right next to it, there is father's quarters, and on the other side, the one of Sister Ophelia's."

The priest was silent for a moment, clearly surprised.

"Have I understood well? Is Sister Ophelia of Angels here?" he asked finally.

The officers exchanged glances.

"I saw a penguin here, but I don't know its name," said Michałow.

"To tell the truth, I thought it was a delusion."

"No, it wasn't a delusion. Sister Ophelia was assigned because, according to the new encyclical, nuns have the right to confess women, and there are a lot of women here," Arek explained.

"These newfangled inventions only damage religion," the priest muttered sourly. "Alright, I'm going to inspect the chapel, my children, I don't interfere with this secular council," he said and left majestically, closing the door behind him.

"Has he gotten something against Ophelia?" Mayher was surprised. Arek chuckled.

"No, my dear," he explained cheerfully. "She is simply not only a nun, but also his real sister ... whom he fears like fire."

XVI.

Captain Zakrzevska was sitting in the repaired armchair, chewing on her unhappy thoughts. The mysterious asteroid had already reached the secluded planet and the screen image showed jellyfish creatures, apparently building a kind of house on the surface. The Clingorgs were circling somewhere nearby, but they probably had trouble tracking because they were searching blindly. The scan made by Veronika confirmed that the artificial asteroid remaining in the orbit of the planet was empty. The Clingorgs had not yet tracked 'Hermash', but they could do it at any moment.

For a while she watched as one of the strange creatures picked up some plants with its dorsal process, while the rest erected a makeshift shelter. They looked well organized.

"What do you think, they'll be fine here?" she asked ArCer.

The Uoltan nodded slightly.

"They are intelligent and their appearance suggests the ability to adapt to almost any conditions," he replied. "The concentrate you ordered to prepare, however, will be a valuable reserve for them."

Immediately after the conference, the captain ordered the science department to prepare as many concentrated copper salts as possible in the configuration found in the Uoltans' blood. Along with them, a strange biocomputer was sent to the planet, and now 'Hermash' was getting ready to take the artificial asteroid from the planet's orbit. If it had stayed there, it would have been an excellent signpost for the Clingorgs. Engineer Michałow finished stabilization of the traction beam emitters, while Christopher Mayher went to the armory and inspected the equipment there. Having finished, he went to the engine room.

"Mr. Mikhalov, will you help me check the mazers and launchers?" he asked.

"Willingly," replied the engineer. "If you stop talking nonsense about saber charges against tanks. You should know this is plain libel."

"I know it, but they don't know it in Armada's HQ, and they don't care anyway."

"That's true too. They are probably convinced that we have white bears walking our streets. Greg, finish the job!"

Mikhalov wiped the grease off his hands and followed Mayher to the sniper positions, while his deputy took care of the emitters. They required a lot of work because they had been assembled quickly and carelessly, and if you had used them "on the go", they would have not only disintegrated themselves, but probably the generated feedback pulse would have destroyed the warp reactor.

"Really great job," Greg muttered, picking the links of the thrust.

"What to expect from people, especially such people," SyTar laughed maliciously and added: "Watch out to the left. Better take the magnetic probe, not the clamp, or you will short-circuit."

"If you hadn't distracted me, I would have known myself," the engineer grunted, hurriedly changing the tool. The cursed vatra in his head could be helpful, but Greg would have gladly given up such help. The awareness that around the clock he was not alone even for a moment disturbed him at times, and in his private life it was an insurmountable obstacle. He would have liked to get rid of the intruder, but he didn't know how to do it and if it was possible at all.

The two 'M' gentlemen started checking the mazer guns and torpedo launchers. They were both in their element and everything around them temporarily ceased to exist for them, so much so that they even got rid of the service, sending it to rest. They cared much less about the asteroid and strange creatures than the state of armament, admittedly, not the best.

Meanwhile, the captain gloomily finished the report for Star Armada Command and went to the infirmary, where she expected to obtain an attachment to the report. Doctor TiShan was supposed to have it prepared, meanwhile, unexpectedly, Lilianna found the Uoltan shedding tears over her desk like an ordinary Earthwoman. It was a sight so unexpected and so illogical that the captain promptly summoned ArCer through her personal communicator. Then she tried to find out what was wrong with TiShan, but she couldn't get her to make any meaningful answers to the questions asked.

"It's some kind of nervous attack," she said when ArCer arrived at the infirmary. "As far as I know, the Uoltans don't cry."

"Being educated on Earth is harmful, and not just for the Uoltans," ArCer replied sarcastically. "I will take care of her, Captain, and you should return to the bridge. The engine room has just reported that the traction beam emitter is ready for use."

"I hope you will bring this baby to a working condition. I don't want the mentally ill head doctor to come here," Lilianna muttered dissatisfiedly and left the infirmary. The time had come to put her plan into action, and she couldn't be prevented by TiShan's snuffling due to what she guessed was the asteroid survivor.

XVII.

ArCer stayed in the infirmary with tearful TiShan. For a moment he wondered what to do to make her stop crying. After all, it didn't befit the Uoltan. Finally, he came close to her and crouched down to look at her tearful face.

"Crying is a highly illogical waste of body water, especially on planet Uoltan," he began sternly to get attention, but only caused that she cried even more.

He sighed and tried from other side.

"Please tell me what happened. Why are you crying?"

"He's so young ..." she stammered through tears.

"Are you talking about SiWok?" he asked gently and she nodded.

"I don't know if he will survive. I can't help him. And I remember when he was a little child ..."

"We have strong bodies and we don't give up easily. I think that for now it is enough to feed him well and he will do the rest himself."

"But I found something weird in his body," she began to calm down as the conversation turned to medical matters.

"And?"

"I can't identify it. It's some strange substance and he has no leukocytes at all."

"If you want, I'll help. After all, I'm a science officer." He smiled and the girl looked at him, surprised. She stopped crying.

If ArCer had known that a simple smile would have helped her, he would have done it at once. For TiShan, it was as if the sun had been shining. She had never imagined that the Uoltan had such a skill. After all, it is a result of emotions, and emotions are illogical. In addition, ArCer's smile was really special. The doctor stared at him and opened her mouth involuntarily. When he grew serious, the sun went out and TiShan sobered up.

"Thank you. Help will be very useful to me."

"So, I am asking for a blood sample from SiWok for testing."

The doctor got up and left the office for a moment. When she returned, she was holding a sealed test tube with the green blood of the young Uoltan. ArCer took the given item.

"So I'm going to work on this material. If I find out anything, I will let you know immediately." He smiled gently at TiShan again, turned on his heel, and left. The young woman was left alone. She sat for a while, wiping her eyes, which took a while, because, like all Uoltans, inhabitants of a semi-arid planet, she had very long and thick eyelashes. She was surprised by her own reaction to ArCer - she usually disliked and distrusted men. She had bad experiences with them, both with the Uoltans and with people, and here this officer ... She shook her head in disbelief.

***

On the bridge, Captain Zakrzevska directed the action of taking the asteroid into the open space. The towing beam turned out to be stable enough to overcome the gravitational force of the orbit, although it turned out that also a jerk was necessary, which shook the entire 'Hermash'. So strong that on the bridge the intercom rang, through which the crewmen shouted disrespectfully what they thought about such helmsmen and way of moving. After a while, everything calmed down because nobody was hurt except Professor Trekovsky who cut himself with the broken test tube, fortunately clean. He made, however, so much noise about it as if he had at least been cut with a battle sword.

"I can't work here!" he screamed, stamping his feet on the floor with such energy as if he was getting ready to take part in the "Got Talent" program, tap dance competition. "What a damn idiot is shaking the ship so much?!"

The testers explained to him that it was the emitter of the traction beam, which riled him even more. Finally, he calmed down and, having used a handy skin regenerator, went back to his work.

All the confusion, of course, didn't bother ArCer, who was able to disconnect from his surroundings when he had some tense work to do. He was starting to come to very interesting conclusions, but to be sure, he still had to test the sample with the latest generation chromatograph - and since no one had used it before, it had to be scaled first. Busy with this arduous work, he paid no attention to what was happening. And there was happening a lot.

After catching the artificial asteroid with a towline and taking it out of its orbit, 'Hermash' set off with full allowable thrust as far as possible from Planet Haribo, as it was tentatively named due to the association of strange creatures with jelly beans. The ship flew so all night to be far from the planet in order to pull the Clingorgian pursuit from it. According to the plan, when encountering the remains of the artificial asteroid, the Clingorgs were to become certain that the fugitives were killed in the blast, which guaranteed the survival of the remnants of the strange race. Being at a reasonable, as she thought, distance, the captain ordered to release the object and destroy it with mazer gun fire.

Christopher Mayher took care of it; he was very pleased that he finally had something to shoot at and that he could test the on-board arsenal. He hit the asteroid first using the port and starboard cannons, then the bow ones, and would have also gladly fired a torpedo, but first of all, he had already nothing to fire at, and secondly, it was better not to waste disposable ammunition.

"How is the situation?" the captain asked nervously through the intercom, as the energy wave jammed the bridge sensors for a long moment.

"Went to hell!" the chief navigator reported.

"What?!"

"Not you, but this asteroid," said Mayher. "It's an ash and a diamond now. So, can I go to dinner now? Maciek promised that he would make paprikash especially for me today."

"Then enjoy it."

Captain Zakrzevska sat down comfortably in the command chair and signed the report brought by Johnnie.

"We're back on course, full speed ahead," she ordered.

XVIII.

"And how are the moods on the ship?" Captain Zakrzevska asked when, having handed over the command on the bridge to Arek, she went down to her quarters for a well-deserved rest.

"There was a row in the eighth corridor, Mrs. Tekla hit her husband in the face," Johnnie reported eagerly. "This Russian, who is our gun foreman, left the hospital. The chaplain says that he will hang holy pictures everywhere, otherwise evil will destroy us. And he announced a universal retreat, because what he sees here is a gang of pagans, not real Christians. The cook said that he can make cheese dumplings on Friday if the priest wants to fast, but he won't hang anyone, because he is not a hangman. The chief engineer doesn't believe in anything, so he didn't want to hang, and the reverend father told him then that he will turn back all of us, Jewish minions, to people ..."

"Convert," the captain corrected him, and sighed. "Just what I needed here, the loony in the cassock. And what does Sister Ophelia think about it all?"

Johnnie laughed against the regulations, but happily.

"The monastic lady said that diplomacy cannot be required of men," he replied with delight. "And that the Reverend Father failed to complete the course of toleration for the differently wise people. And that he would better go to pray, because he naps until noon, and already before sunrise he should kneel with the breviary ... And the priest told her not to lecture him, because already Saint Augustine wrote that every woman is stupid and prone to sin ... and the young lady said that if it weren't for the guys, there would be no one to sin with, and also there would be no reason to sin, because it is they who accost women. And she added that Saint Augustine was a villain himself, and when he had gotten old and had no strength to sin, he had become a saint and shifted all the blame onto the women ... and then they noticed me and threw me out of the chapel on my ear."

Lilianna choked on a laugh, but got serious right away. The order of suffragette sisters was known for their demanding attitude towards the Vatican and had won the extension of powers for nuns over a hundred years earlier, but it was still not enough for them. As they argued, centuries of humiliating and deprecating women couldn't be so easily forgotten or compensated. For understandable reasons, most of the priests were opposed to the programmatically rebellious sisters, but there was little they could do - the times when excommunication was thrown as easily as a ball into a basket were gone, now it would have only resulted in ridiculing the church authorities, and no one wanted to risk it. However, having on board NXY -

much larger than a standard unit of its class - the conservative priest and progressive nun, however, must have resulted in trouble.

"And besides, peace?" she asked.

"You can say that," Johnnie replied enigmatically. As if on order, the ship was thrown, and the captain bumped into her orderly.

"The commander is asked to come to the bridge!" said the intercom with Arek's soprano trembling with emotion. "The Clingorgs have just made direct contact with us!"

"Jesus!" Johnnie grunted devoutly.

"Take care of Gizia," the captain told him. "I'm going to the bridge."

"And we were left here alone," the highlander sighed, moving his huge arm to the ferret sitting on the top of the bookcase.

On the bridge Lilianna was greeted by Malvinka, shouting something in Clingorgian to the communications apparatus.

"They don't want to listen to me," she complained, taking the receiver out of her ear.

"Call von Braun, he's a specialist in such contacts," the captain said.

"I've already tried. He doesn't want to come, he says that cream in his Nelsonian roulades would burn," said Jürgen.

"Unbelievable, two Germans on board and they can't get along," technician Watery muttered from his console. The left eye with purple halo clearly indicated that Johnnie didn't exaggerate when describing his incident with his wife.

"Matias von Braun is just as German as a German Shepherd," the captain said sternly. "His name is such, because his stepfather adopted him after marrying his mother ..."

"...Where is this Wanda today, who didn't want a German ..." Watery sighed.

"Don't be smart, Ensign! Summon him again."

Jürgen obediently switched on the communicator and sent the summons, but not to Matias, but to the security section, ordering the diplomat to be brought to the bridge regardless of his opinion. The communicator gurgled, growled, and after a few minutes Matias, grumpy and angry, appeared on the bridge.

"If the dinner is impossible to eat, blame yourself," he said furiously.

"We'll blame ourselves," the captain assured him. "Talk to those Clingorgs and find out why they shoot at us."

"Maybe we told them something or we didn't tell them something?" added Arek.

Matias took the receiver Malvinka had given him and for a moment tried to fulfill the captain's request as best he could.

"Nothing of that," he said after a moment. "As far as I understand, they accuse us of destroying Imperial property and killing the ship's crew. They want revenge, not talk. I think it's about that counterfeit asteroid. Can I go back to the kitchen now?"

"Yes, if the kitchen isn't destroyed, you can come back."

"They haven't destroyed it yet, and the dinner has to be made on time."

After making this philosophical remark, Matias left the bridge, and Lilianna took the receiver from Malvinka, screamed to it what she thought about the attackers, and ordered:

"Red alert! Raise the shields, return fire on my cue."

XIX.

"Captain, they're calling us," Malvinka reported after both ships exchanged a pair of practice volleys.

"On the screen," Zakrzevska ordered from her armchair.

A huge Clingorg appeared on the main screen, shaking his shaggy hair angrily.

"Who's in charge?" he inquired.

"Me," Lilianna replied calmly. "What is it about?"

"I'm not going to talk to a woman about military matters," said the Clingorg.

"Then talk to yourself, lettuce man," suggested the captain, making a clear allusion to the crimped shape of the Clingorgian forehead.

"Lower your shields and surrender. Otherwise, you will be destroyed immediately."

"Surrender? I don't know this word. Get away from us, we are not accosting you."

"You destroyed the Imperial ship and killed its crew."

"First of all, the crew hadn't been on board for a long time and we don't know what happened to them. Secondly, maybe we can talk a bit about what was the purpose of this ship and its 'cargo'? Because we know it too."

The Clingorg was silent for a moment.

"Prepare to be annihilated," he said ominously, and the screen went blank.

"So, should we prepare?" Arek asked doubtfully.

"Heck to the no, forget that," replied the captain sharply (sometimes, in moments of great agitation, she spoke in Silesian dialect) and turned on the communicator. "Engine room, turn off all systems except life support and weapons. Strengthen the guards to the maximum and keep the mazer batteries charged. Attention all crew! Get ready for heavy fire!"

"He hid behind the outhouse, and he was still under fire..." Malvinka recited in a merry falsetto.

"Miss Bumblebee, evasion maneuvers," the captain ordered, ignoring her.

"Mr. Mayher, join the snipers. Ensign Watery, to the spare rudders."

"Cool!" rejoiced Joe Watery, who wanted to steer from the very beginning but was forced to be bored at the engine room console. Christopher Mayher gave him the helm and left, muttering for the sake of order:

"Aye, Ma'am."

He preferred the sniper position. He had become famous on the USS Rodan as an excellent artilleryman, who hadn't lost his cold blood and an accurate eye in even the most difficult situations, and the current situation was also not the easiest one. As he could realize, the Clingorgian cruiser looked no better equipped than Hermash, but it didn't mean it wasn't dangerous. It was, and very.

In the sniper position, he found a blue-skinned T'enga, a young Pandorian from the Communications Department, and Second Lieutenant Zaychik, cursing in Russian with utmost passion and making very damaging assumptions about the morality of the moms attacking the Clingorgs.

"What's up, Vashka?" he asked amiably.

"Vsie strelki ostalis na Ziemlie!" Zaychik cried out indignantly. "Eta galubaya ptica gavarit ..."[2]

---

[2] *(Rus)* All the shooters stayed on Earth ... this blue bird says.

"Go to Polish, Vashka, do not tire people," Mayher interrupted him.

"...she says that she can shoot ...maybe she can ...well, she is responsible for communications, not rifles..."

"We don't have a choice anyway. I take the bow mazers, you sit at the starboard mazers, Cadet T'enga at the portboard ones. I open the communication channel, and we are acting on the direct orders of the captain."

Gasping with nervousness, Vasyl Anecdotych sat down at the starboard gun console, and Mayher took his place at the bow. On the screen, he could see the Klingon unit straight ahead, preparing to attack. He activated a homing scan and followed its calculations with one eye, ready to open fire at any moment.

The Clingorgs made hay while the sun shone. They hit the 'Hermash' bow deflectors twice, before Mayher finished tracking, but the delay paid off - he detected a weakened spot in the cover of their cruiser's third shield and shot the strongest available cannon payload at it. The Clingorgian craft was visibly thrown, and the blast tore the hull plating.

"Otlich'no,"[3] said Zaychik happily.

"Not bad, Chris," she praised the captain through the intercom. "Their cover is destroyed. Aim at this spot and prepare a torpedo."

[3] *(Rus)* Great.

"Do you want to torpedo them?" Jürgen asked uncertainly.

"Only as a last resort," the captain assured him.

The comm console buzzed and Malvinka Krencik gracefully picked up the receiver. She listened for a moment, then turned to her commander:

"Captain, the Clingorgs say they filed a complaint against us to Star Armada's command."

"Advise them, darling, to complain also to their moms," the captain said.

"They are insolent!" technician Watery exclaimed. "Not only are they attacking us, but also they write complaints that we are defending ourselves!"

Malvinka dutifully repeated to the Clingorgian liaison officer what Captain Zakrzevska had said and on her own initiative added also what Watery had told her.

"I don't think they mean that we are defending ourselves now, but that destroyed asteroid," Jürgen said thoughtfully. "Fräu Hauptmann, I don't want to be a bad prophet, but they can present the case so that the command won't even want to listen to our explanations. I would advise you to prepare a good line of defense in advance, because I'm afraid that when you return to Earth, a court-martial will be waiting for you."

XX.

Contrary to the expectations of Captain Zakrzevska, the Clingorgs didn't let them put them off their stroke and continued firing, having cautiously changed the angle of their position in relation to 'Hermash'. The covers, which turned out to be admirably strong, were still in their place, but, as Gregory Brzenchyshchykievich noted, it was a "temporary state". Damage could occur at any moment, which would have made the Polish ship helpless against the Clingorgian cruiser. Nevertheless, some of the crew quietly went to dinner, assuming that, even in the worst case, what they would eat would be theirs. The occasional shocks from hits, they took with an almost Uoltanian calm, as if they had been just an interesting diversion to the boring journey.

"Interesting, will they destroy us or we'll blow ourselves up because of the overheating of the reactor, and we will scatter in atoms all over the area?" Engineer Michałow wondered aloud, getting sensational roulades prepared by Matias despite objective difficulties.

Several of the security boys eating at the next table turned a little green.

"I propose a joint prayer for the salvation of the ship," said Father Toadstool from his table.

"Forgive me, father, but I'm an atheist." Michałow smiled. "And like many crew members, I'm not going to indulge in magical practices"

"Ya magu malit'sya, ya pravoslavnyi,"[4] said Vasyl Anecdotych Zaychik from the corner of the room, busy dressing roasted flounder, or at least something that reminded it very much.

"I profess Islam in the reformed version."

"And I, the Mosaic religion."

"I am a Protestant."

"I'm a Seventh-day Adventist!" membership declarations came from everywhere.

"As you all want, just don't be surprised at the Judgment of God, because I will not defend you," the priest got offended and took care of his lunch with an involvement that was slightly inappropriate for a clergyman.

---

[4] *(Rus)* I can pray, I'm Orthodox.

"So, let's drink to our damnation! Maciek, give me half a liter!" Michałow called to the kitchen.

"I've already gathered speed to make the captain peck me to death. Boozing in full alert is forbidden," Matias von Braun decisively replied, straightening the chef's cap that he put fancifully on his left ear.

"Damn it, this is just a battle with the Clingorgs, not the end of the world! Give us at least beer ..."

"Not even a droplet. We'll all have a drink, but only when it's all over."

"Crawler."

"What did you say?" Matias grabbed the handle of a heavy saucepan eloquently. His gaze made it clear that he was going to use it. The colleagues managed to ease the dispute and they all accordingly started to consume the dessert.

***

In the infirmary, Dr. TiShan watched over the still unconscious SiWok. The ship functioned weirdly, ArCer didn't come back - generally she felt terrible about that. Her situation was so bad also because she didn't realize how foolish it was to renounce Uoltanian practices - it was the abandonment of them that caused her emotional disturbance. Under normal circumstances it was of less importance, but under conditions of space travel it became more and more pronounced. Anger against "that moron who thinks herself a captain" was growing in her. "How could she risk a conflict with the Clingorgs!" It took someone really smart to get them out of this impasse. Someone like that nice Mr. ArCer, for example.

Plans for ArCer to take command slowly emerged in TiShan's mind. When Jacob Zmiyevski, still yawning after his nap, entered the infirmary, the plan was ready.

"Please take the patient," she said, standing up. "I have to handle something."

"Okay, why not?" replied sadly Jacob, who still dreamed of going back to bed, because he liked to sleep above all.

TiShan entered the nearest quick-elevator.

"Bridge," she said.

The elevator screeched, jerked, and obediently moved.

On the bridge, no one noticed the newcomer. The entire crew's attention was focused on the Clingorgian cruiser, which was clearly looking for some gaps in the earthly ship's cover. Both units maneuvered around each other like circling wolves, and neither showed the desire to retreat.

"Captain, please leave the bridge," TiShan said loudly. "Your behavior indicates mental imbalance. As the ship's chief physician, I am exempting you from duty."

"What the hell is she saying? Is she out of mind?" Arek was amazed.

"Apparently." Captain Zakrzevska looked at TiShan with moderate curiosity. "You explain yourself, or you will be arrested and maybe also hit in the face."

"You're not fit for duty. Your decisions put the ship and crew at risk. Command will be taken by the most experienced officer."

"And the pigs will fly," the captain turned on the intercom. "Lieutenant Gvizdak, please send the security team to the bridge."

"You're crazy. I'm the chief physician and the only surgeon here. Your conduct proves the correctness of my diagnosis: you are endangering the health and life of the crew by depriving them of proper medical care!"

"Don't worry about it," the captain answered. And to the three red-uniformed bullies who had just entered she said: "Escort Dr. TiShan to her quarters and put-up guard."

When the soldiers took the agitated doctor from the bridge, Jürgen turned to Lilianna:

"And yet Fräulein Doctor was right that we can't keep her in custody. We need an experienced doctor."

"I know. And from the very beginning I was prepared for such an action. I was warned that the Uoltans might try to seize the ship." Lilianna turned on the intercom again. "Science department? Commander ArCer and Mr. Nbeba are to report to the bridge."

XXI.

The black crewman stepped onto the bridge, where curious glances greeted him, then stood upright.

"Rest," said Captain Zakrzevska. "End of the masquerade, Dr. Nbeba. Please go to the infirmary and temporarily assume the duties of the head physician. Dr. TiShan broke down a bit under the burden of responsibility, it seems to me..."

"I understand, Captain."

Nbeba made the "right about" accordant with the rules and marched off, followed by already very surprised looks.

"Does this mean that from the very beginning you have taken into account ...?" Malvinka asked in bewilderment.

"I maybe not, but General Jaruzelski has," replied Lilianna. "Dr. Nbeba was supposed to accompany us without revealing himself, at least until we reach the colony on Deneva. The general thought, rightly so, as you can see, that the Uoltans would try to take control of the ship ... though I don't know whether to treat TiShan's carrying-on as an honest rebellion or as a real collapse. We'll see what ArCer says. Listen on and keep an eye on the Clingorgs."

ArCer and the second security team, sent by Maura Gvizdak, got onto the bridge. The Uoltan seemed to be completely calm and not know what had happened.

"Yes, Captain," he said, standing in front of the command seat. Lilianna Zakrzevska looked at him carefully and came to the conclusion that he probably had nothing to do with TiShan's carrying on. His face, handsome by earthly standards, exuded honesty and seriousness that ruled out such irresponsible behavior.

"Commander, your fellow countryman has just tried to deprive me of command to, I believe, your advantage," she said. "Do you realize that I can charge you both with mutiny in times of danger?"

ArCer was silent, pondering what he had just heard. He hadn't expected TiShan to do something so unwise, even if her mental balance was indeed debatable.

"Captain, I would like to remind you that the Star Armada forbids sentence people to death," interjected in a trembling soprano Arek, who, it is not known why, thought about it.

"Nobody sentences anyone, after all, death is inevitable for everybody ... but I can set a date for everyone here to meet the

Creator if they piss me off, so you'd better shut up, darling," the captain replied. "Mr. ArCer, what do you have to say about this?"

"I have nothing concrete to defend myself," replied the Uoltan. "I can only assure you that I didn't try to take command and I have nothing to do with what Dr. TiShan did."

"Will you deny that your headquarters has instructed you to take command in the event of my incompetence?" the captain said blindly.

Although she didn't consider herself a seer, she was quite smart and knew how to draw conclusions from even flimsy premises. Such an order, given to ArCer, seemed to her simply something logical, and yet even General Jaruzelski admitted that the Uoltans were very logical.

"I won't deny it," ArCer replied, looking his captain straight in the eye with unfazed, dignified calm. "But it was more of a suggestion than an official order. It was never my intention to start a rebellion on board 'Hermash'. Of course, I am aware that you have the right not to trust me, and I am willing to give up my service voluntarily."

The security squad soldiers stood ready and kept their eyes on him. The entire bridge froze in tension, waiting for the commander's words. For a moment there was a silence in which only the faint humming of the console transducers was heard.

"No, that won't be necessary," said the captain at last. "Maybe it's crazy of me, but I trust you. However, please take care of Dr.

TiShan, you have your ways ... I wish she would start acting quite normally. Dr. Nbeba is not bound by any contract and may at any time request that we drop him off at some base we pass by, and I don't want to be left without the chief physician. Anyway, it seems to me that she is only sick, not rebellious. Please send Lieutenant Karpiel here and take care only of her now. I want to give her a chance," she finished a little more quietly.

ArCer nodded with the movement of his eyelids. Even on Earth, before departure, he had been warned that captain 'Hermash' might have been ill-disposed towards the Uoltans, but it seemed that Zakrzevska was not clearly hostile, but perhaps distrustful, and that was understandable in these circumstances.

"I'll find out what caused Dr. TiShan's behavior," he said. "I would like to assure you that we, Uoltans, usually don't behave in such a crazy and illogical way. And although the doctor is a bit different than the typical representatives of my species, I will find out what the reason is and try to eliminate it."

He reported off and left the bridge, followed by the slightly confused security team.

"I wouldn't believe him," muttered Joe Watery.

"And you'd have right to it if you were in my place, sweetheart." The captain stretched until her bones crackled, then turned to Malvinka. "How are our Clingorgks?"

"They have patched the plating and are probably getting ready to attack again. We should have finished them off right away, not coddle them as if they were friends."

Contrary to these words, the great cruiser didn't attack, although it did remain fully alert. There was something menacing and, above all, incomprehensible in his silence and lurking. The Clingorgs seemed to be waiting for something, but for what? Only the sudden subspace distortion showed that they knew what they were doing, although...

Nobody really expected that. When it became clear that the ship that had just emerged from subspace was the famous USS Superprice, everyone was shocked. An additional reason for stupor was the fact that the Armada flagship fired a warning salvo from all cannons at 'Hermash' before it lost speed. It was only thanks to Captain Zakrzevska's immediate reaction that the indignant Christopher Mayher didn't respond with a fire, and with a better aimed one. The Clingorgian cruiser immediately began its retreat, while the comm console rang and flashed its lights.

"They are calling us, captain," Malvinka Krencik said instinctively.

"I can see, can't I? I'm not blind. Get them on the screen."

"A handsome, well-built man appeared on the screen.

"I'm Captain Jeeves R. Kerk," he said. "I'm on the orders of Star Armada HQ, which received the complaint about your behavior. Please lower the shields and prepare to receive me and my first mate for official arrest."

XXII.

"What?" Captain Zakrzevska frowned.

"Please follow my instructions, otherwise we will force you to do so. Are you aware of your position?"

"I think so. I'm sitting in an armchair, my feet are on the floor, I'm looking at the screen, oh, and I'm listening to some idiot who has taken into his head that he can give me orders."

"We won't talk in this tone through the connection. Please bring us and I will present you with an official warrant."

"I told you so." Jürgen said softly.

The captain snaped her fingers at him.

"I invite you aboard then, Captain Kerk," she said, rising from her chair. "We'll talk, if you're so eager to talk. Arek, you will take over the bridge."

Lilianna took the speed-elevator down to the corridor and headed for the transport hall, whistling happily. At the bend, she was joined by Bear, which didn't like to stay in his mistress' quarters and wandered freely around the ship, which wasn't a problem for anyone.

"Forget it. Stay there," the captain ordered him sternly and entered the hall, where Lalevich, jaded as usual, was preparing to receive the transport.

Soon, two cylindrical, elongated shapes appeared on the platform, composed of spinning particles that finally fused into two human figures. After a while, Captain Kerk and the skinny, tall Uoltan who accompanied him, in whom Mr. Spox could be easily recognized, stepped off the platform.

"You are under arrest by the order of Star Armada Headquarters," he said to Lilianna. "Your incompetence may cause the breaking of the truce with the Clingorgs."

"I deny the accusations," Lilianna said calmly.

"I'm not asking you about that. You are living proof that women are not fit to be captains. The appointment of the lady to such an honorable position was the greatest mistake of Armada in history," Jeeves R. Kerk was clearly agitated and struggled to control himself.

"Shut your mouth, because if I hit you in the ear, you will lose the stripes on the sleeves..." growled Johnnie Caterpillar menacingly, rising next to his captain like out of the ground.

Kerk couldn't quite understand what he meant, despite the translator's efforts - maybe that was better.

"Easy, Johnnie, I took care of worse people. If he pisses me off, he will be only the slippers and passport," Lilianna assured her aide.

"On behalf of Star Armada, I am arresting you for causing the tension with the Clingorgs!" Captain Kerk repeated, even more angrily than before.

"Typically like a man. The fellow judges me before finding out the facts only because I'm a woman," Lilianna snorted, tossing the braid over her back. "Arrest your grandmother, wise man, and first of all, explain yourself for the shots in our direction."

"Captain, perhaps we really should find out exactly what happened," said Mr. Spox. "So far, we have only the words of the Clingorgs, who didn't necessarily say everything ..."

"...but they are still more trustworthy than some woman, right?" Lilianna cut in.

"You will explain yourself in the headquarters!"

"It's interesting, because I'm not going anywhere from here! I will not interrupt the maiden voyage of 'Hermash' because of the Clingorgian lies."

"Pax, pax vobiscum, beloved." Father Toadstool appeared beside both captains and raised his hands in a reassuring gesture. "What's with this unchristian behavior?"

Kerk's jaw dropped at the sight of the figure in the cassock, and Spox's eyebrows rose under the bangs.

"Our chaplain, Father Thaddeus Toadstool," introduced Father Lilianna. "Father, this is Captain Kerk and his first mate, Mr. Spox."

"Chap-lain?!"

"Don't try to understand."

The intercom clanked and sounded across the entire transport hall with Arek's voice:

"Captain, the Clingorgs are turning!"

"They are turning to the true faith?!" Father Toadstool cried hopefully.

"No, father, they are turning their ship back toward us!"

"Everyone to the positions!" the captain ordered. "Red alert. Raise the covers. Dish, you block the transporter. Warn Superprice, they come on strong with everybody!"

She ran to the quick-elevator, leaving her confused guests with yawning Lalevich, who sat down and, ignoring them, plunged into his reading again.

XXIII.

Wait, I'm not finished yet!" Captain Kerk exclaimed, running after Lilianna while wondering intensely what the hell was going on there ... why was the Clingorgian cruiser attacking when it knows that the Star Armada took over this case?

Just outside the hall door, he bumped into the mass of brown fur, which barked with a bass and pressed him to the floor with the paws. At first Kerk thought it was a bear, but then he remembered that bears didn't bark.

"Good boy," he grunted, trying to push the amused animal off him.

However, Bear didn't think to give up the unexpected entertainment. The nice guy was saved from oppression only by Johnnie Caterpillar, who turned back and boomed:

"Go away, you son of a dog! Shoo!"

This way he managed to chase the dog away enough for Kerk to get up and brush off the hair.

He felt more and more dumbfounded - the Polish ship really looked like a madhouse, and what's worse, this insolent captain, barely reaching his chin, didn't look like one that allowed herself to be arrested easily. And if she didn't, what to do? Fight with them, I mean with the Poles? A bit stupid, after all, the same service.

He looked helplessly at the unmoved Spox.

"What do you think, did the Clingorgs tell the truth?" he asked.

"No data," the Uoltan replied stiffly. "We'd better go to the bridge."

The suggestion was as logical as ever, so they both got into the quick-elevator and appeared on the bridge just as the Clingorgs got close enough to fire. And they fired.

"Full reverse!" the captain commanded.

"What is it?" Deadskull shouted, struggling with the controls.

"Probably a torpedo, but I have never seen such one," Arek groaned with admiration and fear.

The flying object resembled an elongated paralite crystal, pointing with its blunt end towards 'Hermash'. It was definitely some kind of weapon, but not only Arek, none of those present, including Kerk and Spox, knew what it might have been. However, they all quickly came to the unanimous conclusion that if the Clingorgs were shooting it, it must have been something devilishly dangerous.

The situation matured quickly, turning into drama. Although Deadskull and the young boy accompanying him did their best at the spare console, the mysterious object copied all their evasion maneuvers, approaching inevitably as if it had its own warp drive. Lilianna grabbed the communicator.

"Chris, shoot at it as hard as possible!" she screamed. "It can't hit us! To everyone: prepare for a strong shock!"

"Yes, ma'am!"

Christopher Mayher clung to the sight, caught the moment when two bearing fields met at one point, and fired all the energy available to him at the mysterious torpedo.

"All at covers!" the captain managed to shout, switching to the engine room channel before the shockwave generated by the explosion reached the ship.

Unknown energy hit 'Hermash' with such force that it flashed through space like a stupefied ball hit by a baseball bat. Anyone who happened not to hold on to something, hit the wall, floor, or the nearest object, many of which turned out to be unpleasantly angular. The energy apparently triggered some wandering impulse in the superlumination system, as the engines began to increase the output power by themselves, not responding to commands from the engine room computer.

"Everyone is okay? Report, goddamn it, or I'll tear your legs off your asses!!!" the captain roared into the intercom, wiping the blood from the gash on her forehead cut against the edge of the science console.

Andy Karpiel helped her up, even though his arm was dislocated. Mstislav Deadskull was lying unconscious on the edge of his armchair, while his young companion, who had not suffered somehow, made every effort to ensure that 'Hermash', flying faster and faster, didn't bump into something big. Jeeves Kerk struggled to get up from the floor and stood unsteadily, clinging to the command chair, for he was less fortunate than Spox, who only bruised his elbow - he banged his head against the wall and felt an imposing bump grow on it at an Olympic rate. The rest wasn't seriously injured.

After a while, reports, or rather lamentations from the entire ship, began to come through the intercom. The damage was considerable, the rescue operation was made more difficult by the fact that 'Hermash' was still accelerating. The engine room was doing what it could. The technicians trembled with fear that the ship wouldn't be able to withstand the overload, but so far they had failed to stop the alien program that had infected their computer. At last, in the final despair, engineer Mikhalov slammed the main link with a bottle of moonshine, which Greg and Karpiel had bootlegged with Johnnie Caterpillar, it is unknown from what. The bottle broke and the high proof fluid flooded the system, causing an immediate short circuit. The ship slowed down so suddenly that they all flew in all directions once more.

"No, I'm not playing like that," Captain Zakrzevska grunted, getting up again from the floor. "Engine room, what's going on?!"

"I report that the paralite crystals have broken down," reported Charles Mikhalov succinctly. "The end, fin, finito, basta, kaniec filma. Kancerta nie budiet, Sasha swallowed the saxophone. Reaching the warp speed is also not possible and will not be."

"And to hell," the captain quoted the famous line from the classic movie 'Two Killers'. "We flew."

She sat helplessly in the command chair and looked at Captain Kerk, whose head was just being examined by Spox. The famous Uoltan was as calm as if he had been sitting in an Anglican church during a Sunday sermon, but Jeeves T. Kerk cursed under his breath like a drunken cowboy. By coincidence, he had hit the exact same spot as the first time.

"I'm afraid we can forget about the arrest for the time being," Lilianna said finally, meeting Kerk's fierce glare. "Although I am starting to like the idea itself. A cozy cell, walks, regular meals and no responsibility. Eh, dreams..."

XXIV.

The whole brawl practically went unnoticed for ArCer and TiShan. To understand why this happened, we should go back to the point when ArCer, having left the bridge, knocked on the door of the young doctor's quarters. Not receiving a reply, he simply slid the door open and entered. TiShan sat curled up in her bed and wept copiously.

ArCer shook his head disapprovingly.

"I already told you that this is an illogical waste of water and electrolytes," he said scoldingly. "All your behavior indicates emotional instability. We have to deal with this before anything really bad happens."

"Leave me alone."

"It's too late for peace. You've already rocked the boat. What were you thinking?"

"You should be in charge, not that chit who pretends to be captain!"

ArCer sat down next to the doctor and gently took her hands. Even such tearful she was beautiful and he liked her more and more.

"I'm just an observer here," he said emphatically. "I don't want to take command, especially since I might face a rebellion. Do you understand? I promised Captain Zakrzevska that I would teach you how to control your emotions. You may not be aware of this, but in the Uoltans they are very strong if they are not suppressed. In the past, because of them, we almost destroyed our civilization."

The doctor nodded meekly. She looked like a hurt child now, and ArCer felt a sudden urge to hug her. It was an illogical but very pleasant feeling that he had never known before - he had never felt anything like this for his wife TeM, who was the antithesis of this girl. She was always cool and composed, and treated her husband as a necessary evil. Their parents brought them together and they didn't protest because they were children. Later, when they grew up, their relationship seemed natural in an orderly society, even desirable, because they could create a family, have children. Until now, ArCer had seen himself as someone who had done well in life. He had a nice, cultured and intelligent wife, successful son, beautiful house, but since he was on this ship, which was full of emotions, he wondered involuntarily why something was missing in his life, something he couldn't even name.

He reached out to touch TiShan's temples with his fingers, but the girl jerked suddenly backwards.

"I don't want to," she said, and her eyes widened with sudden fear. It was disturbing, and ArCer turned serious.

"Has anyone done something to you in this way?" He asked.

TiShan shook her head first, then nodded.

"My parents wanted me to marry one scientist," she said, stumbling slightly. "He was my father's age, but they said it would be for the best ... They left me alone with him, and he made a connection, though I asked him not to. He said that if we were to be married, we must have established a bond ... The next day I ran away from home."

"Yeah. It was really careless of him. Instead of making a telepathic link with him, you got a permanent trauma. Someday I will convince you that it was only an unfortunate coincidence, but now let's limit ourselves to the current affairs."

He put TiShan's hands together, keeping her two fingers straight, index and middle ones, and bending the rest.

"Please close your eyes now and concentrate," he said. "Please direct all negative energy to the tips of your extended fingers. In this way, you will release it and dissipate it without any harm."

The doctor obediently closed her eyes, trying to do as he instructed her. She had never tried it before, because although her parents had taught her various meditation techniques, she had been too rebellious to them to benefit from these teachings. Now she found that they weren't that stupid ... though she'd have had a hard time telling if this "energy dissipation" really helped her or it was the touch of ArCer's hand, so confident and calm. The commander felt the girl calming down slowly, her stress level dropping, and the Uoltan logic of reasoning taking his place.

"It's better now? he asked softly, with a friendly smile.

"Better," TiShan replied, opening her eyes.

She looked at ArCer with such gratitude that he felt like hugging her again ... and this time he didn't stop. He even went a little further, much further in fact. Preoccupied with other people's problems, he clean forgot that the period of hormonal storm was fast approaching for him, and that he hadn't relieved the tension in time.

The young woman gave as good as she got. Therefore, it is easy to understand why they were awakened only by the shock of sudden braking.

"What's that?" TiShan asked sleepily, hugging ArCer.

The latter listened for a while, but the doctor's quarters were soundproofed, so he was not able to hear what was unleashed on board.

"I don't know," he said finally. "I have to check it out. Before, I thought the ship shook, but I couldn't wake up."

"No wonder," TiShan chuckled without a trace of shame.

Someone banged violently on the door, then slid it open, giving no time for a reply. The tall, thin woman in a habit and cornet burst into the quarters. At the sight of the two Uoltans naked as newborns, she braked sharply with her heels.

"Sodom and Gomorrah!" she exclaimed, scandalized. At least cover yourselves with something when you see a religious person, adulterers!"

"Am I supposed to be Sodom or Gomorrah?" ArCer asked, stupefied.

The doctor silenced him with a slight hiss and turned to the nun:

"We are sorry, Sister Ophelia, we didn't know that you planned a visit to my quarters."

"I didn't plan," the nun huffed. "What a moment you chose to break the sixth commandment ... We have been fired upon, there is a lot of damage, and together with others, I'm looking for those who suffered. Once you both deign to get dressed, it would be nice if you joined us ... for you are fine, there is no doubt about it."

She glanced at them angrily once more and stepped out into the corridor. The Uoltans dressed quickly and joined her in searching the sections.

XXV.

Reports of damage to the plating and the ruin of individual sections were pouring in from all over the ship. First the acceleration, well beyond the safety scale, then the sudden braking made a terrible mess. The ship withstood, but required repairs, and for now it was not even known how many crewmen would be able to participate in them. The infirmary refused to provide data because there was so much work that nobody had time to count.

Luckily for 'Hermash', the engine room didn't suffer too much. Almost everything except the superlumination reactor was working, and the engineering team took care of the repairs right away.

"The batteries are full, and if we manage to start the backup power reactor, we will survive," Mikhalov reported to Captain Zakrzevska. "If not, we'll be choking in fifteen hours."

"So, get cracking, handyman engineer," the captain sighed.

Malvinka, Jürgen, Karpiel, Arek, both steersmen - all looked at her expectantly, as does each crew, believing that the captain, second to God, would get them out of this cesspool in which they were stuck up to their necks. And it didn't matter that in their case the commander was a tiny young woman with no cosmic experience - the captain has to deal with it, and that's it. Lilianna knew what they were thinking, and she wanted to weep, but held back. Such a demonstration wouldn't have helped, and somehow the crew had to be kept in check.

"Ensign, I give you praise," she said, addressing the young steersman. "You handled the difficult circumstances perfectly well. What is your name, sir?"

The boy jumped up from her chair.

"Bequiet," he choked out. Seeing the astonished glances around, he added hastily:

"Xavier Bequiet. Such a surname .... Do you think it's easy to live with? Wherever I go, I introduce myself politely, and everyone dummies up."

"Man, it would be better to be called just Shutup," Malvinka muttered.

"Do you know where we are, Ensign?" asked the captain, smoothly glozing over the case of the unusual name of her helmsman.

Confused, the boy shook his head.

"Computer, where are we?" Andy Karpiel asked, turning to the library console.

"I don't know," was the reply.

Captain Kerk was unpleasantly surprised that Hermash's on-board computer spoke in a hoarse schnapsbaritone, as if belonging to an old drunkard who has merits in the field of alcohol consumption. It was nothing like the soft female voice of a computer on Superprice.

Karpiel stared at his console. He hadn't expected such an answer.

"How come you don't know it? It's an information connection!"

"So, I'm just informing you that I don't know," this time the voice of the computer was clearly offended.

"Lieutenant Krencik, what do you see?" asked the captain, abandoning the mechanical assistant for the time being.

"I see clouds, I see flowers, I see Superman's undercrackers," Malvinka replied, resting her cheek on her hand. "Oh, you're asking seriously? Eavesdropping is silent. When it comes to visual content, we have chaos."

"Father Toadstool would say it's very good, because there was chaos in the beginning," the captain said. "Let someone take the navigator to the infirmary ..."

She paused as Spox approached her and examined the wound on her forehead.

"You should see a doctor, too," he decided after a moment.

"Forget it. I just need to wash my dial and it'll be okay. It will heal by the wedding."

"I don't know when you are having this wedding, but this wound needs to be dressed, otherwise it will cause trouble and you will have a scar."

The captain waved her hand impatiently.

"Alright. Arek, bridge. Get to know our location, I'll be right back."

Reaching the infirmary, the captain saw that she couldn't squeeze through quickly and gave up. She returned to her quarters, and on the way, she found the completely stupefied Johnnie, who was carrying Gizia on his shoulder, and the frightened Bear was running at his feet.

"They were shooting at us," he said when he saw his captain. "Weasel escaped, I caught her with difficulty."

Gizia snuggled against his neck, and her hair was sticking out in all directions. She was clearly terrified of what was happening.

"You have to find a cage for her, or something similar... You will talk to Mikhalov. And what about Veronika?" asked the captain, soothingly stroking the squeaking Bear.

"I don't know anything, they are looking for the girl, and the doggie stayed alone, so I took him. And something happened also to you, let all saints save us ..."

"It's nothing, a simple scratch." Lilianna entered her ruined quarters, found the hand-held regenerator effortfully, and, helping herself with the compact mirror, she somehow closed the wound on her forehead with it.

Now she was ready to overcome the mess that had arisen on the ship.

XXVI.

Despite the heavy damage, few crew members were seriously injured. The rest suffered more from fear than from wounds that, on closer inspection, proved to be superficial and harmless. One person, unfortunately, died - the helmsman Veronika Bumblebee, or actually not so much died as got lost without a trace. Finally, she was deemed to have been sucked into the vacuum when part of the deck had depressurized - there was no way to confirm this as most of the sensors had failed.

Engineer Mikhalov and his team worked in the engine room on the engines and the damaged computer. Greg was sitting at the control panel, armed with all the tools he might have needed and a bottle of something stronger at his disposal. He had to drink, struggling bravely with the processors of the computer and SyTar, which for some reason became very active and put his two cents in everything. Working with such a companion inside the brain was not easy, even though Greg got used to it.

Sister Ophelia, accompanied by the Uoltans, whom she had chosen as her team, was bravely digging through the mounds of debris in her sector, looking for the wounded. They were accompanied by Malvinka Krencik, who interrupted her shift and handed over the comm console to Inga Laush. The nun showed great energy and efficiency in finding and digging out the victims. She had already dispatched a few to the infirmary and had given a strong slap to one hysterical crewwoman to sober her up, and she hadn't lost her positive attitude even for a moment. Having reached the headquarters of the engineer, the three rescuers concluded that the headquarters was virtually gone - only the force field kept the room airtight. Even so, it was possible to pick up a weak signal of life from within.

"Something small ... Some animal. Alive," ArCer said. "Probably the chief engineer's favorite."

He was eager to pull the creature out, but he was too well built for that. The only place through which one could get inside was too narrow for him. It turned out, however, that he was unnecessarily worried. Sister Ophelia removed her cornet and squeezed between the remnants, ignoring objection of ArCer who feared for the stability of the force fields. After a moment she crawled out with a terrified vall in her hands.

"It seems that this oversized rat belongs to our engineer," she said, handing him to TiShan. "He must be returned to him."

The doctor gave the pet to Malvinka with disgust that was difficult to hide. She didn't like animals, and she was simply afraid of most of them.

"You risked for something like this?" she asked in surprise.

"It is also a creation of God," replied the nun sternly, strapping the cornet on her head again and moving vigorously to continue searching.

Malvinka followed her, hugging the trembling Vuvu against her. The poor furry dog was snapping his teeth and snarling at his unseen enemy, pretending to be more formidable than he had ever been. Having reached the end of the designated section, the team encountered Captain Zakrzevska, who was running around the ship, trying to grasp the extent of the damage.

"Oh, hello, sister," she said, stopping beside them. "Where's your brother? I mean, Father Thaddeus? I'll go crazy with these family connotations ..."

"Tadek is praying in the chapel. He is fit only for that, and not very much."

Sister Ophelia nervously adjusted the cornet, and Captain Zakrzevska almost laughed. Someone "up there" must have had a great sense of humor, since he gave 'Hermash' these two antagonists as spiritual protection.

Slowly, the commotion on the ship calmed down, mainly as a result of the coordinated activities of the rescue teams led by Lieutenant Maura Gvizdak who kept her cool. The wounded were treated, the badly wounded were operated on, and those who were not seriously ill were divided into repair teams. The commencement of works couldn't be postponed, although it was not known whether the repairs would be of benefit. If the reserve reactor hadn't been put into operation, the fate of 'Hermash' would have been sealed anyway. Few, however, were aware of this - the captain preferred not to inform the crew about the threat, so as not to cause a dangerous panic.

Having briefly acquainted herself with the damage, she ordered a quick repair schedule to be drawn up and without delay to get to work, then together with Malvinka Krencik she went down to the engine room.

"Mr. Mikhalov, how's it going?" she called as she entered.

"I don't know yet, goddamn it!" the engineer shouted back from the backup reactor chamber.

"I guess it can be started, but I won't risk initial launching without checking all the circuits. If it explodes, we will die. I need two more hours. Oh, don't you know the captain, what about my quarters?"

"Unfortunately, it's gone with the wind. Until the coverings are patched up, you can't even get in there."

There was a rumble in the chamber, then the chief engineer jumped out, with maddened eyes and an old-fashioned wrench in his hand.

"What about my Vuvu?!" he screamed with such fear as if they had been just nosediving with the whole ship to a fading star.

"All right, he's here," Malvinka handed him Vall, which, whimpering mournfully, leapt into his master's arms.

Mikhalov threw the wrench to the floor, only miraculously missing a foot of the technician who was bent over the circuits of the auxiliary computer. He hugged the pet and began to whisper something to him, while stroking his spiky back. It seemed that he forgot about the reactor, the power supply, the repairs, and the whole ship in general.

"Alright, alright," the captain decided to break this idyll at last. "Miss Krencik will take care of your favorite, and let you restore the power supply. Then we'll worry about what to do next. Oh, and when you finish the job here, talk to the main computer. I may be wrong, but it looks like some peculiar program has been activated on it. A moment ago, when I asked what time, it was, it replied:

"Sweetheart, half past the chimney."

XXVII.

For Captain Kerk and Mr. Spox, what was happening with 'Hermash' was at first irritating, then terrifying, and then it brought them to a state close to total confusion. Despite the apparent chaos on board, the Poles pulled themselves together surprisingly quickly and took action. The damaged plating was repaired by a crew working in vacuum, the rest took care of the interior and partially restored it as such, even before the chief engineer announced in triumph that the backup reactor was working fine. He had sat at it for nearly ten hours, meticulously checking all parameters before deciding he had the right to say something like this and go to sleep. As his quarters was still "in shambles", he lay down on the floor in the library, leaving the engine room in the care of Greg and Jolka Stern. He needed to get some sleep.

Captain Zakrzevska, who had already caught a few hours of sleep, did herself up a little and called a meeting of senior officers.

"But the chief engineer is sleeping like a log," said Christopher Mayher, who assisted in driving the command section to the conference room. "Shall I wake him up?"

"There is no such need," replied the captain. "Bring Jolka Stern, she knows everything about engines. Oh, and find me Kerk and his sidekick too."

The commander of Superprice and his first mate, who were ignored by everyone, walked around Hermash, examining everything and wondering who had agreed to send this joyful creation, staffed by a random jumble of crazy people, on such a serious mission, and during what attack of insanity. They both tried to talk to the on-board computer, but it talked nonsense, or got into verbal scuffles with them, and finally declared that they were not authorized personnel and that it had no obligation to talk to them at all. Apparently, it had a personality of its own, and an unpleasant one. It was rather surprising, especially since the Uoltan ArCer, one of the science officers on 'Hermash', swore that such a thing didn't exist in the construction plans. They accepted the invitation to the conference with relief and joy, because it was a chance to learn something specific, especially why the hell they couldn't connect with their ship.

In the conference room, first of all, they saw a table set with platters and bottles, like a buffet.

"Excuse me, gentlemen," said Captain Zakrzevska in response to their astonished glances. "Our cook says that you need to refresh yourself for such a conference and he has prepared all this, so please help yourself without hesitation."

Lilianna finished braiding her hair still damp after washing, then wrapped the braid around her head and attached it with large hair clips. She gave the impression of a person who was already accustomed to the new conditions, whatever they might be.

"Is everyone present?" she asked rhetorically and tapped her hand on the table top. "We're starting the briefing. I am asking the first officer to highlight the situation."

Arek got up and in one breath drank a glass of water with some juice, given to him by Matias.

"Ladies, gentlemen," he began. "The mysterious Clingorgian torpedo turned out to be a generator of an unknown type of energy. The impulse it created, threw us into a place that has not yet been mapped, a place that may even lie beyond the boundaries of our galaxy. No communication can be established. We only have white noise on all channels. Our databases are useless as benchmarks. Briefly: we don't know where we are, we don't know in which direction we should go, and to make matters worse, only the propulsion engines are working. The only paralite crystal we have left is currently feeding the reserve reactor, without which we would be doomed to a quick death. However, since the reactor is working, we'll keep living for some time."

"It's unbelievable that the fate of the whole ship depends on some ornament from Swarovski's advertisement ..." muttered Lieutenant Krencik with disgust.

Captain Zakrzevska looked at the guests.

"Gentlemen," she said. "I'm sorry it turned out that way, but for now you are both condemned to our company and for the common good I advise you to accept it. If you have any questions, keep them until the end of the briefing."

At that moment, Joe Watery burst into the conference room, gasping for breath.

"Miss ... miss Captain," he choked out. "Please, have me arrested!"

"What happened?"

"I threw ... at my wife ... a broken lever."

"Is she hurt badly?" Dr. TiShan asked, rising from her chair.

"No, I missed ... But she'll be here right away!"

Were it not for the apparent horror of poor Joe, everyone would have laughed, and so compassion prevailed, though the exchanged glances were very amused. Everyone knew Mrs. Tekla's bloody temperament and her views on what consensus in a marriage should have looked like.

"Miss Gvizdak, take Ensign Watery to the arrest where he will stay until his wife cool down a bit," the captain said, struggling to suppress a smile.

"Yes, ma'am," replied Maura Gvizdak. Together with two members of the security section, she solemnly escorted the happy Joe to the arrest, set up a guard in front of his cell door and returned to the room where the briefing was still in progress.

"Mr. von Braun, what are our supplies?" the captain just asked Matias.

"It's not bad," replied the young diplomat, and a passionate cook. "It may be enough for us for a very long time, although I don't know if long enough for us to get anywhere. If only the propulsion engines are working ..."

"Miss Stern, what is the condition of the engines?"

"The engines are working, Captain," said Engineer Jolanta, with her mouth full of vegetable salad. "Even the superlumination system should work if we had new crystals.The old ones were burnt."

"Doctor TiShan, the report."

"The injured are in a stable condition," said the Uoltanian doctor. "Two of the crew died before we were able to help them, five others won't get back on their feet soon, but will survive. The rest will be back in service in a few days. Drs Zmiyevski and

Nbeba are taking stock, but even a cursory look at the inventory allows for cautious optimism. We shouldn't run out of drugs."

"Research department, Mr. Karpiel?"

"Little damage, no casualties."

"Communications department, Miss Krencik?"

"As the First said, we only have noise in the headphones. Everything is operational, but we can't connect to anyone. Internal communication works flawlessly."

"Weapons?"

"Everything works, the armory is well stocked, the mazer batteries are eighty percent full," Vasyl Anecdotych Zaychik reported servicely. "Come on, Kristof, let's charge them to one hundred percent."

"All right," the captain nodded. "Then listen: our priority is to seek paralite. We have to find it, no matter how. Scanners are supposed to constantly check every litter on our way, every rock crumb, not to mention meteors and asteroids. Are there any questions?"

"I have a question," Captain Kerk said, then stood up, leaned his hands on the table top, and cleared his throat so that he almost ripped off his throat.

"If I understand correctly, for now my first mate and I are trapped in this ... ship," he mispronounced an unflattering epithet and continued. "As there is nothing, we can do about it, I would like to at least fill the gaps in our knowledge. What's the matter with those Clingorgs which attacked us?"

"He's askang about it noo, lowlander," Andrew Karpiel snorted, unable to resist.

"Be quiet, Andy. Better late than never, a necrophile used to say that," the captain said, and turned to Kerk. "What exactly do you want to know? Where did we meet them, what did we argue about ... or better, what was their complaint based on?"

"Oh, the last one."

"Well, the whole matter will be presented to you by Mr. ArCer, because he's been up to his ears in it all from the beginning. Talk to each other. Commander, you have my permission to show our guests all material relating to the artificial asteroid and its crew. Dr. TiShan, by the way, what about that boy we brought on board?"

SiWok woke up during the firing. "His condition is stable," the doctor replied.

Spox shuddered at the boy's name and pricked up his ears.

"Sorry, doctor, but what's his name?" he asked. "SiBok? Who is this boy?"

"SiWok. He is less than twenty years old. He's a third-year cadet at the Armada Star Academy, and I think he'll tell our guests some interesting things about the Clingorgs allegedly wronged by us."

Spox looked disappointed, though it would have been hard to guess why. In any case, he was silent. Later it became known that his stepbrother had a similar name, hence the questions.

"That's the end of the briefing. I'm asking all officers to take care of the morale of the crew in this difficult situation," said Captain Zakrzevska.

"Entschuldigung, Fräu Hauptmann,[5] but how are we to take care of something that is not here from the very beginning?" Jürgen asked coldly.

"Mr. von Ravensburg, if you talk such heresies, I will demote you to private and send you to clean the plasma lines!" Captain Zakrzevska screamed and banged her hand on the table so that even Jeeves T. Kerk curled up reflexively. "If I catch someone sowing defeatism, let God's hand protect him from me, because God maybe sometimes forgive, but I never!"

"Do I have to sit here and listen to these blasphemies?" asked matter-of-factly Father Toadstool, who, as the deck chaplain, was also present at the meeting, though he had not yet spoken.

---

[5] *(Ger)* Forgive me, Miss Captain.

"No, you don't have to! And I don't blaspheme, I warn! We are in a bad enough situation, and I will not tolerate any obstruction here! Understood?! End of the briefing!"

She left, unsuccessfully trying to slam the door behind her, which didn't make much sense, because the photocell was working flawlessly, annoyingly enough.

The officers looked at each other.

"For obstruction, the best are prunes," muttered Arek. "You eat a full glass of it, and it's gone."

"We don't have prunes," sighed Matias von Braun, resting his cheek on his hand.

"What happened to your captain?" Captain Kerk asked helplessly.

"Nothing, dear," Karpiel informed him kindly. "She's been always like that. Help yourself to the cheese toasts, they are delicious."

XXVIII.

For almost two weeks the starship 'Hermash' had been flying in an unknown direction, searching for paralite crystals. After solidly patching the outer coatings, the rest of the work was carried out on the fly, as it didn't require going into a vacuum. Life in the crew panned out somehow, though not always very auspiciously. The Watery's marriage continued to quarrel, there were even fisticuffs in it, but slowly everyone got used to it. Chief engineer Mikhalov made friends with Malvinka Krencik and they spent every free moment together, which made Gregory Brzenchyshchykievich extremely angry - not only was he lumbered with the engine room more and more often, but he also felt jealous. He, too, liked the pretty lieutenant, but she ignored him.

"If I, damn it, had a six-legged groundhog as a bait ..." Greg muttered furiously, checking the valves during one of the routine rounds that he was forced to do for his boss.

Somewhere in his head there was an unpleasant chuckle.

"Get rid of him. It's the only logical solution," SyTar advised him.

Greg only shrugged his shoulders impatiently and didn't reply. He had the impression for a long time that Uoltan himself considered Malvinka a very attractive person and resented his 'host' for not following her all the time.

Captain Kerk and Mr. Spox had already become a bit used to the crazy ship and its explosive commander, although they still wanted nothing more than to return to their unit. What happened here was so different from the orderly atmosphere of the USS Superprice that they felt like in an asylum for the insane, the more so because when they asked anyone:

"Is it always so bizarre here?"

the person replied with amazement:

"What do you mean?"

Interestingly, even the good Dr. Nbeba, who had served on Superprice, and therefore their colleague, reacted in this way. The black doctor with Polish roots perfectly adapted to 'Hermash', he made friends with Jacob Zmiyevski and the sister superior, Lolita Icant, and received the nickname 'Shaman' among the crew, which he was not at all angry about. His cheerful and gentle manner won him universal sympathy, despite his poor beginnings and, one could say, people had more confidence in him than in Dr. TiShan.

The most surprising thing for Kerk and Spox was that every calendar Sunday they were herded together with the remaining officer elders to the chapel, where they had to attend the service and listen to the sermon, most often phantasmagoric and completely out of touch with life. Father Toadstool followed this very strictly - interestingly, all the officers allowed themselves to be quite easily terrorized, although not all were Catholics, or even believers. This was something neither Kerk nor Spox could understand, as well as the fact that the priest personally found them and chased them to the chapel. This was a clear violation of the religious freedom section.

"Don't object, believe that it will be faster and calmer this way," the captain told them, so they decided to accommodate her. Ultimately, heroes like them couldn't be hurt by a little forced prayer. Bored at most, but on the other hand, listening to Fr. Toadstool's blather wasn't the worst entertainment - Spox even said one Sunday that he had no idea how in a ten-minute part you could contain so many conflicting views and erroneous information. He clearly treated the sermons of the chaplain as an opportunity to study human nature and discover its hitherto unknown aspects.

So somehow things were going on, though there were some unexpected events as well. One fine day, two-meter-long snakes appeared on the second deck, causing a wild panic. One of them decided to visit the bathroom, which caused Mstislav Deadskull, who was there in silent contemplation, to jump out into the corridor with his pants lowered to his knees and a roll of toilet paper in his hand, and accidentally run into Sister Ophelia passing by. He screamed then:

"Watch your step, victim!"

It was completely illogical, as it was, he who caused the collision. The nun, surprised and clearly shocked, pushed him all the way against the wall, shouting:

"Pervert!"

"Where's the pervert?" asked a passing security patrol consisting of three young girls.

"You have only one thing on your minds," Sister Ophelia replied not very to the point, while Deadskull was hastily pulling up his pants. He had no intention of returning to the bathroom, as he had lost the necessity with emotion, but the girls looked in there and made such a screeching sound that alerted crewmen began to flock from everywhere. Father Toadstool came first and at the sight of the reptile crawling calmly, he screamed excruciatingly, then fell to the floor as if cut down.

"Shall I call the infirmary?" Deadskull worried, shifting the toilet paper from hand to hand.

"What for? Is it the first time? He suffers from herpetophobia. Hit him, and he'll come around. Unbelievable, this ship is not a ship, it is Noah's ark," replied Sister Ophelia, who shook out, and then grabbed the snake expertly right behind its head.

However, there was still the second one. Before it became clear that both snakes belonged to Professor Trekovsky and were completely harmless, a fuss was made, which had to be finally calmed down by the security under the personal command of Maura Gvizdak. The captain got furious and ordered a strict inventory of all the 'favorites' aboard the 'Hermash'. When she was provided with the detailed list, she sat down with shock.

It turned out that Gizia, Vuvu and Bear were completely innocent pets. On the ship there were, with great talent, smuggled in briefcases, under a jacket or in a pocket, such specimens as: four Brazilian tarantulas, one Australian, the aforementioned Dinoslaw Trekovsky's pythons, a young Iberian lynx, a frilled-neck lizard, two flying phalangers, a siberian chipmunk, raccoon, an adult large flying fox, a capybara named Whisper, pot-bellied piglet, white-tufted marmoset, a pair of guinea pigs and fifteen chameleons of different varieties. Maura, who took the inventory, honestly admitted that she wasn't entirely sure if that was all.

The captain locked herself in her quarters, and she was heard swearing there with the utmost passion. Still, no one was scolded - Lilianna had a sufficiently developed sense of justice to believe that since she had smuggled Gizia on board, she couldn't reproach anyone. She only wondered why, with such a diverse zoo aboard, the innocent pythons had caused such a commotion, but she didn't dwell on the subject. She only recommended that they keep an eye on what they had there, mostly spiders, which, being small creatures, could get anywhere and even lead someone who stumbled upon them into a heart attack.

The case of a persistent rash that plagued many crew members was also explained. The lynx had fleas which, like fleas, didn't respect Armada's regulations and jumped from one to the other.

"Let the science department produce some fleasol, or something similar ..." the captain said when she was informed of the unwanted stowaways.

"And the spiders won't be poisoned?" Malvinka asked with concern.

"Spiders are not insects. Anyway, they will be closed in something sealed for the time of spraying," answered Karpiel happily.

From the beginning of the flight, he had been waiting for some tasks that only his department could handle, because until now his staff had been mostly occupied with playing cards and social flirting. Only professor Trekovsky worked, but he didn't tell anyone on what. And there was also ArCer, but he was independent and not subject to Karpiel, and Andy respected him too much to inquire about the subject of his research.

Flea poison was soon produced and used. Although all fleas become extinct, now half of the crew got an allergic rash, and the capybara and guinea pigs got conjunctivitis so that they couldn't see.

"Damn it, I'm a doctor, not a zootechnician," Jacob Zmiyevski was angry when he was called for home visits to suffering rodents and, which made sense in this situation, he treated the animals as if they had been human.

"Unless he starts treating people as if they were horses, that's all right," Captain Zakrzevska said when Sister Lolita Icant told her about the troubles of the nice doctor. Lolita, a cheerful, sociable and not very intelligent girl, loved gossip above all else, which is why the events in the infirmary were always an open secret. However, it must be honestly admitted that she was the first to learn about all the novelties of the captain - Lolita strictly followed the official hierarchy.

XXIX.

Dr. TiShan knew better than the others what the threat to the crew was, as she assisted ArCer during scientific analysis. They both discovered that the ship was affected by a field of unknown energy, possibly related to the sector they found themselves in. It was impossible to figure out what this interaction was yet, but ArCer felt it existed. He knew how it worked on him, so he suspected that it must also have had some vague influence on people.

"Could it be dangerous?" TiShan asked, looking up at him with her big, gentle eyes.

"It's hard to say. For me, it causes the degeneration of an emotional block, in people it can cause irrational behavior," the commander replied her. "I mean, more irrational than usual."

ArCer himself couldn't quite understand why he was still thinking about the girl after satisfying the desire that had resulted from the advent of the mating season. Perhaps it was the emanation of this place, the space into which the torpedo launched by the Clingorgs had driven them. Oh yeah, the torpedo ...

"Captain, I have already figured out the case of the missile that was sent to us from the Clingorgian ship," he said, having found Captain Zakrzevska in the gym. "It was a mini-generator of energy similar to the tachyon jet, but much more powerful. If it had hit us, it would have sprayed our atoms all over the area, and so it only released the shockwave. It's a mystery to me where the Clingorgs got it. No race I know has such a thing."

The captain looked at him with the crossed eyes, then put the barbells back on the rack and stood up. She looked tempting in her gym clothes, especially that it could be seen that she had nice legs.

"Well, an interesting academic achievement," she said. "At the moment, however, this news won't help us much. We can only use it when we get back."

Ignoring the officer still standing in the basic position, she hanged herself upside down on the ladders and started doing crunches. At the same time, she continued to say:

"The ship is now patched, people have recovered, no immediate threat hangs over us, so we can work normally. The morale of the crew is very important, I think you yourself understand. Everyone has to take care of it as much as they can. Sister Ophelia offered to organize a theater club, Father Thaddeus watches over the mass ... yes, I know that you think it is at least a gross weirdness, but I assure you that regular services have a therapeutic effect. At least in a situation like ours. The universal rite, adopted at the general assembly of representatives of earthly religions eighty years ago, does not offend anyone, and all religious people can participate in it. In fact, you too..."

"We Uoltans have our own beliefs. But if you like, I will take part in what our chaplain does, it's okay for me."

"I don't give a damn, Mr. ArCer. It's your thing, your circus. But Father Toadstool will probably storm, so decide for yourself if you want to be in conflict with him ..."

Here Lilianna paused, because Captain Kerk burst into the gym, angry and red in the face like a crushed tomato.

"Do you know that such a preserve on the Star Armada ship is against the regulations?!" he asked abruptly.

ArCer looked at him with cold interest, not understanding why he was saying about it now, when such statements were already a forgotten matter.

"Dear, I don't care about regulations," Zakrzevska replied nonchalantly, continuing her exercises. "You are too irritated, I can see, in the end you will die of a heart attack here and how will I explain this in the command? Now who the hell is that?!"

The hell brought the grumpy Johnnie Caterpillar, carrying Gizia on his shoulder. The inseparable Bear was walking heavily by his leg.

"Sir-ma'am, I swear to God it's not the fault of the God's creation," the highlander said, hitting his massive chest with a kulak. "It was this stranger who came to the mess and sat down on the chair without looking if there was anything on it..."

"She bit my right chee ... buttock!" Kerk shouted, forgetting about his captain's dignity.

"And what did you expect when you crushed her?" Johnnie replied. "If you had hurt her, our captain would have torn your head off, and before something else too..."

"Is she okay?" Lilianna made sure with concern.

"No. She's healthy and cheerful as always."

"And won't you ask if I'm okay?" Kerk hissed angrily, rubbing the injured part of his body.

"I don't have to. I can see and hear it. Go to the infirmary, the doctors are having lunch at this time, but Sister Lolita will be happy to take care of you, and vice versa, I suppose."

At this point, ArCer's communicator beeped softly. The Uoltan apologized to those present and took out a device that he had improved himself about a week ago, equipping it with a screen and a receiver, coupled with long-range sensors. Now he turned on the screen, and for a moment he traced the stripes of spectral analysis glowing on it before looking back at Captain Zakrzevska. His eyes remained cool and calm, his face unmoved.

"Captain," he said, "I'm reporting that we have paralite."

The detected cluster of valuable crystals was located on a small asteroid, practically airless. Its surface was covered in places with remnants of some structures, which clearly indicated that it was the remains of a once inhabited planet that had undergone an unknown catastrophe. According to the scans, the paralite was several dozen meters below the surface and after determining the exact place, the science and engineering department formed an ad hoc mining team, which, blessed by Father Thaddeus, went to work briskly and with a song on its lips. It returned only two hours later with a load of crystals enough for several ships. The deposit was easily accessible, and although it turned out to be smaller than it had been thought, for the needs of 'Hermash', it was even too rich.

"The crystals are irregular, so their use may result in uncontrolled energy fluctuations, but give me a few hours and I will grind them into the desired shape," judged Jolka Stern after examining the prize. "As for cleanliness, they are in good condition. The inclusions are few and of no practical importance."

If Jolka said it, it had to be like that. Charles Mikhalov always claimed that she was an excellent specialist in superlumination engines, and he respected her much more than the rest of his team. Probably not without significance was the fact that Miss

Jola was able to pull up anyone like Saint Michael the devil, and she knew the "Dictionary of abusive words" backward and forward because the chief engineer didn't like meek women.

The crew celebrated the acquisition of the crystals in their own way. As Captain Kerk and Mr Spox passed the lounge, they heard a choral singing:

Drank!

It's true that we drank!

We blowed chunks, oh

With barf, we stunned

the world!

We drank!

Oh, how much we drank ...!

After looking into the lounge, both guests realized that the crew in it had already meticulously gotten drunk and are clearly striving to break the world record in this field. Disgusted, they found Captain Zakrzevska.

"Your crew is getting drunk," Kerk said in a tone of rebuke as he sat down at her distracted invitation.

"If you grudge, get drunk, too," replied Lilianna, not looking up from the tablet. "Don't worry, they are the ones who are off-duty. The watch and both uber-watches are sober."

"Doesn't it bother you?" Mr. Spox asked without any particular surprise in his voice.

"What's to bother me? That the watch is sober?" Captain Zakrzevska answered the question with a question, this time lifting her head and tossing the braid over her back.

"No, that the rest is drunk."

"After the service, everyone can have a drink. Besides, they have to celebrate the acquisition of the paralite somehow. And besides, who taught you such a snitching on others?"

"And if someone attacks us now?" Spox dwelled on the subject, smoothly avoiding the thorny subject of the 'snitching'.

"So, bloody what? Why do you care about him so much? He attacked first, let him defend himself alone. Have you never heard that a Pole is the best soldier when he is well oiled? Read about Kozietulski's charge at Samosierra."

"I don't understand you at all," Captain Kerk sighed with palpable resignation.

"And you don't have to," Lilianna consoled him. Just don't worry about all this and it'll be nice. When we turn on the warp drive, we will find the Superprice and you can go back to your people ... you don't want to arrest me anymore, do you?"

Kerk shrugged slightly. "No," he admitted reluctantly. "We have examined the materials you collected and it is clear from them that you weren't the aggressors. Moreover, it seems that you prevented the utter destruction of the hitherto unknown, peaceful and intelligent race.

Lilianna stroked casually the sleeping Gizia, curled up on the table.

"They were lucky to stumble upon us," she said after a moment. "The Clingorgs wanted to use them, possibly to attack the Uoltans. As these creatures reproduce by division, it only takes a few individuals to rebuild their populations, and let's hope they would be able to do so."

"What if it wasn't planet Uoltan that was about to be attacked?" Spox suggested suddenly, putting his hands behind his back in his own way. "The Clingorgs wouldn't have risked attacking one of the Union's planets, and so important one. In my opinion, their target was rather Camulus. When we come back, we will need to report it."

All three fell silent. From the corridor came the barking of Bear, who was playing with Johnnie Carerpillar, as well as the MP20 player. The atmosphere was relaxed and charged with some illogical carelessness in this situation.

"Will we be back?" Kerk asked softly.

"Certainly, Jeeves," Lilianna assured him unceremoniously. "One has not been born yet, which would harm Poles."

Meanwhile, in the engine room, Charles Mikhalov enjoyed watching the paralite crystals processed by Jolka with masterful precision. Currently, they had a regular shape with a 'pavilion' elongated according with the rules as well as facets equal to a fraction of a millimeter.

"It's ideal for a club," he said. "We can assemble."

Greg and Joe Stelmach went to work, whistling briskly, and Mikhalov helped them by controlling the installation process at the main computer console of the engine room. Vuvu sat, snuggled against his leg, grunting softly, wanting to attract his attention. Little vall didn't care where the ship was and where it would go, it was only important for him to be with his master. No one noticed the small, faintly visible cloud of energy that penetrated into the engine room, twirled for a moment under the ceiling, and flowed out through the wall.

An hour later, Captain Zakrzevska was sitting on the bridge, trying to determine some reasonably route to return to civilized regions. Despite repeated attempts, the navigators got lost hopelessly, because the most important thing, a point of reference, was missing. Even Christopher Mayher couldn't do anything about it.

"If it was about breaking through the enemy army, I would be able to offer advice and help," he said. "But I can't get to know how to get back to our lands if I can't figure out where we are."

The captain entered into the computer all the data at their disposal at the time and, after waiting a moment, asked:

"Computer, how can we get back to the Sol system region?"

"How do I know?" the computer muttered.

"From the data."

"From what data? What I got are shabby scraps."

"Computer, don't be like that. Try a little for the common good."

"I'm a computer, not a clairvoyant."

Captain Zakrzevska leaned helplessly against the science console. She was beginning to lose hope that she could do anything to get her crew home and she suddenly felt desperately alone.

"Little computer, help me, I must have someone to count on," she moaned tearfully.

"Captain, my queen, what can I do, little angel, if I can't find the way?" the touched computer sobbed.

Kerk and Mr Spox exchanged glances before Spox said to Lilianna:

"Captain, don't you think this computer is not fully operational? I could check it. I have A7 specialist class, maybe I can find something ... it is possible that it is a minor defect and if we remove it, the computer will work properly."

"What do you not like about me, you stray?" the loudspeaker growled, but Lilianna quickly turned it off so it wouldn't have time to protest.

"You can get into the program only from the panel next to the holo-room," she said. "My chief engineer tried elsewhere but only got a kick."

"What?"

"I mean, the electricity kicked him. And since Mr. Mikhalov wasn't inferior, he kicked it back and there was a need to use the help of the infirmary. This computer knows how to defend itself."

Spox winced slightly, looked at Kerek, then back at Lilianna.

"Maybe let's go to that link by the holo-room, I'll see what I can do," he suggested.

Lilianna nodded, turned on communication with the computer again, and left with the Uoltan and Johnnie Caterpillar, who was following them, gliding like a shadow. In the corridor they encountered an unusual sight - Joe Stelmach, smeared from head to toe was walking in the middle, clearly angry and probably not very sober.

"Eh, chick, the engines ready," he grunted, seeing the captain.

"We are not on 'chick' terms," Lilianna shouted. "Please express yourself according to regulations and wash yourself before going into the corridor!"

"I will say what I like! Look at her, if you give a mouse a cookie ..."

He didn't have time to say more, because Johnnie grabbed him by the neck and asked factually:

"Shall I arrest that bastard or at once beat him without a trial?"

"Order security to lock him up for forty-eight hours, let him cool down, just have them wash him first," the captain replied lightly.

The summoned security took the screaming Stelmach, who threatened everyone around with some unspecified consequences, with particular emphasis on the mean captain. Spox watched this scene with all the more astonishment as Lilianna herself, it seemed, didn't see anything unusual in it.

"Are we going?" she asked cheerfully, as if nothing had happened as soon as Stelmach's screams ceased in the distance.

"Okay, we can," Spox replied hesitantly. He wasn't sure of anything anymore, but a vague suspicion began to form in his mind.

XXX.

The huge holo-room, which took up half the fourth deck, had been closed since it was new. No one was eager to find out what was wrong with the circuits of this technical recreation room, because everyone had different things on their mind. Besides, the affairs of 'Hermash' were so peculiar that no one felt the need for artificial stimulus.

Mr. Spox removed the control panel cover and began checking the circuits. After a while he grabbed his head and sent Johnnie Caterpillar to the engine room with a list of parts and tools he needed.

"Who gave him the right to interfere with my work?!" Mikhailov shouted menacingly, glancing at the list.

"I don't know anything! I just had to ask about the little things Mr. Uoltan had requested."

"I will teach him a lesson," Mikhalov growled and headed for the holo-room.

He was truly furious, and when he saw Spox at the open panel, his anger reached its boiling point.

"Let it go!" he screamed. "I'd rather let you hold my personal fiancée's bust than touch the computer under my care!"

Spox looked at him out of the corner of his eye and replied calmly, without a trace of offense:

"I haven't seen you taking care of it. These are not complicated damages and they could be repaired at any time ... although on the other hand, I have never seen anyone put together logical circuits together with a tape for paper."

"Beloved, don't sulk, it's not healthy," the captain interjected. "This junk needs to be fixed and that's it, and you have more serious things on your mind. How are the warp engines? When will it be possible to start them?"

"We have some unforeseen difficulties, but we should finish it by the night watch," the engineer replied. "The science department promised to help us. We still need purified rubidium, additional coolant, and donuts with cherry marmalade."

Spox dropped the magnetic probe and looked at Mikhalov with sky-high amazement.

"Did I hear you wrong?" he asked.

"You didn't hear me wrong. It's Fat Thursday. Matias has been working hard since morning to make doughnuts for the whole crew from what we have, but Polish, honest ones, not some fraudulent rings."

Spox's ascetic face showed that he was trying to associate the existence of Thursday with the fact that it was supposed to be "fat" and with the need to make "doughnuts" by the cook, something he had never heard about - because it was probably not about flower buds or gemmating amoebas.

"What are doughnuts?" he asked finally.

"A type of cakes fried in pork lard, stuffed with preserves and glazed on top," the captain informed him. "I myself signed an order in the morning to deliver the spirit from the scientific department to the kitchen ... you know, when you use the spirit, the lard doesn't soak that much into the dough and it's tastier. On Fat Thursday you have to eat at least one donut, otherwise you will be unlucky all year round."

"Do you believe it?"

"No, but it's a very tasty superstition."

"It's something ..." Sopox finally picked up the probe. "So this is a Polish customary holiday?"

"Something like that. Next week we have Ash Wednesday and Lent begins, so today we are starting to organize a carnival party. Mr. and Captain Kerk are also invited, of course."

"In this situation, you want to have fun?"

"Yeah, what's the harm? Mr. Mikhalov, when the donuts are ready, I will personally make sure that the engine room gets the entire dish."

The engineer smiled; his anger was gone. He picked up Vuvu from the floor, put him on his shoulder, and strode away, whistling happily. Spox shook his head and went back to his interrupted work. In the fallen silence, one could clearly hear the rumor and the terrible curses of Joe Stelmach, who was brawling in the arrest - the cells were beside. Spox listened to this endless monologue for some time, finally couldn't stand it and asked:

"Is this young man suffering from Tourret syndrome?"

"No, he's just plain yap," Lilianna replied carelessly. "Don't worry about him, when he cools down, he will fell silent. You better tell me; can you do something about it?"

"Oh yes, but unfortunately it looks like the strange behavior of the main computer is unchangeable. For its construction, experimental matrices were used, based on the engrams of the human brain. The main memory core has been animated, and now your ship is in a sense a living creature. It has a brain that thinks for itself, which is very interesting, but it can also be dangerous."

"Hmm ... and can you change its powers so that it can't take the controls, disconnect the systems, etc?"

"Of course. From here I can do everything. I'll take care of it right away."

Spox worked in silence for a while, then decided everything was fine and turned to Lilianna:

"Please, Captain, choose a program now."

"Sea, beach, tropics," Lilianna demanded after a short thought, and stared at the open door.

Palm trees, a rustling ocean and the setting sun over the lagoon appeared in the holo-room. The air smelled of sea salt, wet sand and grass, the whole space was filled with the scream of gulls. The invigorating breeze was harmoniously woven with the sweet, hot scent of fried dough, as Sister Icant had just arrived on the fourth deck with a huge platter of tasty brown and white frosted doughnuts.

"Captain, help yourself," she said in her thin, singing voice. "And you, commander, too, please. They are great, although there was no cherry jam and we took strawberry one."

The captain grabbed a hot doughnut and happily stuck her teeth in it. Spox followed her, albeit with some reluctance and only at the pleading look of Lolita, who had, according to the description of the first mate, the eyes of a Disney spaniel and could achieve anything with their help.

"Great indeed," admitted the captain after a moment, licking her lips deliciously, and reached for her communicator. "Jasio, I know that you are in the mess and you are just binging. Take the plate of donuts from the cook and take it to the engine room. Plate them enough for them to be stuffed until the evening."

"I'll be there in a moment, miss," said from the loudspeaker the slightly mumbling bass of the orderly, in fact having his mouth full of hot dough.

"I admit that this baking has a nice effect on the sense of taste, said Spox, trying to eat with dignity, which is never easy with frosted lips. "However, I have doubts as to whether it is healthy."

"Because it isn't, like all that is sweet," replied Lilianna with all her calmness and with such a peculiar intonation that Uoltan almost choked on jam. So, will we check to what extent the holoprojections are real?"

***

What the captain and Spox were doing in the holo-room was unknown, but they came out after four hours, in a state of animation that seemed to exceed the excitement of a normal recreational program. At least that's what the leading gossipers of 'Hermash' said, mainly on the basis of the captain's tousled hairstyle and Mr. Spox's very suspiciously glittering, usually Uoltanian-style gloomy eyes.

"And that's good, refusing them a little moment alone would have been unchristian," said to Mikhalov Malvinka Krencik, who was getting ready to talk to Father Toadstool and was very rebellious about it.

The chaplain conducted such talks with each member of the crew individually. The assessment of these private "retreats" was different, ranging from "he bored me like a milk skin", through "he talked gibberish" to "a devil put on a chasuble and is ringing for a mass" as expressed his dissatisfaction Mstislav Deadskull, a staunch Lutheran.

However, in fairness it should be added that some of the crew members were satisfied with such talks, although there were also two factions among them. One claimed that it was simply a great way to diversify the trip, while the other believed that Father Thaddeus was an excellent chaplain and could lift a person's spirits. A peculiarity was that the latter group included the Pandorian T'enga and ... SiWok, a young Uoltan, rescued from the paws (or rather legs) of the bizarre jellies with bloodsucking tendencies.

SiWok recovered, although according to medical rules he should have been dead for a long time. There was little he could add to what ArCer had learned, but he had had a long, confidential conversation with Captain Kerk and Spox. Johnnie, who, in the simplicity of his spirit, believed that his duties included not only serving the captain, but also being her eyes and ears, snatched from the infirmary a demonstration stethoscope (held by Dr. Zmiyevski as a museum piece) and with its help he eavesdropped on the entire conversation.

"This boy said that the Clingorgs catched him and locked him up with them," he reported to Lilianna later. "And then they did something, and the Clingorgs had to escape. He remained, because they didn't want to let him go, nay, he says that they are friendly."

"Because they are, but one can't talk to them," the captain sighed. "Johnnie, call the senior officers to the conference room, the intercom is broken again ... They are supposed to be there in half an hour."

"Yes, I'm going!" Johnnie called and ran, and Lilianna walked slowly to the conference room.

The recovery of the superluminal drive improved the situation of 'Hermash', but not entirely. If they hadn't managed to find out where they came from, it might have even turned out to be of no use to them.

"Computer, prepare charts," she ordered, sitting down in her seat.

The computer grunted furiously for a moment, then said reproachfully:

"You don't trust me, angel?"

"Why?"

"You took away from me the possibility of independent control over the systems. You think I'd sabotage my own crew?"

This equipment was starting to show far too much freedom in formulating thoughts.

"I don't think so," Lilianna replied diplomatically. "You think for yourself, but you are, don't be angry, a computer ... if someone infects you with some virus, some foreign program, you can kill us, even if you don't want to. You don't want that, do you?"

"No, of course not," the computer replied thoughtfully. "Perhaps you are right, princess. And you know what? Maybe call me 'Hermash' not a 'computer'. There are a multitude of computers in the world, but 'Hermash' is the only one, and I'm its brain."

"Of course, if you wish. So 'Hermash', prepare all the charts. Let everyone in the meeting have them on the screen."

"Yes, Captain."

Johnnie soon showed up, bringing coffee and cakes for the participants of the meeting, and later the officers started to come. When the scuffling died away as well as exchanging the words of malice in an undertone, each took their place, and the captain spoke these words:

"Ladies and Gentlemen, each of you has a chart on the screen showing the routes we have traveled recently. Unfortunately, the most important one is missing, in other words, a living or mechanical soul doesn't know how we got here and where this "here" is located. Without this data, we can choose the route blindly, but we risk going the devil knows where. So, does any of the honorable members of the audience have a suggestion on how to calculate the route to our regions?"

"With your permission," said Commander ArCer. "Mr. Spox drew attention to a fact in his conversation with me. Namely, the on-board equipment has registered a certain ion trace, which may be a clue. It almost certainly comes from the torpedo that sent us here."

"That 'almost' could cost us dearly," muttered Jürgen.

"You're right, but do we have a choice?" Christopher Mayher asked sarcastically. "Or maybe you prefer to call the Gypsy, so that she can tell us the next route, reading cards in a home way?"

"Do we have a gypsy on board?" the first mate asked.

"We have. Azalia Kviek and her husband are Gypsies."

"And where are they here?" asked the captain somewhat calmly.

"In the supply section, of course. Azalia bodes well with cards and has also a crystal ball."

"As a last resort, I'll probably use it, too," Lilianna said, ignoring the terrified looks of the Uoltans present at the conference. "For now, however, let's try to find the way with more, hmm, verifiable methods."

"If we fail, we will have to find a quiet planet and set up a colony there," Andy Karpiel sighed, looking at Malvinka Krencik with greedy eyes.

"Don't even think about it, I certainly won't give birth to your children," the girl scolded him, taking on a pouting face.

"It's not for me, it's for the cause."

"Not even then."

The promising quarrel was interrupted by an extremely strange phenomenon. Above the heads of the gathered, a cloud of light appeared suddenly, which began to rummage in the corners, then twisted, shrank down, thickened, and finally took the form deceptively resembling a large, profusely hairy melon. It sat heavily on the table and began to make noises, irresistibly reminiscent of a toddler's crying.

XXXI.

"A fine kettle of fish," the captain sighed, staring at the strange creature. "What could it be? Andy, you are the head of the scientific department here. Mr. ArCer, do you have the best knowledge, what is it?"

Andrew Karpiel got up, reached across the table and took the creature in his hands. It squealed louder, so he stroked it, and then it began to purr trustingly.

"It will sound idiotic," he said. "But it's a baby. I mean ..." he broke off, not knowing how to formulate his thought.

"A biologically immature specimen," ArCer helped him. "It does look like it. Judging by the fact that first it was an energetic creation, it is probably a being capable of transitioning from an energetic to a material form. This is not so unusual when you consider that matter is actually a form of energy ..."

"Sir, don't grumble," the chief engineer interrupted him. "This maggot damaged the synthesizers on deck 5 and the recovery circuit in the engine room. Now I know why there were these sudden failures. Where did it come from?"

"All indications are that it got in through the wall. What's the problem for it to penetrate the shields?"

Arek took the creature from Karpiel and started to stroke it himself. "We'd better find its mom, because we can't keep it here. If it gets scared of something, it will break our home."

"How do you know it has mommy?" Captain Kerk asked sarcastically.

"It's simple. Because it acts like any lost cub. The conclusion is that so far someone has looked after it."

The captain slapped her palm against the table.

"Gentlemen ArCer and Karpiel go to the scanners. Enter the parameters of this thing and look for a similar creature. Arek is right, we'd better find its mother and give her the cub, because if she finds us, we can have a lot of trouble."

"Hihi, how sweet it is," Malvinka chuckled, taking the fluffy creature from the Arek's hands. It hugged her with full confidence and began to purr.

"What about the conference, Captain?" Jürgen wanted to know.

"Hell with the conference. We can resume it when we find something that can be used somehow. For now, we are treading water, anyway."

The news of the finding of the bizarre creature spread across 'Hermash' like wildfire. In some sections it took the form of a rumor like "The Martians are attacking", in others it inspired people to dream of world-wide fame as discoverers of new life forms. The research department wanted to investigate the strange creature immediately, but Malvinka and Arek opposed it vigorously, voluntarily taking on the role of "godparents" or rather "legal guardians" of the fur ball. Besides, the ball kept changing dimensions, shape, and even color, at times it shocked accidentally with electricity, although it was obvious that it was trying to behave correctly. It was undoubtedly a friendly and rather gentle creature.

"May its mother be like that too," Karpiel sighed, analyzing the scans of the area.

"It might as well be father or just an ancestor," ArCer instructed. "Not all creatures are gender specific. Captain, I've found something."

One of the scanners showed parameters almost identical to the parameters of their charge. The captain rushed to the screen, checking everything herself, and arresthtened, seeing that there was indeed a creature relatively short distance away, which could be an adult of the species of their guest.

"I have a suggestion, Captain," ArCer said. "I would like to try to establish telepathic contact with this being. She may mistake us for her child's kidnappers, and you only need to look at the scan to see that she is very strong. The potential difference at the ends of this cloud is about 6 million amperes."

"Try it," the captain said.

The Uoltan sat down in the chair in front of the comm console and concentrated to the maximum, placing his hands on the instruments. For a while, there was no visible effect. The cloud, pulsating with pale light, was thrashing around the area, in fact resembling a worried female, looking for her offspring. At one point she stopped, turned around and headed towards 'Hermash'. She braked only a few kilometers from the bow of the ship. ArCer, pale as death, didn't even move, but there were greenish veins at his temples, and his lips turned white.

After a while, the creature in Malvinka's hands began to squirm and squeal, then escaped from the girl, jumped and spread into a cloud - a smaller copy of the one on the screen. Then it moved towards the nearest wall and penetrated through it.

Soon the people gathered on the bridge saw it approach the larger cloud, changing the color and intensity of the light pulsation as she did. Both creations intertwined with each other, creating an extraordinary spectacle that is difficult not only to see but also to describe. It was unspeakably beautiful.

"Captain, she says she wants to help us," ArCer said after a long moment in his voice coming as if from a great distance. "She is grateful to us that we gave her the child. She will show us the way to the place we came from."

"But it means that you will have to stay in touch with her for a while longer. It could overwhelm you to death," Spox warned him.

"It's a logical choice," ArCer replied in the same, distant voice. "Captain, give the order to start the warp drive at the highest speed that can be squeezed out of it. This being will guide us."

"Mr. Mikhalov, make it so," the captain instructed.

The chief engineer nodded and got the lead out to the engine room while Lilianna, struggling to suppress her excitement, called to her orderly.

"Johnnie, run around the ship and tell everyone to prepare for the flight with increased thrust. We're going home."

"Mother of God from the Polish mountains, thank you ..." Johnnie groaned with joy and disappeared behind the door.

The captain sat down in her chair and said:

"Mr. Deadskull, Mr. Mayher, stay on course for this being. Highest permitted speed. Engage."

***

Nobody suspected that after what 'Hermash' had been through, it would be able to maintain a constant superluminal speed of the fifth degree, even a little more, for four days continuously. It turned out, however, that the ship passed the test smoothly. On the fourth day, Christopher Mayher and Ensign Bequiet gave a shout of joy together, because suddenly they saw a well-known configuration on the screen - 'Hermash' returned to the mapped regions, which would probably never have been possible without the help of the mysterious creature.

"She's saying that she'll say goodbye to us here," ArCer said in a dead voice, still sitting at the communications console. "She has to go back to her homestead."

"Tell her we're grateful!" Captain Zakrzevska exclaimed, literally jumping with glee at the command post.

"Yes of course ..."

"Are you well?" Spox asked anxiously, helping ArCer to get up from the chair by which he had spent four days.

The Uoltan didn't answer. He stood up and with his fingers clasped on Spox's helpful arm, he walked a few unsteadily steps, then collapsed to the floor. He was deadly exhausted.

"Medical team to the bridge!" the captain yelled into the intercom, which had been repaired in the meantime, and worked for the time being.

The paramedics arrived quickly. Taking the unconscious ArCer away, they found out that 'Hermash' returned home and, which was to be expected, the entire ship learned about it at an almost magical pace. As a result, when Captain Kerk and Spox left the bridge, they were greeted in the corridor by joyful toasts and a choral song from everywhere:

"We'll return allegiant!

We, the Four Tankmen!

Ginger and our dog ..."

"Do you understand any of this?" Spox asked his captain.

"Nothing at all," Kerk replied grimly. "But apparently it must be so."

Meanwhile, on the bridge, the navigators worked like crazy, calculating the route, and Malvinka Krencik sat down at the communication console and corrected the parameters, completely out of tune due to communication with the energetic being.

"Captain, it's okay," she finally reported. "We can connect with whoever we want."

"Try calling USS Superprice, sweetheart," Lilianna told her. "They must be losing their minds there, mourning their commander and the First."

Malvinka nodded irregularly and started calling. First a transport ship answered, then a shuttle station, and finally, to the relief of everyone on the bridge, the girl caught the distant signal of the Armada flagship. The audibility was faint, the image couldn't be obtained at all, but communication was established, whatever one might say. It is true that the crackles made communication a bit more difficult, but after a short exchange, Malvinka managed to convince the lieutenant with a sonorous name Hura Hura, who was sitting on the other side of the link, that these were not stupid jokes.

"Superprice is saying we should go along the course 3.12/4.59," she said to Lilianna. "We'll meet them in a week or so if we keep the steady speed of grade three."

"Then, we will keep it," Zakrzevska decided. "What else?"

"They ask what about their captain."

"Tell them that both of our guests are fine, they are not missing any vital body part. We will give them back upon receipt as soon as we meet."

Having said that, Lilianna suddenly grew serious and called the infirmary.

"Dr. Nbeba, what about Mr. ArCer?"

"Captain ..." Dr. Nbeba hesitated obviously. "I don't know if he'll survive. I really cannot vouch for anything."

Lilianna's eyes filled with tears involuntarily. She liked ArCer more than she was willing to admit.

"Oh God, don't say that, sir ..." she whispered through her tight throat.

"I'm sorry, Captain."

"He was so exhausted from contact with this creature?"

"No, Captain, that was nothing ... but Dr. TiShan just got a pregnancy test ... and I'd rather not repeat what she said."

XXXII.

As soon as 'Hermash' left the zone to which the Clingorgian torpedo had dispatched it, Dr. TiShan seemed to wake up from a long sleep. It was a very pleasant dream, full of unfettered feelings, but still only a dream. Right now, she felt only embarrassment at letting herself be carried away by her senses as well as astonishment that ArCer had allowed himself to be so overwhelmed by them. It was so ... non-Uoltan. Apparently, the commander was right when he said that the place to which they had been thrown was having a destructive effect on them. The influence passed as they crossed the boundary of the world known to them, guided by the energetic being, but the effect of the outpouring could no longer be undone.

"Wonderful, a baby, just what we needed here," Captain Zakrzevska sighed as she somehow digested the information received from Nbeba. "If it cries all night, we will go crazy here. You can get mad anyway. It is supposed to be a Polish ship, and on board there are Germans, Russians, Gypsies, Uoltans, Pandorians and the devil knows who else. It is a military unit, but we will have to open a nursery here. Shame, a doctor, and she doesn't know how to prevent getting up the duff."

"Too late to worry about it now," Jürgen remarked reasonably. "If Fräulein TiShan decides to give birth, we will have to support her."

"She didn't need our support to get pregnant."

"Fräu Hauptmann..."

"Okay, okay ..." interrupted the captain. "I know perfectly well what you said and what you mean. Well, I'm not going to order her to strangle the baby with a pillow! If she gives birth, we will accept it. We'll all be godparents to this pointy-eared brat, and whoever calls it a bastard, they will deal with all of us. First with me."

"And if TiShan decides to terminate the pregnancy?" Arek asked.

"It will also be her choice and we will respect that too."

"With your permission, but it's hard to imagine Father Toadstool respect that. Not to mention what he will say when he gets news of the extramarital child, an artificial miscarriage is definitely out of the question for him. He's ready to excommunicate poor TiShan," Malvinka said from her console.

"You think it'll make a difference to her? After all, she doesn't follow any of the earthly religions," noted Arek.

"Well, she doesn't confess, but it is always not pleasant ..."

"I'm just wondering what ArCer will say about it ... What about him?" Lilianna asked loudly, seeing her orderly who had just returned from the infirmary.

"He is lying, poor fellow, white as a handkerchief," Johnnie replied sadly, but immediately cheered up. "Is it true that he made a baby?"

"That's true," the captain sighed. "Now complete Chinese dance will be here."

While there was this perhaps not-so-normal debate on the bridge, things were slowly normalizing on the ship. Professor Trekovsky was still cursing due to the Clingorgian torpedo case, Andy Karpiel and Charles Mikhalov, beaming, threw fresh mash into the moonshine vessel in the engine room (it was necessary to celebrate the return), and TiShan was sitting by ArCer's bed. The commander was still unconscious as the four-day connection with the alien life form had caused severe damage to his nervous system as well as purely physical exhaustion.

Even though the doctor apparently no longer cared about ArCer, she was as worried about him as she was about any patient. Besides ...

"He has to survive, if only to hear what I have to say to him," she explained to Jacob Zmiyevski.

"Right. Curse that baby-maker, teach him a lesson," her friend agreed with her.

For now, however, a nice moment of "cursing" had to be postponed, because ArCer was resting on a mecha-bed table, pale as a wall, and the indicators on the scoreboard were pulsing lazily at the lowest acceptable level. Despite all her anger, TiShan was very worried about him until Mr. Spox came into the infirmary and explained that the Uoltan had simply put himself into a healing trance.

"Good," she said with relief. "He has to survive so that I can kill him."

So, PSS Hermash was flying to meet USS Superprice, and Captain Kerk and Mr. Spox were completing their report to Star Armada Command. It showed that, although Captain Zakrzevska was completely irresponsible, the ship was put together sloppy, and the crew consisted of suspicious individuals, they were an inseparable whole and could work effectively. At the same time, they responded to the Clingorgian accusations, dealing with them thoroughly and devastatingly.

"Although," said Captain Kerk, "I would like to see this captain before a military court, and her crew in the penal colony."

"It's illogical," said Spox coolly. "And also undignified."

"Yes," sighed Kerk, resting his cheek on his hand, "but it's very human."

"I think that's what I said, Captain ..."

***

The meeting with USS Superprice occured almost exactly at the place designated by the interim commander of the unit. The slight deviation was due to the fact that, as the computer 'Hermash' said, "it had mistaken something". Fortunately, there wasn't much of this, and the ships managed to determine the coordinates without too much trouble. Having received this message, Captain Kerk and Mr. Spox rushed with enormous relief to the transport hall, where Lalevich, yawning as usual, was setting the transport coordinates sleepily.

"Oh, the gentlemen already came," Captain Zakrzevska greeted them cheerfully. "That's good. Dish is about to send you back to your famous vessel, and we'll go further as we already have a long delay in our schedule and we should make up for lost time."

"Glorious reliability," muttered Captain Kerk.

"It's not reliability. We simply have no choice but to stick to what has been agreed in advance. What else could we do, desert?"

"I would advise against that," said Mr. Spox seriously.

"I'd be surprised if you advised it. Well then, politely go to the platform. Hasta la vista and if anything, bad happens, it's not us."

Captain Kerk grimaced painfully and shook the great tarantula out of his sleeve.

"I knew something was tickling me," he said. "Whose is this?"

"If my eyes don't deceive me, it is Chikita of Kazik Piskorz," said Lalevich, picking up the eight-legged monster from the floor and threatening it with his finger. "I'll give it back after the service. Other spiders sit quietly in terrariums, and this lady is like Johnnie Walker ..."

He put Chikita on his shoulder, where she clung, very pleased with the warm and safe place next to the human - though not very clean - neck.

Father Toadstool, out of breath, burst into the transmission room, stepped back abruptly at the sight of Chikita, and slammed his back on the door.

"Reverend, don't be afraid, she is gentle," Lalevich said kindly.

The priest winced and walked around her.

"I'm not afraid," he said.

"Then why do you, reverend have such a sour face?"

"I don't question your words, son, but I prefer not to check it. Understood? I don't trust something with so many paws."

"The spider might say it's hard to trust a cripple who is missing six legs, but let's drop it," said Captain Zakrzevska. "Did something happen because, you, father ran into this room so quickly?"

"No, I just wanted to bless our guests for the journey."

"What? What for?" Spox was surprised.

"So that the "bad" doesn't confuse you during the transfer," muttered Lalevich with amusement.

"Dish, you better check the coordinates. The priest should do his job, and you do yours."

Spox looked at Lilianna, then decided to approach. He was clearly embarrassed and unsure of himself.

"I wanted to say that ..." he began.

"I will never forget you, it meant a lot to me, I will think about you and other nonsense," the captain interrupted cheerfully. "You wouldn't even count how many times in my life I've heard this text. No, no, my beautiful pointy-eared creature, let's just say goodbye like friends."

She stood on her toes and kissed Spox on the cheek. Kerk looked at it with discreet amusement, Father Thaddeus with obvious scandal, and the first officer of Superprice himself looked at that moment as if a large bone had stuck in his esophagus.

"The end of the official part. Please go to the transportation place," Lalevich exclaimed cheerfully.

The guests climbed onto the platform.

"Are you two ...?" Captain Kerk asked, unable to refrain.

"No comment," Spox cut off dryly, putting his hands behind his back in his way. After a while, the dematerialization ray turned them both into two clouds of spinning molecules.

"Sometimes I wonder if this way of traveling is in some way inconsistent with the Bible," said Father Toadstool thoughtfully, looking at the platform and discreetly saying goodbye.

"Where is it written: don't use a molecular transporter?" Lalevich was surprised.

"It is also not written: "don't put your hand into a grinder", and yet you shouldn't do it," the priest returned the ball.

Since this type of religious dispute could take a long time, Captain Zakrzevska decided to retreat and return to the bridge, where Malvinka Krencik happily chatted through the link with Lieutenant Hura Hura, Ensign Bequiet was bantering with the helmsman of Superprice, and the first and second officers were playing cards on the scientific console. At the sight of their captain, they got so embarrassed that they dropped the entire deck on the floor, and several cards flew up to Lilianna's feet. The captain got down, lifted one of them, and watched it.

"Ace of hearts," she said, settling herself in the command chair. "For certain I will meet a heart-to-heart boy. Okay, ladies and gentlemen, we end the gossip and go back to the course."

Everyone rushed to their positions. The front screen flickered, and after a while, "High vacuum" was displayed on it. Then the text faded out and an image of the departing Superprice appeared in its place.

"Good riddance," muttered Christopher Mayher.

"See you later, alligator, after a while, croco..." added Ensign Bequiet.

"Alright, alright, enough," the captain stopped him. "So, let's go ahead, my dear. The warp speed, factor three."

XXXIII.

"And you say that somehow everything is going well there?" Admiral Cormack asked, clearly disappointed.

"They're doing well. I think this crew can be trusted despite all the objections, although the investigation into the Clingorgs' mysterious weapon that sent the ship somewhere in hell will probably surpass them," Captain Kerk replied, without getting into his own doubts.

Then he submitted a recording of his conversation with ArCer, SiWok and a few crew members, as well as a detailed account of the weeks spent on 'Hermash', which now seemed to him a madman's dream.

A successful report should have pleased the admiral, but it didn't. The lack of grounds for recalling the crew of the Polish ship from the mission was very unfortunate for him, but for now he couldn't do anything about it. After this report, 'Hermash' officially became part of the Star Armada, and he would have to struggle with its undisciplined crew and the madwoman playing the role of captain.

At the time when Kerk was talking to the admiral, PSS 'Hermash' was already flying towards the phenomenon known as the Murasaki 400. It was ordered to find out what it was, but for now the crew was finishing the renovation of the ship and the ongoing repair of the damaged equipment. The admiral's surprise that they could somehow cope with it was not known to them, and it would have surely offended them. It had been known for a long time that a Pole will always manage, not matter what, and whoever doubted it, committed almost blasphemy.

Life on board went on in its own mode, like that square circle, as the first mate Arek had termed it. Watery's marriage regularly woke up all the neighbors every few days with a marital quarrel that turned into fisticuffs. Dr. TiShan didn't speak to ArCer and was hysterical when she was admonished in any case (she took the beginning of her pregnancy very badly). Jacob Zmiyevski fell in love with a laboratory technician from the hydroponics department and completely lost his head. Professor Dinoslav Trekovsky started a new research project, he did not tell anyone what it was, but he loudly demanded that two assistants be assigned to him. The theater club, founded by Sister Ophelia, rehearsed in her spare time and promised to stage a play "soon". Father Thaddeus turned his nose at this idea, he preferred a church choir, but he was afraid to oppose his sister, who increasingly dominated the "government of souls" on the ship. Engineer Mikhalov and Malvinka Krencik tried to get along somehow, which was not easy, because whenever they wanted to get a date, something happened that either disturbed their meeting or spoiled the date completely. They suspected someone was deliberately interrupting them, but so far, they hadn't been able to trace that person.

As for Captain Zakrzevska, as always, she tried to maintain her position of the "dominant female on board", which was greatly helped by the constant presence of Johnnie Caterpillar behind her back. The young highlander was very serious about his duties of an orderly, that is, helper and gorilla in one. Thus, in general, one could observe a peculiar retinue: Captain Zakrzevska was leading the way, Johnnie with the ferret on his shoulder followed her, and in the end Bear, who had already recognized Johnnie as his surrogate master. So that there would be no problem during the possible inspection, Lilianna entered Bear on the crew list as a junior 'cabin boy' Mikhail Shaggov, with a security assignment as an investigator. Despite such a promotion, Bear didn't stay in the duty room, but voluntarily served Johnnie as additional support.

There was even a saying among the crew:

"Oh, the captain and her gobs are coming."

"It was used for the first time by Charles Mikhalov and gained instant popularity among the entire crew. In addition to inventing funny phrases, the engineer tried to make at least a general, approximate technical sketch of the strange torpedo, but so far, the hours spent in Trekovsky's studio gave a round zero. It was unknown what the Clingorgs had actually used and where they had gotten it from.

Keeping order in a crew like this was certainly not easy, but Lilianna Zakrzevska somehow handled it. When Professor Trekovsky bothered her, she assigned to him SiWok and Joe Stelmach from the engine room, the latter as a punishment. Since the Wateries had taken their toll on the entire deck, she changed their quarters to another, in one of the holds, away from the rest of the crew. And since Father Toadstool constantly complained about the lack of morality among the crew members, she issued an official circular obliging everyone to perform morally reprehensible acts only during the quiet hours when, as she knew, Father Thaddeus slept like the righteous among the nations of the world. Thus, as she stated, "the wolf will be sated and the virgin will be saved."

In the multitude of various matters, no one noticed that the deputy chief engineer talked to himself more and more often, or maybe nobody cared about it. "Is he talking to himself? Let him do it, let it be good for his health. Apparently, he likes to talk to someone intelligent," people said. Meanwhile, Greg was going through an unpleasant idyll with his "roommate", who became more and more independent and liked to put his two cents' worth in everything. The worst thing was that he really fell in love with Malvinka Krencik, and more than once Greg went somewhere, got thoughtful for a moment and suddenly it turned out that he was unknowingly headed towards the bridge or the quarters of the beautiful Malva.

"What are you thinking, SyTar?" he was angry. "You can't take control of my body whenever you want!"

"Then whenever I can," SyTar suggested, knowing in advance that Greg wouldn't agree to something like that.

The Uoltan also didn't feel comfortable as a "squatter" in the mind of the man, and the man prejudiced against Uoltans. However, the two had no choice but to share one body and put up with each other somehow. Perhaps somehow it would have been if Mrs. Krencik hadn't intervened in their fragile agreement - unknowingly anyway. It wouldn't have occured to the beautiful lieutenant that not only the chief engineer wanted to meet her, and besides she didn't think of Mikhalov otherwise than in terms of friendship. As one of the pillars of the amateur theater group founded by Sister Ophelia, she spent every moment free from service rehearsing for a play that was to be staged after Easter. And it was coming up.

"Is it really impossible to celebrate such a great holiday without some pagan texts?" Father Toadstool was indignant, when one day he came to rehearsal and heard Malvinka reciting with excitement:

"Dear fox, fox little

Where is Backwardness? Where's this locality?

'Sir,' the fox will say, 'there's something in it of harassing people!

Maybe you think it's the Vatican City?"

Arek, dressed as a fox, stared at the priest.

"It's a classic, Galchynski," he said.

"Was it impossible to choose something better?"

"We also had a choice of 'The Ballade of Three Happy Angels' or the play 'If Adam Were Polish'," interjected Matias von Braun, who voluntarily took on the role of stage manager. "Believe me, father, it wouldn't be better."

"Do you have any matter to discuss, Tadek, or you came to disturb?" Sister Ophelia asked sternly.

Father Toadstool got his hackles up.

"I just wanted to remind you, Ophe, that Easter is around the corner and you haven't made the confession schedule yet," he said with dignity.

However, it was to no avail, as the suffragette sister only shrugged.

"You and your bureaucracy ... Whoever wants a confession, will come themselves."

"This isn't right! We are responsible for their souls!"

"They won't bring them in chains. I have hung the hours of admission on the door of my quarters, whoever wants it, will come. I respect freedom of choice. I advise you the same, because so far you just walk and win, and everyone runs away from you like from a plague."

"It's not true!"

"True! You are puffy, narrow-minded, hidebound, pompous and stupid."

"Not true!" Father Thaddeus crowed indignantly. "I was entrusted with this ship as a token of trust!"

"What token of trust? The opportunity was taken to get you out of the country, because you were so disturbing that it was impossible to endure," the nun retorted, correcting the cornet with a nervous movement, as a result of which it tilted sideways. "You interfered with everything, you wanted to have the last word everywhere, due to any sitter, you made hell in the mass brainwashing media ... so when the possibility appeared, you were sent, the farther the better. You won't pull the wool over my eyes."

"This is disrespectful! You're undermining my authority in the eyes of the crew! I'll file a report!"

"Complain even to our grandmother, but don't disturb me in my work, or I don't know what I will do. Look at him, how smart he is ... as a rule you should say midnight prayers and get up early to pray, and how many times have you done it since the beginning of the cruise? I counted twice. If you want respect, you have to earn it."

"You're insolent! If you give a mouse a cookie, he will tear your whole arm away, right?!"

The raised voices of both ministers finally lured ArCer and Jürgen to the library where the rehearsals took place. The two unsuccessfully tried to calm the quarrellers, but gained only so much that they were threatened with immediate excommunication. This worried ArCer little, especially since he had no idea what the word meant in practice ... He understood, however, that the row had reached a point where it had to be stopped and he called for security. Here, however, a surprise awaited him, as the security refused to intervene, explaining that it wouldn't afoul of the Vatican by persecuting the clergy. Completely devastated, he went to Captain Zakrzevska for further instructions.

XXXIV.

Lilianna was just eating dinner. Bear put his huge head on her lap, begging with his warm gaze for culinary evidence of sympathy. At the next table, three lab technicians were discussing an experiment, using meatballs with pasta as symbolic demonstration objects, and Malvinka Krencik and Inga Lausch in the corner tried to program a dessert synthesizer to make a cheesecake with coconut shreds. What they had made so far was more like oatmeal in vanilla sauce.

"Can I take you some time?" ArCer asked as he approached the captain's table.

"Sit down," Lilianna showed him the place in front of her, continuing her busy chewing. "Would you like to eat something? Matias is busy but he left a pretty good set in the slot machines."

"Thank you, I've already eaten. Captain, I would like to ask if it is normal for security to refuse to intervene when two crew members are in each other's eyes?"

"Why? The Wateries quarreled again? Be understanding, they are married, so they probably must have a fight once a week."

ArCer shook slightly at hearing such heresy, but decided not to delve into the subject and cut to the chase:

"The point is that your priests got into a very loud dispute and security refused to intervene.

"Ah, that," the captain put down a fork and smiled indulgently. "Commander, you can't ask too much. The clergy is somewhat outside of our jurisdiction, it is subject only to the Vatican City."

"It's ridiculous!"

"Of course, it is, but so what? Anyway, they will not fight each other, so if they argue, let them argue for their health."

"Yes, but how does this affect the morale of the crew?"

"At all. The crew probably treats it like a cabaret for free. You should take care of your own affairs and not worry about the role; they will ream you anyway."

ArCer's eyes got rounded a little, for although he was used to the captain's casual expression, he was still surprised by her sayings. Not finding the words of the comeback, he hurriedly reported off and left the mess. Lately he had felt that being assigned to this ship was the worst thing that had happened to him in his life. On the way he looked into the infirmary, he himself didn't know why he had thought to turn this way.

Dr. TiShan was sitting at her desk, pale as a wall. It was evident that she was nauseous and very unwell.

"Could I do something for you?" He asked uncertainly. TiShan just muttered something incomprehensible, so he approached her and bent over her anxiously.

"I am terribly unhappy," the doctor moaned and cried out. ArCer hugged her awkwardly, unused to comforting pregnant women - his wife had a completely different disposition and always acted like an iceberg, even in the different state. Maybe that's why he felt so attracted to TiShan - she was so different, although she was also a Uoltan.

"Don't worry," he whispered. "Everything will be fine. We will take care of our baby together. You won't be left alone."

"Bullshit," Lolita's voice said from the corner behind the screen. "Every guy says that, and when it comes down to it, he draws in his horns and he's not seen anymore. A man must not be taken seriously. He will tempt you first, and then he will run away from mummy to the end of the world."

ArCer twitched, startled. He had no idea that there was someone else in the infirmary besides him and TiShan, and in addition the leading gossip girl of 'Hermash', to whom there was nothing sacred.

"The doctor felt bad, I just wanted to calm her down," he started to excuse himself. Lolita came out from behind the screen with a hypo-syringe, full of specific to alleviate pregnancy ailments. She looked as if she had come on board straight from a space fashion magazine, and her appearance was the result of the joint work of a clothing designer, beautician, make-up artist and hairdresser. Nobody knew how she did it, but she always looked like that.

"You want to console her in the only way you know, don't you?" she asked ironically "You, Uoltans, are such hypocrites. Why the heck won't you admit that you love our doctor?"

ArCer stiffened, raised his eyebrows, and assumed dignified, cold expression.

"That would be highly illogical," he said. "I'm a Uoltan and such feelings are alien to me."

"You say so," Lolita muttered sarcastically and she pressed the hypo-syringe against the doctor's arm.

The Uoltan commander stiffened even more.

"You mean to say I'm lying?"

"Rather, that you are lying through your teeth. If I were blind in my both eyes, and as stupid as table legs, then maybe I would believe it, but that also not for sure."

"It's illogical! First of all, animals are organically incapable of lying, and second ... " Here ArCer fell silent, as he had just realized that he didn't know what was the second.

Lolita snorted contemptuously and went to the storeroom to count the supplies (she had been doing it for a long time and couldn't figure them up in any way, because Dr. Zmiyevski treated very lightly the obligation to accurately enter the goods issued notes in the register).

Once they were alone, ArCer looked at TiShan with a guilty gaze. He didn't want her to believe what he had said, which he had had to say, because one of the guiding principles in Uoltan's dealings with other races was not to disclose certain things.

"It's not like that," he said softly. "I really care about you, much more than I ever thought ... than I supposed that I might care for someone else. I think about you all the time."

TiShan looked up at him and smiled through her tears. She slowly raised her hand. ArCer lifted his, and their fingers intertwined in a Uoltan love gesture.

So, let's leave our lovers and see what happened elsewhere in the ship. And something very interesting and incomprehensible occured there.

XXXV.

Greg Brzenchyshchykievich left the engine room after duty and went to rest. He was terribly tired. He had hardly slept lately, though it seemed to him that he slept like a log. He didn't feel like eating or even talking to anyone. Nobody paid any attention to it, because the engineer was still doing his job and was as unsociable as ever, which was a shame. Something was definitely going on.

So, Greg finished his shift and, without even taking off his shoes, fell to the bed. It would have seemed that he fell asleep like a top, but after less than an hour he got up, left his quarters and went to the backup control room. After recent events, not everything had been ordered there, so the presence of Brzenchyshchykievich might have not surprised anyone, if it hadn't been for the fact that engineer Mikhalov strictly ordered that no one else take care of the control room. However, no one asked unnecessary questions, as no one was there.

The engineer stood at one of the consoles, opened the panel and began to manipulate something inside. After some time, he closed the lid, left and, unnoticed by anyone, returned to his quarters, where he went back to bed, as if nothing had happened. After another half an hour, he got up, shaved in front of the mirror and went to the conservatory, where usually at this time, the communications officer, Krencik, enjoyed a little relaxation under the artificial sun.

Malvinka noticed, because it was impossible not to notice that the deputy chief engineer 'revolved' around her, that he visited her very often during those moments of rest, but she didn't mind. She thought that Greg was nice and quiet handsome, and although she sensed something mysterious and incomprehensible in him at the same time, it didn't bother her. If Commander ArCer had wanted to adore her, she would have probably felt much more embarrassed, because this Uoltan aroused in her not only respect but also an undefined fear, as if he had been some superman, sent, it is not known why, to this junk pretending to be a ship ...

"What is there to be afraid of?" Inga Lausch was simply surprised when she confided in her once. "Same guy as the others. He eats, drinks, he has to go to the latrine, and if he catches a common cold, his nose runs and he needs a handkerchief.

There was no poetry in Inga, which after all was a nice girl. As people used to say about her, "she was life's walking prose". No wonder then that she was not influenced by the authority and personal charm of ArCer, with which more and more female members fell in love.

"They just have nothing to do," Inga said disparagingly when Malvinka reminded her of it. "Anyway, he follows our doctor like a tomcat in the spring."

The fact was still a fact, so the commander, although Malvina liked him very much, was out of the question as a possible pickup object. However, it was different with Mikhalov and Greg. They were both handsome and interesting in their own way. She herself didn't know which one she liked more. She was only a little surprised why Greg was so kind and talkative alone with her, and in other situations it was difficult to get a word out of him and you got the impression that he was a different person. However, she didn't bother her head about it, especially since there were more interesting things going on aboard.

At the request of the captain, Christopher Mayher organized exercises for the entire crew. He personally went to the holo-room, fine-tuned computer simulations and prepared the appropriate weapons. The maneuvers, he said in the announcement, would also include hand-to-hand combat and the throwing of a klingat knife. The latter was very interesting for the crew, because everyone from a force of armed Tartars had educational gaps and no one knew what a 'klingat' was.

"A kind of hand-thrown weapon used by the inhabitants of planet Patella," ArCer explained to the people gathered in front of the sign. "Yes, factually speaking, it can be considered a knife. At a distance of up to one hundred meters, it is as deadly as a mazer, provided it is in skilled hands."

"For God's sake, no!" shouted Joe Watery. "If you teach Tekla how to throw it, you can arrange a first-class burial for me right now! Eight mourners, silver lanterns, the flag ..."

"What a whim!" huffed Maura Gvizdak, who was also present. "Second class is not enough for you? I can delegate four people, the rest, I will need."

"Or third class, is it bad?" Mikhalov supported her. "Two mourners will carry you easily, although you have your gut, and for a deceased a plywood chest is as good as a mahogany case."

"I don't need your grace, I can walk," the technician grumbled. He was the perfect joke object because he had always taken everything seriously.

"You know, Joe, the least trouble would be if you were eaten by something," said Mstislav Deadskull after deep reflection.

Watery got very offended and slapped him in his ear, as his temperament in no way was inferior to that of his half. In the corridor there was a turmoil like a cockfight, because also the shreds of uniforms flew in all directions like feathers torn out. The gathered people immediately divided into two camps and began to cheer the wrestlers, shouting slogans such as: "Legia rulers, Cracovia beggars!" (Deadskull was from Cracow), "Eagles, go for it!", "Slavus, punch him like Golota!", "Don't tire the boy, kill him!" and so on.

"Hush!" roared Captain Zakrzevska, who appeared out of nowhere, as was her custom. "Hush, because if I get pissed off, you both won't recover!"

"Have you heard?!" she was backed by inseparable Johnnie Caterpillar. "It must be quiet, or I will beat you both with the ice ax!"

Since the gladiators showed a selective deafness at that moment, Janek gave Gizia sitting on his shoulder to Lilianna and, as announced, began to separate the feuding colleagues. The two immediately joined forces against a common enemy, but it did not help, because Maura came to Johnnie's aid and the quarrellers went to the detention center. The captain looked sternly at the crew members who were clearly disappointed by such a sudden interruption of the good entertainment, walked over to Mayher's advertisement, with a few keystrokes added the inscription "Attendance required. Captain" at the bottom and authorized the note with her code.

Then she looked sternly at ArCer.

"Why didn't you intervene?" She asked.

The Uoltan raised his right eyebrow slightly.

"I don't know when or what is adopted here," he replied. "I didn't want to break some Polish tradition that I have not known yet."

"You are insolent. I promise that if you allow the fight again in your presence, I will write the rebuke in your files and hang on the middeck."

Seeing ArCer's indistinct expression, Lilianna added hurriedly:

"Of course, I will hang the rebuke, not you. We are not in the British Navy, but on the other hand it is a pity, because I would like to whip those two."

"I have no doubt that they would be delighted if you did it yourself," ArCer muttered as he watched the captain walk away. Only day earlier SiWok had drawn his attention to the fact that she was quite a charming woman, previously the commander hadn't noticed it, seeing only the commander in his captain. Now that he looked at Lilianna from this angle, he understood SiWok's interest, though he was a little worried at the same time. His young compatriot shouldn't have been interested in Captain Zakrzevska, he shouldn't have paid attention to earthly women at all. He decided to talk to him honestly at the earliest opportunity.

When this happened, Chris Mayher finished tuning the parameters of the training program, which he baptized with the mysterious code name "Kazik's dad versus Gidorah" and together with Vasyl Anecdotych, who was to conduct the training with him, tried the demo version. They were both very pleased with the test results, although the creatures programmed by Mayher surprised the Russian a bit.

"The participant is to fight on the side of etih gchuchilov,[6] not the people?" he assured himself. "I szto eto, do they have hvosty[7]? Pure behemoths!"

"These are not bogies, but intelligent creatures. In addition, the test participant have to understand that not always the one who comes from his or her own race is right in the dispute with the representative of the Aliens," Mayher explained to him accessibly.

"And eta bolshaya lizard is shto, koshka[8]?"

"This is a test whether our brave soldier knows how to go beyond the anthropomorphic thinking diagram," Christopher replied, looked lovingly at the giant reptile plunging into the holographic sea and called the first five from the list of crew members.

The exercise scheme was quite simple - no one was to know whether they passed the test or failed until the official results were announced, and of course no one also could find out what the determining factors were. The holographic sensei was to teach how to throw the shuriken-like klingat and how to shoot primitive weapons. Hand-to-hand combat, everyone had to

---

[6] *(Rus)* These loonies.

[7] *(Rus)* Do they have tails?

[8] *(Rus)* This big lizard is what, kitty?

perfect on their own. They all learned the essentials in basic training, now they were going to learn how to use them practically.

XXXVI.

The maneuvers were in full swing. Every day two groups of five finished the test and, completely exhausted, went to the mess to replenish their calories, drink, and complain about "that moron who was setting this goddamn thing up." The exercise program was difficult and had so many options that no situation happened the same way, so even letting others know what to expect wouldn't have helped them. The humanoids programmed by Mayher, armed with knives and bows, behaved so unpredictably that the crewmen cursed like a sailor the chief navigator's ingenuity, calling him himself, using absolutely unprintable words.

Captain Zakrzevska didn't care about the maneuvers or the fact that, according to Chris Mayher, the level of the crew was terrifying, as she had her own problems, and quite unexpected ones. SiWok, who on the ship, hold an intermediate position, between the senior passenger and the junior apprentice, began to show a strange interest in her. It couldn't be said that she disliked the boy - on the contrary, he was very handsome, like most Uoltans, and he had an exceptionally pleasant disposition - but she didn't consider appropriate to meet him. However, it was impossible to her not to notice the physical and spiritual qualities of this young man. SiWok was not only intelligent and logical, like all Uoltans, he had also masculine strength and charm, and at the same time, a strangely feminine sensitivity and gentleness.

Until now, she had known such a melange only in her close friend from Earth, who was a 'recovered' man - he was born and raised as a girl. However, as far as she knew, this was not the case with SiWok. And how she judged him shouldn't have mattered. She, as a captain, couldn't consort with such a punk.

"Punk? He's twenty-five!" exclaimed in amazement Jürgen, in whom she confided in her moment of weakness.

"He's a kid for a Uolt. After all, our TiShan is forty years old," the captain replied. "When I saw her, I thought she was eighteen, well, twenty. Uoltans live longer, and their age is counted differently. But that is not the point. What am I supposed to do with this SiWok?"

"Well, Fräu Hauptmann, what you want. You're both adults, I don't think HQ would interfere with your relationship. You can boldly get involved with him."

"But I can't get involved with him in any way! It would be dangerous to the authority of the captain."

"Then don't get involved."

"But I like him, fiddlesticks!"

"Then get involved."

"What an advice you've given me!"

Jürgen spread his hands as if to say "I won't come up with anything else." Meanwhile, the problem was getting serious because Lilianna, although she was the captain, was not a wooden doll and prolonged loneliness didn't affect her well. Perhaps it would have been less important if there hadn't been so many married, engaged or simply "dating" couples on the ship.

"You could say it's not a Star Ship, but a flying tryst house," Father Toadstool, very displeased, used to say, whenever he found a cooing pair somewhere.

"A good brothel is not bad," said Dr. Zmiyevski when he found out about that term.

"If that were true, at least everyone would smile."

Meanwhile, not all were. Doctor TiShan still felt bad, engineer Mikhalov complained about persistent headaches, the Watery couple still waged a loud war, and Greg Brzenchyshchykievich walked as if unconscious and it happened that he fell asleep in the mess over a meal. Nevertheless, he turned out to be one of the few who gained the recognition of

Christopher Mayher during the holo-room maneuvers. The manner in which he solved all the tasks before him aroused the admiration of the chief navigator and Vasyl Zaychik - they had no idea that the engineer had a good advisor during the test, SyTar, whose reflexes and intuition were very useful. Greg himself, however, took praise and good notes with surprising indifference. He just wanted to sleep - and this time he managed it for real, as if the mysterious demon that had haunted him, had taken pity and let go for a moment.

Of course, Sister Ophelia of the Angels didn't take part in the maneuvers. As she said herself, she wouldn't beat anyone or shoot anyone, so her presence in the holo-room was completely unnecessary. Instead, she worked on the set for the Christmas performance. She had not only a sharp tongue that didn't fit the habit, but also an artistic sense and the ability to impose her authority on others. She even put to work on decorations the Father, who was indignant at her lack of respect for authorities, but he couldn't do anything about it.

"Why do you boss everybody around?" he shouted so loudly that the whole deck heard him. "Men are to rule, it has always been so, from the beginning of the world! Don't you know that God gave Adam two more measures of reason than Eve?!"

"I know," Sister Ophelia replied calmly. "So, take the tools and work, because I won't do it for you."

For such a dictum, Father Toadstool found no argument and, grinding his teeth with impotent rage, meekly set to work on the decorations. He was assisted by Johnnie Caterpillar, his unofficial favorite among the crew, uncritically worshiping the entire clergy and volunteering as an altar boy at all religious ceremonies. As a result, they contained an unintended note of comedy: the small, full-bodied priest and the soaring mountain of muscles with the thatch of hemp hair, wearing a tight surplice and thundering piously and with the highlander accent:

"Aaaameeen!"

As Arek used to say, it was worth participating in Sunday services for this itself.

***

After a few days of practice, everyone knew that it wouldn't be possible to finish the tests in the holo-room before Christmas. In the meantime, research on the newly discovered miniature quasar had to be carried out, and not only that caused the delay. There were too many crew members, and the program itself required repairs several times, so that some of the crew had this pleasure announced for after Christmas. So new acids were created - those who were to pass the tests before Christmas envied the other group that they still had time to prepare. In turn those who were to pass after Christmas envied the first group that it would soon have it out of their 'coconuts'.

The crew members were delighted with the fact that Commander ArCer, having passed the first part of the test, failed miserably the second, because he suddenly panicked at the sight of a huge reptile that stuck its head out of the holographic sea and roared directly at him. As a result, ArCer threw himself backwards, capsizing the fragile boat on which he was about to reach the submarine, and it became apparent that ... he couldn't swim. Few of the Uoltans possessed this ability (planet Uoltan was dry and desert), but all assumed that ArCer, like Mr. Spox, had the ability to swim. Unfortunately, the reality exceeded their expectations.

"I don't understand what's so funny, the commander said in an insulted voice as he appeared on the bridge after the mishap.

"Don't even try to understand," the captain advised kindly. "The human sense of humor is incomprehensible to Uoltans. Better tell me what you think about all this ... Strange signals.

ArCer leaned over the scanner and was silent for a moment, staring at the readings.

"Something unusual," he said finally, straightening up. "It seems we are dealing with a phenomenon that has not yet been classified: a planet orbiting a mini-quasar. It is not a planetoid or an asteroid, it is a planet, and with its own atmosphere."

"What does this atmosphere consist of?"

"It's a gas mixture. Oxygen and helium dominate, there is also a lot of water vapor and carbon dioxide. In turn, nitrogen is present in trace amounts."

"Well, it would be fun if we landed there. We would all talk in soooo thin voices ..." Andy Karpiel laughed.

"Better not to land on it. The surface temperature is seventy degrees Celsius, the water temperature in lakes and oceans reaches eighty."

"Life?"

"It's strange, but ... plants and animals."

ArCer paused and looked again at what he saw through the scanner. The blue glow on his face pulsed slightly under the sequence of changing spectra and series of numbers.

"Creations of advanced technology," he said finally in an uncertain voice.

"This is interesting. Some unknown intelligent animals?" asked the captain somewhat calmly.

"It is certainly not any of the known breeds, as far as that is what you mean. We can safely assume that it is reluctant to make contact, since it hasn't let us know about its existence so far ... Although no ... It must be a precosmic civilization, it rather doesn't fly beyond its planet."

"So, we cannot interfere with their development. The first point of the code is bowing here," said Jürgen firmly.

"But we won't bow," said Captain Zakrzevska carelessly. "We're going to explore the quasar, and we'll explore the planet, too, though not necessarily very violently. We will be careful and we will not land. It's too hot there and I don't feel like singing in a high voice."

"So how will we do it?"

"Commander, I should ask you that! Apparently, your mind is not yet balanced after your holo-room experience."

If ArCer were human, he would have probably blushed with embarrassment, but he was a Uoltan, so he only turned a little green. Indeed, the question didn't sound very wise, and even seemed completely mindless. The 'Hermash' scientific section had been equipped before the start with all kinds of stationary, flying, crawling and lying probes, ie broken from the beginning, because almost half of them were not fit for use, even though they were 'brand new'.

"No wonder," as Charles Mikhalov said after he had seen some of them. "Made in the PRC. Chinese scrap and that's it."

He then made a devastating remark about the legitimate appearance of both probe makers and those who purchased them for the mission, and set about saving what he could.

During the preparations, Father Toadstool came up with a weird idea. He unexpectedly announced that as the chaplain of the unit he must have been ready for anything, so he would also pass the holodeck test. Chris Mayher stated that he would not object to it, that Father Toadstool was the same crewman as everyone else, and he signed the priest up for one of the groups, anticipating a lot of fun.

XXXVII.

"So, you say that it breaks down for no reason?" Jolka Stern was diagnosing the backup console circuits in the head mechanic's quarters one by one, while trying to find out what had happened that the boss needed her help instead of dealing with such a trifle on his own.

"Damn it. When a cow craps, it goes on, and this bastardness, when it gets crapped up, everything is stopped here," muttered Charles Michalow, at the same time scratching Vuvu's back. "And what breaks down there all the time? When I take it apart and assemble it, it works like gold ... and the next day it's the same."

"Everything seems to be working, although ..." the laser probe caught something unexpected and Jolka fell silent, absorbed in her discovery.

"What is there?"

"Someone picked it, and it wasn't you. Even more so not me."

Jolka took a long tweezer from her bag and, maneuvering it, carefully pulled five long, thinner than a hair, transparent threads from the circuits of the console. She packed them carefully in a plastic bag.

"I've never seen anything like it," she said. "I'll have it checked by the science department."

"This devilish thing was breaking my console?" Mikhalov was surprised, looking at the handbag against the light. The mysterious threads were slightly iridescent, and practically invisible. Only Jolka's hawk eyes could see them.

"Looks like it, boss. I don't see any other reason for these continuous failures."

The chief mechanic shrugged, handed her the bag, and yawned desperately.

"So, give it to the eggheads, Jola. I'll go to bed for a while, because I really want to sleep," he muttered, then returned to his quarters and stretched out on his bed. Vuvu curled up on his chest, panting with happiness.

Jolka put the console back together, checked that it worked, then threw her bag over her shoulder and left. The mysterious find intrigued her, but even more so that someone had put these threads in the console - for what purpose? And who? She hoped the study would reveal at least part of the answer. In addition, in the research department, worked Andy Karpiel whom she liked very much.

On the way, the engineer encountered a strange procession. Four security men carried the unconscious Father Toadstool on a blanket, singing grimly:

The Pole has died and is lying on a tray.

Drunken compatriots make speeches!

And then suddenly the cock crows

The Pole gets up and ... sober!

If they knew such consequences

they would have given more vodka![9]

"The priest is dead?!" Jolka was scared.

"No, miss," Tuniek Afdieyev from Lviv calmed her singingly. "He just fainted out of fear like some brat when he saw those creatures with tails."

"And yet he had a gun in hand, like all of us, and a knife at his side," added Kaziek Piskorz from Warsaw's Praga. And he got so scared that he collapsed in a heap. I said from the beginning that the Reverend is not fit for any maneuvers. The

---

[9] Olga Lipińska's cabaret.

penguin would be better, because she has bigger balls than this man."

This statement clearly illustrated the attitude of the entire crew to the two ministers - in general, Sister Ofelia enjoyed much more respect than her titled brother, and for good reason.

"Kazik, have you seen Karpiel?" Jolka asked, knowing that Ensign Piskorz was one of the soldiers guarding the science department.

"He's with Trekovsky in his lab. With my own ears, I heard them cursing the assistant, because she measured something wrong. She took offense, because as you know, every woman is honorable, and she went to our missus to complain," the ensign replied with a cheerful smile.

"I see. Then take the priest to the infirmary, and if anyone asks about me, say that I went to Mr. Karpiel."

"Of course."

Jolka got into the nearest quick-elevator and went two levels down, to the science department. In the hydroponics section, three lab technicians were playing poker while their supervisor was snoring on a sofa. When asked by the lieutenant, the lab technicians explained blithely that "they didn't play at all, but foretold what the result of the experiment would be". After receiving this answer, Jola preferred not to ask anything and went on. In the physics section, a name day were celebrated loudly, other sections were closed due to the failure of the electric subnetwork. Only the biochemistry section Jola headed for, worked relatively normally, because Professor Trekovsky, a real divine punishment for every research institute, was a committed workaholic and always worked, regardless of the failures that haunted his laboratory, even by candlelight. He had smuggled an old-fashioned Bunsen burner, a gas cylinder, and an antique microscope in his luggage, so he could continue his experiments even when the power went out. Andy Karpiel got along with him right away and they were happy to work together without telling anyone what they actually worked on.

"Hello, Jedrus," said Jolka, entering the laboratory. "I have a little work for both of you."

She put the bag with threads on the table.

"What's that?" Trekovsky became interested. With his unmistakable eye, he immediately recognized a RIDDLE and, grasping the bag, began to study its content intently.

"I don't know what it is, but when placed in some device it interferes with its operation and is practically undetectable," Jola replied. "I only noticed a slight refraction of the 'halo' around the laser beam and thanks to that I found it. Check what it is and where it could have come from to the backup engine room console."

"Sure, we'll check it," Andy gave her a mischievous smile. "Hey, Jola, Me orderang the ferst dance at the festol party. Will yeh remembor?"

"Of course. As long as the captain doesn't kill you sooner. What did you both say to Marzenka?"

Trekovsky stopped looking at the thread for a moment and snorted.

"We? Almost nothing," he replied. "And certainly, much less than was due. She is a complete idiot."

"But she is the first woman who has withstood you for more than two weeks," Jola pointed out to him. "Okay, that's none of my business, but don't be surprised when the captain gives you hell."

She said and she left. She had to go back to the engine room and take care of the whole business, since Mikhalov took a nap, and Greg was completely lunar from the morning and it was impossible to get along with him.

Jola was right to say that Trekovsky and Karpiel would be in trouble. When Trekovsky's assistant told Captain Zakrzevska what had happened in the studio, and she burst into tears, Lilianna felt a powerful, truly Sarmatian anger.

"What's that supposed to mean?!" she roared so loudly that the whole deck heard her, and the next two. "As long as I am in charge here, no superior except me will offend my subordinates!"

"And you are allowed?" ArCer asked before he could bite his tongue.

"Privilege of rank."

"I don't see the point in it, if you are allowed to yell at everyone and trash them, and the professor and ..."

"Do as I say, not as I do ... Mr. Dupelecki," interrupted Lilanna. "You better take care of TiShan, who got up the duff because of you ... I wonder how."

"How? In the traditional way."

"I don't mean the technical side! But how did that come about if you Uoltans are so composed and emotionless like a kitchen mixer with target programming. How could you both forget yourselves to such an extent?"

ArCer got confused and looked away.

"We don't talk about these topics even with each other, let alone with representatives of foreign races and cultures," he finally said.

"It's a very convenient answer. I mean, doing different things is okay, but talking about the problem isn't, right?"

"No, not at all!"

ArCer felt himself losing his composure, which was not so new to him in dealing with the captain. Personally, he was of the opinion that the supreme Uoltan philosopher alone wouldn't have been able to stand this woman for more than an hour. She was just awful. Even with all his Uoltanian restraint, he could find no other word.

"Think for a moment," he said finally, summoning all the control techniques he knew to help. "Do you know what is the most characteristic feature of Uoltans?"

"I know. Pride."

"Exactly. How can a logical, proud being, without problems accept the state in which he or she turns into an animal, ruled by the most primitive of instincts? Unfortunately, we have not managed to eliminate the cyclical nature of this phenomenon, but at least we try to control it, and one of the tools for this is to avoid this topic in conversations and even thoughts. Is it so hard to understand?"

"No, why hard?" the captain replied politely. "On Earth, they were also such wise men, and for centuries. They ended up going haywire and they either arranged bloody witch hunts to get back at the wicked gender, leading into temptation, or they fell into all sorts of other deviations. Nature doesn't get fooled that easily, Mr. ArCer. Even a freak like Father Toadstool understands it, although he probably not quite ... He is, in a straight line, the heir of the old masochistic monks who tormented themselves and demanded the same for everyone around, because no one likes to be alone in misfortune."

"You don't understand Uoltans. We believe that only by getting rid of all emotions, including those related to the mating season, you can become a perfectly logical being, that is ..."

"... a computer in sneakers," Lilianna cut in on him. "It's not pride, Mr. ArCer, that speaks through you, it's haughtiness. You want to be better than others so much that you get paranoid. It's fortune and God's grace that you are not interested in imposing your model of happiness on other races, because it could easily happen to you what happened to a certain Igor Sebastian Tichy, who invented an Obnoxynol[10]."

"What did he invent?" ArCer asked dejectedly.

"Obnoxynol, a nontoxic drug when taken in microscopic amounts, was causing the act of procreation to be highly unpleasant. He meant more or less what you want, to free yourself from the bodily desires. And it would have been good if only he had used it, but no, he decided to make everyone happy with it, and it ended very badly for him. Read Lem. Now, please go to the research department and reprimand Trekovsky. Please tell him that if I hear one more complaint of this type against him, he will find out how difficult it is to pick teeth off the floor with broken hands. Is it clear?"

"I think ... I understand."

ArCer stepped out into the corridor, wondering how to pass along the captain's words in a form that would be acceptable to the Star Armada rules, and at the same time conveying the merits of the case. Turning behind the corner of the corridor, he almost ran into the first mate, who was walking with his hands

---

[10] "The Star Diaries" by Stanislaw Lem.

in his pockets, whistling, despite the fact that he should have been on the bridge for ten minutes.

"Oh, sorry, Mr. Uoltan," Arek cried cheerfully. "Why are you so sour? I mean, more than usual?"

"The captain called me by a term I don't understand," the commander replied. "My translator didn't find it in its database, and it must mean something."

"What is that term?"

"She said to me: Mr. Dupelecki."

"Khem ... yeah. It's a kind of Polish idiom ..." Arek made every effort not to laugh, but he could barely refrain. "It's actually hard to translate, but it's not a compliment."

"I figured that much out myself. If you're looking for me, I'll be in the science department for now."

"All right, you can go. There is peace everywhere."

Arek saluted in the old-fashioned way and continued on his way. For the next twelve hours he was to command 'Hermash' and he was not eager to do so, because the main computer, now strangely independent in the process of thinking, didn't like him much...

XXXVIII.

When ArCer entered Professor Trekovsky's laboratory, both the professor and Karpiel were engrossed in their work and didn't even look at him.

"My gentlemen," said the Uoltan, standing proudly in the doorway. "The captain instructed me to convey to you her disapproval in relation to the case of ensign Marzena Szkwał."

Both officers stopped their work as if on command and looked at him in amazement.

"Convey disapproval? It's probably not our captain," said Karpiel, scratching his head.

"Our boss would say much more and much more bluntly."

ArCer got ruffled, and hesitated.

"Well, she put it more bluntly," he admitted, stuttering slightly. "But the meaning was more or less the same. You are to stop harassing Miss Szkwał."

"She's not a miss, but a two-time divorced woman," Trekovsky snorted, not taking his eyes off the spectrograph.

Andy Karpiel nudged him slightly in the side. ArCer couldn't take a joke, sense of humor was completely unfamiliar to him, and he understood no irony.

"We'll try, Commander," he promised. "But why don't you take a look at what we have here in the meantime? Because we don't really know what we're looking at."

ArCer walked over to the analytical equipment and looked at the readings, more for courtesy than for some other reason. After a while, however, there was a faint interest on his face. He turned the indicator.

"Where did you get this?" he asked. "Certainly not from the standard equipment."

"It was in the backup console in the head mechanic's quarters."

ArCer was silent for a moment, closely following what showed on the scanner screen. It was evident that strange readings were not alien to him at all.

"Beryllium diramian," he finally muttered.

"What does it mean?" Trekovsky asked, exchanging stupid looks with Karpiel.

"It means we have a saboteur on board," the commander replied calmly, and left the lab, leaving them both completely stunned.

Ramin, an element derived from planet Uoltan, combined with the Earth's beryllium, formed the radioactive substance, almost invisible due to its molecular structure, but very dangerous. Its presence on 'Hermash' was disturbing to say the least, especially since it was unknown where it might have come from. Only a successful synthesis attempt by someone who really knew his stuff was considered - but who could it be? ArCer took the sensor and went with it to the head engineer headquarters. As he suspected, the radiation levels were well above normal, and Mikhalov, who was fast asleep, showed clear signs of irradiation.

The Uoltan shook him vigorously.

"Mr. Mikhalov, you will immediately report to the infirmary for examinations," he said when Charles opened his sleepy eyelids. "And take your rat with you."

"Mr. ArCer, sod off, or your nose will have a close encounter with my fist," Mikhailov grumbled, half-conscious and not fully awake.

It didn't help him, because the Uoltan forcefully sat him down and poured water on his head from a cup on the table. The chief engineer tried to implement his announcement, but ArCer without hesitation made him feel his physical advantage, and

Charles finally got revived, but this didn't change his behavior at all.

"Ah, you deprived of the feeling, scrub of drunken toad, I will teach a lesson for waking up the hard-working man from his first dream!" he screamed, and there was a need to bind his hands with a sheet.

After a short tumult, which ended with the above-mentioned action, ArCer could finally get a word in edgewise and calmly, without offense, explain:

"Mr. Michalow, someone sabotaged your backup console with a radioactive agent. It is highly probable that you have been irradiated. You must undergo a detailed examination, as well as your pet, who is dressing my left calf at the moment."

Despite all his anger, Mikhalov laughed shortly.

"You really have to be a Uoltan to speak so calmly when my Vuvu bites your leg," he pointed out. "Okay, untie me, I'll be good now. I will go straight to the infirmary."

Having dealt with this difficult matter, ArCer went to Captain Zakrzevska, to whom he had to report on the discovery of the scientific department and his own findings. Along the way, he came across Sister Ophelia, who was very bustling. He almost smiled - though he still didn't understand the essence of earthly religion, he liked this fighting woman, and so did everyone on the ship.

"Hello," he greeted her politely. "What's up with our chaplain?"

Sister Ophelia shrugged and adjusted the cornet, which was tilted as always.

"He's still confused," she replied. "He asks everyone if these horrible creatures for sure won't come out of the holo-room, and he has to take some calming pills. What I have to deal with ... do you know, Commander, that while still in the seminary he tried to force his thesis about the devilish origin of Uoltans as something perfectly sensible?"

"What? Why did something like that come to his mind?"

"You know, those ears and eyebrows of yours, and the general appearance ... The bishop himself had to get involved in this and ban his work from being published, because it would have been an embarrassment across the entire Planetary Union."

"Somehow that doesn't surprise me," ArCer thought, but didn't say it out loud. Nothing surprised him anymore about Father Toadstool. He said goodbye to the nun politely and headed for the captain's quarters. He had more serious things on his mind now than the ideas of the haunted priest.

In the infirmary, sister Lolita Icant was preparing another sedative injection for Father Toadstool. The deck chaplain was really in deplorable condition. As it turned out, he had never been in the holo-room before the memorable tests, and therefore he was completely unprepared for the plasticity of the impressions. Since he was not a holographic expert, he also couldn't understand that the strange creatures he had come into contact with couldn't leave the room and haunt him outside, and he therefore fell into severe neurosis.

"This guy is a divine punishment," growled Jacob Zmiyevski, who, as a sworn atheist, didn't understand the point of having a chaplain on board the Star Ship. "Not only is he useless, but he also causes trouble with his respectable person."

"We can't help it, that was the order of the command," the captain told him, watching with a certain amusement the priest who lay on the bed in the pose of a dying swan and waited for the injection.

"Shall I give him two milliliters, or one will be enough, doctor?" Lolita asked, shifting her innocent gaze to the doctor.

"One and three quarters, you victim of the health reform!" Cuba replied angrily. "Finally learn how to calculate the dose!"

"I tried. I counted according to two different formulas and once I got one, and then two, and you are telling me otherwise ..."

"Because if I hadn't, you might have thougt that I'm not needed here, and you only need a handy pharmacopoeia."

Lolita made an offended face first, and then the injection to the priest. Father Toadstool sighed excruciatingly, as if the nurse had used a rusty needle instead of a hypoinjector, and assumed a martyr's face. Cuba, watching him, checked the readings and nodded approvingly.

"Father, you can go now."

"Will he recover by the end of the mission?" asked the captain when the priest left like a badly exhausted miner, returning from a twelve-hour shift in front."

"I don't know. He's even dumber than Lolita, he probably wouldn't be able to solve a one-color Rubik's cube. Nobody can explain to him that Chris' blue elves won't jump out of the holo-room to eat him raw."

"Sure, he would be much more digestible when roasted, especially since he is such a fat priest ... What's up, Commander?"

The last question was, of course, to ArCer, who stood patiently in the doorway, waiting to be noticed.

"Captain, we have a saboteur on board," said the Uoltan. "Someone put a very dangerous substance in the backup console, in the headquarters of the chief engineer ... who, by the way, should be here by now. I told him to come for a checkup.

"He probably decided to kill something on the way. Are you sure it was sabotage?"

"I confirm. A synthetic radioactive compound was used, the production of which in our conditions requires many days of work, but it is possible. However, it is not included in anything that we might have packed before we took off at the dock."

Sister Lolita made a sound intermediate between a cry of fear and a groan of admiration, but it was not a reaction to the commander's words. The chief engineer was walking down the corridor, clearly visible thanks to the opened door. His head and upper body were decorated with pasta and chopped liver, and plentifully covered in tomato sauce. In his left hand he held a cup bent in all directions and sipped something from it, in his right he carried a half-nibbled leg of an unidentified poultry. Instead of pants, he wore some pathetic, tattered and charred remnants. Following Mikhalov, Vuvu was so smeared with goulash and vegetable salad that at first glance he resembled the famous Pizza Man from the classic comedy "Spaceballs". Every few steps he stopped and licked his lips deliciously, then ran, so as not to lose sight of his master.

"Sodom and Gomorrah," the captain muttered with interest.

"Those are probably the favorite words on this ship," remarked ArCer, in which the unusual sight caused only a slight wrinkling of his beautiful forehead. Not much could surprise him now.

"Mr. Mikhalov, what happened?" asked Jacob Zmiyevski, inviting the engineer to the infirmary with a friendly gesture.

"The synthesizer blew right in my face," Mikhalov replied calmly. "It's good that it didn't have time to heat anything, it was barely warm. I came for a checkup, but maybe I'll wash before it."

"Indeed, maybe it will be for the better," agreed Jacob. "Lola, go to the supply room for a new uniform, men's, size L, engine room."

"I'm not a messenger," the nurse pouted, but she left anyway.

Mikhalov took his pet in his arms and went to the shower.

"Hmmm, as I'm already here, doctor, could you please check my calf?" ArCer asked.

"And what is?" the captain asked.

"When I woke the chief engineer, this creature expressed its far-reaching disapproval of my actions."

Jacob Zmiyevski crouched down and lifted the torn leg of the Uoltan's uniform. He studied Vuvu's teeth marks in concentration for a moment, then took the regenerator out of the cabinet and went to work, whistling the "White March" at the same time. ("Psychosis, thrombosis, tuberculosis cough ... Tuberculosis, yes, it's all us .... Psychosis, sclerosis, creaking in a back, paradentosis, this is a kickup ..."[11]). ArCer stood patiently, waiting for the doctor to finish his work while explaining to his

---

[11] "White March" Jaromir Nohavica.

captain how difficult the process of obtaining beryllium diramian was.

"And do you have any idea who and why packed this stuff into the console of our nightmarish Charles?" Lilianna finally asked him, having glozed over the fact that she didn't understand all dilatations of the learned commander.

"Unfortunately, not. A thorough investigation will have to be made."

"So, you and Miss Gvizdak will take care of it immediately. Jacob, examine Mikhalov and his pet, and I will go to the bridge. This quasar-like creature, which replaces the sun for the race from the new planet, emits very interesting impulses."

"I already know. Initially, we thought it was a type B quasar, a very small equivalent of a proper quasar, but the parameters don't match. It is some stellar form unknown to science. Astrophysicists are already working on it."

"Did they find out anything?"

"No, for now they are arguing about who this phenomenon is to be named after. Everyone thinks they have more rights in this regard than others, so you understand ..."

"I understand, chit-chat, and the peasant are picking up plums. When you change your pants, you will go and say that they should enter the name of 'Hermash', because without our ship we wouldn't have discovered anything. And if any of them protests, take him to the arrest and you're done with it."

"Thank you, princess, you are an angel," said the touched bass of the on-board computer from the loudspeaker. As usual, the hotheaded spirit of 'Hermash' was watching and was present everywhere.

ArCer wanted to say something, but bit his tongue. Even the main computer on this ship was crazy, so what could be expected of its crew?

XXXIX.

The Hermasian phenomenon, as the quasi-quasar was eventually called, was indeed something very interesting. It emitted both the radiation typical of a small star and radio waves, which certainly prevented the development of radio communication on the planet, as they caused unbreakable background noise. Probably thanks to this, the civilization that had developed on the planet, dubbed Mothra by Christopher Mayher, hadn't been previously discovered.

"Actually, why is Chris to name the planet?" pouted Andy Karpiel during the scientific conference, when everyone had already sat down comfortably and tasted the delicacies with which the invaluable Matias von Braun decorated the table.

"Because he was the first to determine the location of this planet," the captain replied. "And if you don't like it, you can get a punch in the face."

"But why Mothra?" asked the first mate, scratching his head anxiously.

"And why not?" the chief navigator replied with a shrug.

"Ladies and gentlemen, let us not stray from the topic. The name of the planet is secondary, especially as it probably has nothing to do with its proper name, used by the inhabitants," ArCer said aloud. "We now need to study its surface and, if possible, the race that lives there. Study without interfering, as everything indicates that we are dealing with the pre-cosmic civilization, probably convinced that there is no other rational race in the universe apart from it. Professor Trekovsky will now highlight the probable parameters of the creatures we will come into contact with, though rather not directly.

Dinoslav Trekovsky got up and, having assumed a dignified face, drank water from the glass in front of him. He choked due to the importance of the moment, and for a long time was unable to suppress his coughing, until the captain, impatient, approached him and punched him on the back.

"Oh God, she killed me!" the professor yelled, losing his balance and falling face down into the dish of herring salad.

"Male hysteric," Lilianna growled in displeasure as everyone else was laughing.

The professor finally caught his breath, then his balance, wiped the salad off his face with a towel handed to him by the obliging assistant, and began his speech with a slightly offended voice:

"Ladies and gentlemen, the race that has developed on this planet, may not resemble any rational race known to us. By analyzing the data provided by astrophysicists and applying general biological laws to them, it can be concluded that, first of all, it must be a race resistant to ultraviolet radiation to a much greater degree than, for example, humans. It is also characterized by high resistance to increased pressure and high temperatures. The respiratory system of these creatures must be extremely efficient and probably has an anatomical structure different from what we already know. I would venture to say that due to the high content of water vapor in the atmosphere, it may be a gill-like system, and the creatures inhabiting Mothra may be dipnoan, as such a property would be very functional from the point of view of their evolution.

Closer analysis shows that for much of the year Mothra's atmosphere resembles a very dense fog rather than typical air, and therefore, in the course of evolution, the gills may not have disappeared, but rather turned into something like spiracles, closing in a drier atmosphere, and opening in a wetter one. The same is true of all terrestrial creatures on this planet. Further: because we have discovered products of technical thought, in addition characterized by artificially applied dyes, these creatures must have both grasping and visual organs. We can also assume that they have mastered the exact sciences, and thus they know both some form of writing and mathematical signs. Based on the architecture, their height was estimated at just over a meter, but we still don't know what they look like. We know that they can see, but we don't know if they can hear or smell, although it seems they should do both."

"Uh, why?" Malvinka Krencik blurted out.

"Because, miss, evolution is just like the survival of the fittest. Basic senses help a lot - if you have your hearing, you can hear when someone hunts you, and if you have a sense of smell, you can smell an invisible and inaudible dinner."

"Do you have something to say, or you just wanted to disturb?" the captain asked sternly.

"I do," Malvinka replied with dignity. "These beings use something like a radio, although it is obviously not a radio as we understand it. Their devices operate on the principle of electrical impulses transmitted through a wired network. This network literally covers the entire planet and serves only for communication between inhabitants."

"Did you decode their signals?"

"No, I have not succeeded in this art yet. However, I'm on the right track, because it is a typical verbal communication, although to our ears it would be more like mouse squeals than normal chatter."

"The conclusion is that they also have a vocal apparatus capable of making such sounds, i.e., that they have something like a mouth and larynx. And if so, we would probably be able to communicate with them somehow."

"We are not allowed to do that," ArCer reminded her.

Captain Zakrzevska waved her hand.

"Yeah, yeah, I know," she muttered reluctantly. "But I'm more and more interested in these creatures. Unfortunately, landing on the planet that is constantly flooded with ultraviolet, whose atmosphere resembles either unsaturated water vapor or saturated vapor, depending on whether it is dry season or not, would be an unintelligent move. We will send a research drone. When could it be ready?"

"In two days, Captain," said Andy Karpiel. "We have to adapt it."

"Well, we are starting in two days," Captain Zakrzevska decided, standing up. "Until then, I hope it will become clear what an idiot is playing sabotages here ..."

It was easy to say - explain what an idiot ... ArCer, who was casually promoted to the head of the local investigative office, had to start by examining who among the crew was educated enough to be able to obtain a dangerous substance without the help of a properly experienced team and specialist apparatus. After examining the files of everyone on board, which took him three full days, without food or sleep, he concluded that no one was skilled enough, erased his notes and fell into deep reverie. The conclusion was not only unexpected, but also complicating everything remarkably - no one, not even Professor Trekovsky, had participated in an adequate training, because the production of beryllium diramian was a highly specialized undertaking and required an adapted laboratory. In fact, even ArCer itself couldn't cope with such a challenge. It was known that no one had brought it on board in the luggage, because the transporter would have blocked the transmission, having detected such a dangerous substance, and it also hadn't been smuggled in the shipyard, because the receiving committee would have noticed the malfunctioning console. Besides, trouble had only recently started.

"We are dealing with something that is not possible, but it has happened," he finally noted in his personal journal and went out into the corridor to unkink a little. He was immediately struck by an unexpected sight. Extremely lively crew members ran here and there with some decorative baskets in which various food products and twigs of plants, mostly artificial, were arranged. Everyone headed for the chapel, where every fifteen minutes Father Toadstool gave a solemn speech, said a prayer and solemnly sprinkled the baskets with water. Since on the table placed in the chapel decorated with the greenery could fit no more than ten baskets at a time, the ritual had to be performed in parts, and the crew members fighting for priority covered themselves with malice and pushed like preschoolers.

The Uoltan understanding nothing of it, caught Sister Ophelia passing by and asked:

"Excuse me, but what's all this supposed to mean?"

"Today, it's Holy Saturday, people went with Easter baskets," the nun kindly explained to him, which of course didn't explain anything.

"What did they go with?"

"It's such a Catholic religious rite."

"So why do I see also representatives of other religions?"

"You see, in Poland this tradition is so deeply entrenched that even representatives of Polish Islam can come with Easter baskets," sister Ophelia replied. "Of course, this is possible only in this enlightened age, but it is. You know, this is an opportunity for integration, kindness and mutual forgiveness."

"Don't get in front of me, you blue cow, because if I slap you on the dial, you will take seriousness immediately," came the nervous voice of engineer Joe Stelmach.

"You bloody foundling, how do you speak to my girlfriend? I'll teach you good manners!" answered the voice of Gustaw Jopek, quartermaster and personnel officer in one person.

"Come on, Gusto! Hit him against the wall!" prompted him Honoratka Kalisiak, supplier, which had been Gustav's girlfriend from elementary school.

"There are much braver people in the cemetery because of their lack of social sophistication!"

"There are people stronger than you which were taken by an ambulance after fight with me!"

"Peace, children, peace be to people of good will," Father Toadstool tried to soften the controversy, but no one listened to him, the quarrel began to spread, because, as it usually happened, the other gathered began to take one side or the other.

"Hush you both! The rest too!" Johnnie Caterpillar's bass boomed finally. "We have Easter, we should love each other, not argue! If someone doesn't respect the holy day, I swear to God that I will move the ice ax over their back! Amen."

ArCer looked at Sister Ophelia, who shrugged helplessly and adjusted the cornet.

"Polish temperament, you shouldn't be surprised," she said. "They'll make it up over the egg."

The Uoltan decided not to dwell on the subject any longer, having come to the conclusion that he would have understood little anyway, he said excuse me to the nun and set off in search of Captain Zakrzevska. He found her in the briefing room, where she was working on some reports, resting her feet on the back of Bear sleeping under the table. Of course, she also had her own basket, with eggs, a chocolate lamb, dry sausage, a piece of cake and salt in a crystal container on a white napkin. The basket stood quietly on the table and the captain worked unconcerned.

At ArCer's footsteps, she looked up.

"Hello, Commander. Any news?" she asked.

"Only that no one on board could, due to the lack of appropriate knowledge and apparatus, produce beryllium diramian."

"Hmmm ... and if they had knowledge, the apparatus wouldn't be so necessary?"

"Well, it's an inconvenience that could be avoided," admitted ArCer. "However, none of the crew, including myself, has the appropriate education."

"Yeah, yeah ... And how is Mr. Mikhalov?"

"The effects of irradiation have already made themselves known. He is in the infirmary, his condition is stable, although not the best. TiShan said he would be confused for a while ... he has already started losing his mind but she should recover."

"I hope he's our chief engineer, we're in the shit without him."

A loudspeaker on the wall creaked, then the main computer's schnappsbaritone spoke from it:

"Princess, your communicator fucked up. Our doctors have been calling for an hour. They ask you to come to the hospital section. They have an unexpected problem there, Dr. Zmiyevski must have stuck to Sister Icant with a plaster, heh."

"What problem are you talking about ...? Be serious, Hermus, did they say something specific?"

"We may have a dodger on board."

Even though Captain Zakrzevska was used to the way her main computer spoke, it took her some time to realize it meant a stowaway. But in the infirmary? It is true that miracles happened on this ship, but it seemed to be at least improbable.

'Hermash', tell them I'll be there soon," she said and got up from the table. "Commander, I have a request: take my Easter basket to the chapel, bless it and then return it to Johnnie, he will know what to do next. I don't have time."

ArCer wanted to say something, but was speechless. Meanwhile, the captain left, and Bear followed her, waving his tail. The Uoltan was alone. For a moment he looked uncertainly at the Easter basket, then grabbed its handle and with a heavy step returned to the chapel, where he was greeted by surprised and even discreetly amused glances. As he later noted in his personal journal, he had never felt so stupid in his life.

XL.

In the infirmary, the entire areopagus - Nbeba, Zmiyevski, TiShan, Sister Lolita and two male nurses - was discussing animatedly in front of the closed stasis chamber. Everyone looked very excited wondering who might have been locked in it.

"Lie down," Captain Zakrzevska said to Bear, who reluctantly lay down in front of the door, put his huge head on his paws and began to whine softly.

"No way, this is the infirmary, not the common room," Lilianna tried to comply with the regulations, even though she usually declared complete contempt for them. Bear knew it well and listened to her as befited a well-mannered dog.

The captain closed the door behind her and turned to the medics:

"How is it possible that no one has checked the stasis chamber for so many months?"

"It was not needed, so no one checked it," replied Jacob Zmiyevski with his usual nonchalance.

"There were other problems," added Dr. Nbeba.

"The problem is nobody takes anything seriously here," the captain grumbled. "What are you waiting for? Open this contraption!"

Dr. Nbeba hurriedly typed in the traditional Armada Star code, but to his surprise, nothing happened.

"Enter the date of the Battle of Grunwald," Sister Icant suggested.

"And when was that?" Nbeba was surprised.

"Oh, a nice couple of years ago ..."

This is where Jacob Zmiyevski entered, chose the correct code and the lid of the stasis chamber opened noiselessly. The time inside again began to flow normally and after a while a slim, girlish figure emerged into the world of God.

"Holy Mother, Veronica!" Lolita shouted.

"Yes, that's my name," stated the helmswoman, who had gone missing without a trace, standing up unsteadily. "Why are you staring at me as if you went haywire in a body? Oh, Captain, I'm sorry I haven't noticed you."

"What were you doing in this chamber?" TiShan asked sternly.

"For months we've thought you went missing during the ship disaster, and you, as we can see, were in the chamber the whole time."

"I went in to see what was there, and that damn thing had to shut up," the girl began to explain, and only now she realized what the doctor said. "How is it, for months? You mean you found me dead?"

Dr. Nbeba tried to explain to Veronica the circumstances of the incident, but the steerswoman unexpectedly became utterly hysterical. She started screaming that no one was looking for her, no one needed her, no one loved her, and that she was going to kill herself. One of the nurses tried to cheer her up, but he got such a slap that it whistled and echoed throughout the infirmary. It is not known how it would have ended had it not been for Malvinka Krencik, who had just decided to visit the sick Mikhalov and opened the door. There was a bass "wow" and the mass of brown fur leapt onto the hysterical Veronica, knocking her to the floor. The helmswoman having her face scrubbed by the pink tongue, lost confidence, barely able to breathe under the pressure of several dozen raging kilograms of the shepherd dog unconscious with joy.

"Bear, little Bear," she grunted at last, trying to get up. "My pup, baby ... Have you missed me? Who took care of you while I was away?"

The huge dog whimpered, squealed, barked and jumped, showing in every way how much he had missed and how glad he was to see his mistress back.

"No harm happened to him. Johnnie cared for him no worse than for my Gizia," said the captain, observing the scene with undisturbed calm. "Okay, enough of the fun. Ensign Bumblebee, attention!"

Veronika jumped up from the floor, assuming a basic posture, which was not easy due to the fact that Bear was jumping around her.

"On your order, Captain," she gasped.

"First, you will report to the personal department, then to Chris Mayher to include you on the duty list. Then you will go to Father Toadstool and explain to him what happened, because he has already performed three services for the peace of your unfortunate soul and I don't know if he will not be personally offended by the fact that you are alive ..."

"He may think it is making fun of holy things," Cuba chuckled.

"It was accidentally ..." Veronika frowned and after a while she realized that the doctor was joking. She assumed a dignified face, reported off and left, followed by Bear jumping merrily.

In the corridor, she came across Johnnie Caterpillar, who had already finished his shift in the chapel. The orderly was carrying a tray from the mess on which stood a bowl of soup, a plate of noodles, and a pot of coffee. It was supposed to be a lunch for the hard-working captain. Upon seeing Veronica, the highlander screamed riotously:

"Oh, most gracious Jesus!"

and instinctively threw the tray up until it hit the ceiling. The soup, pasta with cheese and coffee splashed all over the corridor, while Johnnie went round the astonished helmswoman, burst into the infirmary and fell to his knees in front of equally astonished doctors.

"Save me, doctors, I'm crazy, I see ghosts!" he howled in a voice like a fireman's siren. " Give me some injection or something ..."

"Calm down, Johnny!" the captain shouted, struggling to hold back a very unkind laugh. " Veronika is not a ghost. She just spent all this time in our on-board immobility room. Come on, get up and don't protest, or I'll hit you in that stupid face."

"My ancestor, the voivode, used to say: 'if you don't slap a peasant in the morning, he walks stupid all day," murmured Jacob Zmiyevski, unable to resist. The captain gave him a sharp look and left, with difficulty suppressing a smile, and the completely detonated Johnnie trailed after her like a beaten dog.

***

The return of Veronica, whom everyone had already mourned, was treated as an Easter miracle, although it had nothing to do with a miracle. Malvinka Krencik quickly spread the word among the crew members and organized a welcome party. In order to avoid any surprises, the ship was then decided to "park" in a relatively quiet and safe zone. Preparations for the dance began immediately, sliding all tables and chairs in the common room against one wall and decorating the walls with festoons. This caused enormous anger of Father Toadstool, who said that Holy Saturday was still fast and no boisterous celebration was not allowed. Not wanting to annoy the stern chaplain, it was decided that at midnight everyone would share an egg and the fun would start only after that.

"Excuses," growled the unhappy priest as it reached him.

"Come on, Tadzio," Sister Ophelia persuaded him kindly. "After all, this is an unusual, completely unexpected occasion. You can't tell me you're not glad."

"I'm glad, but that's no reason to break the rules. I'm going to the captain with this."

"I can already see our Lilka listening to you," Ophelia snorted, but her brother didn't listen to her anymore, but, as he had promised, went in search of the ship's commander. He found her halfway between the common room and the conservatory, listening patiently to ArCer's grumbling at the lack of discipline and the dangers it might have posed.

The chaplain waited for the Uoltan to stop speaking, then laid out his complaint, ending it with a categorical demand that no play be allowed.

"I don't want them to caw to me," replied Lilianna calmly. "I don't see any reason to spoil people's joy at the return of the friend. Don't try to be holier than the Pope himself."

"Cephas VII certainly wouldn't approve of it!"

"And where does this certainty come from? I heard that he is a cheerful old man, he eagerly listens to youth music and reads comics."

The priest was out of breath with indignation. SiWok, who was walking down the corridor, stopped and listened to the conversation with evident anxiety on his narrow face.

"Will the dance take place?" he asked finally.

"Of course, don't worry."

"It's very good then. May I ask you to dance with me first?"

"Unbelievable," ArCer muttered in shock, and the cheered captain replied:

"Naturally, SiWok. I'm booking this dance for you."

The young Uoltan smiled happily and moved on, while the commander looked at Lilianna reproachfully. However, he said nothing. He should have gotten used to the fact that his young compatriot was not a typical Uoltan, but he couldn't and tired SiWok with long lectures on logic, duties and the need to control emotions, which the boy let in with one pointed ear and released with the other. The years spent at the Armada Star Academy completely destroyed the careful upbringing he had received. He became no better than an average Earthling, which was beyond ArCer's law-abiding mind.

So, everyone waited for fun decorating the common room or helped Matias von Braun to prepare snacks. Johnnie Caterpillar opened his special hiding place for this occasion, where he kept some of the moonshine, unscrewed the bottles and seasoned the noble liquid with concentrates of different juices, thus obtaining high-percentage liquors with various, often surprising flavors. Matias and a few volunteers who didn't feel disgusted with working in the kitchen set about cooking. First of all, he had to prepare something to replace the hard-boiled eggs. The Easter eggs for an Easter basket were obviously artificial, but Matias managed to obtain a protein and yolk substitute with an almost natural taste and appropriate color from the synthesized ingredients. He made hand-formed quarters of eggs from the obtained masses, and for those willing he also managed to make a kind of mayonnaise, which was very useful for decorating tiny sandwiches. There were also caviar toasts and hot sausages with cheese, aside from other snacks that could satisfy the most discerning astronautic tastes.

At midnight, the host computer announced in its drunken voice:

"End of the fast, gentry! Happy Easter!"

Immediately afterwards, a veritable orgy of merriment broke out in the common room. For almost an hour, all one could hear was loud greetings, resonant kisses, and mutual patting on the back. There was also almost an equally loud argument, because Joe Watery accused Joe Stelmach that what he patted his wife on was definitely not the back, but the ladies present, somehow smoothed the conflict. As the last counterfeit egg vanished from the platters, music began to blast. SiWok bowed courtly to the captain, who, as promised, danced with him a dance of honor in the middle of the common room, after which all the pairs danced.

Jürgen and Trekovsky's doctoral student, Ewelina Siwak, and Greg with Malvinka danced the Hungarian csárdás, Jacob Zmiyevski and sister Icant tried to adjust the Argentine tango to what they heard, and the rest didn't care about any dance canon at all. Most preferred a style, defined as something between twist and obertas, with the advantage of being suitable for all kinds of music. The exception was Johnnie, who to his joy discovered that Inga Lausch from the communications department had grown up in Poronin and briskly danced the robber dance, shouting the loud "Hey!" at the same time. They were both completely undisturbed by the fact that the music played through the loudspeakers completely didn't fit the fiery highlander dance.

Doctor TiShan, whose pregnancy was already very visible, didn't dance, but it was evident that she got into the spirit of the general atmosphere, because she gossiped happily with two researchers from the science department, as well as sister Ophelia and Maura Gvizdak, who had sprained her ankle the previous day and preferred not to strain it yet. The whole party was watched by Father Toadstool, still gloomy and offended, but not enough to deny himself Matias' delicacies. He even let himself be persuaded to have a drink. Arek, who voluntarily assumed the position of a cupbearer, poured him with his generous hand the moonshine, seasoned with raspberry concentrate and candied ginger, in the hope that a decent "schnapps" would make the gloomy priest relax a bit. The effect was that the chaplain started to cough and he had to be hit on the back for a long time, but the anger actually passed.

XLI.

One person didn't succumb to the mood of champagne fun - ArCer, of course. Driven by the Uoltan's typical sense of duty, instead of going to the common room, he went to the bridge, where he decided to make the necessary scans and calculations. There was no danger anywhere, but just in case...

'Hermash', scan the immediate area," he demanded, sitting down at the science console.

"And where is the magic word?" the computer croaked, sounding like it was completely drunk.

ArCer frowned in displeasure, opened the access panel and found there what he was looking for - a high frequency transducer turned on. On artificial intelligence systems, high frequency acted like alcohol on a human being, so it is no wonder that the on-board computer simply ... got drunk, following the example of the amused crew members. ArCer shut down and locked the transducer, then sat down again, waiting for the computer to regain its balance of mind. When he felt it should have happened, he repeated the request for the scans.

"You're mean," the offended schnappsbaritone announced from the loudspeaker. "And I'm not giving you shit."

"Why?" ArCer asked calmly. "I asked for the magic word."

"What, abracadabra?" ArCer's amazement infuriated the computer even more, and it now gurgled up something the translator refused to translate. The commander was just wondering what he should have done in such a situation, when the door slid open and the sleepy Charles Mikhalov marched on the bridge, barefoot, in a disheveled pajamas consisting of a shirt, to the navel but wide as if for a sumo wrestler, and fustian pants with an elastic band. It was evident that when Mikhalov got up, he tried to somehow hide the wide flaps of his shirt in these pants, because he had somehow stuffed the corner of the sheet behind the elastic band, which now trailed behind the engineer like a train.

"Sir, you are pointing to the consumption," ArCer choked, to which Mikhalov only waved his hand indulgently and went to the engine room console. For a moment he checked the settings, then in a surprisingly sober voice he shouted:

"Jesus Mary, what idiot worked on this?!"

He opened the cupboard under the console, took out a meter and a few small tools, then set to tweaking the console's parameters. The Uoltan watched him for a moment, then discreetly connected with Captain Zakrzevska.

"Captain, the chief engineer is on the bridge rummaging in the engine room console," he said.

"So, he's in the right place," came the calm reply.

ArCer grimaced in displeasure.

"But is he mentally stable?"

"Certainly, more than the rest of the crew. Don't worry about the role, because anyway you will be ... Jacob told me that Charles's condition was almost perfect. The treatment went brilliantly, and in fact, he may be returning to duty. If you have a different opinion, then observe him and overpower him if necessary."

"Why did I ask ..." the Uoltan muttered reluctantly, turning off the communicator. Meanwhile, Mikhalov clearly didn't like something about the lower circuits, because he was kneeling in front of the console, with his nose near the floor, and he was rummaging among the logic systems, sticking his half-naked butt out towards ArCer in a gesture of innocent provocation. At the same time, he cursed in an undertone with incomparable flowery, completely not caring about the presence of the commander.

At one point, a sensor on the science console beeped, signaling communication with the trial probe. It was evident that the science department had secured the equipment well, because the Mothra atmosphere, unfriendly to delicate devices, didn't hurt them. ArCer turned on the preview and saw a type of city on the screen, but different from the cities he knew. All the buildings were connected with each other, creating an extremely complicated structure, which apparently protected the inhabitants from unfavorable weather conditions not only during home rest, but also work and walks. This could mean that the creatures inhabiting Mothra were not as well adapted as they appeared, which could lead to interesting conclusions.

ArCer would have been happy to discuss it with Karpiel or Trekovsky, but they were both at the party and were certainly not suitable for a conversation right now. The Uoltan entered everything he could into the main computer's memory and ordered the probe to continue the exploration. He almost forgot about Mikhalov, who by that time had finished tuning the console and stood up, wiping the sweat from his forehead.

"Anyway, where is everyone?" he asked, looking around the bridge. "Are they striking?"

"No. A lot of fun is taking place in the common room, and you have not been invited, because you should still be in bed."

The chief engineer said what he thought about lying down, jerked his pants up nervously, noticed the sheet at last, unhooked it, threw it over his shoulder and went to the common room, where the fun was in full swing. Johnnie Caterpillar was just placing empty bottles in a huge basket when he saw him. At the sight of the chief engineer in shabby pajamas and with a stubble, he was so dumbfounded that with his dexterity, he dropped the basket to the floor. The hellish noise the bottles made alerted everyone.

"Mr. Mikhalov, what are you doing?!" cried Jacob Zmiyevski, pushing his way through the crowd. "How do you feel?"

"Okay, can't you see? Only this tailcoat you gave me is such big that three men like me would get into it."

"And couldn't you leave that damn sheet, take a shower and change?"

"It's a good idea." Mikhalov turned and stepped on Bear's paw, which in retaliation bit his buttock, not hard, but demonstratively. The engineer jumped up almost half a meter, cursed violently and burst into the corridor.

Veronika pushed her way through the crew and grabbed Bear by the neck.

"I'm so sorry!" she exclaimed. "He certainly didn't want to!"

"Die, get lost, you unclean specter!" Mikhailov shouted at the sight of her. "Ghosts! Apparitions! This ship is haunted! Parish priest, help me!!!"

"Oh, when in fear, God is near ..." Father Toadstool began venomously, but Sister Ophelia closed his mouth with her hand and explained to the engineer as shortly as possible what had happened. However, only after having a bigger drink served by the helpful Johnnie, Mikhalov recovered enough to be able to stagger away towards his cabin, muttering at the same time.

"And let somebody tell me that our 'Hermash' is just an ordinary ship..."

XLII.

If anyone had thought that ArCer had forgotten to investigate the assassination of the chief engineer, they would have been wrong. The Uoltan continued to work on the case, although he had virtually no starting points. Nobody on board wished Mikhalov so ill as to want to irradiate him, and even if they had, they would have not been able to produce a dangerous substance without drawing anyone's attention. Despite being absolutely certain that this was the case, ArCer couldn't help feeling that he was missing something, something important. But he hadn't the faintest idea what it might have been, and he struggled with it terribly.

The Uoltan worked, and the Easter celebration on board was in full swing. Nobody but ArCer cared about Mothra, the coup and anything else. Only on the third day, hungover, Karpiel-Bagietka called a meeting of the scientific department and the researchers plunged into the analysis of the data sent by the probe. ArCer, who didn't want to participate in their quarrels, only presented his report and left, deciding to focus on the investigative work, especially since the person of the mysterious bomber intrigued him much more than the creatures inhabiting the planet inhospitable to humans. He was assisted in the investigation by Maura Gvizdak, as security chief, and SiWok, who simply liked puzzles. The two of them nosed wherever they could while ArCer sat down to study the crew files again, hoping he had missed something.

After several hours of persistent work in this direction, he came to the conclusion that either someone had turned off the light or he had lost his eyesight. Since there were no screams of panic, no curses anywhere, and no frantic running around with the question what the hell happened, he found it logical to stick to the latter solution. So he meticulously put together all the padds and calmly left, deciding to reach the infirmary by the seat of his pants. Fortunately, he didn't have to bother with it for a long time, because after a dozen or so steps he ran into the ubiquitous Johnnie.

"Sorry, officer, I haven't seen you ..." the highlander began to excuse himself.

"It's okay, I haven't seen you," ArCer interrupted. "Would you be kind enough to lead me to the infirmary? I seem to have lost my sight."

"Oh, Blessed Mother ..." Johnnie groaned sympathetically, then took the Uoltan by his elbow and dragged him to the hospital section.

There was just a shortage of patients in the infirmary, so Dr. Nbeba and Zmiyevski played cards with Father Toadstool, and

Dr. TiShan gave lectures for the mid-level staff. The mid-level staff sat on their chairs with despairing expressions as everyone together and individually thought they had more interesting things to do than listen to the next training session.

At the sight of ArCer, the doctor paused in half a word.

"What happened?" she asked anxiously.

"I don't know, doctor, I only found him," Johnnie replied, helping ArCer to lie down on the diagnostic bed.

"I was working and suddenly stopped seeing," the commander explained. "As this has never happened to me before, I would like to ask for a complete diagnosis."

"And not also for the treatment?"

"Mr. Caterpillar, please take away this bacterial depot from here! The hospital is not a place for such creatures," it was directed to Johnnie, on whose arm Gizia sat and watched TiShan's actions from above.

"She is cleaner than many here," Johnnie got offended and left the infirmary with dignity.

Over time, he began to treat the ferret almost like a sacred cow and treated every word of criticism towards her as a personal offense. It was dangerous because the fair-haired highlander had the strength of a young bull, but fortunately he was also quite disciplined and, having received a clear ban from his captain, wasn't gagging to fight.

Doctor TiShan, assisted by Nbeba and Zmiyevski, diligently examined ArCer, trying to hide, without success, that she had an overly emotional attitude towards this patient. They all knew it anyway, but they politely played possums.

"There is no damage to the eyeballs or the visual cortex," the doctor said finally. "According to my medical knowledge, you should be able to see unhindered."

"I'm far from questioning your expertise, but I can't see," ArCer replied.

Nbeba and Zmiyevski exchanged glances, then the darker-colored doctor suggested:

"Why don't we put the patient to sleep for twenty-four hours and see what happens? Sleep treatment can be very effective in psychosomatic disorders, especially when assisted with brain electrostimulation."

"Are you suggesting that I'm emotionally unstable?" the Uoltan got offended (as much as a representative of his race could be offended).

"I'm suggesting that something nonphysical is happening to you, since we can't capture it with scans. This is a logical conclusion."

ArCer thought and decided that Nbeba might have been right. He decided to undergo the treatment he recommended and hope that it would work.

"You'd better confess, son," Father Toadstool advised ArCer kindly. "What happened to you may be heaven's punishment for your dissolute life. Confess your sins and repent, and if that happens, you will have a lighter case in the Last Judgment."

"I'm sorry, but I only partially understand what you are saying to me," ArCer confessed with astonishment exorbitant for him.

"Father, give him a break, he's a Uoltan, he's not even baptized," Zmiyevski tried to intervene.

"He can always be baptized so that he is not a pagan. It would be more helpful than your doctoral hocus pocus. But if you prefer to act like godless people, go ahead, vuala," said the chaplain and offended, moved into the corridor.

The doctors quickly agreed on the anesthetic dosing schedule and the stimulation system, and then proceeded to act. At the same time, Lolita Icant and her two subordinate nurses decided to go to Captain Zakrzevska and ask for permission to search ArCer's headquarters. It was not without reason that Dr. Zmiyevski assumed that there might have been the cause of the commander's sudden blindness - as he used to say, Dr. House was crazy, but usually he hit the nail on the head, and searching the home of a patient whose disease wasn't known was his favorite method of operation.

Captain Zakrzevska listened to sister Icant's request with some reserve.

"All right," she said finally. "I, too, heard about the methods of this legendary freak, Gregory House. Just don't mess up, or ArCer will tear your heads off. He's absolutely crazy about order. Is he nervous or what?"

Sister Lolita made a solemn promise that they would be careful, then went with her helpers to ArCer's quarters.

"Indeed, like in a museum," she murmured, looking around the cabin, gleaming with order and cleanliness. At first glance, it seemed impossible that there could be something that found itself there without the knowledge and permission of the tenant, but Sister Lolita nevertheless began the search, telling the nurses accompanying her to put every little thing in its place. So, the girls started to look carefully at everything - a Uoltanian harp, a chess set, a lot of padds, some devices and knick-knacks, the meaning of which they could not even guess. They looked through the sheets and bed, dresser drawers, personal computer and all access panels, but found nothing suspicious. Only a paramedic Cezary Prank, who volunteered, found a small piece of plastic while examining the walls, perfectly matching the color of the substrate and practically invisible.

"It's some electronics," he said after examining the find with a mini-scanner. "It definitely shouldn't be here."

Despite the sincere intentions, nothing else could be found that, with some imagination, would have been considered suspect. After a few hours of searching, the team of sister Icant officially went to the research department, where they handed over their find to Andrew Karpiel.

"Are you practicing for the next procession?" Karpiel asked ironically. "Wouldn't it be enough if one of you came?"

"Father announces the procession?" Lolita asked.

"Probably one for the first of May," added Prank. "I bet he thinks about it."

"No, on the 1st of May, it will rather be a May Day parade."

"In the morning a parade, and in the evening a procession. Normally, like every year."

"It's raining evenly on the first of May. One time it will fall on a flower, another time on ... pansy ..." sang in falsetto docent Benek Saturator from the archeology department, who had just visited Trekovsky's assistant, Marzena Szkwał, for immoral, as Trekovsky used to say, purposes.

"We can laugh, but what will we do if, from one side, Matias von Braun and Zaychik start calling for the singing of the Internationale, and from the other, Father Toadstool will yell 'Hello, May's dawn'?" Karpiel wondered.

Contrary to appearances, it was not a pointless question. Matias von Braun and Vasyl Anecdotych Zaychik constituted a modest but decisive atheist faction of 'Hermash', and in addition one with a clearly Marxist deviation. As opposition to Father Toadstool's weekly sermons, they established their own tradition, and every Wednesday one of them gave a lecture in the Leninist spirit in the common room. The ship's chaplain was furious about the fact that these talks attracted no less listeners than his services. Both von Braun and Zaychik had the advantage of speaking in an interesting and imaginative manner, so their readings were treated as great entertainment. It was possible that they would try to organize a May Day parade - the insiders even claimed that they had already sewed red banners and prepared appropriate placards, and Malvinka Krencik swore that she had heard Captain Zakrzevska practicing singing "Bandiera Rossa", and in two languages. Since it was difficult to consider this matter 'dry', when nothing was known yet, Karpiel took care of what he could catch his hands on and after two hours he knocked on the commander's quarters' door.

"Come in!" the captain shouted from inside.

Karpiel entered and he got shocked a little. The captain had just washed her head, and was now drying her hair, which, loose, reached below her back. SiWok was standing at her desk, correcting something in the computer panel and casting furtive, delighted glances at Lilianna, by no means Uoltan ones.

"Er, Captain, I already know what Lolitka found in Commander ArCer's quarters," reported Karpiel, having slightly recovered.

"What?"

"It's a micro relay. It emits specific texts below the hearing threshold. In this case, someone had gone to great lengths to convince the guy that he couldn't see. As soon as his brain recognized the words as true due to repetition, ArCer went blind.

"That means he can see, but just doesn't acknowledge it, right?"

"Yes."

With a sigh, the captain put down the towel she had used to dry her silky weaves with and picked up a brush.

"Now what shall we do with the hypnotized Uoltan?" she murmured after a moment.

"With your permission," SiWok interrupted. "Only a connection of minds can help here, so it's either me or Dr. TiShan. Due to the different state of the latter, she should be excluded. So, I remain."

He smiled slightly only with his eyes. He loved being useful, because although in principle he should have disembarked at the nearest base, he had nailed the assignment to this crew and at all costs wanted to prove that he was a valuable member to it. So far there had been no opportunity to prove it, but the young Uoltan decided to act according to the principle 'let the living not lose hope'.

"Try it," the captain said. "We need ArCer very much. Besides ... as one detective said, solving the serial killer case, 'A few more dead bodies, and I will really start to lose my patience.' Someone on this ship is playing with us like a cat with a mouse, and we need to quickly find out who started it."

"And then?" Karpiel asked quite stupidly.

"And then we will convince him that such fun doesn't pay at all," the captain answered him calmly, tied her still wet hair with a decorative buckle and followed SiWok to the infirmary.

XLIII.

"Wouldn't it be better if I tried meditation techniques?" ArCer asked after listening impassively to the captain's tirade. "If it's just a matter of some kind of subliminal hypnosis ... then I should be able to deal with it."

"I have no doubts, Commander, but it will be much faster and easier this way," SiWok replied. "I'll get you on your feet quickly, and when you fall into a trance, we won't know when you'll come out of it. And yet there is a saboteur on the ship who has now attacked you, before the chief engineer, and who knows what their next target will be. Maybe he or she will try to get to our captain?"

"Let them try and it will be their fault," Lilianna growled with her expression showing that the saboteur would have then only had a choice between the morgue and the hospital.

"It may be their fault, but first we need to figure out who that person is," SiWok said with overwhelming logic. "And I'm afraid it would be difficult without Commander ArCer. Therefore, I'm asking for permission to merge our minds."

The captain shrugged slightly.

"Merge, but clean up after it," she allowed. "I will not interfere with Uoltanian conceits, with one exception: ArCer, you have to regain your eyesight, do you understand? That's an order."

"It is not enough to order someone to heal," TiShan interjected, scandalized.

"Why is that? Someone told him to stop seeing, and he obeyed, now let him hear me."

It was hard to deny such logic, and ArCer reasonably abstained from commenting. He himself was curious why - despite realizing the facts - he still couldn't see, and he knew that the connection of the self with SiWok would allow him to look at what was going on in his cerebral cortex through somebody else's eyes. This was why he agreed to this form of treatment, although the thought that the connection was to be initiated by SiWok scared him a bit. This reckless, rebellious boy was not someone to be trusted on such a delicate matter.

"Okay, but we're making a bipolar connection," he conditioned.

"Why not?" SiWok agreed.

"So, I'm going," said Captain Zakrzevska brightly. "I will not disturb you. Anyway, I have my own job. Reports to headquarters won't write themselves."

"I wouldn't be surprised if they wrote themselves, everything is possible on this crazy ship," chuckled Dr. Zmiyevski, but the captain clearly didn't believe it, because she left.

Writing reports to headquarters was not Lilianna's favorite thing to do. Unfortunately, it was one of her duties as the captain of the unit in the service of the Star Armada. It is true that the Star Armada didn't expect much from 'Hermash' and its crew, but that was an insignificant detail. Anyway, contrary to all doubts, the ship did good somehow, it already had a history of the successful rescue operation and interesting scientific discoveries, which was the cause of constant surprise in the headquarters.

"And how did they do it with such equipment? After all, it is impossible to work with what they took with them," people asked and no one could explain it satisfactorily. If someone from the crew of the Polish ship had been asked directly, they would have probably given an evasive answer, which hardly anyone would have understood. Meanwhile, the matter was simple - the crew members of 'Hermash' either didn't know that something couldn't be done, or they had deep contempt for it, applying the old rule that if a fact contradicted the theory they liked, so much the worse for the fact. And their main assumption was that they were able to handle everything, and they were adamant about it.

As the captain stepped out into the corridor, she immediately heard raised voices from the chapel and, having sighed heavily, quickened her pace. As she suspected, Father Toadstool was arguing with Sister Ophelia. The stone of the offense was, as always, the nun's tolerance and good terms with everyone on the ship, regardless of their views. The chaplain was of the opinion that all crew members should have been converted and baptized, preferably without asking for their opinion (and he had a hidden grudge against Captain Zakrzevska as she didn't want to give her crew an adequate order). In turn Sister Ophelia followed the guidelines of the order of the suffragette sisters - she didn't impose anything on anyone and respected the right of everyone in the crew to have their own views.

"Such permissiveness leads to unrepentant atheism!" Father Toadstool roared. "The Christian spirit is suffocated by Satan of pride and unbelief![12] You of all people, as a representative of the clergy, should fight it!"

"Perhaps with a sword and a stake," the nun retorted. "Don't expect this from me. Every man is the architect of his own fortune, and an adult is not a child, which you will take by the hand and lead wherever you want. They make the decisions themselves."

"How did you end up in the convent, woman?!"

"How? Our father was a Shakespeare fan, he kept saying 'Ophelia, go to the convent', so I went. Should have I gone against our father's will? Honor thy father and thy mother."

"Both of you, stop yelling," the captain demanded. "This type of conversation should be conducted culturally. If you wish, I

---

[12] "The Source of All Evil" - Jacek Kaczmarski, quote.

can organize a panel discussion on the value of religion in today's world, and then you can argue as much as you can. But not in the corridor, but in the conference room."

"But why?" asked roughly Father Toadstool, who didn't like being interrupted.

"So as not to lower the morale of the crew."

"How can we lower something that is practically non-existent?"

"Did you, Father hear about negative values?"

"Maybe you will tell me it's my fault? I will write to the Vatican City that I'm harassed and persecuted here, and all that with the consent of the unit commander," the chaplain raised his chin proudly and hid in the sacristy.

"I'll shoot myself. Bury me at Wawel," the captain sighed with resignation. Sister Ophelia patted her shoulder.

"There would be a nationwide uproar, marches, demonstrations of supporters and opponents, and as a grand finale a fight with the use of baseball bats," she said. "Besides, it's not fun lying in such a stiff company. From the soul of my heart, I advise you to choose Powązki in Warsaw."

***

If someone had peeked in the infirmary then, they would have seen interesting scenes. SiWok, although not very adhering to the teachings of WuRak - planet Uoltan's leading philosopher - proved to be skillful in the art of connecting minds. He made it to the ArCer's subconscious zone without trouble, but was stuck here.

"What a complicated tangle," he muttered after a moment.

"Something is bad?" TiShan asked nervously, unconsciously putting a hand to her stomach.

"Bad? Probably not. I just need to discern it," SiWok replied reassuringly.

His young, handsome face paled a little. TiShan, who had known him from childhood, knew very well that it meant a lot of effort. On the one hand, she was afraid for ArCer, who was the father of her child, and on the other, for the former protégé, whom she liked very much. She still couldn't get over the fear of connecting minds. Her observation was interrupted by Professor Trekovsky, who burst into the infirmary, cursing like a bricklayer on Saturday after payment, and squeezing his right wrist, of which blood was coming out, with his left hand. Andy Karpiel was running after him, shouting:

"Calm down, Dinoslav, or you will hurt yourself even more!"

The professor in very flowery words told Karpiel where he could stick such advice and turned to the bewildered TiShan:

"I need help, Doctor."

"I can see it, but what happened?" TiShan hurriedly took the regenerator out of the drawer.

"Shit ... I mean, nothing."

"He slapped his hand on the table during the discussion with Marzenka and hit a pile of cell-culture dishes," explained Karpiel. They were blown to bits, and Dinek cut his hand."

With a sigh, TiShan took the microscanner and tweezers, then began to remove shards of glass from the professor's injured hand. Trekovsky cursed in an undertone all the time, offending the absent assistant and commenting on the general order on the ship and the women sticking their noses everywhere. Having removed the last shard of glass, the doctor scanned the professor's hand again, just in case, disinfected the wounds and closed them with the regenerator.

"Done," she said. "The next time you have an argument with your assistant, be careful what you hit."

"Next time, I'll hit her in that stupid head," growled Trekovsky.

"Calm down, Dinoslav," Karpiel scolded him in fear that the captain would hear these threats and make hell. "You know very well that you were wrong. Such experiments must not be carried out with a damaged extractor fan."

"You know nothing about it! Keep your nose in your inorganic chemistry and don't stick it into my organic one!" Trekovsky roared. "You're just a stinker, not a chemist! You have no idea how important things I'm working on!"

"Big deal, everyone knows it!" Andy retorted. "You are trying to create a virus that would induce intoxication by breaking down sugar directly in the blood. You just think about getting overdrunk!"

Trekovsky crowed with indignation.

"It's not true!" he screamed. "I work for the good of mankind!"

"I know many people who would admit you are right, because they themselves walk around the clock with a pickled brain, but I have my own opinion on this. Don't be such an important professor, because it'll hurt you in the end."

The professor looked around nervously, clearly searching for something to throw at Andy, but here TiShan protested, chucking them both out of the room into the corridor, where they could continue arguing. Then she wanted to go back to the office where the Uoltanian ceremony was taking place, but it turned out that it was no longer necessary. Both ArCer and SiWok left, pale and exhausted, but on their own.

"Is everything okay?" she asked tensely.

SiWok nodded, too tired to go into details. The doctor scanned him hastily, but aside from some dehydration and a drop in electrolytes, there was no change. Then she looked at the commander, who returned her emotionless, cold gaze.

"Did you really recover?" she asked, trying to be formal.

ArCer nodded with typical Uoltanian calm.

"I confirm," he said. "The blindness is gone. Can I go back to work now, doctor?"

LXIV.

"I'll kill you! I'll tear to shreds!" the shrill scream brought the entire second deck to its feet. It was two in the morning. Frightened crewmen jumped into the corridor, asking if there was a fire, if it was a Camulan attack, or maybe just a meteor strike. Joe Watery must have been screaming. After getting there, you could see that the human hearing was right. The technician literally breathed fire, and his wife was standing nearby, leaning against the wall with her arms folded over her chest, and watching her husband with undisturbed composure.

After a while, the screaming Joe was joined by Father Toadstool, indignant with the naked condition of most of the crew members.

"Sodom and Gomorrah, such a scandal ...!" he shouted, and when he saw Greg yawning, covered only with a padd, on which he had been reading a novel before going to sleep, he got completely furious.

"Damn it, does Father want us to lie down to sleep in nylon coats, bras with fur and valenki?!" the nervous helmsman Deadskull finally roared at him.

"Valonki, valonki, prachyet moya maminka. Vsyo ravno ya ye naydu. Na svidaniya paydu ..."[13] sang innocently Vasyl Zaychik, who, before going to bed, abused a bit of the excellent product of the local moonshine team (Johnnie Caterpillar, Andrew Karpiel and Jolanta Stern). Then he took Anetka Piekutek from the cartography department by the hand and tried to dance kozachok with her, but she hit him in the ear with a truly Warsaw kindness.

"This time you won't get away with it! I have been too good so far and you have swollen asses. I will ...!" Joe screamed further, paying no attention to anything. His wife watched him with the curiosity of a viewer in a cheap cabaret.

"Calm down, man, what's going on?" Greg, one of the closest friends of Watery, mitigated him, but he kept shouting, until finally, he blurted out furiously the original cause of the whole brawl:

"Tekla is pregnant!"

This news did look quite electrifying, considering that Joe was sterile, as was well known. Everyone's eyes turned to the culprit who shrugged.

---

[13] My mother is hiding my valonki. It doesn't matter, I'll find them and go to the meeting anyway - Rus.

"I tested positive, she said. "Yesterday evening ..." She didn't finish because Joe jumped to her and waved his clenched fist in front of her.

"She is lucky today to be a woman!" he screamed.

"Which one?!"

Tekla spread her hands, then looked around the corridor.

"This one," she said, pointing at random with her finger. "Or this ..."

"Oh no, certainly not me!" Malvinka Krencik protested, offended, when the accusing finger pointed also at her.

"Who can be sure, in this era of the loosening of morals and the divine offense," recited Father Toadstool without thinking about what he was saying.

Joe Watery took a breath, and then again blasphemed across the entire corridor:

"She doesn't know who she's pregnant with! She doesn't know it herself; did you hear?! Dammit, goddamn it! But I will not leave it like this! The entire ship will test the DNA, I'll see to it! I will find that slouch even underground!"

"Under what ground?" Jürgen wanted to know, attracted by shouts and confusion. "We're in outer space."

The second mate's cold and measured words didn't somehow cool the atmosphere, which was starting to get quite tense and unpleasant.

"I will not allow myself to be tested," declared Greg, shifting the padd from hand to hand. "What is the reason?"

"Oh, then it's probably you if you're scared!" the betrayed husband rushed to him.

"I'm scared, you cuckold?! Are you nuts?! I would have to be blind and mindless to be into such an old amoeba."

"Just not old!" Tekla got mortally offended and struck Greg with the back of her hand.

No one but her noticed that for a moment the engineer's eyes flashed red as a grimace of rage appeared on his face. Greg made a move as if he had wanted to throw himself at Mrs. Watery, but Mstislav Deadskull tripped him and to the accompaniment of an indignant shout:

'Are you going to beat a woman, you rascal?!',

he set about him. It boiled like in the stands with the cheapest seats during a football match for the national championship, which gave the slogan for a general fight according to the principle: everyone against all. Even the venerable chaplain was involved in the brawl, and only Tekla stood in the middle, bypassed by all, wailing piercingly just in case:

"Don't you dare touch me! I'm pregnant!"

"And I'm wearing sneakers," finally answered her Jacob Zmiyevski, who appeared in the corridor with a medical scanner in his hand. "Hey you, CALM DOWN!!!"

The quarreling crew members instinctively stopped and looked at the doctor, surprised that he dared interrupt their discussion.

"Why are you fighting?" Cuba asked with open pity. "Mrs. Watery is not in the different state at all. She just took a water hardness test from the infirmary by mistake instead of a pregnancy test."

***

Gregory Brzenchyshchykievich returned to his cabin more furious than he could have expected.

"Actually," he monologized quietly, "it's not my business whether Tekla Watery will have a child or not. Neither am I her brother nor a matchmaker. Let her be damned, and her stupid husband. Anyway, I'm only interested in Malvinka ... Malva ..."

"I don't think you're saying it seriously," said the intrusive, low voice in his skull. "You sigh, you groan, but you do nothing to get her."

"Back off, SyTar. What else should I do? Tie her up and put her in the broom closet until she agrees to date me?"

"And that wouldn't be a bad idea ..."

Greg grimaced with dissatisfaction. Since he had to carry a Uoltan's soul within him, he might have gotten a more typical, logical, and serene copy, not a freak like SyTar. Unchristian bad luck - not only they had to transplant the Uoltanian heart into him, but also with such an undesirable addition. Good thing no one on board knew about it, like they didn't know about his past at Terra First. He was sometimes tempted to stop taking eucuprum, which would have eventually resulted in rejection of the transplant - the heart muscle, although artificially adapted, still required an increased supply of copper in the blood. If something was holding him back, it was knowing that this way he would not get rid of the problem. SyTar's goddamn 'vatra' was stuck in his mind, in his brain, not in the piece of carcass that had been transplanted into him. It was stuck, it was fine and had no intention of abandoning the secluded corner.

The engineer undressed, took a long shower, and collapsed onto the bed with relief. Constant fatigue took its toll, he couldn't cope with it, and he preferred not to use the help of doctors. Generally speaking, they didn't inspire his trust. His first dream had just started, he was already envisioning a meadow on which he was walking with Malvinka Krencik with his arm around her, above them there were nosediving fighters singing (there was an air show nearby), and the mechanical milking machines were yelling longingly from the distance, when a sudden banging on the door put him on his feet.

"Who the hell is that?!" he screamed furiously, opening his sleepy eyes. The automatic opening, as usual, didn't work, so he had to, whether he liked it or not, get up and open it by hand.

At the door there was standing ArCer accompanied by three security guys.

"Gregory Brzenchyshchykievich?" the Uoltan asked matter-of-factly, as if seeing him for the first time in his life.

"No, Yanush Palikot," the engineer replied, tapping his forehead meaningfully. "Have you lost your Uoltanian mind, or what?"

"Get dressed, come with us. You are under arrest on the charge of assassinating lieutenant Charles Mikhalov," said ArCer, seemed not to notice the open attack.

Greg's jaw dropped.

"What?" he asked incredulously. "That I ...? This is a joke? 'Hahaha.' laughed in the French style the prince lord ..."

"Don't resist, or you will be immediately stunned," ArCer continued, uniformly like a robot, without a trace of emotion.

Perhaps that is why Greg couldn't stand it and attacked him. The Uoltan grabbed him by his clenched fist, very convincingly twisted his arm back, and pushed him at the soldiers. One of them efficiently intercepted the outraged prisoner.

"You be with us," he said imperiously.

"Not true!" Greg denied violently. "They say 'The Lord be with you' and that could be said by Father Toadstool, and not such a shitkicker as, without pointing a finger, you."

The soldier got stunned for a moment, and the engineer pushed him away and ran like an arrow down the corridor. It's hard to say what he was counting on, but he miscalculated anyway, because ArCer carried out his announcement without delay and stunned him with a mazer shot.

"Take the engineer to the cell," he ordered the soldiers and went to the bridge, where Captain Zakrzevska was studying Greg's files, delivered to her before this action.

"I'm reporting that the suspect has been arrested," ArCer said, standing by the captain's chair and folding his hands behind his back.

"Uhm," muttered the captain contrary to the regulations. "We have the suspect, Mr. ArCer, but the wrong one."

"But the recording from the camera ..."

"I know, the camera recording. But Greg's files show that he can't know what is needed for the synthesis of beryllium diramian. He failed his physicochemistry exam twice, and he was forced to study space engineering."

"So what?"

"It means, Mr. ArCer, that he can't hit the side of a barn when it comes to the production of chemicals, including isotopes. It can't be him."

LXV.

After a careful study of Greg's files, containing the history of his education and the course of his service, ArCer pondered severely. The captain seemed to be right, the deputy chief engineer simply didn't have the necessary qualifications to carry out this attack. And although it could also be linked to the subliminal transmission device found in ArCer's cabin, it was clear that he wouldn't have come up with something like that. In addition, he and Charles Mikhalov had been friends for years and there was probably no serious argument between them. The opinion of Armada's psychologists also questioned this interpretation. It showed that having something against Mikhalov, Greg would have rather beaten him at once, making so much noise that he would have drawn people from the entire deck. His psychological profile didn't match at all his silent, cold-planned revenge. From all this, there was only one conclusion - something periodically took control over his body. Anything else would have been meaningless and would have not fit into the logical association sequence.

"But why exactly Greg? And why does this thing work so stupidly in fact?" Lilianna asked when ArCer shared his insights with her.

"This is what we should find out. And I think it would be good to talk to the engineer."

"Then let's sit down and talk."

Gregory Brzenchyshchykievich initially refused to testify. In fact, not so much refused as gave a longer monologue, consisting of words commonly regarded as offensive, some of which probably even had still an undetermined spelling. When the repertoire was finally exhausted, the captain - listening with great interest - looked questioningly at ArCer which was as unmoved as ever.

"What do you think, that means 'yes' or 'no'?" she asked.

"I think this young man is very badly brought up," the Uoltan replied stiffly.

"That is beyond doubt, but rather not his manners are under investigation."

ArCer played recording from surveillance cameras, which showed Greg visiting places where he shouldn't have been, at a time when, as he claimed, he had been asleep. The engineer stared at the screen, muttered something the captain preferred not to hear, and loudly declared:

"It's a manipula... I don't remember anything like that!"

The Uoltan raised his eyebrows slightly, because in the engineer's voice there was absolute sincerity and such an insult, as if someone had accused his mother of a dissolute life, and him of the unlawful origin. After reflecting for a moment, he suggested:

"Let me know your thoughts, Lieutenant. In this way, we will settle all doubts."

"What?!" Greg roared indignantly.

"Lieutenant, get tested. That's an order," the captain said sharply.

"Such an order, I ..." Brzeczyszczykiewicz sprang up from his chair, bursting with anger. His eyes flashed red suddenly, like carbuncles.

ArCer jumped and caught his wrists just as the engineer tried to grab a heavy paperweight lying on the table. However, he didn't fully realize who he was dealing with and a little disregarded the human - and therefore weaker - opponent. The prisoner hit him with his knee, and then with venomous precision, struck the neck with his straightened fingers, hitting the appropriate nerve endings unmistakably. The Uoltan went limp and fell. Captain Zakrzevska, surprised by such a development of the situation, didn't manage to reach for the weapon when Greg burst into the corridor and ran in a direction known only to him.

'Hermash', follow the deputy chief engineer!" the captain shouted, and leaned over ArCer. Fortunately, he was already regaining consciousness and after a few seconds he sat down.

"That ... was a Uoltanian paralyzing blow," he grunted with difficulty. "We deal with the possession by the carrier."

"What carrier?!"

"Carrier of the self. Someone had implanted their *vatra* in the mind of the lieutenant ... sort of a soul ... some Uoltan.

"What Uoltan, Greg hates Uoltans!"

"I don't know what, we'll find out. But the case is evident, Captain. We have to catch him or it'll be bad."

With a little wobbly legs, ArCer got up and went out into the corridor. Opening the link, he gave the entire security order to detain Lieutenant Brzenchyshchykievich and, after a moment's hesitation, added:

"But please don't hurt him unless absolutely necessary."

Before he closed the link, he heard the comment from one of the security soldiers:

"I bet Greg wasn't ordered not to hurt us."

ArCer grimaced with dissatisfaction, but decided not to dwell on the subject anymore. The engineer had to be caught and that's it, and if the Uoltan's suspicions were correct, it might have not been so easy. Suddenly, despite all his emotional control, he flinched, as the on-board computer yelled hysterically just above his ear:

"The fugitive is on the hangar deck! You drunk scoundrel, leave that panel!"

It took the Uoltan a dozen seconds to understand that the 'drunk scoundrel' didn't refer to him, while the computer kept screaming, hurling at the young engineer various invectives and threats, the mildest of which deserved at least three days' arrest.

'Hermash'! 'Hermash', what's going on?" Captain Zakrzevska asked feverishly.

"Queen, this monkey is trying to fumble my circuits!" the computer croaked indignantly.

"He wants to manually open the hangar airlock! Damn it! Let go of this processor or I'll kick ...!"

"Kick him, 'Hermash'! Just not too strongly so that he doesn't turn up his toes."

"According to your order, sweetie."

There was a crackling noise, a broken scream came from the loudspeaker, and everything went silent. After a moment the communicator clicked and Maura Gvizdak's voice announced:

"Captain, I'm reporting that the deputy chief engineer was shocked, but he's breathing. What am I supposed to do?"

"Breathe with him," Lilianna advised sarcastically. "Take that Tarzan for two cents to the infirmary. And tie well."

"She didn't manage to turn off the loudspeaker yet, when something crackled, the source indicators switched to the 'Bridge', and the voice of Veronika Bumblebee announced:

"And ass."

"Whose ass, Ensign?" the captain wanted to know.

"I'm afraid that something is following us, Captain ... maybe you can come here, because the officers went to dinner, and I'm here alone with my friend Bequiet and Miss Lausch ..."

The captain mispronounced a curse against Arek and Andy, who were on watch, and ran to the bridge. After her, was rushing, jumping the delighted Gizia, who, commotion, eternally reigning on the ship, liked very much.

After taking the elevator to the bridge, Lilianna ran inside with the intention of doing her usual hell, but she tripped over Bear stretched at the very entrance, flew forward and stopped only on the scientific console.

"Captain, look at the screen, can you see this distortion?" Steersman Bequiet, absorbed in his calculations, probably didn't notice the incident with Bear at all. "We are followed by a camouflaged ship. I can't figure out whose."

"Yellow alert, Miss Lausch," Lilianna ordered, discreetly rubbing the various parts of the body that had been injured in the fall. "Let Mayher fill the firing positions just in case. I don't want wasting of energy during a battle, so let it be shooters this time, not the night watchmen of the roundup."

"Ah, you flea bastard of a leper hyena!" she coughed up, gasping for breath. The hairy culprit raised his head and looked at the petite captain with reproach and surprise. Since he had regained his missing mistress, he had never left her and he couldn't understand why this surprised anyone.

LXVI.

Doctor TiShan watched ArCer as he finished his examination of unconscious Gregory. The sight was rather macabre, for although the indicators on the control panel clearly showed a lack of awareness, the engineer had open eyes flashing red, and from his mouth was coming angry mumbling in pure Uoltanian - with a distinct South Coast accent. At last, ArCer broke the contact and, exhausted by the long effort, sat down beside the bed in the chair that had been shifted to him by the prudent sister Icant.

"Calm down, brother," he said. "It's all clear now. I think you are aware of how great risk you put your host at and that you committed a crime."

"So what?" SyTar growled with Greg's mouth.

"So what? We'll see. What is your name and how did you get into this Earthling's mind?"

Greg's body struggled with the bonds for a while, then it gave up.

"My name is SyTar, son of KelSar," the deceased Uoltan said reluctantly. "I was a PhD student at the Uoltanian Embassy on Earth science lab. My body was killed in a clash with the extremist organization Terra First, and my heart was transplanted into the dock engineer ... who, incidentally, was involved in the same clash and was hospitalized for a massive unmanageable heart attack. I found myself in his mind along with my heart. Somehow we made up."

"Okay, I understand that," the commander nodded. "But why did you do all this? Why did you seek Charles Mikhalov's life?"

"I didn't seek anyone's life!"

"Then what was the radioactive compound in his console for?"

"I wanted him to go bald, so that Miss Malvina wouldn't want to date him. She disgusts the bald."

"Words fail me," TiShan sighed.

The ingrained fear of self-bonding made additional sense when she looked at the unconscious engineer, whose body was guided by the soul of the emotionally unstable Uoltan. Because that SyTar must have been shaky a long time before there was the accidental implantation, it didn't require any explanation. Ultimately, even in this remarkable nation, in which everyone was taught from an early age logic and emotional control, there were individuals with a weaker psyche.

"Well, it's better than poisoning Mikhalov with thallium. It also causes baldness," said sister Icant, a little hesitantly.

"SyTar, you must calm down," TiShan said flatly. "Do you know what situation you caused? You committed a serious crime, you exposed your crew members for your whim, and we can't even lock you up because it's not the carrier's fault."

"We can try the transfer ... I could handle it ..." ArCer said after some thought.

A grim chuckle came from the engineer's mouth.

"I don't intend to go anywhere," said SyTar. "I'm fine here. I'm used to it, and this man has my heart. I have the right to be in this body."

"I have a different opinion on this. You nestled in the mind of the host without his consent and you are damaging his career and personal life by entangling him in criminal activities. You have to be removed from there."

Gregory's body was shaken by a paroxysm of rage. For a long time, SyTar tried to break the belts, but failed to do so, and finally, defeated, gave up.

"Don't do this," he pleaded. "I promise I won't go crazy anymore. I won't disturb anything, on the contrary, I will help as best I can ... just don't take me away from this body. I like Greg, we get along well ... well, maybe not always well, but it will be better, I promise."

He was clearly terrified and desperate. ArCer didn't say it out loud, but decided it would be better to avoid a drastic situation. SyTar would have definitely fought him fiercely, and such a fight could have a very negative impact on the health of the host.

"Let's agree that the decision will be made by engineer Brzenchyshchykievich when the effect of the anesthetic wears off," he said coldly. "Now think about your behavior and draw conclusions."

He got up from the chair.

"TiShan, keep an eye on him," he said. "I'm going to the bridge. There's a yellow alert going on, so surely something unusual is happening. Unusual, I mean, even for this ship ..."

***

By the time the Uoltan reached the bridge, the alarm changed from yellow to red. There was a commotion on the bridge, because Xavier Bequiet was trying to establish the exact parameters of the attackers and he was doing poorly, because each of those present contributed put in their two cents' worth. Finally, Veronika managed to capture the energy signature of both vehicles and enter it into the computer a moment before ArCer appeared on the bridge, followed by the sleepy Arek Liljew.

"What's happening?" he asked between two yawns.

"And what is to happen? They're shooting at us," the captain replied, somewhat calmly. "Johnnie, bring coffee for the first officer, or he will swallow all of us raw here!"

"Sure, sir-ma'am!" the highlander shouted briskly and rushed to the door, stepping on Bear's tail on the way. The animal calmly, without a single snarl, sank his enormous fangs into his pants.

"Oh, Most Gracious Mother of God, I didn't want to!" Johnnie screamed at the top of his lungs, grabbing his bitten calf.

"How are our friends?" the captain asked the helmsmen, ignoring it.

"Judging from the signature analysis, they are Pornions," Veronika reported, turning to face Lilianna, who was just sitting in her chair. "Two Hawk-class chasers with standard equipment. Bear, ugh, don't eat Johnnie, you'll get dinner soon!"

"For now, our shields endure, but their power is starting to decline," said Bequiet.

"Snipers, respond with fire!" Lilianna shouted into the communicator's microphone. "Johnnie, stop playing the victim of fate and finally bring this coffee. And grab some salty sticks along the way."

"I'm coming," the orderly moaned obediently and disappeared behind the door.

During all this confusion, Father Toadstool and Sister Ophelia tried, despite the shelling, to continue catechesis. The parish classes were the idea of Father Thaddeus, and the nun went to them so that he didn't teach women. When he did it once, then a delegation of offended female crew members went to the captain and made a fuss that they didn't allow themselves to be offended. Captain Zakrzevska called the priest for a conversation.

"Did you say, father, that wives are to be subject to their husbands, women should be humble, and pain in childbirth is the result of sin committed by Eve and should be endured as penance?" she asked as if it had been a survey.

"It is written in the Bible," replied the priest with dignity.

"And did the father add that a woman by her very nature is prone to sin and obedient to diabolical prompts, and therefore must be kept on a short leash by men for her own good?"

"I think that someone must have made these unfortunate creatures aware of it."

"Sorry," the captain said. "Are you, father in his right mind?"

Here, Father Thaddeus got terribly offended, and for the next few days he didn't want to talk to the captain at all. However, everything slowly panned out and from then on he taught men and Sister Ophelia taught women. The male part of the faithful listened with curiosity to the image of what awaited them for their multiple sins (as they said themselves, it was better than Shakespeare and Dante together). And the women shared recipes for various cakes, talked about the books they had read, discussed needlework techniques and solved crosswords together. Sister Ophelia usually limited herself to writing on a large board the subject of the catechesis and its content in several points, and then she actively participated in what her listeners wanted to do. By an unwritten agreement, only male and female matters were excluded, so each such 'catechesis' turned into a kind of social gathering with substitute coffee and synthetic cookies.

Currently, despite the red alert, classes in both groups weren't interrupted. Everyone on board had gotten used to the fact that a siren wailed every now and then, and no one was paying more attention than it was necessary. Unless the loudspeakers said 'Everyone to arms!', the fun could be continued.

XLVII.

Pornion chasers maneuvered much more gracefully than the heavy 'Hermash', and their mazers bit the shields of the Union ship over and over again. The 'Hermash' snipers did what they could, but it could be seen that they couldn't do much, as they missed disgracefully.

"What idiots are there?" the captain on the bridge was furious. "I'll talk to them now, let this kolomyjka end! Inga, call Chris Mayher and let him go to the turret to see what they are playing there."

Inga Lausch stopped adjusting her makeup and called the chief navigator, who first determined what he thought about the Pornions and such shooters, and then acknowledged receipt of the order. Then he looked for Vasyl Zaychik, who, despite the fire, was sleeping in his own bed, picked up Pandorian T'enga along the way and went with them to the sniper positions.

This room, located in the lower part of the ship's hull, was additionally secured, which caused that it was called a "turret" for internal use, and on the door, there was painted the image of the tank and the inscription "T-102 GINGER[14]". As Chris knew, 'Hermash' already had its own sniper corps, assembled from security soldiers by the only member of the original team who had checked in on the day of departure. As it turned out, they were snipers only by name, because using the mazer cannons was hard going, and none of them could activate the torpedo launchers.

"Maybe it is better, because they would have caused some misfortune," said Mayher, chased the whole unit into the corridor and reported to Captain Zakrzevska readiness to fulfill her orders.

"Ugh, nie hvatayet, shto baba nami komandiruyet, no yeshcho strielki niprichiom,"[15] muttered Vasyl Anecdotych, adjusting the coupling of the sights with the screen in his position.

"Is a woman a worse commander because she is a woman?" Blue-skinned T'enga asked curiously, not fully aware of all aspects of Earth's culture.

"On a combat ship a woman brings misfortune."

---

[14] A reference to a tank from a cult polish series "Four tankmen and a dog"

[15] *(Rus)* Not only is the woman in charge, but also the shooters are useless.

"As well as on land," said Mayher. "There is no difference. You better watch your sight, Vashka, because they are turning back to us again."

"Are you there, armored sardines?" Lilianna's voice said in the communicator. "Forward Grab 1[16], launch a fragmentation missile!"

"Grab? I think you mean 'Hermash'?!" T'enga didn't understand, having some shortcomings in the field of Polish cinematography.

"Never mind! Hit them so that their pants fall off, now!"

"Yes, baryshnia[17] captain," Vasyl Anecdotych replied servicely.

He took aim calmly and after a while his cannon began to breathe well-aimed fire. Christopher Mayher didn't lag behind him, and T'enga was on duty at the launcher, wagging her antennae with excitement, ready to stick the torpedo in the indicated target on the commander's order. The attackers were clearly frightened. Previously, they had gotten daring when the attacked ship had missed them over and over again, but now it seemed that they would fail.

---

[16] 'Grab 1' - that was a code name for a tank named GINGER from series "Four tankmen and a dog".

[17] *(Rus)* Title of honor.

Justice had to be done to the dock installers. Despite a thousand minor flaws, they had made the whole thing quite solidly, and they had done their best, working on the covers. The team responsible for the construction of 'Hermash' had bought them in the army surplus store - they were heavy battleship covers from a Pandorian navy, with double reinforcement and additional shock absorption. With relatively low energy consumption, they hugged the ship like an impenetrable cocoon. The only problem the engineers had with them was that initially no one could configure them properly. It was only when Jolka Stern came up with the idea to ask T'enga for help that the real control code was established. This became a key issue, as the Pornion pursuers were equipped with heavy-caliber cannons, much more powerful than their classification would have suggested.

"Captain, what do they want exactly?" Arek asked, watching the Pornion pursuers, which stubbornly refused to back off.

"They want to get hit, as we can see," Lilianna snarled, lazily brushing her nails. She was also wondering about the stubbornness of the Pornions, who should have realized long ago that they would not be able to cope with 'Hermash', and yet they didn't yield, despite the shielding fire.

"If we stuck the torpedo under their left wing, they would back off right away," snarled from the controls Xavier Bequiet.

Finally, the captain heard his displeased grunts and smiled involuntarily.

"When you're an ensign, dear, everything seems lovely simple," she said. "But I prefer not to have the whole Pornion Syndicate after us. Miss Lausch, have any of the commanders responded to our message?"

"No, gracious lady," sighed Inga, adjusting the receiver in her ear. "There is such silence on their channel, that my ears are ringing. I even wondered if the equipment was functional, but after I switched to long range for a moment, I clearly heard Excelsior talking to Lancaster that the first mate and the chief doctor were goers, and they would even have a baby together."

"Flight doctor pregnant?"

"Not exactly. It is the first mate who got up the duff, not the doctor. She is a Gammazoid and has no resistance at all, and the doctor is an Earthling, supposedly a terrible cock. He doesn't miss any nurse during a night shift."

ArCer, who hated rumors, especially erotic ones, stared Inga out with his icy eyes, but that didn't help. So he said wryly:

"Call the pursuit commanders, Miss Lausch."

"I keep calling them, but they don't give a damn about me," Inga was offended. "Try it yourself."

"Give, dear, a warning: 'Beware, Pornions, you have ten standard seconds to cease pursuit and fire. Otherwise, we will have to neutralize you permanently," the captain ordered, hiding a smile.

"Something constructive at last," muttered Jürgen, who in the meantime had arrived on the bridge, lured by the red alert, and was still chewing his supper. In his hand he held a paper tray with a half-eaten hot German sausage, a hunk of bread, and a portion of mustard.

Inga dutifully repeated the words of Captain Zakrzevska on the calling frequency. There was silence for a moment, then was heard a broken Staccato of a native Pornion, translated by a translator into quite understandable words:

"I got your number, you bitch! You will not escape us, you harlot!"

Upset Lilianna took the receiver from Inga and answered:

"I will give you a bitch! I will give you a harlot, you green checkered monkeys! When I kick the sh... out of you, motherfuc..., using our whole fu... arsenal, you will be fu... up!"

"Captain, not in the presence of Veronika, she is practically a child!" Jürgen groaned desperately, almost choking on the remnants of the sausage.

"I heard worse things at home when my father and grandfather got drunk," said Veronika disparagingly. "At least the captain doesn't beat me, and they did."

"What? After all, it's forbidden ... We are not in the Middle Ages!" ArCer was visibly shaken, and much more than befited a Uoltan.

"I'm from the early twenty-first century, not from here. In those times, I found myself with Bear by accident, coming through an incidental time vortal," the helmswoman explained to him, scratching the favorite on the back. "Cool, isn't it? One day I will tell you how I end up on 'Hermash' and ..."

"Not now, for the love of outer space!"

Captain Zakrzevska's speech must have somehow detonated the Pornions, because for a moment both chasers were talking to each other, then they unblocked video communication, and on the screen, divided in half, two green-skinned men appeared.

"Oh, we are so sorry," one of them said as soon as he looked at the people on the bridge. "There was a mistake due to incorrect information."

"I'm Vint, and this is my brother Tevint. We are chasing our wife," added the second. "She robbed us to the last thread and ran off with some Muld. We received information that they were flying on a ship with false markings."

"Ours are real," said Lilianna coldly. "Star Armada Headquarters will confirm that 'Hermash' is a Union ship. Your attack is a typical casus bello."

"We didn't want to bother anyone. We just want back what belongs to us."

"Do you have the joint wife?" Arek asked with interest.

"In our place it is allowed," explained the Pornion. "Sorry again. The syndicate is not at war with the Union, and we are not interested in having it."

"You have five minutes. If after this time my sensors detect you nearby, I'll turn you both into fried frog legs, is that clear?!" Captain Zakrzevska shouted.

Vint mumbled one more inaccurate apology and turned off. The two chasers turned back and disappeared into the distance at full acceleration.

"And we're done with it," Inga sighed with relief.

"I don't think so," the captain snorted. "We have to take care of our snipers. Let Chris train them, because it's not normal to have such bumblers on the decent ship."

Christopher Mayher accepted the order to train snipers with mixed feelings. He knew it wasn't going to be easy, and he turned out to be right. The commander of the sniper team, Corporal Konstanty Night-heron, wasn't a private enemy of Chris, but he couldn't let him try to order him. He expressed his dissatisfaction by smashing a peer wine bottle on the head of the chief navigator. Mayher stated that this was a provocation that allowed a drastic reaction, and he replied so that the snipers felt it appropriate to act in defense of their commander. Armorer Zaychik, T'enga and Johnnie Caterpillar, who was just passing along the corridor, sided with Chris and one of the most famous skirmishes on the ship broke out. It ended with the arrest of all participants, who two days later paraded in front of the captain and were rewarded for their patriotic attitude with sentences ranging from one day to a week of arrest.

Unfortunately, this didn't solve the main problem. Gregory Brzenchyshchykievich, Charles Mikhalov and Jolka Stern thoroughly checked all the weapons from the technical side and together they wrote a report, which clearly showed that the mazer guns were 100% operational, the deviation of the sights was not more than some minor percentile, and the torpedo launchers were "creme de la creme", as the chief engineer said contrary to the regulations. In the light of this report, it was impossible not to acknowledge that all the problems resulted from the insufficient training of the sniper team, which made Chris Mayher laugh the most. The chief navigator, who knew how to shoot anything from the Roman slingshot, through all kinds of small arms, including all kinds of bazookas, to the heaviest caliber cannons, didn't hide his amazement as to who and for what purpose appointed people without any experience, who in addition, wouldn't have hit a barn.

"Instead of being surprised, you'd better train them," the captain advised. In view of receiving the official blessing, Mayher set up an appropriate training program in the holo-room, and then got down to work briskly. Corporal Night-heron, though seriously offended by him, relented, as he called it, "before force and law", and reported to the holo-room with his men. The events that followed were of such a nature that Father Toadstool preached about them for several more weeks. Captain Zakrzevska received only a brief report that after shooting for some time, the soldiers got bored with maneuvers and - having tied Chris to a tree - invited some female crew members and organized such a picnic in a computer setting that had never taken place before.

"Let one of you miss during the action, and his hour will be wasted," summed up the captain. "Like children, only moonshine and asses are on your minds, and service in your asses. Oh, Chris ... you couldn't somehow control this company?"

Mayher spread his hands in a gesture of excuse, though in fact it was clear that simply he wouldn't have achieved anything, opposing all the snipers and their commander. Lilianna would have liked to dismiss Night-heron, but he enjoyed such a reputation among the security forces that she preferred not to risk additional perturbations. Instead, she organized an individual commission exam for all snipers, and since only Night-heron was 100% effective in it, she directed the rest to additional maneuvers under the supervision of ArCer and Maura Gvizdak. They buckled down to the task seriously, putting the culprits through the hoops.

The maneuvers lasted three full days, and after their completion, the entire unit took sick leave due to exhaustion.

"At least one thing is certain: it is not a simulation," said succinctly Jacob Zmiyevski, who issued the excuses. And it really wasn't.

XLVIII.

While the procession with the sniper corps was underway, the captain finally decided to talk to Greg. The matter was not easy, and Lilianna didn't feel like she was Solomon. Meanwhile, she faced the dilemma of the Siamese sisters - how could she isolate SyTar without punishing Greg for something he hadn't done? On the other hand, how could she release on his own 'recognizance' someone as dangerous as SyTar? According to ArCer, the Uoltan from whom the heart used for the transplant, and therefore vatra, was derived, was emotionally unstable and had already during his lifetime pulled weird stunts many times. Weird for a Uoltan, of course. In this context, his actions took on some crazy sense.

"I would have strangled the bastard if he were still alive," Mikhalov said grimly.

He was recovering, but still wasn't completely healthy.

"You can strangle Greg," Malvinka offered him maliciously, but Charles only waved his hand.

"It's not such a pleasure."

He scratched the head of Vuvu, who was lying belly up on his blanket and moaning in ecstasy. Something that for his master was a great inconvenience, that is, the compulsion to lie down, for the little vall was the pinnacle of dreams. In turn Charles was simply fuming - discharged only three days earlier, he had to return to the hospital due to nasty gastric ailments.

Despite persistent thinking, Captain Zakrzevska didn't manage to find a satisfactory way out of this mess. ArCer, whom she asked for a consultation just spread his hands.

"I won't get him out of there by force," he said. "I wouldn't even know how to go about it, because it's an unprecedented matter. It is true that in our archives there is an account of how a certain Earthly Captain Harper was taken over by the soul of a Uoltanian philosopher from two thousand years ago, but SchuRak wasn't like this madman."

"If you say so," muttered the captain, and after some thought, accompanied by the Uoltan, she went back to the infirmary.

"I want to talk to SyTar," she demanded, standing by Greg's bed.

"Not only you," said Mikhalov, who had just come to find out about the condition of his deputy and at the same time to say as exhaustively as possible what he thought about him. He stood, shifting from foot to foot, and pulling a shortened hospital gown over his bare ass. Greg's eyes glowed red and after a while the engineer spoke in a deep voice, a tone lower than his own:

"Yes, Captain."

Before Lilianna could speak, Mikhalov interrupted and delivered the following message in one breath:

"Wait, let me say something first. You scoundrel, rat, player, pig tit, son of a bitch, scavenger, bastard, bald monkey without a penis, I would rip your guts out and wind them on barbed wire if you were still alive, but you died, and it's very good. That's it."

With a very pleased expression, he spun on his heel and walked out, leaving his audience in utter amazement.

After a good moment, ArCer looked at Lilianna and asked:

"Have I already told you that you have an exceptionally ill-mannered crew?"

"Yes, several times," Lilianna replied absently. "Sometimes I wonder how Juliusz Mrozik would fare in my position ..."

"I have no idea. In fact, why is it not Captain Mrozik in charge?"

"Because he turned out to be shrewder than me and went to jail just before the start. But enough about that. The job is waiting."

She looked at Greg. His eyes were still glowing red, so she sighed and asked:

"SyTar, do you promise you won't sabotage anything again?"

ArCer jumped up, hearing such a lack of logic (who takes the promises of a madman seriously?), and Greg replied with the voice of the late Uoltan:

"I promise. I will never be a problem again and I will try to be of help in everything."

"I hope so," said Lilianna sternly. "Due to the extraordinary nature of this situation, Gregory will permanently wear a brain scanner monitored by a computer. It's not that I don't believe you, but as the captain of this boat, I can't afford to be overly trusting. I prefer to avoid any surprises."

"I see. I agree on everything," SyTar said meekly.

**

"This is unbelievable," said Father Toadstool, scandalized, having heard Greg's confession. "This is the first time I see a man who has two souls, including one unbaptized! I wonder what the catechism has to say about it."

"What can I do about it, Father? SyTar is not a Catholic, and I don't know what he believes at all, because the Uoltans never talk to strangers about their religion," replied the oppressed penitent.

"It's good if they believe in anything at all. Listen, son, I have to consult the Vatican about your case. I can't come up with anything myself."

Gregory left the chapel even more frustrated than when he had entered it. In the corridor he came across Johnnie, who was waiting for him with a worried look on his good face, stroking Gizia, curled up on his shoulder.

"And, man?" he asked. "Did Reverend Father reprimand you?"

"No ... He was rather embarrassed about what to do with me. Johnnie, do you have some of your moonshine? I have to drink."

"Of course, I have!" Johnnie beamed. "Officer Karpiel is carrying out a tasting right now. Let's go to him."

Meanwhile, on the bridge, Jürgen and Arek had a little battle. It turned out that the order with the destination of the flight was lost somewhere and it was not known where the 'Hermash' was flying and what for.

"We need to contact HQ because we can't fly on spec," argued Jürgen calmly and logically.

"And what will we tell them? That we have here such a mess? No way, I would burn with shame," the first officer replied.

"Does it mean that the mess itself is not a cause for shame in your opinion, but the mere fact that the hauptquartier[18] can find out about it?" Jürgen asked.

"And why should we wash our dirty linen? It will spread and everyone will laugh at us."

"But we must know where we are going so unwashed. Fräu Krencik, please add a question about the purpose of the mission."

"Malva, don't you dare, or I will relegate you to a kitchenette!"

"Typical male. What do you think that a woman should only cook?" Malvinka growled dissatisfied.

"No, because those prettier should go for ballet," Watery chuckled from over his console.

"Eh, Joe, you would better stick it to your wife."

"And what do you have against Tekla, you mangy linnet?!" Watery got mad, at which Malvinka got up from her position and slapped him across the face heavily.

"You musty praying mantis!" the technician yelled, holding the injured face.

---

[18] *(Ger)* Headquarters.

Ms Krencik added to him on the other side, speaking the verbal comment:

"Be silent when you talk to me, you damn gentleman!"

"Gentlemen, don't you see that the officers are being beaten here?" Watery asked Jürgen and Arek.

"Slouch! Snitch! Informer!" Malvinka screamed.

"Do you hear, gentlemen, what that bi...ddy is saying?"

"I don't know what Mr. Jürgen heard," Arek replied, "but I didn't hear and seen any gentleman here offended."

"Du bist kein[19] 'gentleman', Joe," Jürgen said. "A gentleman doesn't throw various animal insults at the lady. Possibly flowers, that he can."

"If they were in pots, I would have thrown them at her, and willingly," growled offended Watery and turned his back demonstratively.

"Maybe let's contact the engine room?" Malvinka suggested, returning to her seat. "They should keep backup records."

"Connect, Malva," Arek agreed.

---

[19] *(Ger)* You're not a ...

Krencik opened the channel to the emergency command section in the engine room, but to everyone's amazement instead of the standard "Engine Room is Reporting Readiness", the screaming song in three voices came from the loudspeaker:

"In Spiš and Orava, there is a squall!

Giewont murmurs 'I don't like it at all.'

Krupówki and Roztoka bleat!

They trounced Janicek, and that's it ..."

"A fine kettle of fish, all are drunk there again ..." Arek moaned aloud.

"Oonly not druunk," the loudspeaker got offended. "Iden ... Iden ... intensify yourself ... oh! who are you?"

"This is first officer Liljew! Who am I dealing with?!"

"With the deputy chief engineer, Lil'jew, why? You don't like such 'giszeft'[20]? Sy git[21], Polish army!"

---

[20] "Giszeft" or "geszeft" - it's a word in Yidish and it mean "a deal". "

[21] "Sy git" is also from Yidish and mean "all right". A phrase "Sy git, polish army" is a popular offence for a polish soldier with jewish roots - A first oficer from 'Hermash' has a last name which sounds like "A little Jew".

Jürgen closed the internal communicator firmly and left, heading for the engine room. On the way, he stopped a security patrol consisting of three militant girls and one visibly harassed young man, and ordered them to go with him. Upon entering the engine room, he announced the immediate arrest of Gregory Brzenchyshchykievich on charges of drunkenness on duty and insulting the senior officer. Johnnie and Andy Karpiel were speechless. Greg protested vigorously, but one of the girls twisted his arm, the other tripped him, and the third efficiently put on the handcuffs, ignoring the desperate wailing:

"Women are beating me, help!"

XLIX.

The case of accusing the deputy chief engineer of violating the regulations got complicated very quickly. First of all, it turned out that he hadn't been on duty at the time. In addition, Arek declared that he wouldn't file a complaint, because privately he liked Greg very much, and Captain Zakrzevska, on which the case finally leaned, only stated:

"If I got rid of all the drunks and violators on board, I'd be the loneliest Star Armada commander."

"I don't understand it at all," ArCer complained in a conversation with Dr. TiShan, when he visualized the fetus with mutual consent. "She doesn't worry about anything."

"Maybe she has reasons not to worry? After all, her command style works well on the ship." The doctor replied, not taking her fascinated eyes away from the screen, which displayed the image of what was happening in the belly.

"On such a ship ... nothing will surprise me. And I've finished. The little one looks healthy. With the time dilation we have on board, even the time of pregnancy won't agree, but it's about sixth month. All the organs are fully developed, and, as Earthlings say, all fingers in place.

"Are you happy?"

"It would be a fully human emotion. I accept the facts, as befits a Uoltan."

TiShan sighed. She was used to the fact that ArCer's reactions were not what she expected, because he was "a real Uoltan" after all. SiWok understood her better, especially since he was subject to quite human emotions. He was hopelessly in love with Captain Zakrzevska, and she, instead of keeping a cool distance, as befited a star ship captain, seemed to be very pleased with his attentions. It was really indecent.

When the doctor was buttoning her blouse, Johnnie Caterpillar marched into the office, followed by limping Bear.

"Where are you going with this bacterial depot?" TiShan exclaimed angrily.

"Doctor, Veronika is on duty, and this poor creature stepped on something sharp," said the highlander with worried bass. "Look at his leg ..."

"I'm not a vet," TiShan growled, but she reluctantly leaned down and examined the bloody leg of the sheepdog sitting with his head hanging sadly. He allowed her to watch, but when she tried to touch the injured limb, he straightened up and presented her with all his impressive fangs.

"What a mean bastard!" the doctor stepped back cautiously.

"My sheepdog from my home village was even worse," Johnnie consoled her. "Even his doghouse was impossible to approach."

"He was so bad?"

"Bad, no, it was just so shitty ..."

"I will summon Shaman ... sorry, I mean Dr. Nbeba," ArCer interrupted this probably not very wise conversation. "In your condition you shouldn't risk."

Dr. Nbeba dealt with the matter methodically - first of all he bandaged Bear's mouth, then gave him a premedication and, having cleaned the wound, closed it with a regenerator. Nevertheless, until the end of the day, Bear walked with his paw up and moved it to anyone who showed interest, whimpering demonstratively and demanding any culinary comforting methods.

***

The study of the Murasaki 1061 phenomenon, to which 'Hermash' was ultimately directed by an order of the headquarters, almost ended in disaster. The peculiar magnetic pulsation completely stupefied the ship's sensors, cut off communication and disrupted the operation of devices on all decks. Worst of all, for some reason, the synthesizers suffered the most. They did work, but in a completely surprising way, producing various bizarre creations, and the crew members even used them for a kind of lottery - they bet what would pop up after entering a given command. Almost no one could guess, and if anyone did, it was simply a matter of luck, not deduction.

Captain Zakrzevska, on whose plate, instead of borscht, formed a shoe from a left leg, generously poured with ketchup and decorated with an umbrella from a Hawaiian drink, uttered a longer monologue, even a transcript of which would have caused a public scandal, and then she got the technicians to work, very flowily presenting what and how she would have ripped them off, if they hadn't fixed the devices quickly.

"It's easy for her to say," Jolka Stern grumbled, while her full-time assistant, Andrew Lepek, tried to demagnetize the power circuit inputs. "Will you play with this for a long time?"

"I'm an agronomist, not an electronics engineer, my specialty is agricultural harvesters and milking machines," Lepek growled angrily in response.

"Then why the hell did you volunteer to work in the engine room?!" Miss Stern's astonishment knew no bounds, though she should have been used to the fact that on Hermash there were mainly people completely unfit for space service.

"I didn't volunteer for it! I joined the space program to spite my missus, and they sent me to the engine room because I know plumbing. You know what, Jolka, sometimes I wonder if it wasn't better to stay on Earth after all. There, I was in danger of at most stepping into a cow pie, not being smashed by some furious meteor ... and now also of starving to death."

"Damn it. What shall I do with this scrap? According to the diagnostics, everything should work like a dream. Watery, how's the situation?"

"Synthesizers number three and four work, but they still mix the formulas," Joe replied. "Synthesizer nine had minor damage, caused by those on the crew kicking into its wall who wanted to somehow show dissatisfaction with the products they received. I fixed it, but it still doesn't work properly."

Jolka mispronounced a curse, while wondering how the hell to handle the task, if the broken synthesizers were not broken at all? After some thought, she reached for her communicator and called the engine room:

"Gregory, everything works here. Only the final product sucks. I don't know what else we could do."

"It is important that I know," a voice replied, strangely deep and somewhat non-gregorian. "You have to modify the deflectors in such a way as to eliminate the magnetic pulses. All you need to do is obtain the captain's authorization."

"So, obtain it!"

"Communication with the bridge is broken. Be so good and go there in person." Jolka angrily turned off the communicator, told her team to finish checking the synthesizers, even if it looked like a stupid job, hit Lepek in the neck to work it off somehow, and went to the bridge.

On the bridge, the engineer found the entire watch - Inga Lausch, helmsman Bequiet, the first officer, Andy Karpiel and Tekla Watery - gathered around the scientific console, on which swarthy Azalia Kviek from the supply department was laying out cards.

"What are you doing?" she asked in amazement.

"Hush, we are trying to determine where to fly," Karpiel replied, not taking his fascinated eyes from the cards. "Everything failed, and we need to know what to stick to."

"You want to foretell further course from cards?!"

"Do you have a better idea? The captain told us to think of something, so we brainstormed."

Jolka came to the console with a determined step.

"Ensign Kviek, please stop this witchcraft immediately," she demanded angrily.

"The gypsy will tell you the truth, miss. Put the piece of paper on the card and I will read the whole truth ..." Azalia replied in a characteristic style, counting the cards. "The first, second, third

... the enemy is waiting for us, the intransigent enemy ... death is lurking ... but near the captain I see love. Someone loves her, someone is close ..."

"You have to be blind not to notice it. SiWok follows her like a calf follows a cow," Jolka growled. "Maybe enough of this fu... nonsense?"

"Course, Aza, give me a course," the steersman cut in on her.

"The card will tell the truth ... Two of hearts, jack of spades and ten of clubs ... Course 312.03."

"I'm wondering how you calculated it."

Bequiet rushed to the control console and entered the coordinates given by the Gypsy into the analyzer.

"Damn, you know it looks quite logical?" he exclaimed in amazement as he compared the plot with the data from the automatic map.

"Where's the captain?" Jolka asked with a sigh, resigning from further disputes.

"She went to the mess!"

The engineer left the bridge, with confusion in her mind, deciding to give the commander as comprehensive a report as possible on what she had seen, but by the time she got to the mess she forgot about the non-standard course calculation, fascinated by what she saw. Namely Father Toadstool, who it is not known what he imagined, decided to perform a general exorcism and now he was standing on the middeck, waving his sprinkler and shouting darkly and solemnly:

"Go away, Satan! I curse you! I command you, get out of here and leave us alone!"

"Call the infirmary. Let them come with a straitjacket," Jolka groaned at this unusual sight, rubbing her eyes at the same time and wondering if she hallucinated. After a while, however, she concluded that even if she had dreamed continuously for two years, she couldn't have imagined something like that.

"Calm down, it's nothing," consoled her Sister Ophelia, who of course was also nearby. "Tadek is a fanatic of understanding certain things literally. He insisted on banishing evil from the ship, and he tries. Let him have fun."

"And you, sister don't believe in devils?" inquired Matias von Braun, who followed the priest's activities with the interest of the viewer of the comedy de arte.

"I believe. But not that they have any other worries than our junk pile. Unfortunately, Tadek is quite old-fashioned ... He believes that when something inexplicable happens, there must be some impure force in it."

At that moment, Father Toadstool turned in the corridor and stepped straight on a Vietnamese pig that had escaped from his master's, Lieutenant Antoni Dudek's quarters. The piglet, who had grown into a large pig during the journey, made a loud squeal, tripped Toadstool and ran down the corridor, finally bumping into Ensign Kinderman.

"Oy vavoy, this is shady!" the ensign shouted, jumping hastily backward. "I can't be on one ship with this!"

"Let's say that this is the first kosher pig in history and it will be fine," said Captain Zakrzevska, who had just appeared in the corridor with a plate full of food cubes. "Hey, everybody help yourself. We have a full load of it, but be warned, it tastes like cat food mixed with washing powder."

L.

It is not known whether the exorcisms of Father Toadstool helped, or rather the engineering division, terrified by the prospect of eating "iron rations" for a longer time, started a gallop, but the synthesizers could be turned on the next day in the evening. That same night, Greg, working tirelessly on the shield modulators, finally set the correct code and the harmful influence of the alternating magnetic field was eliminated. All the systems were activated at once, and so effectively that Vasyl Anecdotych, who was setting up the 'turret' targeting devices, inadvertently sent two photon torpedoes somewhere into space.

"Yob tvoyu mat!"[22] he screamed in fear. "Tfu, chiort pobieri takoy karabl!"[23]

Captain Zakrzevska, delighted with such a turn of events, set all the staff to work checking the parameters of everything that could be checked, and after two days of hard work, the ship's

---

[22] *(Rus)* A vulgar curse.

[23] *(Rus)* Damn such a ship.

staff found that everything that should have worked was working properly enough to move on. The only thing that permanently "failed" was the gravity as well as the water oxygenation system in the aquarium, which stood in the middle of the conservatory, fixed to the floor and secured in all possible ways. The spare device was included in the inventory, but it was physically non-existent, as confirmed by Colorado Kviek, responsible for small equipment in the warehouses. Ensign Cucumber, who was a gardener in the 'Hermash' conservatory, dismantled the pump into prime factors, then with disarming frankness stated that he couldn't put it back together and carried a box of miserable remains to the engine room, demanding that "they do something about it".

"Hell, and Satans!" Charles Mikhalov shouted at him. "It seems that your head withered, you cucumber, and before that, also your both hands and dick!"

The gardener was very offended and, regardless of the fact that he was only an ensign, and his opponent a lieutenant, he hit him in the head with a box. Of course, the chief engineer responded in a very similar way to such an attack, and there was a struggle during which the elements of the aquarium pump were scattered throughout the engine room, and some of them couldn't be found at all. From what was left, plus a few extras, they managed to put together a 'joyful creativity' which was then placed by Joe Stelmach in the aquarium near gravel.

"The performance will be lower, but we can live with that," he said. "Let the fish harden. As do we all."

Artificial gravity was also not fully dealt with. It is true that the system worked, but like this pump - with reduced efficiency. The vessel's force of gravity was now 0.6 G, and that was all they could squeeze out of the circuits. Doctor Zmiyevski was very grumpy about this inconvenience and prescribed injections to prevent bone decalcification to all members of the crew, especially pregnant TiShan. Also to pets. However, when he administered the injection to Bear, he himself had to seek the help of a doctor, because the sheepdog treated it as an attack on him and gave it a very toothy expression.

Having left the area of dangerous pulsations, 'Hermash' flew on, but it turned out that what had happened then wasn't left without repercussions. They had barely covered a parsec when the ship was hit in the port side with a solid payload.

"They're shooting at us!" the on-board computer screamed hoarsely so that the entire crew heard it.

"Thank you, 'Hermash'. Without you, we wouldn't have guessed," Captain Zakrzevska answered him calmly, tied a braid around her head and turned on the intercom.

"Attention crew, red alert! Engine room, shields at full power! Snipers go to the turret! Infirmary, prepare to receive the wounded! Kitchen, put out all vending machines and stoves! Combat team go to the bridge!"

A chaotic hustle and bustle ensued on all decks. Everywhere could be heard nervous comments like:

"Damn, what a cruise!"

"What a scoundrel is hitting us again?!"

"Probably another admirer of our missus ..."

"Where the hell are you going?! Now it's my turn (this was next to one of the few operating toilets)!

And so on. Still, amazingly quickly, everyone found themselves in their post, except for one of the security shifts. The six-man squad had previously secretly feasted on canned food stashed away, which turned out to be contaminated with some kind of bacteria, and now it occupied two of the five active toilets, and was unfit for combat at all.

On the bridge there was a combat cast - ArCer, Jürgen, Maura Gvizdak, Christopher Mayher with philosophical calmness eating a portion of paprikash, Malvinka Krencik and Mstislav Deadskull.

"All in their places?" the captain asked. "Chris, leave this plate at last!"

"When a Pole is hungry, is angry," Mayher replied with his mouth full. "I sneeze at fighting with an empty stomach."

"They are catching up with us," Malvinka reported. "Judging from the signature, it's a Sheolian ship."

"A fine kettle of fish," muttered the captain. "Try to call them out."

This time she was a bit worried because what she knew about the Sheolians didn't make her feel optimistic. This inhuman race was not particularly hostile to the Union, but it had made itself known as a ruthless pursuer of its rights, and it was better not to get in its way without a really good reason. It is true that Captain Zakrzevska didn't remember getting in the way of the Sheolians, but who could be sure? It could have happened accidentally - it was enough that 'Hermash' somehow touched the space of these insect-like creatures and they could have a grudge.

"Captain, Commander Loskine on the phone," said Malvinka, who had finally managed to tune the frequency to Sheolian's communications equipment.

"Good job. Commander Loskine, this is Captain Zakrzevska from the Star Armada. Why are you shooting at us?"

The loudspeaker screeched, squealed and replied:

"You are the aggressors. Give up or die."

Malvinka looked uncertainly at her captain.

"He said ..." she began.

"I heard," Lilianna interrupted. "Wait a minute, Loskine, we don't seem to be in Sheolian space right now, so what is it about?"

"You shelled our ship for no reason."

"Us?! When?"

"About four-time units ago."

It didn't explain much, because a time unit could be anything - a minute, an hour, or a day. Captain Zakrzevska looked helplessly at her officers, who could only shrug their shoulders. Nobody knew anything.

"Let me check the records," she said finally. "I don't know anything about shooting, but maybe something like that really took place. I would like to clarify this sad matter somehow."

"You can get our records now," Loskine replied unfriendly, and displayed on the screen an image of torpedoes hitting the shields of the Sheolian ship. It was impossible to miscue, they were the union torpedoes.

"If this is the case, and we are the only Union ship in this sector, then we did indeed shoot," said Jürgen after some thought.

"Shut up, freak," the captain muttered, and called Vasyl Zaychik. "Vashka, talk like in a confession: what is this shooting without my order?"

"Kakoya strielanina..." Vasyl began with a raised voice, but then he reflected and replied, embarrassed: "My Baryshnia, kogda systema dzialac nachaly[24], two torpedoes went to hell. Nie znayu, v co papaly."[25]

"But, I znayu," the captain said grimly, and turned off, postponing the scolding of the chief armorer until later. "Commander Loskine, are you there? Well, I figured out that our torpedoes flew towards you as a result of a villainous accident. There was no ill-will in it, just a simple glitch."

"I don't believe you," the Sheolian replied firmly. "We can't believe dioecious races."

"I'm sorry, but what does dioeciousness have to do with it?" was stunned the captain, to whom the cultural prejudices of races such as insectoidal Sheolians and Zoindi against humanoid mammals were alien.

"Excuse me, Captain," ArCer said hurriedly at the sight of her expression. "The sexuality of the hominids offends the moral sense of Sheolians, in general our reproductive structure disgusts them. From here, it is only a step to various other prejudices."

"And why do they about our sex? It's such a fun activity for free hours."

"For full hours, Captain!" Malvinka exclaimed animatedly.

---

[24] *(Rus)* When the systems started workings.

[25] *(Rus)* I don't know what they hit.

"Where did you get such a fantastic man?"

ArCer looked up in mute terror, and got speechless. Lilianna just waved her hand and turned to Loskene again.

"Commander you may not believe it, but it was an accident caused by a failure. We don't think about giving up, so please tell me what the other options are."

"There are no other options," Loskine screeched ominously. "Get ready to die."

"Damn it, threaten your grandma, you fucking trampled cockroach with the guts on top, coated with grain weevils!" the eager captain finally lost her temper, and she banged her fist on the console. "You want war? Then you will have it! I will kick your abdomen so that even your grandchildren will jump!"

At the mention of the deliciously prepared cockroaches, Christopher Mayher, who had just finished the spicy paprikash, turned green and dropped his empty plate. Meanwhile, the captain ordered the shields to be raised and all guns to be ready.

"Er ... I can't raise all of them," Mayher stuttered, with difficulty controlling the hiccups. "Only the bow ones works."

"Well, then move the bow ones!"

Loskine disappeared from the screen and after a while 'Hermash' was shaken by a blow.

"Answer them, but so that they will shit themselves," the captain roared into the intercom. The turret breathed a volley of mazers, hitting the Sheolian ship in the starboard side. The snipers fired another payload and after a while Loskine retreated beyond the range of the shots.

"He must be gathering strength," said Deadskull. The captain thought so too.

"Let's not give him time for that," she said. "Hyperspace jump, warp speed, factor eight."

LI.

No one objected to the captain's orders, not even the engine room, where the dangers of such a sudden jump into the warp speed were well known. Nobody was surprised when, after the jump, the engine room reported that it couldn't slow down because the drive regulator seized up.

"Well, we'll fall apart soon," said, somewhat calmly, the younger technician, Cezary Monkey, who was on duty on the bridge.

"The sheathing won't endure," added Jürgen.

"Princess, do something!" the computer creaked. "I can't turn on safeguards! I can't slow down!"

"It's even pointless to try, these circuits are beyond central control," the captain reminded him ruthlessly. "Calm down and let me think."

Suddenly, the comm console beeped, and a nervous female voice came from the loudspeaker:

"Arek, why didn't you call back? How do you treat me? I repeat the question: how dare you leave such a mess in your room?! Socks under the laptop, panties on the cactus, and the cap in the aquarium!"

The First Officer's expression changed and he grabbed the microphone.

"But, Mom, this is not the best time ..." he began.

"Don't hedge, brat! Do you think that because you went to the other end of the galaxy, I will forgive you? Forget it! You have to come back someday, and then you will be so grounded that you will remember your great-grandmother."

Captain Zakrzevska got roused from stupor.

"At least we already know we jumped towards Earth," she murmured and took the microphone from Arek. "This is Captain Zakrzevska. Ma'am, we have a little crisis now. Would you like to scold your son some other time?"

The loudspeaker spat, huffed, and replied:

"I don't know how you stand him there. Arek is messy, careless and lazy. But if you don't mind, why I should care. Just remember that he has weak sinuses and he catches the runny nose and then he gets scabs near his nose. And make sure he doesn't eat chocolate because he gets a rash from it. And if he doesn't move the bowels every so often ..."

At that moment, luckily, the private channel was drowned out by communication with the headquarters and it was high time, because poor Arek didn't know where to look.

'Hermash', report how's the situation."

"Great. We contrived a military incident with the Sheolians, and we are currently going at high warp speed and can't slow down. It couldn't be better," the captain answered politely.

"What incident, what are you talking about?" the headquarters got angry, glozing over the threat to the life of the crew.

Lilianna explained as easily as possible what had happened and why, and reported the reaction of the Sheolian commander. The headquarters fell into deep reverie.

"You got into mischief," she said finally. "Please prepare a detailed report of this incident and attach to it the record from the on-board recorders."

"Okay, unless we don't fall apart, because for now we're accelerating instead of braking."

"Fall apart?! No! I don't want to die!" the on-board computer squeaked.

"Who is this?" the headquarters asked.

"Our computer. Some idiot has assembled into him an artificial intelligence circuit modeled on the engrams of the human brain, so that we have a basically intelligent ship ... but not very predictable," the captain explained.

"Princess, Empress, do something, I don't want to die like that ..." the computer sobbed, shaking at the same time so that the whole ship shivered.

"Hush, 'Hermash', it won't be that bad for sure," the captain consoled him and turned to headquarters again. "Forgive me, I have to get over this chaos. I will make contact whenever possible."

She dropped the microphone and rushed to the elevator. Exactly ten seconds later she found herself in the engine room and run to the chief engineer, locked in the drive chamber.

"And?!" she called, braking with her heels right before the protective pane.

"Shit, Captain!" Mikhalov exclaimed in despair. "I can't unlock the drive adjustment! The sheathing won't endure it!"

Left by his master in the middle of the engine room, Vuvu wandered and squealed pitifully, and for some reason this squeal suddenly triggered some association sequence in the captain's mind. She grabbed the intercom."

"Attention, everyone prepares for a strong shock!" she called, then turned to the engine room staff: "Turn off all systems. Now!"

There was consternation among the engineers. This kind of braking required the rejection of the energy core, with various consequences. Charles Mikhalov jumped out of the drive chamber as if burned.

"It could paralyze us," he warned for the record, tearing off his protective suit.

"If our sheathing gets torn apart, the whole crew will die. I'd rather risk paralyzing the ship," the captain growled. "Where's the emergency switch?"

"On the wall, under the calendar. Let's hope it hasn't failed."

The calendar presented caricatures of the world's leading politicians and certainly came from one of the niche printing houses, very popular in Poland. Under it there was indeed a red painted box with a pane, with the inscription "In case of danger, hammer it." Underneath it, in slightly smaller letters, the other said: "I said, in case of danger, you idiot." Joe Stelmach, who was closest, swung his wrench and the glass broke into thousands of pieces.

"Everyone to the floor!" the captain commanded over the intercom and lay down herself in a defensive position. Others in the engine room followed her example, except for Mikhalov, because someone had to pull the switch after all.

As soon as this happened, the ship's force of gravity increased tenfold for a fraction of a second, and then it dropped to zero, as a result of which everyone jumped to the ceiling, and immediately fell back, when it returned to the previous 0.6 G. 'Hermash' flew driven by the force of inertia a few thousand more miles until it finally stopped.

For a long moment, only curses were heard in the engine room, but then the entire crew got up from the floor and briskly set about the inspection. In turn Captain Zakrzevska went to the bridge.

"All sections, report," she demanded, sinking into the command chair. "Miss Bumblebee, Mr. Mayher, you will both report to the hangar and fly the shuttle to get the energy core. The main module will give you the bearing."

"Not main module but 'Hermash'," the offended computer screeched. "I will send the data directly to the shuttle dashboard."

"All right, 'Hermash'. Send it."

Reports started pouring in from all sides, mostly of minor lesions and small bumps. Nothing serious happened to anyone, even spiders, relatively fragile creatures, survived the sudden increase of the force of gravity and were just very scared. The reptiles also showed anxiety, let alone the mammals. The piglet squealed like crazy, the lynx crawled into the ventilation duct, and Gizia out of fear bit Johnnie on the right ear, to which it was closest to her. Bear lay pressed into the corner of his mistress's cabin and growled. Only Vuvu didn't care about all this, because with his master he had experienced worse situations.

The only more serious accident was that Joe Watery, characterized by a somewhat abundant shape, and founding himself in a secluded place during braking, got stuck with his backside in the toilet bowl when the gravity force increased. He got stuck in it so thoroughly that there was no question that he would break free on his own and finally he had to resort to a vocal call for help. This event gave the crew a lot of fun and an opportunity to weave against this background a fantastic story that Malvinka immediately passed on to the nearest station.

***

Veronika Bumblebee and Christopher Mayher found the discarded core, but in order to do so, they had to move far away from the ship. Chris didn't mind, but Veronika, against her will, was shaking like a leaf. It was the first time she traveled on a shuttle in a deep vacuum, and such a distance. To someone who has never experienced something like this, it is difficult to explain in an accessible way what the vastness of the universe around the meaningless speck is - a shuttle of several people. The impression is so overwhelming that someone unprepared may fall into quite hysteria, but luckily Miss Bumblebee was able to contain herself enough not to chatter her teeth ... too loudly.

Lieutenant Mayher kindly ignored the nervousness of his young companion, focusing on keeping an eye on the indicators. Being an experienced pilot, he found the core without difficulty, grabbed it with the transporter beam and hauled it onto the deck, then turned the shuttle back.

"Hmmm, there are some traces here," he muttered after a moment. "Miss Veronica, please enable automatic external registration."

"Lieutenant, I catch a call for help," Veronika reported with amazement after a moment. "In addition, it's like ours ... It's so weird."

"Rather disturbing. Connect, miss, with 'Hermash', and quickly."

"It's impossible! The apparatus doesn't want!"

"Holy moly ..." Christopher mispronounced much worse words and focused on the readings. Something was happening, and he didn't like such surprises. Especially when he was on his own, and he looked after a completely green teenager who probably received the title of helmsman as a gift for Christmas from people who sympathized with her due to breaking of her from her own timeline.

LII.

On the deck of the ship, Johnnie was running, nervous, clearly looking for something.

"Andy, how do you call a flittermouse? Tas tas, Chip chip...?" he asked helplessly when in one of the corridors he saw Andrew Karpiel conferring with the Pandorian T'enga, or rather clearly hitting her.

"What and how do you want to call?" T'enga asked in amazement, cocking the antennae that replaced her ears.

"Flittermouse."

"What is this, by all the Pandorian glaciers?"

"Flittermouse ... well, this is a flittermouse, blue miss ... You know, miss, it's like a mouse ... such a mouse that ate a candle in a church and experienced ascension ..."

"A bat," explained to the Pandorian, Karpiel, almost choking with laughter. All the translators, even the best-programmed ones, stuttered at the Silesian-highland dialect used by the commander's orderly.

"This is what I mean. Miss, it gets into your hair, and God forbid such a grunge flies over a cow because it takes its milk right away!"

Slowly, a meaningful picture emerged from Johnnie's story. A beautiful, tame kalong belonging to one of the crew members escaped from her quarters during emergency braking and sank like a stone. The crew member, second lieutenant Marlena Wróbka, made a terrible lamentation, and even more lamented those of the crew who were afraid of the bats. As it turned out, there were more of them than those who feared snakes and spiders. Johnnie, who had already been promoted in the internal system to a specialist in "house livestock", went in search of the Indian beauty and spread panic on all decks, announcing everywhere with his loud voice what a dangerous beast this was on the loose.

"This ship looks more and more like a madhouse," grumbled Jacob Zmiyevski, and words failed him completely when docent Polikarp Hołuj from the cartography department, commonly known as Karpik, entered the infirmary, carrying his capybara in his hands, and in a tragic voice announced:

"Doctor, the Whisper passed out of fear ..."

Jack gave the rodent a stimulant injection, the capybara jumped to its feet briskly, huffed, spat and, having made a large puddle in the center of the infirmary, ran out into the corridor.

Beaming, Karpik embraced the doctor profusely, patted sister Icant on different places, and ran after his favorite. Sister Lolita sighed heavily and went to the back room to get a cloth (the cleaning machines, as usual, didn't work).

After a while there was a deafening scream in the storeroom and the girl burst out of there as if she had been chased by a pack of demons.

"There is a devil!" she roared and ran into the corridor, where, stumbling over the ubiquitous Bear, she landed in the arms of von Braun, lured by the commotion.

"Devil? True?" Matias asked.

"Father Thaddeus! You are asked to come to the infirmary with the sprinkler and holy water!"

Father Toadstool, overjoyed at the prospect of demonstrating the appropriate competences, hastily armed himself with the standard tools of an average exorcist and appeared in record time in front of the infirmary. Sister Ophelia ran after him, shouting:

"You damn idiot! They are kidding you, and you are taking it seriously?"

The news of the devil in the broom closet spread like wildfire across all decks. There was a great deal of gossip as to whether, if it was in fact the devil, he had gotten in somehow along the way, or had been picked up from Earth. Atheists mistrusted, but since almost all of them believed in ghosts and supernatural phenomena anyway, they themselves inadvertently fell into the discussion of what a devil is, what he could do on the star ship, and finally, how many devils fit on the tip of a pin. All the confusion was finally cut off by Johnnie, who, lavishly sprinkled by the priest with holy water, entered the storeroom and announced in a loud word that "this was not a devil, but a flittermouse!" After a while he left, carrying on his outstretched forearm a stately black kalong, clung upside down on his sleeve, turning its head and opening its mouth amusingly at the sight of the crewmen staring at him.

"Are you kidding the representative of the clergy?!" Father Toadstool asked angry, hiding the sprinkler.

"No, Holy Father," Lieutenant Marlena reassured him, grasping the favorite with relief. "The hook looks so weird that anyone who came across it in the dark could really get scared. Especially such a frigging moron like Sister Icant."

"Mean cow," the nurse was offended.

So, the devil's case was successfully dealt with. On the bridge, no one even knew about it, for they had much bigger worry there than some stupid devil in the storeroom.

***

The call for help from the shuttle was formulated so vaguely and without obligation that Captain Zakrzevska didn't know how to respond to it. Attempts to specify the type of defect or problem didn't bring results, because the contact broke off, although all measurements indicated that it should have been available.

"I'll fly over to them and find out what's going on," ArCer suggested.

"Okay," agreed the captain. "Let Lieutenant Gvizdak give you some fool from security and you can go on the other shuttle. Just keep in touch."

ArCer made his way to the hangar deck, where after a short thought, he chose the shuttle aptly named "Adam's Rib", not because he liked the name, but because it was the best equipped. A moment later, Ensign Dysentery entered the hangar, furious because he had to quit a promising game of poker. He clearly wanted to say something unpleasant, but the sight of ArCer's pointed ears stopped him. He might have started an argument with the deputy chief of security and the senior officer alone, but with the Uoltan, he didn't want to mess.

The shuttle 'Adam's Rib' took off at 0:15 PM, the boarding time, after which it got so completely lost that all attempts to locate it failed. Initially, the officers on the bridge weren't concerned about this, as there were disturbances in the entire apparatus caused by the passage of a large comet, but when the disturbing field receded and attempts to locate the shuttle failed, Captain Zakrzevska cursed everyone and demanded immediate diagnosis of scanners, a subradio and other devices.

"Don't curse us, captain," Malvinka replied to her speech. "You won't be able to track them either. Please try."

Encouraged to redouble her efforts by the threat of immediate confinement in the arrest cell, she puffed up with insult, but began checking all connections on the comm console while the steersmen took care of the scanners. While feverish diagnostics was going on, a shuttle suddenly appeared at the hangar hatch. However, it was not the missing 'Adam's Rib', but 'Kashpirovski', which Mayher and Veronika Bumblebee flew. Only in direct contact was it possible to detect their frequency. The captain immediately gave permission to dock, almost pulled poor Chris from the shuttle and made him a tavern brawl entitled: "And what a message you sent, you Dardanelles donkeys?!"

"We didn't send anything, Captain!" Veronika cried tearfully. "It's someone else! We caught it too!"

It surprised Lilianna. She released Chris, whom she was shaking like a ratler, a large bull terrier, and looked at Veronika with stupefied eyes.

"How is it, you didn't send? Then who?" she was suddenly scared. "ArCer and Dysentery went to look for you and they are gone ..."

"Maybe we will turn back and look for them?" Mayher suggested, adjusting the crumpled uniform.

"No way, are you stupid?! Nobody will fly again until we clear this up!"

The news about the disappearance of Commander ArCer and Ensign Dysentery swiftly reached everyone on the ship. Charles Mikhalov, who had already gotten drunk after leaving the duty office, inadvertently expressed the opinion that both missing people sought solitude because ... they fell in love with each other. When this ingenious slander reached Dr. TiShan, she found Mikhalov and hit him in the face so that it made him sober up with surprise. Then she had a regular bout of hysteria, and Dr. Nbeba had to give her some Uoltanian calming concoction.

The case of the disappearance of the shuttle 'Adam's Rib' absorbed the entire crew of 'Hermash'. In particular, SiWok took care of it together with SyTar who, due to the circumstances, was allowed by Greg Brzenchyshchykievich to take over his body for a longer time. His own consciousness seized the opportunity to take a nap and muttered in his sleep so that SyTar's soul could barely concentrate on the work. Both Uoltans managed, after many days of fruitless efforts, to extract the ion trace that couldn't be explained, so, for lack of a better trail, a joint resolution was made to follow this trace. Joint, because - as the captain noticed - democracy didn't reign on star ships, but absolute monarchy was not in Polish style and it was better not to try to introduce it on a Polish ship.

LIII.

For many weeks 'Hermash' had been following the barely perceptible trail of ionic disturbances, the only thing left of the lost shuttle. Captain Zakrzevska ordered that this trail be followed and threatened to throw overboard anyone who dared to protest. She had reason to be upset. Pregnant TiShan, ignoring her and her unborn child's safety, stole one of the remaining shuttles and tried to find her lover on her own. Since the shuttle's life-support system had failed before she was found, she was severely hypoxic, and Dr. Nbeba had no hope of keeping her and the baby alive. All he could do was to hurrily put TiShan in the stasis chamber and wait for the miracle.

The incident made a very dark impression on the entire crew, especially on SiWok, who cared so about TiShan as if she had been his older sister. In these difficult moments for him, Captain Zakrzevska gave him unexpected help. She assigned him to the infirmary as a junior paramedic so that he had specific activities and, at the same time, could watch over TiShan, who was sleeping in stasis. She also gave him permission to eat at the captain's table so that they could meet at mealtimes to talk quietly. The mischievous claimed that SiWok deliberately celebrated a tragic face in order to be able to get closer to the adored woman, but there was no shortage of tauters anywhere.

The headquarters gave 'Hermash' permission to search, on the condition that it would collect scientific data along the way, because the trail led through areas that had so far been a white spot in stellar cartography. About the fact that the Polish ship might have faced some completely unknown danger, no one cared.

"And let it face, the sooner the better," Admiral Cormack said when someone made such a supposition. People immediately started whispering that he couldn't forget the facer that the Polish captain had given him, but in fact 'Hermash' was still considered in the Star Armada as a kind of Trojan horse that could do some unspecified damage and that it would have been good to get rid of it.

Nobody on the Polish ship knew, of course, about such an attitude in the command, and if they had known, they wouldn't have cared either. The crew of 'Hermash' considered the command of the Star Armada to be a gang of old guys who had no idea about anything, and they accepted the mapping order with such indignation that would probably overwhelm the Academy of Fine Arts graduates who would be ordered to color the books with Winnie the Pooh and Piglet with wax crayons.

"What do they think? That we went on a sightseeing trip?" Mstislav Deadskull vented his indignation.

"These lazybones don't even know what we look like," summed up Arek. " They gave us the task just to be done with it, probably such one that no one else wanted to take."

"We can't expect that they let us negotiate a treaty with the Cumulus Empire. Especially after we messed up with the Pornions and got under the skin of the Clingorgians," Matias von Braun remarked reasonably.

"Do we play or talk?" Malvinka Krencik asked matter-of-factly.

"All four sat in the mess, playing bridge, taking advantage of their free time and not worrying too much about anything. As uberwatch, they had to be on the alert to take over duties of people finishing their shift, but nothing else. Matias von Braun, who was not an officer in principle, but a diplomat assigned to the ship, to his displeasure, also had to serve on the bridge. He tried to avoid this boring duty, but Captain Zakrzevska was relentless.

"I know that you are to negotiate, like an ass is to shit," she said kindly. "But we can't afford such a narrow specialization here. The service on the bridge is compulsory for everyone."

If for everyone, then for everyone. Worse, the captain really treated it literally, and therefore the service on the bridge had to be performed also by professor Trekovsky, red-faced due to the interruption of his work in his beloved laboratory, Gregory Brzenchyshchykievich (or SyTar, depending on the activity of the self), head nurse Lolita Icant and even Father Toadstool and sister Ophelia of the Angels. The chaplain of 'Hermash' was so indignant at the captain's order that he became speechless, which rarely occured, but his sister hastily explained to him that, anyway, the captain was "first after God" and he had to obey the order. Thus, Father Thaddeus was on duty on certain days and after some time he even found this job quite interesting. In general, he was then able to preach whatever he wanted without hindrance. Officers were even grateful to him for that, because it added variety to the boredom of the shifts, during which, as a rule, nothing happened.

The uberwatch, busy with bridge, was just playing another part, when - during a rather complicated auction with a redouble and a possible spade vole of one of the players - the tactical alarm sounded.

"Damn it, just when I have such good cards ..." Arek muttered, jumping up from his seat. "What a devil is alarming there?" he asked rudely over the intercom.

"Because we have something on the scanners ..." Inga Lausch's soprano sounded from the loudspeaker. "And Aśka Kubica asks whether to slow down."

Joanna Kubica, one of the helmsmen, descendant of a long line of racing drivers and pilots, slowed down reluctantly and rarely, and never of her own free will, and most willingly piloted anything that flew at crazy speeds, exceeding the limits.

"Let her slow down, let her slow down immediately!" cried Arek. "Overwatch to the bridge, I'm going to wake the captain."

***

The target looked unusual enough, to use the mildest of terms. The officers gathered on the bridge were wondering how to classify it - it was definitely an artificial creation, but was it a ship or a biosphere?

"I have never heard of a ship in my life that looks like a Rubik's Cube monument," Arek said finally.

"Which Rubik? The one from the 'Oratorio'?"[26] asked Inga, who, despite the presence of her co-worker on the bridge, didn't want to leave the communications console for anything.

"No, the one from Caesar," protested Joe Stelmach. "Caesar crossed the Rubik's River and threw the dice ..."

"For what?"

"I don't know, maybe he wanted to predict the weather for the next day."

"He crossed Rubicon, not Rubik, you fool!" von Braun shouted in shock. "From year to year the level of requirements as to historical knowledge in schools is lowered, and here are the consequences."

Arek, without explaining what he meant, strengthened the image on the main screen. Looming against the background of

---

[26] It is about the Polish composer Piotr Rubik.

distant stars, the block looked very solid and completely surreal at the same time - a metal cube with walls covered densely with convex ornaments, with no trace of typical visors, external screens, nacelles or cannons.

"Shall I get closer?" Aśka Kubica suggested, raising her light red head from above the controls.

"Don't you even dare! Whatever it is, shouldn't seen us!" shouted angrily the captain, who, regardless of the seriousness of the function, appeared on the bridge in pajamas and hairy slippers, tousled like a not heavenly creature.

"As you like, but the ion trace leads right there."

"All the more. We don't know what we're dealing with." The captain meditated for a moment, then asked: "Hermas", does what we have on the screen, figure in the Armada database?"

"I'll do a search in a moment, sweetheart," replied the drunken voice of the on-board computer. There was a crash, then a creak like made by a thousand unlubricated hinges, then something that sounded like the flapping of the wings of a hundred pigeons.

Then the computer declared:

"No reference, queen. It is an unknown object."

"Lovely. Can they see us?"

"The devil knows. They see, or they don't see," replied Andrew Karpiel-Baguette, who was just trying to get some data from the scientific console.

"It's a kind of combat cruiser," he said finally. "I detect high-tech weapons and a whole lot of different devices. There are also signatures of biological life, but strangely mixed with cybernetics ones."

"Of life, okay, but what?"

"Various races of creatures, including unclassified ones, and ..." Karpiel paused theatrically, "two Star Armada tag signatures."

"ArCer and Dysentery. It must be them."

The captain considered while the other officers stared at her, waiting for any explanation. The tags were implanted in the 'Hermash' crew experimentally. Their usefulness was tested, and the Polish crew had no idea what injection was actually being administered to them. General Jaruzelski explained the matter in a letter that Lilianna only got on board. Seeing no other option, she explained what was going on as sparingly as possible, which caused a real storm, coupled with promises ranging from knocking all teeth out, through tearing the legs off the butt, to a general thrashing "for those different sons in command."

"Be quiet!" the captain roared at last. "That later, now let me think, you Mongolian baboons!"

"Why baboons ... and Mongolian? As far as I know, there are no primates in Mongolia," noted Matias von Braun.

"And what about the Mongols? Are they prosimian?" Mayher asked skeptically.

"Do you always have to accentuate your racist views?"

"Shut up," the captain demanded angrily, without wondering whether the Mongols were primates or prosimian. The officers fell silent so as not to disturb their commander in thinking.

Finally, Lilianna scratched herself under her pajamas and commanded:

"Arek takes over the bridge. Gentlemen Jürgen, Mayher and Gvizdak will prepare to participate in the boarding group."

"Maura Gvizdak is a woman," Jürgen noted for the sake of order.

"He's twice as male as many of you," the captain grumbled and went to do herself up. As she said herself, boarding was a visit like all the others, and you couldn't start it in inelegant attire.

It is known that every person has a place where they think better than in others. For Lilianna Zakrzevska it had always been a shower. By the time she finished her ablutions, she had a plan of action ready. However, when she appeared on the bridge,

Greg Brzenchyshchykievich was already there and didn't let her speak.

"Captain, SyTar wants to say something," he reported excitedly.

"Come on, SyTar," the captain said, twirling the braid into a bun and pinning it with hairpins.

Greg's eyes flashed red for a moment, as always when SyTar's soul took control of his body, and then he spoke in a deep, full voice, different from the usual engineer's whiskey tenor:

"This ship has one of its shields weakened. Strongly weakened. Work is underway to repair it, but for some reason it's not going well. We can reinforce the transporter beam accordingly and just bring our people on board. There is only one but ..."

"What? Tell me! It rips my guts out ..."

"I analyzed the objects emitting Armada's signal. They are not uniformly organic."

"What does it mean?"

"They got something implanted, I think. We'll bring them, but we don't know what we'll get with them. I advise you to take extreme caution."

"Me too," said Maura Gvizdak. "They can't see us now, because we are motionless in the "blind spot", but when we bring our people, they'll probably figure out what's going on."

"I suppose so," the captain agreed. "That's why we grab what's ours and get the hell out of here at the maximum power of the engines. Mr. Mikhalov, how much can you give at the peak and for how long?"

"You know, such questions in front of everyone ...?! ... oh, you mean from the engines? I think we can keep warp speed eight for about thirty-eight minutes. Certainly not longer, but it will be enough to disappear from their sensors."

The captain mused severely, putting all the information together into a meaningful whole.

"Alright," she finally decided. "Tactical alert for security. The infirmary and research department should be on full alert. Force field around the transporter platform. Lieutenant Gvizdak, you will report to the transport hall with a few gorillas."

Maura nodded and hurried out, while the captain gave additional orders and went to the transport hall, where the technician on duty Lalevich was calibrating the transporter beam in accordance with the guidelines of Greg-SyTar standing over his head.

"When will you be ready, Dish?" she asked.

"Right away," replied Lalevich, connecting the circuits with incredible speed. As he said about himself, he was so lazy that he did every job as best as possible so as not to have to repeat it, and as quickly as possible to get rid of it fast.

At the platform itself, engineers from the engine room, Tekla Watery and Urban Lowsalt, quickly installed force field emitters. In fact, they should have already been installed in the shipyard, but someone missed this point in the plans.

"Done, Captain," they reported after a moment.

"Then get the hell ouf of here," replied Lilianna. "Dish?"

"Yeah, yeah ... Alright, we can bring them."

Lilianna looked at the open door where the security squad stood, and nodded.

"Localize and bring them," she ordered.

LIV.

It was easy to say "Localize and bring them." The transporter acted reluctantly and slower than usual, having clearly encountered a configuration it was not designed for, and the nervous seconds stretched like quarters of an hour. The security guards yawned anxiously, the captain cursed in an undertone in a very sophisticated manner, her orderly bitten his nails involuntarily, and only the technician Lalevich looked as bored as usual. Finally, the transporter made a long-awaited, modulated sound.

"Objects in the buffer," reported Lalevich. "Bridge, full speed ahead!" the captain shouted into the intercom.

"Alright, full speed ahead!" Christopher Mayher shouted back briskly and 'Hermash' fired into hyperspace, away from the mysterious cube.

"Dish, rematerialization," Lilianna ordered.

The technician moved the reluctant lever, but the transporter just screeched.

"We're losing the record! Seventy percent!" Greg, who was observing the indicators, exclaimed and added in SyTar's voice. "Mr. Lalevich, please start the reserve record."

"Don't teach a father how to make babies," the technician said, clicking buttons on the console.

"Why the hell do they all use transporters when they're so unreliable?" Maura Gvizdak muttered, shifting from foot to foot.

"Well, statistically speaking, it is safer to use a transporter than to wear a security uniform," Lalevich replied maliciously, then moved the return transport lever.

Two pillars of light swirled on the platform, and then formed into two extremely material objects. At first none of the gathered people recognized them as ArCer and ensign Dysentery. They both wore some kind of fitted blackish metal armor, and on their shaven heads they had helmets with a visor covering one eye. Oddly enough, these metal parts seemed not superimposed but rooted in their bodies. The skin of both men had an unhealthy gray-white shade and seemed lifeless.

"I think we will have to go to some psychiatrist ..." muttered Captain Zakrzevska, rubbing her eyes with a sudden movement. The two brought crew members descended in a steady movement from the platform, and only coming across the force field did they stop. There was something terrifyingly automatic about their movements, as if they had been remotely controlled.

"What's wrong with you guys?!" exclaimed Maura in amazement.

"Oh, Most Dear Mother of God, what a devil did this to you?" moaned Johnnie Caterpillar, widening his kind eyes until they became completely round.

"We are ZONK. The life you've known so far is over," Dysentery said in a steady voice.

"You're gonna be captured. Resistance is pointless," ArCer echoed in the same mechanical way.

"What are they talking about?" was surprised Charles Mikhalov, who had just appeared in the transport hall to report to the commander that basically everything was okay.

The captain looked at Greg, who was staring with his half-open mouth at the newcomers, hoping that SyTar knew something. But the soul of the Uoltan must have been as bewildered as its host, in any case it remained silent.

'Hermash', check the word "ZONK" in the database!" Lilianna called. The loudspeaker creaked, squealed, and after a while replied:

"Word unknown. No references, princess."

Meanwhile, both crewmen repeated their attempts to get out of the force field cage. The clamps on their forearms turned out to be a kind of firearm, thankfully not strong enough to break through the field. However, it almost overloaded the generators, and its owners had something else as well - some blades popping out of nowhere. The captain decided that it was necessary to remain alert and to be as careful as possible, for the behavior of these two clearly indicated one thing: they didn't recognize anyone, they were obedient to something she had no idea about. She could make further attempts to communicate with them, but concluded that the game was not worth exposing the crew to attack by two apparently brainwashed madmen armed to to their noses.

'Hermash', activate internal defense," she ordered. "Set the mazers to stunning. Start the procedure of neutralizing the objects inside the force field."

"Oh man!" Johnnie groaned, crossing himself piously.

"There's no need to waste energy, angel," the computer screeched fondly. "I have another way to deal with troublemakers."

There was a piercing hiss, and the space, enclosed by the force field, filled with a grayish vapor. Both men, still attacking the invisible barriers, paused for a moment, then collapsed to the floor.

"Ready, queen," said the computer. "You can take them. They won't wake up for six hours or so."

***

Captain Zakrzevska walked nervously around the research department, glancing at the armored pane behind which doctors Nbeba and Zmiyevski, as well as professor Trekovsky and his assistant, Andrew Karpiel, were struggling with their task.

"Lady dear, will they sober up?" Johnnie asked timidly, following his miniature captain with his eyes.

"Why should I know?" Lilianna replied grimly. "I don't even know what exactly was done to them."

"Someone changed them completely ..."

Johnnie paused, because Andy Karpiel had just come out of the screened room, and his expression clearly indicated that he was very baffled.

"It's some technology I don't know," he said. "We removed implants and we are rebuilding damaged organs, but what you can see from the outside is only a small part of the problem, and it's a smaller half."

"What do you mean?"

"I mean that they have nanites in their blood. They change them and, as it were, connect them with other minds of the community. And in order to restore them to the state of public use, we should remove these grunges first. Nbeba says it can be done by exchange transfusion as long as they have not yet penetrated to the bone marrow. We'll be able to deal with Dysentery, but ArCer and his green blood ..."

Lilianna cursed in powerless passion. The research department quickly determined that the minds of both crew members were artificially linked to some great community. Dinoslav Trekovsky was as happy as a child that he had the opportunity to investigate such an unusual phenomenon, and many arguments had to be used to make him start figuring out the problem of feedback blockade. Only the announcement of Captain Zakrzevska that one moment more, and the professor would go to the arrest, and with a broken jaw, was effective. Trekovsky was terribly offended, but in an hour, he figured out what frequency would disturb the transmitting and receiving waves, and the engineers assembled the appropriate devices, working on the principle of a brain scanner. Only this caused a decrease in the activity of both brains, so far, in spite of anesthesia, operating at an increased level.

"Captain," Inga Lausch, who was on duty at the communications console, said over the intercom. "Headquarters are asking for a report."

"Let a dog shit it! I have two crew members here in a state of total schizophrenia, and unless I find out how to help them, I won't write puff pieces for the lazybones from the command!" Lilianna shouted impatiently.

"My daughter, your language cries to heaven," said Father Toadstool, who had come to the science department, hoping that someone would want to be confessed.

"But which heaven? I've already been to a few and I still can't get enough," said Karpiel cheerfully.

"What blood type does ArCer have?" the captain asked him.

"P(+). Do you think about SiWok as a donor? I thought about it, too, but you know that in his blood, leukocytes are replaced by substance X. Its amount is more or less constant, but we don't know how it will act in the case of taking bigger amount of blood that is needed for a transfusion."

"Then you goddamn find out! For what am I keeping you here?!"

"Alright, alright. There's no need to be nervous, boss. You are such a highlander brigand who doesn't let others rest."

Andy called SiWok, who was just off duty and slept away his shift, to the research department. The boy showed up very quickly, looking like he was from a Uoltanian journal, although a moment earlier he was still in bed. While he didn't always behave like a real Uoltan, he kept many features of his species no worse than ArCer, including keeping a flawless appearance, regardless of the time of day or place.

"I'm listening to your orders," he said, glancing fondly at Lilianna.

"Let's not call them orders ... we're having trouble with ArCer and we want to use your blood. However, we don't know how much we can draw at one time," Karpiel explained to him.

"About a liter and a half, I should be able to endure."

"And after the stimulant, how much? It is not known, right? Without stimulant, we won't have enough anyway, and this drug will burden you a lot. Will you agree to such an experiment? We don't know how much it will hurt you."

"Then check it out."

"Are you sure?"

"TiShan is in the stasis chamber. There are no more Uoltans in the crew. I'm the logical choice. Is the commander really in bad shape?"

"I don't know. He's flawless for a cyborg, but as a Uoltan, he has trouble as big as from here to Pandoria."

After this philosophical remark, Karpiel took SiWok to the infirmary, where Sister Lolita Icant was sitting by the stasis chamber and, due to lack of a better task, she was weeping like a child.

"Lola, what's going on?" Andy called. "Why are you crying on duty? Please smile immediately!"

"I can't," the girl wailed even louder. "So much misfortune..."

"What is this for?" SiWok asked in amazement. "Crying is illogical."

"It may be so on planet Uoltan, but on Earth no woman can do without crying. Some can weep all day long. Lola, come on, give me the transfusion blood collection kit, a copper blood preservative, and a Proxilian stimulant. We must have a large supply if we want to save ArCer, and SiWok's organism will not be able to produce as much as needed without support."

LV.

"Has anyone ever used this stimulant?" Captain Zakrzevska asked Dr. Nbeba.

"Occasionally," he replied. "It puts a lot of strain on the liver and spleen, but SiWok is young and strong. He should endure it."

"Damn it. There is no other way?"

"There isn't. We have to get these damn nanites out. Trekovsky figured out how to do it, but I won't risk such an event without a blood supply. The apparatus may break down, there could be lack of energy, and who knows what else? We have to be ready for anything, and besides, there must be at least two liters of blood in the machine before it starts cleaning."

"How is this supposed to work?"

"On one side, there will be collecting and cleaning, and on the other, the return of already purified blood. As far as I know, no one has ever done such a thing to a Uoltan. Anything could happen."

"I know when your head is full of dreams. Now I dream that it will finally get boring, because at the moment it is too interesting."

Lilianna grumbled angrily, trying to cover her anxiety somehow. She was worried about ArCer, she was also worried about SiWok, a young boy who had already been through so much and who had already settled in 'Hermash' for good. Everyone liked him, because despite his typical Uoltanian features, he also had a lot of the usual joy of life as well as kindness to everyone. Contrary to the other Uoltans, he also didn't prance before the Earthlings, and that was a lot.

While both patients were transported to the infirmary where they were prepared for the final surgery, the science department worked on the implants removed from their bodies and on what their blood contained. It also turned out that despite eternal quarrels, slurs, and even fights, when it was needed, they could work there together, and very harmoniously. Professor Trekovsky, who of course was the head of the temporary team, rarely went to bed, as he was very excited about the riddle he encountered. After four days of hard work, however, he faded, a bit from fatigue, and a bit because he hadn't come to any conclusions. Having concluded that he wouldn't be able to figure out such an advanced technology with his methods, in the act of despair, he drank a bottle of "Hermashovka" in one fell swoop and finally went to sleep.

It was then that Andy Karpiel took up the problem and approached it from a completely different angle. Instead of analyzing the collected material, he treated the mysterious mechanisms as if they had been a biological threat - he checked how they reacted to different types of media. The whole science department mistrusted, but it soon turned out that there was a method in this madness. The nanites treated with the human blood medium visibly revived and began to attack the red blood cells, grabbing them and, as it were, armoring them with their microscopic protrusions. It seemed that they were not so much hurting as enslaving them. After some time, they began to send signals whose intended use was very intriguing to the entire science department. They couldn't decode them, and they wondered what that might have meant until Dr. Lemowa from the Data Processing Department came up with the idea of bringing the removed implants to the laboratory where the nanites were tested. It immediately turned out that the emitted signals were intended for them, which didn't solve the mystery of where they came from, but already gave some clues. The implants reacted with movement, sometimes with the extension of blades or some claws, as if they had wanted to do something, but without the support of their biological part, they couldn't.

"In my opinion, these nanites are only transmitters," said Andy. "They don't generate signals by themselves. Let's shield the test site well, and then we'll confirm it."

The team set to work and in a short time carefully screened the test box with lead plates, a reinforced force field and a standard cork.

"The cork will not help here," protested Trekovsky, who in the meantime managed to get enough sleep and, tormented by a monstrous hangover, returned to the research department.

"But it won't hurt either," Karpiel replied. The professor recognized the validity of such a reasoning and fell silent, waiting for the results of the experiment.

The effect turned out to be amazing. All transceiver activity died down, also movement inside the samples stopped. The blood cells infected with nanites were still alive, but looked catatonic, as if they had been waiting for something. The implants also lay still, like any other piece of scrap metal, and they didn't even think about sticking out their steel claws.

"So, we have the answer," concluded Karpiel. "The control is from the outside. I think we have enough materials to send the report to the Star Armada."

***

On the bridge, the first shift ended taking positions. The younger technician, Tekla Watery, was yawning at the engine room console, lazily checking the gauges, the steersmen Kubica and Deadskull were calibrating the thrust, and Arek was sitting in the command chair and eating a sandwich with white cheese ... or something that reminded it. Xavier Bequiet wondered at the communications console how to diplomatically notify Captain Zakrzevska that a response had come from the command, when Lilianna herself burst onto the bridge, still a little sleepy.

"Captain, it's good to see you," said Bequiet. "We already have the answer to our report on the ZONKs."

"How does it sound?"

"You see ... how could I put it ..."

"Gosh, man, talk brutally, don't hedge because I don't have time!"

"They wrote to us: We never laughed so much in life, stop. Congratulations on your imagination, stop. You should be writing fiction books for young people, not explore space, stop. As soon as you sober up, go to station 8, stop. There you will pick up your next task. Over and out," read Xavier, abandoning all diplomacy.

"What donkeys! Alright, it's their business, if they don't believe us," the captain snorted. "If they don't want to, let them not eat, I won't argue with them. Arek! Haven't you seen Malva Krencik here, darling?"

"No, and the communications room is empty too. She must have gone to the holo-room with Inga," replied the first mate, having swallowed the rest of his breakfast so violently that his eyes widened.

"Cool. And the helmsman is sitting on the bridge at the headphones. Where's Cadet T'enga?!"

"You mean our Pandorian? In the armory. Oh, here you have an application from Vasyl Zaychik to transfer her to snipers."

The captain had difficulty reading the scribbles of his armorer, who had made his request half in Roman and half Cyrillic, motivating it with the fact that in his current team of sharpshooters there was no one who would hit a barn from a mazer, and on the entire ship the only real sniper was the main navigator. He added that it was no wonder, since the unit assigned to him didn't consist of snipers at all, but of plain crewmen.

"I don't understand. So, what if they are plain? Would you prefer a team made of hunchbacks?" the captain muttered to herself as she studied Zaychik's report.

"No, he just prefers T'enga," Arek said, brushing off the crumbs carefully. "I think he desires her. I really don't know if it is not pedophilic, she is seventeen, and Zaychik is an old fogey."

"No, it's not, and don't cast such suspicions at all, Number One, because it's a shame. If nothing happens, please govern yourselves here for a while, I go to the infirmary. The shaman told me that today they are awakening our unlucky people."

There was understandably liveliness on the bridge. The condition of ArCer and Ensign Dysentery had been the main subject of rumors on all decks for four days, but what was passed on as the strict, proven truth, in most cases was pure nonsense. For example, engine room personnel claimed that ArCer and Dysentery were dead, and aboard had been brought androids clothed in their skin. The science department told with relish and horror that swarms of intelligent cockroaches had poured out of the bodies of their missing colleagues, and Father Toadstool stubbornly stuck to the version that both were possessed by hellish powers and that a shrine should have been built on the nearest planet to counter the expansion of evil. For this intention, he even carried out a fundraiser among the crew, and he was completely fine with the fact that it was not known what currency on this planet was respected.

Most of the crew didn't want to pay, claiming that it would be a construction lawlessness, for which they would be hit in the face from the inhabitants of the planet, so the priest came up with a bright idea to put up a chapel on an uninhabited planet.

"And who will pray there? Cats?" Charles Mikhalov asked carelessly, in response to which he heard that he was a wicked man, an iconoclast and a dissolute libertine.

The collection ended two minutes later when Sister Ophelia found out about everything. She categorically took the tray away from her brother, scolded him and told everyone who had let themselves to be persuaded to donate to come to the sacristy to take donations. Around evening, it was revealed that more people came than should have, so the ship's sacristy was currently in the red.

"And to think that the Planet Union is implementing a plan of introducing a completely cashless system ..." said Matias von Braun as the crew discussed the whole thing in the mess with delight over dinner.

"Then I don't know how the Vatican will survive it," said Mikhalov in a tone deprived of sympathy.

"The Vatican will cope, but how will the parish priests make it?" Malvinka Krencik wondered. This initiated a heated discussion that lasted until midnight board time, when Captain Zakrzevska entered the mess and chased everyone to sleep. It was no wonder that in the morning everyone, including her, overslept. Fortunately, the work of the infirmary wasn't affected by this.

LVI.

Dr. Nbeba decided to put both patients into a pharmacological coma for the time needed to regenerate the damaged organs. As he himself said, it was a painful process and it was better for the delinquents to sleep through it in peace of mind. He was also not sure how much their psyche had suffered, and he didn't want to find out. However, there was no medical reason to delay waking up both patients, especially that Captain Zakrzevska appeared and immediately started a hellish row that the proper procedure had not yet been started.

"What is this?!" she screamed, stamping her feet on the floor as loudly as if she had wanted to wake up her crewmen on her own, using traditional methods, not chemical stimulation. "You were supposed to start two hours ago! I was sure that I would find them on their feet!"

Doctor Zmiyevski tried to defend his friend, but as he was using rather vague arguments, the captain told him to go to hell and not make a "fool of his aunt". Then Nbeba, with his heart in his mouth, proceeded to awaken his patients.

He gave them the appropriate stimulant, put on pure oxygen, and watched the control boards, trying not to show his nervousness. After a few minutes, life entered both motionless bodies. Ensign Dysentery sat down and uttered a long, very complicated sentence, of which only the initial words "What the ..." were decent. ArCer gasped spasmodically at first and his readings indicated sudden bradycardia, but after a minute or so he recovered and sat down as well.

"Why is it so silent here?" he asked.

"Is he deaf in those pointy ears of his?" The captain looked at Nbeba, raising her eyebrows.

"He shouldn't," the doctor said, grabbing the scanner.

"I'm not deaf," ArCer assured them. "It's so quiet here, you can't hear anything."

"And what the hell would you like to hear? Because if a few words about you, I can scold you like Saint Michael, the devil," Lilianna politely offered him. "I won't lavish you."

The Uoltan cleared his throat.

"That's not the point, Captain ... I had the impression that I was in the midst of the constant presence of a whole collective of minds. I heard their thoughts and they heard mine. Now it is all gone."

"And that's very good. Yes, someone converted you and the ensign into transceiver machines, but we tried to remedy that. I hope you can tell me what actually happened.

"Our shuttle was brought aboard a flying combat station. Then we were injected with something and we lost track of time. Our bodies became strong, resilient, and our minds was emotionless and networked with others. If this collective is hostile to the Union, we will not survive."

"And is it hostile?"

"It has only just found out about it through us, and so far doesn't consider our technology worthy of attention. You know, the cube that caught us is like a research probe. Emits a fake call for help, constructed in a truly fascinating way. The appropriate rhythm of the currents creates such a digital code that, regardless of the race of creators and their language, each computer read it as a call for help. This enables them to study the creatures inhabiting this quadrant."

"Nice. And these headquarters fools don't believe us. We sent them a report of what happened to you, and they laughed at it."

"If such a cube reaches one of the Union planets, they will laugh in a sheepish voice, if you'll pardon the expression, captain," said Dysentery. "This civilization is a degeneration! Oh, oh, I've gone so numb ..."

He got up and, grimacing, began massaging his calves.

"Civilization or race, what do you think?" Captain asked ArCer.

"Civilization," the Uoltan replied firmly. "It is made up of representatives of various breeds, united into one swarm in the shape of a beehive. They act and think as one body with many tentacles. We were just such tentacles."

"Great," the captain muttered. "Okay, you guys are no longer tentacles, you are again yourselves, so go on duty. No more lying around and slacking off. We have to go to base eight, they have something for us there ... and we can leave TiShan there."

"Why?"

"Right, you don't know anything yet ... she had an accident, she's in the stasis chamber. I'm sorry to say this, Commander, but most likely neither she nor her child will survive."

ArCer silently considered for a moment what he heard. His Uoltanian mind didn't receive the news the way a human mind would have received, he was unfamiliar with despair and fear, but the captain saw the hint of feeling on his face and waited anxiously for what he would say.

"It is indeed an unfortunate event," he said finally, standing up. "Can I go to the bridge now?"

Lilianna was speechless for a moment.

"Yes," she replied after a moment.

"Go to the broken street if that's all you can say."

ArCer nodded stiffly to her and left the infirmary. Ensign Dysentery stared at him with his mouth open, then his look met that of the captain.

"What a cold motherfu..." the ensign finally choked up, without a trace of respect for the higher ranks.

"Just a Uoltan," sighed Dr. Nbeba. "It's sad, but they ... are completely heartless."

***

Space station eight glowed in a void like a jewel, lit by positional spot lights. Arek, who was on duty that day on the bridge, ordered the air traffic control to be called for the fifth time, but again, there was a deaf silence.

"Did they get drunk there or what?" he muttered to himself.

"It's unlikely," ArCer said from the science console. "The station commander is Commodore Walter Gibbs; he wouldn't have let that happen."

"Maybe the apparatus failed," suggested Tekla Watery, who was on duty at the engine room console. A huge bruise on her cheek reminded that the previous evening her husband had decided to make her marriage scene, and this time he was the aggressor. Captain Zakrzevska, with a typically female lack of objectivity, sent him to the arrest cell. Joe explained in vain that his wife had repeatedly punched him in the face as much as she could, and he had hit her only once, in vain he was also referring to equal rights. The captain said that on her ship no wife beater would beat his half, and Watery himself finally stopped protesting when he realized that he would have a nice rest from his wife and boring watches. He was lying in the cell now, reading Joe Alex's crime novels, and Tekla was on duty for him at the console, cursing like a sailor.

"I don't think, I would have any message about transmission errors," Malvinka said in a worried voice, trying to probe the silent apparatus of the station somehow.

"Traces of life?" Arek asked.

"It's peculiar, but I don't register any," ArCer replied without taking his eyes off the scanner. "Either this station is extinct, or something no less strange is happening there."

Arek meditated for a moment, looked at the textbook for senior officers just in case, then called Captain Zakrzevska.

"What the hell do you want?!" the captain's contralto bellowed angrily over the loudspeaker. The characteristic background noise clearly indicated that Lilianna was either taking a shower or bathing Bear. Loud whines and reassuring purrings of the helmswoman Veronika let them know after a while that it was the latter. Usually, such an operation had to be performed by two people, because one person couldn't cope with a big like a bear and playful sheepdog.

"Captain, I'm sorry to disturb you, but we have something strange here," Arek reported humbly. "The station looks completely dead. I don't like it ..."

"I'll be there soon."

Within a few minutes, Captain Zakrzevska, visibly concerned about the whole situation, got on the bridge. Behind her, wet as a not heavenly creature, burst Bear, braked in the middle with all four paws and shook himself vigorously, spraying water on everything and everyone. As the owner of long and thick hair, he was able to do it exceptionally generously and usually wasn't embarrassed.

"What a maggot!" Mstislaw Deadskull shouted, wiping the steering console with his sleeve. "Captain, with all due respect, what are you doing?!"

"Nothing unusual," replied Lilianna, unshaken. "We had to bathe him because he entered the engine room and got dirty with grease. Veronika and I scrubbed him for an hour, first with the deactivator, then with the shampoo ... Go to your mistress, canine son!"

Bear explained to himself the captain's scream in his own way, because he lay down on his back and started waving his paws in the air, opening his shaggy mouth in a broad, doggy smile. Lilianna shrugged and turned to Arek:

"What's up, First?"

"I don't know what. The station is not responding. The positional lights function properly, there are no visual warnings anywhere, alarm signals are also absent ... The scanners are not picking up life signals at the station."

'Hermash', what do you say?" Lilianna asked, sinking into the command chair with such force that she almost broke the railing.

The on-board computer gurgled, coughed, and replied in a creaking baritone:

"Queen, I've been trying to communicate with the station's computer for a quarter of an hour, but it's some mechanical idiot. He constantly demands authorization from the K-8 commander and refuses to acknowledge the explanation that if he disappeared, no cosmic force would obtain that authorization."

He was clearly offended and embittered by the unworthy behavior of his mechanical kin.

Lilianna thought for a moment about contacting the command, but decided that she wouldn't "run to daddy" with every little issue and commanded:

"We're not docking yet. Keep the synchronous orbit. Safety protocol as in an emergency. Lieutenant Mayher, you will appoint a reconnaissance party. Let it report to the transport hall, I'll be there in a moment."

"Ya ..." ArCer began, straightening up.

"Ja, Ja, natürlich," the captain interrupted him. "You stay, you are not in shape yet. And don't protest, or I will reprimand you and hang on the relaxation deck!"

ArCer stiffened.

"Armada's regulations prohibit death sentences," he said coldly.

"I will hang a rebuke, dammit, not you. The ceilings are too low anyway," growled Lilianna. "Arek, you rule on the bridge until my return. Please keep an eye on everything and everyone."

LVII.

Generally, Union Planet space stations were busy and noisy. These where the places where people hosted and dispatched ships, traded small things, held informal diplomatic talks and social meetings, but above all, these places were a true breeding ground for various intrigues and 'the buzz', as Johnnie Caterpillar used to say. Through each such station went petty politicians, traders, tourists, thugs, bounty hunters, spies and vagabonds, various blue birds from the associated and non-associated planets. So, it is understood that such a creature must have efficient administration, strong security and a manager who could keep everything in the hollow of his or her hand. Usually, the station supervisor was some Star Armada captain who, for reasons beyond their control, lost the ship and had no chance of getting a new one, although it was not a legal rule. However, attempts to fill this position with civilians usually resulted in great confusion.

"There must simply be someone who can show the whole company who's boss," General Jaruzelski said a long time ago to the young lieutenant Zakrzevska. "Civilians can't get such a respect."

In the exploratory team, as Mayher called selected people, there were: ensign Caterpillar, who was explained with great difficulty that he couldn't take either the ferret or a shepherd's axe with him, SiWok as a medic (assigned to the infirmary, he absorbed knowledge like a sponge and was seriously starting thinking about medical studies), two security guys, Pandorian T'enga, and Second Officer Jürgen.

"Why did you assign Janicek there?" asked Matias von Braun, when having dispatched the unit, Mayher came to him for a portion of his favorite paprikash. "He is a scout like a goat ass reisentasche[27] ..."

"Because of Lilka," Christopher replied. "She always goes where it's dangerous, so it would be better if a bodyguard was with her. With Johnnie, she won't die. He can beat the entire platoon himself and not even get out of breath."

"That's true, a man like a wardrobe. But you know what? I'd rather not be the one to get in our captain's way. She looks like Thumbelina's younger sister, but heck, a concussion grenade isn't too big either ..."

Christopher nodded without a trace of irony. He thought that if Matias had seen the captain in training, shooting with him at practice robots and tearing through the primal jungle in a

---

[27] *(Ger)* Travel bag.

survival time rally, his respect for her would have been even greater.

The captain herself, contrary to her announcement, had not yet reached the transport hall. For on the way, she thought it would be worth asking Professor Trekovsky about the progress of work on the Clingorgian torpedo, and she strayed to the research section.

"Professor, do we have something about the contraption the Clingorgs shot at us?" she asked, entering the studio, where Marzena Szkwał, bitter and twisted, weighed the reagents for the experiments of her supervisor.

"We do," said Trekovsky. "Herring ear and vest sleeves. Give me some Clingorg here, and I will get the truth out of him ... but from the data we have, no reasonable theory can be put together. Not even a conspiracy. The Clingorgs couldn't possess such weapons. It had never been used by anyone before, and none of those I contacted could tell me anything meaningful about it."

Lilianna nodded understandingly.

"So, you don't know shit?" she made sure.

"If only that ... Our main swell made a sketch of a device that could produce a similar effect. The problem is, it would have to be larger than a Miracle-class ship, and built of materials not found on any of the Empire's planets."

"So, the Clingorgs just stole this detail from someone."

"They stole, bought, exchanged for something ... there are many possibilities, but I would like to know, how do you imagine further investigation in this case?"

Unfortunately, this question wasn't answered.

***

The transfer to the station turned out to be unexpectedly complicated. The transporter was secured with a code that no one present could deactivate, but the technician Lalevich worked it out soon, without changing his usual, sleepy expression even for a moment. Thanks to his efforts, the team was finally at the station and could start stubbornly looking for anyone with whom it could talk.

Unfortunately, there was no soul at the station. Captain Zakrzevska found out about it after several hours of searching the extensive structure from the monitoring center. All the cameras showed empty rooms, tools abandoned at workplaces, cups with half-finished coffee, half-eaten sandwiches, browsers open on handheld computers ... Water poured into one of the bathtubs, music played here and there, the holoroom over and over again played the same fragment of relaxation program with dancing Pornion girl in the lead role.

On the hangar deck, there were all the shuttles, which were the station's equipment, and a dozen or so foreign ships, including a tiny fighter of unknown class, one-man, but armed like a military battleship. It aroused great interest from the technicians who examined it thoroughly and to the general delight translated the name painted on its side as "Bastard 1". The pilot was nowhere to be seen, but there was something on the console that they initially mistook for a flashlight, which turned out to be a laser cutlass, a tool as elegant as it was dangerous in the hands of a trained warrior. They watched it with admiration, tried it, and then put it back.

The only living objects that appeared on the screens in the control room were people from 'Hermash' searching the station, more and more confused and minute by minute more succumbing to the mood of horror. Zakrzevska watched them with a vague feeling that some ghoul would pop up out of nowhere and attack the recon, but nothing like that happened. The station was indeed abandoned, not even a poor rat remained. Lilianna felt by analogy like Winnie the Pooh, who the more he looked into the hut, the more Piglet was not there.

"We will have to check the logs," she said to herself at last and started sending to the main library of 'Hermash' all the monitoring records. Then she went in search of the station commander's office. She found it on the main level, wide open. There was a little mess inside, the desk was littered with padds and cookie wrappers, one of the drawers was half-open, and there was an almost empty bottle of Johnny Walker gin stuck endways in it. As in other rooms, everything here gave the impression that the user of the office had only left for a moment. The personal quarters of the commander were very similar, except that there was a nice pile of skin mags on the couch, and in the corner, there was a glass case with a whole set of erotic gadgets. In the opposite corner there was a well-stocked bar.

"Oh man ..." muttered Lilianna, looking at this collection with slightly widened eyes. Commodore Walter Gibbs must have been an extremely entertaining guy, and surely the women under his command couldn't complain about the lack of variety in the boring service on the station.

Having taken her eyes off the glass case, Captain Zakrzevska noticed the recorder with Walter Gibbs' personal notes lying on the desk. It was open for editing - the commodore apparently had made a record when had happened, what had happened. Lilianna touched the "Back" button and rewound it a bit. Then she pressed the "Play" button. A slightly hoarse, yet seductive baritone flowed from the small device:

"...are finishing renovation of the fourth section. Lieutenant Kaori doesn't neglect the training of her subordinate personnel. Her commitment is exceptionally evident. She scheduled internal station defense exercises on Tuesday. I will have to..."

Here the record stopped suddenly and simply. There were no grinding, screeching, shots or other suspicious sounds, just silence filled with white noise. With the disappearance of the commodore's voice, also the audible, albeit faint cacophony of background station sounds died away. Whatever had happened, had happened everywhere at the same time.

"Some dybbuk kidnapped them or what?" Lilianna left the quarters and bumped into running Johnnie, who screamed out of fear and only after a while regained his composure.

"It's ghastly in dis playks," he excused himself in a tremulous voice. "Mys, you aren't afrayn of anytin?"

"Yes, of anytin," Lilianna assured him. "Stick to me, Johnnie, and you won't die."

Despite making up with her expression, Captain Zakrzevska felt extremely uncomfortable in this empty station, especially since she couldn't understand what had happened there. The only clue that could explain anything seemed to be the dancing Pornion holoprogram. According to the technical passport, it had been added just two days before the station crew had disappeared, and not by one of the technicians but by the cook. That is why there was the loop - the cook was probably not the best at programming.

"I'll try to do something about it," SiWok said, and set to work while the rest finished a detailed scan of the station.

"I would advise you to notify the high command," Jürgen said to Lilianna when he came to report to her. "It's not normal."

"You are right, it's not. Please go to the communications room and report to headquarters," the captain replied. "With it, please send all communications logs and the official ship's log to HQ. When can we expect an answer?"

"Not sooner than three or four hours at this distance."

"We will continue to investigate on our own. Maybe we will find something."

"I already have something," T'enga said, with her blue antennae wagging with excitement. "Unusual ionization on all decks. The reading is interpreted by the decoder as a piezoelectric anomaly."

For Captain Zakrzevska it sounded like an abracadabra, so she failed to make a wise face.

"I don't think ions kidnapped them ..." she muttered uncertainly, scratching her crown.

"Maybe it's a trace of a transporter beam, such unusual one?" SiWok said, continuing to work on the holoroom circuits. "Pornions sometimes use one to kidnap people right from the decks of their ships."

"Nonsense, the station covers wouldn't allow something like this ... although, right, they could modify their equipment. This Pornion girl made you come up with this idea?"

"No, I somehow remembered that." SiWok switched some circuit and suddenly the projection was cut off, something hissed, and then in the center of the holoroom cabin the scantily clad, black-haired Pornion girl appeared, the same as in the holoprogram, but very alive - and very nervous.

"What a surprise!" Johnnie exclaimed with joyful amazement. "A girl like that lettuce leaf!"

The dancer wasn't exactly "like lettuce", her skin was rather greyish-green, but no one could have any doubts about her race.

It is true that the inhabitants of the planet Cronus also boasted green skin, but with a more pronounced color, and their hair was pigmentless, white, almost transparent.

The Pornion girl looked around fearfully, but seeing only the members of the scout, she clearly calmed down.

"Vint and Tevint are not here?" she asked distrustfully.

"Who?" Captain Zakrzevska stared at her. The meeting with the Pornions had long vanished from her head and she had no connection with these two names now. However, SiWok had a better memory.

"Your husbands met us a while ago," he replied. "But they flew their way, and we flew ours. Do you know what happened here?"

"Not really. Mr. Delany hid me in the holographic program so that they wouldn't find me," the girl replied, and her beautiful eyes suddenly became as large as saucers and pleading. "They were headed for the station. Please don't hand me over to these two pigs."

LVIII.

The beautiful brunette with green and gray skin looked from one to the other with her pleading eyes. Everyone was scratching their heads involuntarily, as if they had gotten pediculosis, only Johnnie stared at the Pornion girl in silent delight. It was obvious that she made an electrifying impression on him.

"And, Captain?" asked one of the security ensigns at last. "What will we do about it?"

Lilianna shrugged angrily.

"I don't know, damn it! The two Shreks that were chasing her didn't seem doveish to me, but I don't think they were behind the sudden desertion of the station. It's not even that the Pornions don't have the necessary technology at their disposal, because maybe they have ... but their ships were too small to cram so much of such a boisterous nation into them..."

"Captain, I'm reporting that Johnnie Caterpillar is staring at this rusalka like a magpie, at a bone," said the other ensign venomously. By the way, it turned out that, despite appearances, he was a hundred percent woman, because hardly any man would have had such a sonorous soprano.

"Johnnie, mind your manners. Ensign, no denunciations, please," the captain said mechanically and turned back to the Pornion girl. "What's your name, my child?"

"Gayla."

"Great. Don't make such a scared face. I assure you that your husbands can kiss my ass. If you don't want to be with them, make an official request for asylum in writing, and that's sorted for me."

"But I can't write!"

"We'll handle it. You really don't know what might have happened here?"

The girl calmed down a bit.

"I don't know, ma'am. But ...I know Vint traded with some strange creatures who sold him a few weapons. He told Tevint that no one in the Alpha Quadrant had such a weapon and that he would make a fortune from them."

Jürgen, usually reserved, made a loud appeal to a representative of a certain profession, not very respected on Earth.

"Did your husband trade with the Clingorgs?" he asked.

"With anyone who wanted to pay," Gayla assured him.

"And those freaks he bought weapons from ... you don't know who they were?"

"I have no idea."

"And do you even know what they looked like?"

"Yes, I watched them. They were ... funny. They had huge heads, eyes like black glass lanterns, and very small lips ... and they walked around naked."

"Azgartes!" T'enga shouted fearfully.

"Nonsense, Azgartes don't exist," protested Lilianna uncertainly.

"How can you say they don't exist if their weapons sent us out of the galaxy? They got to us through the Spatial Gate and saved the Earth from Govalds, you know, such bullies that pretended to be the ancient gods."

"Oh man," the captain thought deeply. "I thought Azgartes died gloriously along with the Govalds ... that's what we were taught."

"As you can see, they're extinct, but not necessarily," the security tomboy said. "But why did they suddenly start trading in arms? After all, they were peaceful."

The question hung in the air like the sword of Damocles. Only SiWok broke the silence:

"It means that what the Clingorgs fired at us was the ZM!"

"What is it?" Johnnie didn't understand.

"Zero module. A technology that was superficially known to some of our ancestors, but got lost. It wasn't from our galaxy ... and neither were Azgartes."

"What does all this have to do with the station?" asked the highlander in a gawky way.

"That's what we need to find out," Lilianna sighed. "Everyone to work. Get a research team here. We won't leave until we learn something. I'll arrange it with HQ."

"And me?" Gayla asked timidly.

The captain looked at her and smiled warmly.

"For now, I invite you on board Hermash," she said. "Then we'll think about what to do next."

***

While examining all the records from the station and digging through the Armada database, Captain Zakrzevska finally came to the irresistible conclusion that despite the words of the Pornion girl, the mysterious creatures couldn't be the semi-legendary Azgartes. Too much didn't add up. First of all, the specification of their devices didn't match what happened to the 'Hermash' crew, and secondly, no one had yet managed to prove, even theoretically, that the events recorded in the databases had taken place. There was no trace of the technology that was said to have been available, except for one single exhibit at the Museum of the Unexplained Things, exhibit that might have as well been an ordinary counterfeit.

In turn Jürgen, who analyzed the records, found something very interesting. There were once travelers of unknown races at the station, about which there were left unclear records, so Lilianna led by her instinct told him to focus on them. At first, the second mate found this nonsensical, but soon changed his mind.

"The more I think about it, the more these Azgartes don't match," he said.

"Das ist nicht gut,[28] but I don't know what we're dealing with. You're right, let's focus on those guys who couldn't be identified here."

He leaned over the desktop and carefully studied the biometrics of the beings noted as Ostrem, Saga, and Yoghen. German accuracy, often ridiculed on board, brought unexpected, surprising fruits. In the fourth hour of work, Jürgen let out a piercing cry, somewhat reminiscent of the Mescalero

---

[28] *(Ger)* It's not good.

Apache's war howl, which brought all the reconnaissance team to the headquarters.

"Why are you pointing at me?" he asked in surprise as everyone burst into the control room with their weapons unlocked.

"Are you really asking?" Johnnie got upset. "You screamed like an attacked goat! We thought you saw something ..."

"Sorry," the second officer reflected. "But I actually noticed something wunderlich!"[29]

"Then come on," the captain urged.

"This is the biometric data registered in the port next to the station. And here are data from individual sensors on the station. Please see how they differ from each other. And here we have a complete rarity: the measurements of an individual known as Yoghen. Those from the port differ from those from the recreational deck by more than twenty-five percent!"

All heads bent over the panel, studying Jürgen's comparisons. Indeed, the results were astounding, and they certainly didn't match anything they knew.

At first, I thought it was a measurement apparatus error, but then I looked through the camera records and found something interesting."

---

[29] *(Ger)* Wonderful.

He played a record from the week earlier, six o'clock, the station's internal time. The transcript showed Saga, a woman resembling a golden-skinned Corredian, entering the bathroom, and then emerging from it as a perfectly normal Earthwoman. Were it not for the unusual clothes she was wearing, even perceptive Jürgen would have thought that the Earthly girl had been in the bathroom before the Corredian girl and had left first.

"They're a race of shapeshifters ..." Captain Zakrzevska said, opening her eyes wide. "I read about such on Earth, but it was SF literature, not serious studies."

"And we have our mysterious Azgartes," SiWok said with what seemed like disappointment. He, too, had heard of these legendary visitors from another galaxy and was very curious about them.

"What does this mean for us, Mr. SiWok?"

"That we don't know much, Captain. There are legends about this breed as about the Azgartes. Apparently, they are able to take any form, which means that they can personate whoever they want. There is no data as to their home world, culture, technology, intentions ..."

"One thing seems certain: they could take on the figures Gayla saw, and we can assume with a high degree of probability that it was them who sold to the Pornions the weapons from which the Clingorgs hit us. But the question is, what do they have to do with the disappearance of all staff and all station guests?"

SiWok spread his hands helplessly. He didn't know that.

*****

ArCer repeated his pleas every now and then, finally descended to pleading. He had an illogical but strong feeling that he would solve the riddle of the deserted station, and finally the captain, tired of his intrusiveness, allowed him to send himself to the station together with Professor Trekovsky and the reference laboratory. Anyway, she came to the conclusion that it would probably not get any worse.

Dinoslav Trekovsky unfolded his equipment and went around all the rooms of the station, hung with scanners and meters like an abstract parody of a Christmas tree. It took quite a long time and caused a lot of confusion, as the professor either gave out shouts of joy when something matched his earlier theories, or alternately, disappointed, cursed at the top of his voice like a Legia fan during an unlucky match. Finally, he demanded that everyone except ArCer leave the station because they were interfering with his tests. Since the reconnaissance team was fed up with the ghastly place, the captain gave the appropriate orders and both scientists were left alone.

While they were working, beautiful Gayla aroused an understandable sensation on board Hermash, much more than the mysterious beings noticed by Jürgen on the recordings. They were not known where, and the green-skinned beauty was around - a dazzling beauty in skimpy Pornion slave clothes, and in addition very nice and eager to make new friends. The captain let her run freely around the ship, so she sightsaw it with the curiosity of a child in an amusement park, and she was ubiquitous.

"What are we going to do with her?" Arek asked skeptically when the captain finally appeared on the bridge. "After all, we can't take her with us, because in what capacity?"

"Relax, we'll just leave her on some other station," Lilianna assured him. "For now, we just need to explain what happened on this one."

"Ya vam gavariu, shto eto niechystiy biznes,"[30] growled Vasyl Anecdotych, saying goodbye three times from right to left. "Some dybbuk kidnapped them ..."

"You're talking nonsense, Zaychik," the captain interrupted, dissatisfied.

She had reasons to be in a bad mood. She faced the difficult task of making a credible report of it all. In the headquarters, they perceived her reports badly anyway, because they usually contained various strange facts that no one could believe in, and the collected evidence was so far in the 'Hermash' warehouses ...

Just in case, she demanded a connection with the command.

"The station is deserted," she said bluntly. "Is there anything known about it?"

---

[30] *(Rus)* I'm telling you; it is a dirty matter.

"It is known that it fell silent," said Vice Admiral Armadi, Senior Pandorian Nellen, thoughtfully waving his left tentacle. "We also know that the ship "Queren", of the Intrepid class, was hijacked just from this station and no trace of it has been found. Commander Gibbs' last report concerned just the disappearance of this ship. Then everything fell silent."

"What was that report, Vice Admiral?"

"Wait, I have it somewhere ... Oh, here it is. *'Queren moved towards Procyon's system and reached the warp speed before we could send scouts after it. Our summons remained unanswered."*

"A fine kettle of fish ... has something been done about it?"

"Two ships were sent there, 'Tsiolkovsky' and 'Hubble', both of te Miracle class. We are waiting for their reports. You take care of the station. Try to find out as much as possible."

"We'll do our best," Lilianna promised, suppressing a sigh of desperation. "Vice Admiral, I would like to point out something before I turn off myself: there are some Aliens wandering around the Union, trading unclassified weapons. They are probably from outside the cataloged sectors and some traces indicate that they are able to freely change their appearance."

"Do they have any identifying marks?"

"We only know that they are two males and a female. They may be humanoid, but we don't know what their original form looks like and how to recognize them. However, we know that they can also take the form of creatures from legends. It seems they don't quite know who really existed and who didn't."

Captain Zakrzevska uttered the last words a little slower, that was what tormented her - she suddenly understood that these mysterious newcomers simply had stumbled upon the image of an Azgart somewhere in documents or virtual records and were convinced that such creatures existed among civilizations of this quadrant which knew each other. And that meant they weren't well informed.

LIX.

Inga Lausch and Malvinka Krencik knocked on the door of the captain's quarters, ignoring the sign "Please ring, knocking broken". It was only when no one answered their knocking that they came up with the idea of pressing the bell, which resonated across the entire corridor with a sound that resembled a steel hammer hitting a cast-iron pipe. Immediately after that the loudspeaker clanged:

"Come in!" The captain shouted, and the door lock was deactivated.

Lilianna was kneeling by the cage Johnnie had built for Gizia, and was changing the litter. The ferret was playing cheerfully on her back and head, and the common marmoset sat on the table eating something pressed. The monkey, belonging to the Watery couple, often visited other quarters, and of this one she was especially fond. She didn't do this because of the constant quarrels of her masters, but simply because by nature she was very social and liked people.

"What's up, miss?" the captain asked, glancing kindly at both girls. Inga nudged Malvinka in her side and they both started simultaneously:

"Captain, we would like to ... We mean ..."

The girls fell silent, communicated with their eyes and Malvinka, alone, finished:

"... because we know what the Clingorgs really hit us with."

The captain turned to face them, amazed. How is it, these two butterflies solved a puzzle that almost made the entire science department have a heart attack?

"Did you investigate the torpedo remnants?" she asked.

"No, we are not familiar with torpedoes. We checked computers, that is, data banks, logs, everything."

"And what did you find there?"

"Viruses. Lots of viruses that didn't exist before. All Clingorgian ones and all very hard to detect. We found them only because we assumed their presence and searched stubbornly like a maniac. Captain, do you remember what Mikhalov said? That the computers in the engine room got the wrong program. Well, it was from this torpedo, just like the others. They haven't been activated so far because we haven't performed the operations that trigger them."

"Right," Inga agreed with her friend. "For example, one of them would infect our defense system if we recalibrated the deflectors, and the other was to take over the defense system. It's just that it was triggered by the auto-sight sequence code, and our snipers were aiming manually."

"Indeed, Zaychik said something about the fact that our automatic sights were useless and he was supposed to repair them, but he didn't do it ... The deflectors have also never been recalibrated, because it is a job of Greg and his lodger, SyTar, and they are both lazy asses ... one from Earth, the other from Uoltan, but together they avoid work as if they were brothers."

"It will be all to the good, Captain."

"It seems so." Lilianna looked at the ceiling for some reason and said aloud: 'Hermash', can you hear me?"

"Of course, angel," replied the computer's drunk baritone.

"Listen carefully: until further notice, don't load any program except those that are running. Regardless of who orders you to do so. You only listen to me."

"It's clear as a nuclear reaction, sweetheart."

"Doesn't this familiar tone irritate you a bit?" Malvinka asked.

"I'm used to it. Girls, go back to HQ and try to deactivate as many viruses as you can. Write down their configuration, it'll come in handy for the summary report ... and send me Karpiel here if he's sober."

Left alone, Lilianna wrote in the logbook:

"Beyond all doubt, the mysterious torpedo of unknown type was not the Module Zero, as originally assumed, but a computer capable of aggressively broadcasting parasitic programs."

That, she decided, was enough for now. She left the more detailed preparation of the report for later, when she had the results from the research department.

Andrew Karpiel came to the commander's quarters several minutes later. As he explained, he was overseeing a very important experience and really couldn't show up right away. He looked sober, so Lilianna decided not to go into it and went straight to the point:

"What did your department find about the torpedo that sent us somewhere to hell?"

Karpiel scratched his head and squinted. There were little remnants of the torpedo there and, to tell the truth, he had disregarded them so far, as they looked so much like ordinary slag.

"Burned carbides," he said finally. "There was nothing left that could tell us something specific ... or more precisely, we didn't deal with it, there was always so much work..."

"Tell me so and don't hedge ... So, you just put the evidence on the shelf. From your words, I deduce that, despite the lack of progress in this area, your department worked on other matters. For example, on what?"

"Well ... on this and that ..." Andy became entangled and quickly added animatedly: "And now, in turn, we are examining the nanoprobes removed from the bodies of Dysentery and ArCer and we have just discovered something absolutely amazing!"

"Why are you pulling the wool over my eyes?" the captain huffed, but then asked right after: "What is this discovery? But if it turns out that it is some new, sensational kind of coffin varnish, I will have you and Johnnie drowned in the mash!"

The terrible threat didn't make any special impression on Karpiel, especially since he was barely listening.

"Well, we studied these nanomachines, isolated from the blood of ArCer and Dysentery," he reported excitedly. "And they can be freely programmed! We don't quite know how, but they can. If we enter Mrs. TiShan's genetic code into them instead of the program they currently have, and then inject her with a good portion of it, then they should repair all the damage! Do you understand? TiShan and her baby will be able to recover!"

The news was indeed good, but Lilianna Zakrzevska didn't show the enthusiasm that the science officer had hoped for. Of course, it was impossible not to notice that the possibility of healing the Uoltanian doctor, discovered by Karpiel, impressed her, but the captain only nodded her head restrainedly.

"It is very interesting, but can you predict the effect of such treatment?" she asked after a moment. "I really want TiShan to be alive and healthy, and to give birth to a healthy baby with bat ears, but if you give her what turned ArCer and Dysentery into cyborgs, now she may start talking about fusion, pointless resistance, etc."

Andy clearly flagged and faded like a trampled cigarette.

"It is indeed a problem," he admitted. "However, I think that it doesn't work so well without the cooperation of implants, which we won't implant in her. Besides, before we start the operation, we will remove the old program. My team is already working on it.

"We'll think," the captain promised him. "Go back there and get to work."

When Karpiel, clearly in a bad mood, dragged himself out of her quarters, Lilianna pondered what she heard for a moment, and then summoned Malvinka Krencik.

"Malva, I have a request for you," she said. "Send a secret message to Superprice, to Mr. Spox. Tell him I need to contact him urgently."

"Man, sure!" Malvinka called, and lowered her voice. "The captain can count on me ... As for these matters, I can be of help, after all, I have already double-crossed my three husbands."

"Eh, it's not about 'these matters'... you have only one thing in your head. Anyway, write cleverly to Spox to get in touch with me on the coded personal channel, but keep mum, understood?"

"Sure, my lips are sealed!"

Malvinka jumped out of the captain's quarters, glad as hell that something was going on. On the way, she ran into the Arek, who was just returning from the mess, chewing an exorbitant toasted sandwich. As a result of the collision, half of the tasty food flew to the floor, and right away rushed to it a semi-automatic cleaning machine and Bear, which waited for such a turn of events from the very beginning. Bear was faster. He grabbed the sandwich, growled with a bass at the machine, and ran away so no one would take his loot from him.

"Can't you be careful?" Arek snapped.

"What is this rape about?" replied Mrs. Krencik. "After eating what is left, even a hippo would be full!"

"Who's raping whom?" exclaimed Maura Gvizdak, who was just passing by with a security patrol.

"Nobody rapes, who would be willing anyway?" Arek shrugged and shoved another piece of sandwich into his mouth.

"Well, it can be different," said Maura sternly. "Mrs. Krencik, are you molested by the senior officer?"

"No, usually only by Johnnie Caterpillar, but he always salutes me at the same time." Malvinka replied cheerfully and ran towards her cabin. And Arek ate the sandwich, wiped his hands on his uniform and headed for the bridge, where he should have been already twenty minutes earlier.

LX.

Arek was welcomed by a slight commotion. Inga Lausch and Joe Watery argued fiercely, and the two helmsmen and T'enga listened to them with great interest. There was no one in the command seat, and, listening to the argument, the first mate concluded that it was about which of the two was to take the prestigious seat. He settled the dispute by sitting himself on it.

"Report," he demanded briefly.

"We keep a synchronous orbit," reported Aśka Kubica. "So far, peace and quiet. No ship within sensor range."

"The intercept?"

"Nothing special. Half an hour ago, I heard Captain McDaniels asking about the ninth sector maps, and Commander Larp replied that he wasn't his messenger ... and that's pretty much it," Inga replied, sitting down at the console with a grumpy face.

"I know this Larp, he is an acquaintance of my parents," T'enga said. "Awful hothead, it's better not to get in his way."

"From what I've heard, it is better not to accost Pandorians at all," said Joe Watery, reluctantly returning to his seat at the engine room console.

"You heard right," T'enga said proudly, and leaned over the science scanner. Recently, she begged a place for herself among Andy Karpiel's staff and began to seriously prepare for astrophysical studies.

Aśka Kubica, disappointed by the interruption of the merry spectacle, came back sluggishly to penetrating the nearest space and almost immediately noticed something interesting - a ship of undefined specification, which was just entering the range of the sensors.

"Oh shit, we have company!" she exclaimed excitedly.

"What?" Arek asked aggressively, moving his head up violently. He had dozed off, and was actually very unhappy to be roused from his good state.

"I don't know. It is a bit reminiscent of the Kurosawa class, but the signature of the energy is not Union, neither Clingorgian nor Cumulan, it doesn't remind me of anything at all."

"Aśka, you associate everything with the bed or related things ... throw this signature on the command console, I will look at it myself."

"Voyeur," said Miss Kubica and carried out the order.

The First Officer studied the readings, and his face grew longer and longer as he looked through the rows of numbers and symbols. The unit wandering somewhere within the sensor range was something completely unknown, not included in the databases, at least it seemed to be something like that.

"What the hell is that?" he exclaimed finally, losing hope that he would understand anything.

There was a hoarse chuckle across the bridge.

"Why won't you ask me?" the on-board computer inquired.

"What?"

"Nothing. Let me give you a hint: we have already encountered a similar ship. Even two."

Everyone, puzzled, looked around, trying to understand what 'Hermash' meant. Finally, Arem sighed deeply and announced:

"I give up."

"Make a little more effort, lover. Who has come to you recently on board?"

"Pornions! Those two who shot us at the time!" Aśka shouted, turning away from the controls. "They want Gayla back!"

"No way, at most they will get a slap in the face," Veronika was indignant. "Maybe we'll hit them with torpedo right away, huh? Mr. Mayher will be glad he can shoot."

"Wait, miss, what an idea ... Our captain has to make a decision," Arek chilled her.

"The captain's link is blocked," Inga reported. "She's talking to someone, probably on some hellishly important topic, because she has coded all the ways of access."

The first mate thought deeply.

"It's good," he decided finally. "They're not bothering us yet. And when they start, we'll show them Kozakievich's gesture."

"Commander, I dutifully report that it's impossible. Kozakievich is in the infirmary because he was hit with a lever by Jola Stern," Watery interjected, having misinterpreted what Arek had said.

"For what?"

"He patted her, so to speak, on the back ham as she bent down to get the dropped probe, and then said: 'Who bends over, is an offender'. He hit him so strongly that he immediately lost his creditworthiness and operational liquidity."

Watery's voice sounded appreciative. Waldek Kozakievich, a mechanic and sniper in one, was known for his strength and hard head, and Jolka Stern didn't seem to be a wrestler.

"It doesn't matter. Veronika, raise the covers."

"Not in front of Joe, he's married!"

"Inga, please keep your nose in your console and don't confuse, if you please!" Arek shouted angrily. "Raise the shields, yellow alarm!"

***

Locked in her quarters, Captain Zakrzevska didn't hear the alarm. The on-board computer decided there was no reason to disturb her for the time being and sent no signal to her console, and she herself conferred fiercely on the coded link with Spox and paid no attention to anything. Lonely Johnnie Caterpillar wandered on the decks in the company of Bear as well as Gizia, who sat on his shoulder and watched everything with her eyes round like beads. He didn't have anything to do now, and to make matters worse, he was getting tired of longing for his native Polish Highlands. His mood deteriorated minute by minute, and finally he descended into the engine room with a firm resolve to check that fresh moonshine kept the percent at a decent level. The moonshine equipment, assembled in the spare storage room, worked, even so well that one fine day it exploded, frightening the second shift staff and the accidental patrol out of their wits. The engineers quickly repaired the damage and advised not to talk about anything to the captain, fearing that she would also explode and order them to dismantle the 'fountain of life'.

Currently, only Greg Brzenchyshchykievich was in the engine room, as the drive was idle and the rest of the shift took a break. Greg was drowsily walking around his kingdom and arguing in an undertone with SyTar, somehow very active and in a malicious mood.

"Officer, why are you running here like a Jew in an empty shop?" Johnnie was kindly interested. "You are here alone? And the rest, where is?"

"They left for fifteen minutes ..."

"Then they'll be back soon.

"... an hour and a half ago. And you, what, are you bored, do you have nothing to do?"

Johnnie scratched his thick hair in embarrassment, accidentally bumping his elbow against the plasma lines pressure regulation lever. There was a roar in the lines, the frightened highlander recoiled and stepped onto Bear's paw, which screamed excruciatingly and tripped him.

"Be careful, Mr. Beautiful, this is not a sheep herd," Brzenchyshchykievich scolded Johnnie, repairing the damage. "It's easy to make a lot of shit in the engine room when you don't know what you grab."

"I didn't want to ... Officer, I just wanted to have a look at our machine. Bear, don't yell, give me that leg," Johnnie carefully examined the sheepdog's paw, which considered this evidence of concern as a sufficient remedy for his injury, as he licked Johnnie's face and barked happily.

"At the machine? It works like gold, I adjusted the radiator yesterday," Greg beamed. "Come on, it should have dripped half the demijohn by now."

It maybe wasn't half the demijohn yet, but it was enough to make both men smile. They hurriedly poured the moonshine into the prepared bottles and stared at them against the light.

"Like a crystal," said Greg appreciatively. "What do you think, Johnnie, should I make some cognac? Two bottles? We still have some of this onion husk extract."

"There will be color from it, but we won't get the smell," noted the highlander prudently. "I wish we found at least one bedbug somewhere ..."

"There's no way we find it. We need to talk to Andy, let him get some ester for us ..."

"Aster?"

"Not aster, but ester. I don't know if any edible chemical smells like a bedbug, but maybe, who knows. We would have a cognac like a dream."

"When my mother sowed coriander in the garden, it smelled of bedbugs ... But where can we find coriander?"

Greg shrugged helplessly and automatically took a long gulp of the moonshine. He coughed and was breathless for a while. When he finally gasped for breath, his eyes glowed red and the matte baritone of SyTar said categorically:

"I don't want you to poison this body with such a filth. If anyone hasn't noticed, I'm here too."

"Damn it," grunted Greg, regaining control of his body with difficulty. "I would give five-year earnings to whoever takes over you, parasite."

"Parasite? And who tells you most of the solutions?"

"Suh, don't arguet with yourselt," asked scared Johnnie. "Hevt a drin, it will clear yer coconut."

"I can't, this Uoltanian son of a bitch always interferes," explained Greg, resigned. "What are you looking at? Didn't you know I was the carrier of the Uoltanian vatra? It's something like a soul."

"You're just possessed! You should have said that at once. I'm going for the Reverend Father ..."

"Don't you dare! What for is this man needed here? To make a sacrifice of a lamb to Zeus, so that the first Clingorg encountered would beat me?"

"Don't blaspheme ..."

Further exchange of views was prevented by Charles Mikhalov, who entered the engine room with the brisk pace of a well-rested man and started making hell as soon as he realized that Greg was alone 'on the shift'. Finally, he slung Johnnie out and called the rest of the team through the intercom, without sparing words of criticism, which even Palivec, a well-known goop[31], wouldn't have been ashamed of.

[31] A character from the book "The Adventures of the Good Soldier Švejk".

LXI.

The mysterious ship that had so disturbed Arek was still keeping a decent distance away, but it could still be a concern. Vasyl Anecdotych, advised to be on alert, first misunderstood what was going on and went to the infirmary, claiming that he had been told to wait there. And then he panicked and started running around the ship, catching his snipers from different departments where they used to be. In the end, he gathered the entire team, except for Waldek Kozakievich, whom Dr. Nbeba didn't want to discharge because, as he said, the sniper with a concussion was of little use, so Christopher Mayher replaced him. The chief navigator didn't mind because he liked to shoot and was the only one of the team to have combat experience.

"Yes, and he is the only psychopath on this ship," Kozakievich growled, angry that he would miss the shooting due to the conflict with Jolka Stern.

"It's not nice to talk like that about a friend," Lolita Icant gently chided him, changing a compress on his sore head.

"Godzilla is his friend, not me. Did the sister see his quarters? Knives and a Browning gun. He has also ten tasers. It's weird that the captain does nothing about it..."

"Who said that nothing? As far as I know, she is very interested in Chris' collection," said Jacob Zmiyevski, who was just reviewing the staff cards to see who hadn't completed formalities. "They spend hours discussing whether a Magnum 44 or a Colt caliber 9 is better in a direct confrontation and how to throw a Bowie knife, and how a standard bayonet. Damn it, almost half of our people gave me invalid examination cards, the most recent from five years ago!"

"You figured it out only now? Congratulations," Kozakievich sneered ironically, which was a serious mistake, as his aggrieved head responded with a new wave of pain.

At about the same time, Captain Zakrzevska ended her conversation with Spox and left her quarters. The flickering signal of the yellow alert in the corridor surprised her not so much as disturbed her, so she quickened her pace and almost running, burst into the elevator and then onto the bridge.

"What's going on here?" she asked imperiously, having noticed indignantly that Arek, sitting in the command chair, was snoring the most calmly, while Aśka and Veronika were playing charades at the controls.

"We spotted the ship within range of the sensors," Inga Lausch explained. "I think it's Pornions, but they're not coming."

Lilianna gave Arek a nose flick, and he jumped up with a stupid look on his face and looked blankly around.

"Captain on the bridge," he stuttered out, as his sleepy gaze fell on Lilianna.

"And it is dawning in Pińczów," the captain added. "Go to your seat, First Officer."

She sat victoriously on the empty armchair, crossed her feet and stared at the readings.

"They're not coming, are they?" she said. "Then we will get closer to them. Girls, the takeover course. Inga, connect with the station and inform Trekovsky that we are leaving the orbit for now. Let him not panic, we'll be back."

"I can pass it on, but I warn you that Trekovsky will panic anyway," said Inga. "I know him well."

"Then let him go to hell, let him shake. We gotta get these Pornions if it's them."

"And if it's not them?" Watery asked. On the miniature screen in the engine room console, he saw Charles Mikhalov rulling the roost and was glad that he was on duty on the bridge that day, where it was relatively quiet.

"It makes no difference," the captain snapped. Looking at her, it was clear that whoever was not on board the strange ship should have been on their guard.

The pursuit of the mysterious ship was undoubtedly arbitrary, but Lilianna Zakrzevska didn't pay attention to trifles. Konstanty Ślepowron, who, along with his snipers, was herded to the 'turret', could easily add another point in his notebook, where he wrote for posterity all cases of violations of the rules by the crazy captain. How he intended to use his snout report, in which the notebook was slowly changing, he didn't know yet.

There was a tactical alert on the ship, so no one did what they should have done in normal circumstances, only Matias von Braun bustled around the kitchen, locking the prepared meals in the vending machines to keep them fresh. The Pornion girl Gayla, having learned that her husbands were most likely traveling in the chased ship, hid out of fear in the storeroom next to the quick-elevator number four and didn't want to leave, even though Johnnie Caterpillar assured her from the bottom of his benevolent heart that 'these ruffians wouldn't get her,' he swore to God.

"And you, father won't you start thundering?" Mikhalov asked maliciously when, hurrying along with Tekla Watery to the engine room, he came across Father Toadstool. "After all, this lady is untying the marital knot."

"What an idea. Two husbands at the same time, this is an offense to God," grunted the chaplain. "No wonder the poor girl is looking for help."

"Right. Even one husband is sometimes too much." Tekla sighed.

Mikhalov looked into the storeroom.

"Come on, get out," he said persuasively. "You are safe here. We won't let anybody hurt you."

"I won't get out for anything," Gayla insisted tearfully.

"Gosh, girl, you are such a shaky egg, as if your father hung you over the balcony in your infancy to impress papparazzi!" the engineer got impatient. "How did you get the courage to escape?"

"Harnold Muld helped me. But further 1 had to fend for myself."

"My daughter, get out of this closet and dress humanly, because when I see at you, I don't know where to look," the priest admonished her.

"And what do you think about then?" Johnnie became interested, thus causing mad cheerfulness in Mikhalov and his companion.

Father Toadstool was terribly offended, called Johnnie a dim heathen, and then in a firm voice ordered Gayla to leave the storeroom immediately under the threat of anathema. Since the Pornion girl had no idea what anathema was, she quickly jumped out into the corridor, fearing the worst.

"That's better," Mikhalov praised her. "Tekla, take the maiden to the supply workers, let them give her some human clothes, because here the priest will eventually die here due to a heart attack ... anyway, it is nothing strange when you have such a gut ..."

The priest, apparently wanting to prove that he was not inferior to the rest of the crew in defending his personal rights, swung and hit Mikhalov's ear. He wanted to give him back, but Johnnie, deeply indignant at the attempt to physically insult the priest, prevented it with all firmness.

"He can hit me, and I can't hit him?! This is unfair! Discrimination!" the chief engineer yelled so loudly that he brought in a security patrol headed by Maura Gvizdak onto the middeck.

On the bridge, Malvinka Krencik, which replaced the completely exhausted Inga, tried to establish communication with the mysterious ship. But the ship not only didn't respond, but simply also came full circle and began to fly towards the station.

"Vot, svoloch,"[32] commented Vasyl Anecdotych. "Ya b' yemu chvost odstrielil i tol'ko patom gavaril."[33]

The captain, however, preferred to postpone shooting for a better occasion and only ordered to cut off the mysterious intruders. She was determined to find out who they were and

---

32 *(Rus)* What a maggot.

33 *(Rus)* I would blow off his tail and then talk to him.

what they wanted. Her instinct told her that they weren't Pornions, even though the unit was clearly Pornion. Something was wrong here, and definitely.

Having realized that the terrestrial unit wouldn't back off for anything, the foreign ship finally stopped circling around the station and unexpectedly declared its willingness to surrender.

"It could be a trap," said Night-heron grimly as he kept his hand on the trigger.

"Then they will be guilty," said Christopher Mayher.

"He or she," T'enga corrected. "According to scans, there is only one intelligent life form on this ship.

On the bridge it was also known that the "wild horde" that threatened 'Hermash' was in fact one-man. Lilianna Zakrzevska decided to bring the mysterious pilot, since he was kind enough to give up. She took ArCer, Johnnie as well as Tuniek Afdieyev who came acroos her, took tea from the synthesizer on the way and briskly headed for the transmission hall. There, at the sight of the figure that materialized on the landing, first she goggled, then she peered suspiciously into her cup. She sniffed its contents and tasted it carefully.

"Just like I thought, pure tea," she muttered. "So why am I hallucinating?"

The visitor turned out to be a stout, aged man with round as a full moon, good-natured face adorned with carefully curled mustache with sharpened ends. He was dressed in something between a cowboy and a pirate outfit, and in very flashy colors. The whole thing was completed with high beige leather boots, a leather hat with a tucked brim and - it is not known for what - a baldric for a skewer which the newcomer, however, didn't carry. No wonder Lilianna doubted the judgment of her own senses for a moment.

The strange man touched his hat with a courteous movement.

"Harnold Muld, at your, lovely miss' service," he said with a broad smile.

"I'm not a miss, but a captain," Lilianna let him know. "And I have seen many colorful characters, but I must admit that such one like you, I see for the first time."

ArCer standing behind her seemed much more shocked and was speechless. Seeing that she couldn't count on the Uoltan for the time being, Captain Zakrzevska exclaimed:

'Hermash'! Check out our visitor, who he is."

"I'm checking, angel," said a hoarse baritone, and then the familiar symphony of grinding and rattling collapsed.

After a while something squeaked and the computer announced:

"Harnold Muld, age-no data, place of birth-no data, place of permanent residence-no data, tradesman by education, and by passion smuggler, fraudster, pimper, but also a bit of a thief. Therapy in a penitentiary facility with no effect. His carrier's license has been revoked. Pilot license without authorization. An arrest warrant signed by the police of seventeen planets. Main allegations: unauthorized sale and purchase, falsification of documents, notorious evasion of legal liability, escape from the place of solitary confinement. My princess, he is a bezprizorna bradiaga!"[34]

"Nobody's perfect," the captain said thoughtfully. "Mr. Muld, what were you doing near that haunted station?"

"I was counting on your help, beautiful Captain," replied the visitor, not at all discouraged by the crushing evaluation of himself made by the local computer. "My ship's thrust regulator failed and the hold-up system energy is running out. Where was I supposed to turn if not to the nearest space station?"

"Now you are unlikely to get any help. The station is deserted. But there is a way for everything, according to the principle: if possible, it can be done. Mr. Afdieyev, you will deal with our guest for now."

Tuniek Afdieyev didn't seem particularly thrilled with his role, but he didn't protest. He was one of the few truly disciplined crew members aboard 'Hermash'.

---

34 *(Rus)* A homeless tramp, often also a term for a man from an underclass.

"Are you hungry?" he asked carefully. "Would you like to eat something?"

"Since everyone is so polite here ..." Muld replied a little hesitantly. Used to looking for hidden traps in everything, he tried to guess what intentions towards him had the delicate girl in uniform, behind whom stood the tall Uoltan and an even larger man with the ferret on his shoulder.

"Just to be clear: I'm not going to arrest you, because I don't care what you did and where," Lilianna said, guessing what she was thinking. "Unless you come up with the bad idea of doing something stupid aboard my ship, you're safe. Just God forbid you play some prank. Is that clear?"

LXII.

Admittedly, Captain Muld had at first a sincere intention to do some scam aboard the polite unit, but he soon realized that it might have not been that simple. In the first place, nothing looked like it did on the other Star Armada ships. For example, around a corner of the nearest corridor, he came across the enraged priest who jumped on one leg, clutching the other's calf, and shouted nasty insults. The huge, shaggy dog sat against the wall, trying to look like an innocent. The undesirable scene was watched by the thin hook-nosed man, chewing a hunk of bread with a pulpy pate.

"What the hell...?" Tuniek was surprised.

"That porcus[35] bit me!" the priest shouted furiously.

"Taż batiaru,[36] this is not a porcus, this is a canis ovium[37]." Tuniek, who had studied pharmacy in his native Lviv, knew Latin no worse than any priest.

---

[35] *(Latin)* Piglet.
[36] *(Lviv dialect)* But, brother.

The huge shepherd dog, seeing the stranger, barked with a bass and began to jump around him happily, and then climbed up on his shoulders, which caused the balance to break down and the picturesque figure collapsed, because on the cosmic board, Bear had gained healthy weight and already weighed a hundred kilos.

"This brute is dangerous! Biting me wasn't enough for him, now he will bite our guest!" Father Toadstool shouted, but it didn't seem like Bear had any bad intentions. Undeterred by the fact that the man was standing a moment earlier, and now is lying, the sheepdog ran its tongue across his face, then stuck his muzzle without ceremony under his jacket and squealed in amazement.

"Why is he sizzling like that?" Tuniek was surprised and looked suspiciously at Muld. He stood up with a dignified expression, reached under his jacket, and took out something that looked like a ball of gray fur, the size of a medium watermelon. The ball spun and purred amiably. Bear made a "sit", opened his mouth in a wide smile and started wagging his tail as violently as if he had been trying to sweep the floor.

"Oh Jesus, what is this funny hat?" asked Johnnie, who had just appeared in the company of Vasyl Zaychik, attracted by the shouts of the on-board chaplain. Captain Muld didn't quite understand what the fair-haired giant meant, but rushed to explain:

[37] *(Latin)* Shepherd dog.

"It's a trubblat, the nicest little animal in our galaxy. I got him as a gift from Cyrus James, the merchant."

"Tryblet, you say? Let it be tryblet. And where does he have his head? Because I want to stroke him a little."

Muld handed him the trubblat, which distracted Bear from him, and straightened his crumpled clothes.

"What kind of ship is this?" inquired.

"Soviet-Polish," Zaychik replied proudly, which brought upon him all the wrath of Father Toadstool, regardless of other affairs of the fierce anti-communist.

"What heresy you are talking, unbaptized devil?!" he screamed so loudly that the corridor trembled. "Polish! Without any Middle Eastern connotations! I'll give you a Soviet one ..."

Zaychik raged. The Party for the Reactivation of the USSR had been active in Russia for several years, and Vasyl was an ardent supporter of it. Party members and supporters stubbornly used the term "Sovietskiy Soyuz" for their place of birth and residence, and no administrative punishment could convince them not to do so.

"I don't understand something: an Orthodox communist?" Stelmach goggled without stopping chewing his sandwich.

"Exactly, what declaration of faith do you have, dear?" Tuniek Vasyl asked.

"S'nachiala to nichego nie bylo, tol'ko tovarishch' Boh prahażalsia ulicami Maskvy ..."[38] recited Zaychik, thus arousing the madness of everyone present, except for Muld, who didn't understand anything and began to suspect that he had boarded a touring madhouse.

Afdieyev finally noticed his detonated expression and took pity on him.

"Don't you worry, sweetie," he said heartily. "We're just talking to each other. Come to the wardroom, lunch is probably being served now. Johnny, give back the game."

"Hihi, but he's so funny .... He twitters like a sparrow," Johnnie's exhilarated expression left no doubt that the young highlander literally fell in love with the trubblat. Harnold Muld snaped his fingers at it.

"Keep him, boy," he said with suspicious cordiality.

"God bless you!" Johnnie beamed.

Tuniek led Muld to the wardroom, where they both literally bumped into the Pornion girl, dancing for the crew members staring at her, something between belly dance and macarena. Matias von Braun, serving successive portions of that day's "dish of the day", was tapping to the beat a ladle against the edge of a large pot.

---

38 *(Rus)* In the beginning there was nothing, only Comrade God walked the streets of Moscow.

"Gayla!" Muld shouted in amazement.

"Harry! How did you get here?! Did you come back for me?!" The girl interrupted the performance and happily threw herself on his neck. The captain looked a little startled by this meeting, which he tried to mask with jovial gaiety. But Matias, a keen observer, wasn't fooled - Muld was not thrilled about this encounter. If it was true that he had helped Gayla get away from her two husbands, why did he now appear to be afraid of her?

***

After dispensing the last portion of the 'specialty of the day', von Braun closed the kitchen and went in search of the captain, wanting to share his vague suspicions with her. On the way, he came across Kazio Piskorz and Anetka Piekutek, who, with madness in their eyes, searched the entire corridor with scanners. Curious, he stopped and, after a short direct observation, interpellated to explain the phenomenon.

"Diplomat, sod off," he heard in response. "We have such a constitutional disturbance here that it is shocking."

"And more specifically?" Matias asked gently, correctly assuming that with madmen, you need to talk like with children.

"Our chikita littered and the bundles scattered," Anetka replied in a desperate voice.

It took a dozen or so seconds for the diplomat and cook in one person to understand that the female of the beautiful

Brazilian tarantula, the pride of Kazik Piskorz, had decided to change her marital status just before leaving, and now she gave her astonished owner a larger number of extremely mobile tarantulas. During the recent pursuit of Mulda's ship, their terrarium had become somewhat unsealed, and now the nice creatures were the devil knew where.

"Fa-ta-lly," Matias worried. "What will they eat here? There are no flies, beetles or anything like that on the ship ... We poisoned even fleas."

"Well, I wouldn't worry so much about that. In the lower hold we have a nice flock of German cockroaches, which they probably packed with the last goods as a surprise," Piskorz consoled him. "Each animal has its own mind, and the little ones will probably go where they have something to eat as soon as they guess. And you, Mr. beautiful, you have nothing to do?"

"I do. Where's the captain?"

"She's sitting in the infirmary and talking with Blacking ...I mean, with Nbeba and the rest of their gang."

While Captain Muld was looking around 'Hermash', Anetka and Kazik were searching for the small spiders, and von Braun was looking for Captain Zakrzevska, which really conferred with Dr. Nbeba, Jacob Zmiyevski and Andy Karpiel.

"Mr. Spox is of the opinion that even if the chance of success is as low as five percent, it's worth trying," she told them at the end of a long argument, packed with scientific terms so that it wouldn't be understood by outsiders.

"The chance is much bigger, but also the risk is high ... But if this hybrid is for, why not to take the risk?" said Karpiel, who was eager to try the nanite treatment from the very beginning.

"Shouldn't we wait for ArCer and Trekovsky to return from the station?" asked Jacob, scratching his part, which, to his worry, had recently started to widen strangely.

"The devils know when they come back. Recently, they reported that they were on a trail, but didn't explain on what trail. I suggest starting the preparation of nanites without them, and we can wait with the procedure itself. Mr. von Braun, what are you here for?"

"It's not your business," said Matias, who had just entered and immediately refrained. "No, I mean, I wanted to tell you captain that I don't like this Muld."

"Me neither, he's too fat and I don't like guys with a mustache," the captain replied politely.

"And women?" Karpiel became interested.

"Back off, Andy, I have an important matter!" von Braun was irritated. "Captain, this Muld is a bit indistinct! He is guilty of something!"

"You say obvious things. Of course, he is," Lilianna shrugged. "Pornions don't trade ships, and he has the pornion one. I sent Mikhalov with the team there to sniff out what kind of person this guy is. I don't want a conflict with the Pornions, it's enough that the Sheolians have probably issued an arrest warrant for us ..."

By saying that she didn't want a conflict with the Pornions, the captain apparently forgot for a moment about Gayla, who was an enough reason to cause an argument. The inhabitants of the planet Pornia disliked very much any interference in their custom of trafficking in women. Anyway, the ship had to be checked, so a team was quickly completed and sent on board ...

"This boat is not bad, but colors are piss-poor," said Charles Mikhalov, looking around the interior.

It was painted angry orange, which, combined with the azure pattern, was indeed not particularly tasteful, and the dangling here and there drapes of bright pink tulle with fringes were the height of bad taste.

"What idiot made the decor here?" Jolka Stern was clearly scandalized.

"Probably some Pornion," said Andrzej Lepek. "They have such a taste, I heard that they cover themselves with jewelry like Christmas trees, and the more shining, the better for them. What herbs ..."

From the main deck they went into the engine room, which was painted silver and gold, for a change. The propulsion was slightly different from the standard warp reactors - most of all it contained additional equipment that allowed the usage of all the available energy, without the usual reserve, and to make the jump at a speed that exceeded any previous achievements of other races. It was this part that couldn't be activated, which prevented Muld from escaping from 'Hermash'. Mikhalov immediately set about working on the problem, while Jolka was checking the computer, and Lepek started working on the ventilation ducts, in which something unpleasantly snarled.

"Jola, find the "Manual control" option on the computer and turn it on," Mikhalov ordered after a long moment. "Can you handle these Pornion markings?"

"I don't know, it's such chairs, not a decent handwriting," replied the engineer. "Luckily I got familiar with it a little, but I won't bet dollars to doughnuts as I may confuse the option of restoring the life support system with the self-destruct sequence."

"Better avoid it, because our old missus would have to pay compensation for this flying tryst house, and she wouldn't be happy about that."

Having strained all her miserable knowledge of Pornion symbolism, Jola was finally able to identify the appropriate option and activate it, redirecting the drive control systems to the handheld console at the core. Very pleased, Mikhalov began to check the circuits, while making additional documentation, which he intended to use later. Jolka, who had similar godly thoughts, started downloading the trip logs from the computer. They were both so engrossed in their work that only Lepek's loud shout roused them from their trance:

"Oh Saint Jack, watch over me now and always, amen!"

"And he, stone me, came to pray here?!" Mikhalov got pissed off and by surprise released the automatic flap and caught his fingernail.

"Hey, Andrew, the boss is asking why you are praying like that!" Jolka called at the opening of the ventilation shaft.

It took a moment and Lepek crawled out of the duct on all fours. His eyes were completely round and bulging, like that of Peter Lore after an enema.

"Gosh," he gasped. "Do you know what's in there?!"

LXIII.

While an engineering team of three was researching the propulsion of the Pornion ship, Harnold Muld wandered around 'Hermash' in the company of bouncing Gayla and Tuniek. He was examining the ship, peering at every corner and his eyes were shining suspiciously. It was clear to the naked eye that he planned something unfair, but the good-natured Afdieyev didn't suspect anything, especially the semi-childish Pornion girl.

Soon the cosmic tramp, with a clever ruse, got rid of his companions for a moment and disappeared into the tangle of corridors. He was skilled at taking control of other people's ships, and usually all he needed to do was locate the nearest panel, and about fifteen minutes of peace. To his delight, one of the access panels on this bizarre ship was located in a side corridor where apparently rarely anyone was. The second fortunate fact was that the panel was standard and well known to him. He was able to activate it without difficulty. However, when he tried to get to the operating system, he had an unpleasant surprise. He unexpectedly received a solid electric kick, and the furious, drunk baritone declared:

"Try again, beggar, and they will collect you from the wall with a dustpan and pour you through the funnel into a casket!"

"Who's saying that?" Muld grunted, struggling to get up from the floor.

"Local asshole, you already know who?"

The smuggler came to himself quickly and decided not to pay attention to the saucy computer. He had his ways. He quickly took a device out of his pocket and activated it, extinguishing electronic sound waves within several dozen meters. He pulled leather gloves from behind his belt, put them on, then walked over to the panel again and began clicking the keys. However, he miscalculated, or maybe he just didn't know what he was dealing with. Deprived of the possibility of a vocal alarm, 'Hermash' sent a text call to the screen in the control room and to the bridge, and a few minutes later Maura Gvizdak appeared in the corridor with the security team.

"I just ..." Muld began, surprised to see the soldiers.

"Don't say 'just', or a hen will hit you with an egg fast," Maura advised him. "Hands, hands, Kloss! We will wean you off the inside job."

The absurd words of the girl in uniform, armed to the teeth, completely put Muld off his stroke, especially that right after the security department, the filigree captain appeared and with sadistic delight ordered:

"Take him to the arrest, Maura. We are locking him for now, and what will happen next, we will see."

The head of security searched the prisoner, took the weapon hidden behind the uppers of his shoes and the jamming device, which she also immediately smashed under the heel, just in case. The sudden recovery of the ability to speak, 'Hermash' documented with a series of disgusting curses in several languages at once, including Clingorgian and Sheolian, and then declared in an insulted voice:

"I warned you. When you let anyone on board, you have to at least keep an eye on them."

"After all, we have you, you are always watching. So what was our guest trying to do?" the captain asked, folding her hands behind her back like a Uoltan.

"I didn't try anything! I was just curious ..." Muld began with a look of offended innocence, but Maura cut him off and began to recite:

"You hornswoggled your guardian, used the apparatus that jammed internal communication and tried to enter the system stealthily. This is enough for a nice sentence, my lord."

"Curiosity is the first step to hell, Muld," Lilianna said. "And on my ship, to the detention center. And that's where you'll end up. Take him."

The completely broken space tramp allowed himself to be escorted to the cell. Such seclusion had its advantages as well - he had time to think about the situation and come up with something. And in the art of figuring out, he was one of the galaxy's undisputed masters.

Having returned to the bridge, Captain Zakrzevska first of all scolded the steersmen Bequiet and Deadskull, who instead of guarding the console, were arm wrestling, and Malvinka Krencik cheered for them with interest, not paying attention to the fact that the incoming call LED was flashing on the communications console. It was only after Lilianna's scolding that she returned to her seat with a mournful expression and turned on the apparatus.

"Are you sleeping there or what?!" said Professor Trekovsky's nervous falsetto from the loudspeaker. "This is the fifth time we are trying to connect with you!"

"Forgive me, Dinuś, but we had an armwrestling competition here," the captain replied. "Malvinka spaced out. Tell me how's the situation."

"I'm reporting that we solved the problem here. Get us on board and we'll explain you everything."

"I hope so."

The captain called the transport hall and gave the appropriate orders. It was not easy to communicate with Lalevich over the intercom, because the words were drowned out by the loud wailing of Vuvu that Mikhalov had left in the hall. The little vall refused to leave the hall for anything, crouching by the transporter platform and yelping bitterly. Anyone in the world would have been pissed off, but the technician Lalevich was an exception. It was impossible to unhinge him when he sat in the hall reading one of his favorite books.

Trekovsky materialized on the platform next to ArCer, which seemed to be somewhat restless. In contrast, the professor was in a state of euphoric excitement.

"Captain, I know everything!" He called, hopping off the platform and nearly treading on Vuvu.

"You're exaggerating, professor, and do you know the formula for a cold fusion?" Lilianna asked.

"Goddamn cold fusion, I know what happened on the station!" specified Trekovsky.

"He knows?" The captain asked, looking at ArCer.

He gave her a misguided look and ran a hand over his newly regrown hair.

"Supposedly," he replied in a harassed voice. It was evident that he had spent hard time with him, just like anyone who had ever dealt with Dinoslav Trekovsky.

"Not supposedly, but really," the professor was offended. "Captain, please call Zaychik and have him shoot all our mazers at the station. The broadest possible beam, stunning mode."

"Are you sober?"

"Of course, I am, I can breathe!"

Lilianna shrugged and walked over to the intercom.

"Vasyl Anecdotych Zaychik, please report to the turret," she ordered.

Something creaked in the intercom, then Christopher Mayher spoke up, clearly chewing his late supper:

"I report that Vashka went to confession and hasn't returned yet."

"Oh, it might take time. Then, Chris, go to the turret and hit this station with all our mazers, broad spectrum deafening beam."

There was a momentary silence in the intercom, then you could hear Chris actively swallowing, and finally he asked unceremoniously:

"Lilka, did you really say that?"

"And how did it sound? Carry out, soldier!"

"Yes, ma'am!"

Lilianna closed the intercom and turned to the Uoltan, who was shifting from foot to foot:

"What did you discover? Where did those from the station disappear?"

"They didn't disappear," ArCer explained wearily. "According to the professor, they only passed into a different phase. Reverse ionization will make them return to normal, and the mazer beams will ionize the air."

"I've never heard such nonsense in my life," the captain said confidently. "But since the beginning of the voyage, things have happened to us that are contrary to common sense, I won't be surprised when it comes out in the wash that you're right."

Trekovsky began to dwell long and extensively on how he had reached his astonishing conclusions. He waved his hands at the same time, blushed and used more and more complicated sentences that no one but himself seemed to understand. The captain listened politely to the long and broad talk, without even muttering, for she was aware that the professor pathologically hated being interrupted, for whatever reason, which might have been or not important.

The explanations of Dinoslav Trekovsky didn't contribute to the case, as practically no one understood them. They were so convoluted that in the end the professor himself got confused and went silent with a stupefied face. Then ArCer finally pointed to the screeching Vuvu, the wailing of which became more and more pathetic.

"Excuse me, but why is this creature yelping?"

Mikhalov went to Muld's ship to check on its propulsion and left the poor animal ..." Lalevich replied sleepily.

"What Muld?"

The captain explained to the Uoltan the circumstances of the arrival of the star smuggler, as well as the reasons for his arrest and imprisonment in the cell. She hadn't finished speaking yet when the buzzer on the transporter console sounded. The technician pressed the reception button and Mikhalov's voice came from the loudspeaker:

"Dish, I can't connect to our missus, and you have no idea what we found here!"

The captain came over, pushed Lalevich from the console and replied:

"So far, I have chosen myself the guys I connect with, and what do you have?"

"Huge stock of Pornion money! There is so much of it that it would be enough for our entire crew."

Lilianna nodded, though the engineer couldn't see it. She had guessed such a surprise since she had associated facts, such as the story of the green-skinned beauty, the Pornion ship, Muld's dubious reputation and behavior, and the words of Gayla's husbands about the money she allegedly had stolen. It was all clear now.

Harnold Muld noticed that the pretty, child-minded Gayla was very unhappy in the forced marriage. At first he didn't care much, but then he saw it as a unique opportunity to get a large sum free of tax. He knew very well that once Gayla was in the territory of the Union of the Planets, she would be able to claim asylum and it would be granted to her, because the Union didn't tolerate slavery. So far, the Pornion Syndicate had failed to recover any of the slaves who had successfully escaped to Earthlings or any other allied race. Even on planet Uoltan there lived a few green-skinned girls who had managed to break free from slavery and reach this planet of sworn logicians, where they obtained asylum and worked as dance instructors.

"Wait, dance instructors on a volcano ...oh! on Uoltan?!" For the first time Lalevich was surprised enough to be roused from his usual state of jaded indifference.

Lilianna, who disliked being interrupted almost as much as Trekovsky, frowned in displeasure, but explained:

"Uoltans don't give up everything that is beautiful in life just because they are logicians. Besides, their children learn group dance in order to discharge their excess energy and learn that cooperation is the basis for achieving a good result. Am I right, Mr. ArCer?"

"More or less ..." muttered the Uoltan.

He didn't care about this whole matter at all. He only thought of one thing: if the science department had already dealt with the nanite code enough to used them to cure TiShan. He missed her more and more, though he wouldn't have admitted it even at the cost of his life. This, in turn, made him listen to the captain's arguments with only one ear and he preferred to give as evasive an answer as possible. Lilianna realized ArCer was hardly listening, snaped her fingers at it and changed the subject:

"What is this Chris doing in the turret, blackening his eyelashes, or what? He should report the completion of the task already!"

"Maybe he has objective difficulties?" muttered Lalevich shyly.

"What objective difficulties, maybe also artificial fog at the airport and drunk controllers? Come away, I go to the bridge. Dish, bring Mikhalov and his team in, let them finally silence this howling raccoon. You can become deaf from this."

LXIV.

Whatever Christopher Mayher thought about the bizarre order, he kept it to himself. As Vasyl Zaychik hadn't returned from the chapel yet, the chief navigator himself went to the turret, chased Konstanty Ślepowron and his squad away from there, and then set up the mazers. The Night-heron, so unceremoniously taken away, was doing hell in the corridor for so long that it finally lured the security patrol, Ewelina Siwak as well as sister Ophelia, who also came to see what was going on. She listened with interest for a moment to the flow of Night-heron's speech, then, without a hint of warning, she kicked his ankle until he meowed and curled up into a ball.

"You should be ashamed to use such a language in front of the ladies and in the presence of the clergyman," she testified emphatically. "Now please tell me what has happened."

"That ... Mayher ... kicked us off the turret, and I was just about to lecture!" The corporal burst out furiously.

"After all, you can lecture anywhere," Ewelina Siwak remarked, which caused that all the anger of the Night-heron was suddenly directed at her.

"Why do you interfere?! You better watch the kitchen and your man!"

Ewelina was offended, but instead of smacking the corporal in the ear, she launched the traditional woman's fountain. At this point, came Johnnie Caterpillar.

"Damn it, what have you told the girl!" He screamed vigorously, clenching his fists the size of sheep's shoulder blades and shaking them over the Night-heron's head.

"What I wanted," the corporal, who wasn't a coward, bristled sharply and didn't take even a step back. "Don't interfere, bloody elephant! You think you are ideal?! You can, goddamn it, be photographed and your photo hung over the bed instead of a contraceptive!"

Offended Johnnie wanted to punch the corporal with his fist, but at that moment Chris Mayher started all the mazers. The shock after firing the cannons caused the people gathered in the corridor to fly in all directions. The worst of it got sister Ophelia, who literally tumbled across the corridor and ran into Arek.

"Black, white, black, white, black, white, boom," the first mate quoted the famous joke as he helped the nun to her feet. "Stretch the habit, please, because one can see sister's panties."

"You wish, son, I was without them, but forget it," Ophelia retorted, adjusting the outfit.

The intercom on the wall gurgled, coughed and screamed in Malvinka's voice:

"Holy shit, I am picking up the station! They are swearing there like sailors! Damn!"

Arek caught the intercom.

"Malvina, less profanities in the report!" he shouted. "I'm on my way, notify the rest of the elders."

He rushed to the quick-elevator.

"Pooh, elders," Ophelia muttered, buttoning up the cornet. "A bunch of brats and that's it."

Soon most of the senior officers were on the bridge. There were even Father Toadstool and Matias von Braun. Listening excitedly to the complaints of people from the station and trying to put their story together into a meaningful whole, no one noticed that Captain Zakrzevska wasn't with them. It was only after a long time that Jürgen realized that there was no one to report to. Immediate searches yielded no result. Although the ship was examined from A to Z, it was already known before the bugle call that the captain of 'Hermash' had disappeared like camphor. Even the omnipresent main computer knew nothing, because firing all the mazers disrupted his functions for a while. So a terrible thing happened - at a critical moment, the crew was left without the captain.

***

It took a long time for Jürgen, Arek and ArCer to calm down the crew. The disappearance of Captain Zakrzevska caused a panic that 'Hermash' hadn't yet seen. Most of the women cried excruciatingly, and the men started destroying their stocks of moonshine to calm their nerves. The scientific department brainstormed to establish the scientific basis for the disappearance of the flesh and blood person, but the brainstorm ended with an ordinary storm, and this was mainly due to Cezary Monkey, who came in with a simple question whether it was an open or closed party and whether everyone was angry.

Some also sought help from supernatural forces. Azalia Kviek made a cabala from supplies, Dr. Nbeba began to recall some African legends about such kidnappings and offered to make a 'macumba' which was supposed to help, while Father Toadstool started a special service to find the commander.

"And what is a macumba?" Inga Lausch asked.

"Makumba, or the talking tree". Michael Choromanski's novel, I recommend you to read it," Mstislav Deadskull replied from the controls. "This is a kind of African magic with the use of a doll, made of a piece of clothing of a man to whom you want to plant such a 'macumba'."

"How can adult civilized beings believe such nonsense?" ArCer asked with surprise "After all, it won't help."

"But it won't hurt either, Mr. Uoltan. We humans have a peculiar nervous structure: some allogic actions not only calm us down, but also stimulate our minds, making it easier for us to find a solution to the problem."

ArCer suppressed a sigh and resumed viewing the charts.

'Hermash', you really have nothing else?" he asked after a long moment.

"I have nothing! Where is she, my princess?" the computer gabbled with difficulty, then began to play Chopin's 'Funeral March' from a bank of musical memories.

This caused not only another wave of moans on board, but also serious concern on the station, trying to somehow get along with the ship, which, after all, had saved them all from the very embarrassing situation. Fortunately, ArCer finally lost his Uoltanian patience, ordered 'Hermash' to turn off the music in a firm voice, and set about explaining to Commodore Gibbs what had actually happened. Before he finished, SiWok entered the bridge, bringing the news that, according to all readings, the captain's disappearance had nothing to do with the phase shift that the station crew had undergone. Lilianna just disappeared in an unknown way.

Instead of looking inside the ship, look for readings outside," Gibbs advised.

"Outside? After all, there is a void and absolute zero, the captain wouldn't survive there!" Inga got scared.

"Who knows, maybe she managed to grab some warm socks. Propel all the sensors," ordered Arek, who had just remembered that he was the first mate, not ArCer. The Uoltan's behavior was such that at times it was possible to have doubts as to who was who on this ship.

A thorough search of both the decks and the surrounding space didn't reveal any traces of Captain Zakrzevska, but the technician Lalevich insisted that he saw a weak marker of an unusual transporter beam on his sensors.

... And since we had our shields down, it is clear that someone just radiated the captain through the armor," he finished his report. After this announcement, there was a slight commotion, which, however, soon subsided, giving way to a general conference entitled "What to do?"

While almost everyone was conferring and arguing, Veronika Bumblebee entered the bridge and tried to replace Mstislav Deadskull, who, according to the schedule, had just finished the watch.

"Get lost, miss, while I'm still good, because if I kick you in your left butt, you will cover yourself with your legs and fly with your head to the garbage can," replied furiously Deadskull, who wasn't going to hand over the reins at such an interesting moment. Veronika, without thinking for a long time, gave him a strong poke under the left shoulder blade and threw him violently off the armchair.

"Hitting an officer may result in a court martial!" ArCer exclaimed, indignant at such disrespect for the higher charge, and looked around the bridge for support.

"I didn't see anything," Arek replied to his gaze.

"Neither did I," said Mayher.

"Mr. Deadskull ..."

"I was turned away," the steersman interrupted the Uoltan. "What are you thinking, that I will tell in court that the woman is beating me? I'll get her back myself, easy, dress."

"Shut up, all of you, officers, because I can't hear anything," Inga snapped from the comm station.

Over the open link, Commodore Gibbs could be heard ordering his people to scan the immediate space, with the addition of juicy curses. It wasn't long before both teams detected the ion trail left by the alien ship. Closer analysis revealed that the machine hadn't flown away at all, but was close, camouflaged and lurking.

"I wonder who it is," Arek muttered. Then he dropped the communicator, which rolled under the console and, swearing like a sailor, he followed it.

"I bet on Pornions," said Christopher Mayher. "They were probably following us because of Gayla."

"And they kidnapped our captain?" Inga was scared. "It's terrible! We have to notify the infirmary so that they are prepared to save lives. As far as I know our old missus, she doesn't like to be kidnapped, especially by slavers."

"Right, if they don't lock her somewhere, they will be in trouble, that's for sure," said Joe Stelmach, who was just on duty at the engine room console.

"I won't feel sorry for them. They will be guilty themselves if she turns them into goose stomachs in their own sauce."

"Stop it now," ArCer asked disgustedly. "Your comments are not only illogical but also unintelligent. We need to accurately target and call this ship. Stiff negotiations are ahead."

"Very stiff," said Mayher. "Especially since they're flying away."

"Follow them, the keep up course!" Arek yelled, jumping up so violently that he banged his cradle on the protruding railing.

"And don't you dare lose them," he grunted, holding his head. "Anyone got a knife?"

"You wanna cut them?" Mayher asked politely, offering her his own inherent bowie.

"Don't be stupid," Arek replied and put the wide blade of the knife against the bump growing on his crown.

"It's not that stupid! When I served temporarily on the USS Gojira, the combat pilots told among themselves this joke: a fighter was supposed to fire at enemy forces with photon missiles, but the launcher jammed. So he reported: 'I'm going 1000 meters down, I'm going to use manual rifles.' However, after the first volley, the weapon refused to obey. The commander ordered to come back, but the enraged pilot refused. 'I'm going down to the very surface!' He screamed. 'I'll beat them with my belt!"

ArCer couldn't understand why the people on the bridge burst out laughing, but decided not to explore it, and only urged to chase, fearing that the kidnappers would disappear without a trace. So 'Hermash' rushed, following the trail of the unidentified unit, which made efforts to disappear from the sensors, but Mr. Mayher and Mr. Deadskull were too old stagers to get lost.

LXV.

'Hermash' was chasing the kidnappers' ship, keeping enough distance not to lose it, and at the same time to be hard to see. Initially, the ship was escaping at the fastest speed available, but after some time it suddenly slowed down and turned back. Inga, dozing by the sensors, sobered up and screamed:

"Jesus Christ, they are attacking!"

"Nobody is attacking, you joker," Arek muttered. "They have just turned back. Call them out, miss, instead of screaming like a drunken Clingorg."

Inga switched the frequency with trembling fingers, activated the selector, improved noise reduction, and tossed the standard call sign into space. She repeated it three times and was about to ask Arek helplessly what to do next, when the loudspeaker screeched and, on the screen, appeared disheveled, red and apparently angry Captain Zakrzevska.

"Why so long?! They could have raped and strangled me here before you got off your backsides! What a crew I have, God forbid!"

"Captain, we were just afraid not to hurt you, that's why we didn't shoot," Arek excused himself. "And ... and ... where those who kidnapped you?"

"There were only two of them, they are Gayla's quasi-husbands. They were punched in their faces and are lying. And how do you think? Was I supposed to sing for them? Or maybe dance?"

"Didn't I tell you she could handle it?" muttered Christopher Mayher. Knowing Lilianna inside out, he had no doubts about it.

"But ..." ArCer began, and fell silent, suddenly finding his mind completely blank. What had this hellish woman done to dominate two kidnappers, and quite powerful ones?

"But, what? Get me and these two bastards aboard, now! What a moment he found for meditation, pointy-eared hotshot ..."

"I'm going to inform Dish," Veronika squealed and jumped out of the bridge like from a slingshot."

Along the way, she tripped over Bear waiting for her and, with momentum, ran into Father Toadstool, knocking the censer out of his hand, luckily not lit, because the chaplain was carrying it to be repaired.

"Watch out, blind commando creep!" the priest shouted. "What a ship, everyone is rushing somewhere!"

"Especially in the engine room!" the helmswoman shouted back to him with a laugh, not even stopping.

When she reached the transport hall, it turned out that Lalevich, notified by the intercom, was already setting the coordinates for transmission. The five security soldiers under the command of Maura Gvizdak were in full alert.

"Right, I again forgot that there are communicators," Veronica muttered with amusement and stared at the transporter platform. After a while, columns of glowing particles swirled on it, and formed into three figures: the enraged Captain Zakrzevska and two unconscious Pornions.

Even Maura smacked irregularly at the sight of it.

"How did you do it to them?" she asked.

"I didn't look closely, but it seems it was a fire extinguisher, called dyngusovka by Wiech," the captain replied, jumping off the platform. "Lock up these two jerks."

"They didn't tie you up?" Lalevich inquired sleepily.

"They tied up, but not for nothing I was training in Black Berets together with my friend Mayher. What about the station?"

"Okay, when we left, there was a bazaar-like noise there," Maura reported as her soldiers carried the unconscious Pornions out.

"That's good. We come back. We'll leave these cores along with Muld to Gibbs, let him struggle with them," the captain decided. "Verka, find me Johnnie. If he is not sober, use the Broszkiewicz method for him."

"You mean what?"

"Give him salt, ice on his head and fifteen whip strikes in his bare back," Lilianna quoted the line from the novel 'Dumpling, Kefir and Local'. "He has to be in a jiffy in a state of public utility, as is the case with the entire crew. I can already imagine what happened here in my absence. When a cat is away, the mice play."

She pulled nervously her torn uniform down and walked briskly out the door, where right away was heard a joyful 'Wow!' and a thud, clearly indicating that Bear, overjoyed, had knocked the petite captain onto the floor with his manner.

"Shoo, you hairy pile of muscles!" Lilianna shouted. "Jumping on a higher officer is against the rules!"

"I think it depends for what purpose," said with amusement Matias von Braun, who had just appeared in front of the hall. "Bear, come on!"

He helped Lilianna to her feet and kindly dusted off her uniform.

"They're waiting on the bridge," he said. "Commodore Gibbs is trying to talk to you. You see how adored by everyone you are?"

***

It must be admitted that Commodore Gibbs listened to Captain Zakrzevska's speech without twitching his eyelid.

"Those poor men probably thought all women were like their idiot females," he said. "They have a lesson for the future. And what about Muld?"

"Decide for yourself," Lilianna generously allowed. "I don't think to go with him back and forth. On his ship you will find what he stole from these Pornions. They'll probably be content with getting the money back. Gayla didn't lift it, and it wouldn't even have come to her pinhead."

"And what about Gayla?"

Captain Zakrzevska considered. She would have been happy to grant the Pornion girl asylum on board 'Hermash', but she felt that it wasn't a good idea - the green-skinned dancer didn't qualify for a member of any crew, only dancing and having fun were in her head.

"Will you take care of her?" she asked.

"Very willingly. Obtaining asylum for her will be a child's play, then she can work as a dancer in our bar. I'll talk to my entertainment officer."

Commander Gibbs stretched until his bones crackled, and yawned.

"Sorry, Captain. Being in a different phase is bloody tiring and it has taken its toll on all of us."

"Never mind," replied Lilianna politely. "I'm going to send you the prisoners and the official report. I want to get it over with as soon as possible, because something more important than the stupid Pornions awaits me. We will wake up my head doctor. If the experimental therapy fails, we will lose her."

"Good luck."

The captain turned off the communicator and walked over to the deck arrest, where her captors sat on bunks with very silly expressions. It was evident that they felt humiliated by this situation.

"Alright," the captain said, staring at them with pitying eyes.

"Which of you is Vint and which is Tevint?"

It turned out that Vint was the captain and Tevint was his First officer, but aside from the different insignia on their uniforms, the brothers were no different, so which was which, was really a question of trust.

"In a moment you will be handed over to the commander of station number eight," Captain Zakrzevska announced. "You may be interested in the fact that, together with you, I will also hand over Harnold Muld and his ship, on which, by the way, is the entire sum stolen from you. Your wife had nothing to do with the theft you accuse her of."

"Really?" Tevint wondered happily. "So he can come back with us without fear!"

"The thing is, she doesn't want that," Lilianna chilled him. "And if she doesn't want to, you have no right to force her."

"How come, we have no right? We bought her legally at the market!"

"There is no slavery in the territory of the Union. Gayla has the right to choose. And the two of you will be found guilty of kidnapping the Union captain and the act of hostility to the Star Armada, so you now have the bigger problem than your mutual wife's escape."

"We will be a laughingstock throughout the Syndicate," said Vint grimly.

"And rightly so. I would laugh at you myself if I wasn't so mad at you. You are lucky that I have someone to hand you over to, because if I had to conduct a court-martial over you, you wouldn't fall on your feet."

Captain Zakrzevska cast a contemptuous glance at her prisoners and was about to leave when Muld's voice from the neighboring cell stopped her:

"Captain, let's get along. In the end, I didn't do anything particularly bad ... I can be thankful."

"Go to the beets with your gratitude," Lilianna advised him. "I know that guests bring God's blessing, but when such a guest leaves home, thank God. All I can do for you is to emphasize in the report that you took good care of Mr. Gayla after all, and for the help given to her, you shouldn't be released to the Pornions.

"It's something," muttered Muld, who had already visited prisons in his career and hadn't taken good memories from there. The Union prisons had their advantages - first of all, it was much easier to escape from them than from other prisons.

Johnnie Caterpillar, a boy eager to be moved, burst into tears when he was ordered to hand over the trubblat to his rightful owner.

"Vot shchipatiel'naya dusha,"[39] said with sympathy Vasyl Anecdotych, who witnessed this. The captain scratched her head, not quite sure how to react.

"Come on, Johnnie," she said finally. "I'll talk to that old pirate, maybe he'll sell us the furball. Although, damn it, another

---

39 *(Rus)* Here is a sentimental soul.

pet is the last thing we need here. Actually, we should work as a traveling menagerie."

Lilianna was absolutely right, because the pets playing in the corridors were not against the Star Armada regulations just because no one had thought of banning the obvious. None of the admirals, even in their wildest fantasies, had so far thought of any starship where, rushing to the bridge, a man could stumble over the Vietnamese piglet, and in a vent hole, find the guinea pig. In addition, at any time in the warehouse, the Brazilian tarantula could fall behind someone's collar, and in the bathroom, you could come face to face with the chameleon sitting on the shower. All this was the norm on board 'Hermash' and no one, following the example of the commander, made an issue of it, except perhaps Father Toadstool, who was terrified of spiders and reptiles.

The captain kept her word: in exchange for the trubblat, she withdrew the sabotage charge, which meant that now Muld was lumbered only with the accusation of theft. And with both the Pornions he had robbed now having their own troubles, there was a good chance he would be lucky enough to walk away from that whole story.

"No offense, beautiful captain," he said on parting. "One does what one can. It is possible that we will meet again sometime, so see you later."

"Go to hell," replied heartily Lilianna, who, after all, somehow liked the interstellar tramp.

"You can feed the trubblat without fear! He is sterile!" Mudd shouted to her. Then he lay down on the bunk and started whistling cheerfully.

Zakrzevska was confused for a moment, but then, looking in the archives of the station, she found out that well-fed trubblats usually multiply uncontrollably. So, infertility was a big advantage of this particular specimen.

Having returned onto the 'Hermash' board, Lilianna immediately went to the medical section, where the healing team was waiting in full readiness. The research department not only managed to reprogram the ZONK nanoprobe, but also to test it in the laboratory. The results looked very promising, but no one dared begin the procedure without the captain's express orders. So, the whole committee stood at the stasis chamber: Andy Karpiel, Dinoslav Trekovsky, doctors Nbeba and Zmiyevski, ArCer, Lolita Icant with a first aid kit, two paramedics and priest Toadstool.

"And father, what are you here for?" asked the captain in surprise.

"Just in case ... I came to administer the last rites," explained the priest nobly.

"Have you fallen on your head, with all due respect? TiShan is not a Catholic!"

"But maybe she would like to be."

"She's not even human! Father, please leave, it's a secular ceremony."

"I won't leave. It is my duty to look after every soul on this board," the priest insisted.

"Uoltans don't have a normal soul, they have vatra," interjected Sister Icant.

"It's the same, you idiot!"

"Strictly speaking, not quite ..." ArCer began, but the captain gave him such a look that he broke off.

"Let's get this over with at last," she ordered.

She feared no less than the others that the experimental therapy would be useless, but she had dug into Armada's entire medical library during sleepless nights, and she knew well that TiShan and her unborn child were practically without a chance. The choice, then, was only between total failure and little chance of success - and she chose the latter.

Dinoslav Trekovsky placed an automatic injector filled with nanites on the table. It was a device that seemed archaic compared to the hypo-syringe, but was still in use - for example, for administering blood and for traditional drip infusions. It was not so easy to replace it.

"Everyone knows what to do?" Trekovsky asked for the record. "Let's get going. Let us not dwell on the subject any more than necessary."

LXVI.

At the professor's signal, Dr. Nbeba opened the stasis chamber and intubated the unconscious patient with a steady hand. Lolita Icant instantly grabbed her arm and skillfully squeezed it, and Jacob Zmiyevski stuck the injector's needle into the protruding blood vessel. At the same time, the paramedics connected a respirator and, to be sure, closed an oxygen tent over TiShan.

"The nanites have entered the bloodstream," reported Karpiel, whose task was to observe and possibly correct the indicators on the container dial.

"Now we just need to wait," the professor said softly.

TiShan on the diagnostic table looked dead, but the indicators on the board was pulsing lazily - life was still smoldering somewhere in the center of the inert body. This weak spark was supposed to be blown up by properly programmed nanoprobes, but it couldn't happen in a few minutes. It was needed to wait, but not that many people were necessarily needed for that. So almost all of them went back to their normal activities, with the exception of ArCer, Dr. Nbeba, and Lolita, who was tasked with monitoring fetal parameters. The three of them waited for the situation to unfold, ready to react at any moment.

Captain Zakrzevska went to the bridge, where she received thanks from the command for solving the mystery of the silent station and, at the same time, an order to send 'Hermash' in search of the missing ships. Recent bearings of "Queren" and the pursuers 'Tsiolkovsky' and 'Hubble' indicated that all three headed towards the galaxy's core, possibly chasing the mysterious thieves. Then, as it was known, contact broke off and the rest was a matter of guesswork. Lilianna accepted the order without much enthusiasm, but also without protest. For a change, she wouldn't have minded a boring and unarmed mission, during which the crew could somehow come to itself, and such a wild goose chase was supposed to be quite calm.

"In case these shape-shifting creatures want to give us a boo-boo, do we have the right to hit them?" she asked for the record.

"It would be better to establish diplomatic relations with them. Take Captain Kerk's example," Admiral Cormack replied scoldingly. "Don't expect that from me. I'm not going to get along with every alien I come across, even if interplanetary peace depended on it." Lilianna was offended, and she severed the connection to the headquarters, not wanting to waste time on vain discussions. She still had a lot of work to catch up on.

"Maybe with every other?" Cormack muttered with amusement, writing the new Hermash course as a 'research and rescue mission' in the flight schedule. Star Armada's 'dark horse' seemed to be doing quite well.

While the captain was struggling with a pile of unsigned and mostly chaotic reports from all sections, ArCer was watching over the unconscious TiShan, Matias von Braun was preparing a banquet for the No Occasion Day (he invented it himself), and Charles Mikhalov and Greg Brzenchyshchykievich went to the on-board gym to finally take part in the long-announced duel for Malvinka Krencik.

***

If anyone had thought that the two engineers gave up on their rivalry for the favor of the beautiful communications chief, they would have been wrong. Their animosity flourished more and more ferociously, to which SyTar contributed quite a lot, constantly inciting the generally calm Greg. Little by little, everyone on board learned how to recognize whose self was dominant, and when someone was too dumb for it, all they had to do was look at the animals' behavior. Usually gentle Bear growled at SyTar, and little Vuvu bit him on the heels, which terribly upset Greg, or the owner of the bitten body. But never had any of them shown the reluctance to the deputy chief engineer when his body was guided by his own consciousness -

on the contrary, both the vall and the dog liked him very much. In turn, Mruczek, doctor Zmiyevski's wonderful Iberian lynx, adored SyTar, while at Greg, he snorted and spat.

"Cats like Uoltans," ArCer once had said, but hadn't explained why.

The vivid imaginations of the crew members immediately determined that the Uoltans were probably descended from cats, not monkeys, and this theory gained a lot of support.

Anyway, Mikhalov and Brzenchyshchykievich decided to finally settle which of them "deserved" the beautiful Malva and for this purpose they went to the gym to fight the honorable duel. There was some controversy over what system to use, and finally both rivals agreed that wrestling would be the best. Admittedly SyTar was mumbling something that a traditional Uoltanian hand-held weapon, visually resembling giant ear sticks would have been better, but Greg told him to shut up and not disturb. After all, it was not about friends (still and all) killing each other, but about one of them finally establishing his rights to a female homo sapiens.

"I will never understand people," SyTar finally declared and stopped talking, very dissatisfied that he couldn't now take over Greg's body and use his skills.

The news of the duel reached the bridge just as the captain was finishing his conversation with Walter Gibbs. Station eight commandant finally figured out what had caused the phase shift

- or rather who was behind it - and wondered if and in what form to alert command.

"In my opinion, you should submit the usual report," Zakrzevska advised him. "Although they won't believe you anyway, I warn you loyally."

"Those who did it, stole our ship and escaped to their own people with the Union data!"

"You can't do anything about it. Command needs to know about this."

"But I'll look like an idiot who can't watch the computer."

"We can live with that, commodore Gibbs ..."

At that moment, Johnnie appeared, excited.

"Sir-ma'am, they are fighting!" he exclaimed. "The brawl is so drag-out that it echoes!"

Lilianna took her eyes off the screen that showed the cheeky figure of the commodore.

"Slowly, Johnnie. Who's fighting with whom?"

"The gentlemen, engineers! They both want Malvinka, and the girl can't split herself in two, right?"

"Excuse me, Commodore Gibbs, my engineering division seems to go crazy again," sighed the captain. "Miss Gvizdak! Please arrest these two weenies!"

"What a lack of understanding ..." muttered Maura, but executed the order.

Or rather, she tried to execute it, because she had absentmindedly taken with her the unit consisting only of men, and instead of the arrest, there was a regular fight. The row continued until appeared the captain, who ordered punitive maneuvers for all participants of the controversy in a voice that didn't tolerate any objections. Then she looked at Maura and sternly ordered her to join the punished.

***

"You also have to struggle with us?" asked Charles Mikhalov sympathetically, when Christopher Mayher, who led the maneuvers, ordered a two-minute break.

"I got three days of punishment practice," Maura explained to him, panting hard and wiping the sweat off her brow with her sleeve.

"For what?"

"... Including two for such a question."

"She was punished because she couldn't control us and the unit," Greg chuckled, although he was barely catching his breath.

The mere thought that the rest of the maneuvers were about to begin made him sick.

However, the exercise was not resumed, as something ensued which caused a general amnesty and, at the same time, an outburst of wild joy throughout the ship. The main computer suddenly screamed like a pig being slaughtered:

"To the entire crew! Mrs. TiShan is awake!"

He didn't have to say it twice. In the blink of an eye all matters were forgotten, and they all rushed to the infirmary, from which came a faint but recognizable scream. The awakened doctor was giving birth. The racket that broke out on board 'Hermash' clearly indicated that there was happening something unbelievable, which didn't happen under normal conditions, although it was only a banal childbirth.

Arek Liljew at once ran to the supply department with a demand that a bouquet of roses and a box of Wedel chocolates be delivered to the infirmary. Dumbfounded with amazement, Colorado Kviek replied that there were no such delicacies in the warehouse, and never had been, but he had found a piece of red silk, a piece of green one, a wire, and somehow turned it into a very successful imitation of a flower in bloom. However, there were no chocolates.

"If they had been there, we would have probably eaten them anyway," said Arek and went to the medical section.

Having passed through the crowd of crew members, the first officer entered the infirmary, where he saw a sight indeed unusual - unusual, at least for an Earth starship. TiShan was lying on the mecha-bed, apparently in good health, with a small bundle in her arms, from which the small head protruded, adorned with the pair of pointed ears and the sparse hair. Next to them was sitting ArCer, with such an expression as if he had just experienced a revelation of the Uoltanian supreme deity itself.

"Er," the first mate began not very wisely. "Doctor, congratulations ... how are you?"

"Terrible," said TiShan. "You men will never understand what it's like to give birth. It's really no fun."

"We couldn't give you an anesthetic so as not to interfere with the action of the nanites," Nbeba excused himself, preventing the captain from explaining something.

"So, they work?" Arek jumped up from the impression.

"They work like gold. They'll be deactivated in twenty-four hours, and all damage will be repaired by then."

"But ... we will lose evidence for command. They won't take our word for it."

"Let a dog shit them," the captain shrugged. "What matters is that my head doctor and her baby are doing well. ArCer ... ArCer! I'm talking to you!"

"Yes, excuse me, Captain." The commander looked as if he had been roused from sleep.

"What will you call the little one?"

"I don't know yet, we'll both think about it ..."

The First Officer placed a silk flower on top of TiShan's blanket.

"The best wishes," he said with a smile. "Beautiful baby."

From the corridor came an intonated by it's not known whom:

"Hip hip hurray!"

taken up by everyone present and finally so loud that the little Uoltanian girl woke up and squealed softly.

"Well, we got calm over now," muttered sister Icant, trying to hide her satisfaction, as she actually adored little children.

"What calm, it has never been calm here!" Captain Zakrzevska exclaimed. "Hey there, prepare a banquet! Such a scandalous party that has never taken place here before!"

Enriched with the new crew member, 'Hermash' was flashing through space and you can bet any sum that at any given moment in the entire Star Armada there was no happier and more integrated crew.

LXVII.

The banquet in honor of little TiAllia, as ArCer's and TiShan's daughter were finally named, was indeed exceptionally cheerful, and so that halfway through it, the helmsmen 'parked' 'Hermash' in a relatively safe zone, so that there were no surprises. It was better to move on when everyone was sober.

A dozen or so hours later, when the hangover staff of the bridge finally began to return to their workplaces, it found Captain Zakrzevska, sitting in the command chair and reading news from the command on the handy padd. Gizia, curled up in a fluffy ball, was sleeping on the back of the armchair. It wouldn't be surprising, if not for the fact that the captain was wearing a nightgown, bunny slippers, and her hair was wound on curlers. At the sight of her officers, she didn't even get confused.

"Don't look like that, I woke up here," she said. "Probably soon, it will turn out that, to make matters worse, I sleepwalk. While we were partying, headquarters figured out the matter of our Azgartes."

"Oh, and what did they write?" Arek asked.

"They claim that the ZM was an invention of the Starozopryks, not the Azgartes, and that these Pegasus creatures would never trade in such things. In their opinion, we are dealing with the new breed that has access to old technology. The question of why it trades them instead of using them remains open."

"And the Azgartes exist after all or not really?" Veronika made inquiries, sitting at the controls.

"They didn't write that. I think they once existed and visited our planet. I saw a closed portal myself when I was undergoing training in one of the former military bases. Unfortunately, we only have one left, and it's broken ... it's a pity."

They all got thoughtful, trying to imagine what it would have been like if there had still been technology that could move material objects thousands of light-years away like a supertransporter. On the other hand, if the ancient writings are to be believed, nothing good had come from using it, only problems and torments.

"I wonder if the Tokars would be members of the Union today if the Govalds hadn't become extinct," sighed Jürgen, taking his place. The Tokar race was a fraction of the Govald race, preferring gentle coexistence rather than aggression, something like Uoltans in opposition to the Cumulans with whom they had common roots. Whatever had happened to the

Govalds, had also affected the Tokars, as today there was no trace of both factions in the galaxy.

"Who knows. But we shouldn't guess, but rather think how to catch up with those traders. Because that they trade, God be with them, but they hijacked one of our ships and probably immobilized two others," said the captain.

Then she stood up and stretched delightfully.

"I'm going to shower," she said. "Jürgen, you are taking over the bridge. Course 423.81, right into the galaxy's core."

"I wonder if we will ever come back from there," growled Cezary Monkey, who, as a result of a draw, was assigned to be on duty at the engine room console. Being hangover, he always got pessimistic and made very gloomy predictions about the future of the mission. Everyone was used to it and didn't care about it.

"There is something to hurry for?" Lilianna shrugged, scooped Gizia from the back of the armchair and moved to the door. "Don't complain, Monkey, because you will jinx."

"I wonder why we were just commissioned to pursue these what-to-call-them ... Maybe they want to get rid of us."

The captain nodded regretfully and went out, leaving the question unanswered. She wasn't really sure of it herself, but she didn't intend to worry about it. More and more she became convinced that her place was right there, on board 'Hermash'. Not knowing when, she was bitten by the bug of space travel, from which she couldn't free herself - she could only be happy, flashing through the endless black space, marked with flaming fires. She could chase mysterious thieves or deliver vaccines to distant worlds, whatever, just to stay here, among swarms of stars, on the fragile ship, equipped with the hysterical computer and manned by the crazy crew.

***

Before 'Hermash' found any real trace of the hijacked ships, several months passed - how many, no one knew exactly, because the chronometers on this ship worked as they wanted, and the sense of time disintegrated during journeys at superlumination speed. It took quite a long time, anyway. Meanwhile, ArCer found in one of his books a way to bind SyTar's soul, but to his surprise, Greg vehemently protested when he heard about it.

"No way," he said firmly. "I'm used to this bastard, and without his scoffing, I'd feel uncomfortable. Besides, he can be really helpful."

For the next two weeks, ArCer searched the databases for any news about SyTar and was about to quit when he accidentally found information about this Uoltan in ... police chronicles. They showed that SyTar was a troublemaker and hooligan, but at the same time a multi-talented scientist. As a boy he had been in two educational centers, as a teenager in a Military Academy counterpart, and later in college, he shone through extraordinary talents, but his indiscipline and affinity for strange experiments caused him to be expelled from the university. He had been sent to Earth to get rid of the problem from planet Uoltan, in the hope that he would be hastened there, but it got even worse instead of better. First of all, he had fallen into the wrong company, then had taken a liking to earthly alcohol, and finally had gotten into a brawl in which had died from an accidental stabbing with a knife, even not intended for him. For Uoltan, SyTar was an exceptionally colorful character. Besides, his behavior here on 'Hermash' confirmed the common opinion.

"In my opinion, we should neutralize him, ignoring the opinion of engineer Brzenchyshchykievich," ArCer finished the report submitted to the captain.

"In my opinion, too," Lilianna replied. "But without Greg's consent, we won't do it, and besides, SyTar has recently slowed down his entertainment activities. Maybe he will finally settle down, who knows."

ArCer wasn't so optimistic, but he didn't protest, as he had already learned that it would have been useless. People were stubborn and illogical, and when they were also in power, they didn't listen to anyone but themselves. He left his report on the captain's desk and went to the infirmary, where TiShan was just conducting a routine examination of their daughter.

TiAllia was developing properly, growing, gaining weight, and in psychomotor terms she didn't deviate from Uoltan's norms for babies, but the doctor was worried about too low gravity on the ship and the impact it could have on the baby. She was also extremely irritated by the fact that almost all of the crew wanted to take TiAllia in their arms and carry her around a little, as if she had been just another animal on board. Only a few people behaved 'normally' towards her, including the captain and the helmsman Veronika. Both hated little children, so they treated TiAllia relatively neutral.

What irritated TiShan the most was the use of infantile chatter by the crew members when they spoke to her little daughter.

"How is she supposed to learn to speak properly when she heard over and over again "whazh nije lil lejs" or "whoj fingels al they, clap, clap lil paws"? How can she get the idea of who she is when she is told that she is a kitten, fish, frog or the sweetest princess?" the doctor was indignant, but she was powerless in the face of this massive attack on her pointy-eared offspring.

The crewmen sang songs to the little one, from which the logical minds of the doctor and commander ArCer reared, they entertained her with counting rhymes that made no sense ("Here, here, here a waterhen boiled millet ...", "Snail, snail, show the horns ...", "A woman sits on a bench near a stove, says the prayer in German ...") and it was scary to think what kind of education they would give the little Uoltanian girl when she understood anything.

One day, quite unexpectedly, Malvinka Krencik caught the signature signal of Tsiolkovsky from the background noise.

With the excitement, the beautiful lieutenant almost fell out of her chair.

"Captain, there is!" she screamed. "There is Tsiolkovsky!"

"Where?" Captain Zakrzevska, who was dozing in the command chair, curled up like a kitten, moved her head up violently.

"Somewhere there! I have a signature of its engines. Oh, and now I'm catching the other two ..."

"Cool. I commend you for your vigilance. Announce, Miss, yellow alarm, shields endways," the captain sprang up briskly from her chair and ran out. Faithful to the principle that "the master's eye makes the horse fat", she always checked the readiness of the staff personally.

Those of the crew, who weren't touched by the yellow alarm, being scolded by the captain, quickly adjusted to the state of alert. First of all, it was necessary to close the entire zoo in cages and terrariums, then to secure what could have suffered, and only finally to report the readiness for a possible fight. Captain Zakrzevska ran around all decks, checking the condition of the crew, because she rightly suspected that it might have been deviating from perfection, especially after such a long period of relative slack.

Of course, the crew members were not very pleased and they showed it bluntly, especially Father Toadstool, whose meeting of the rosary group was interrupted by the yellow alarm. There was a lark - the good chaplain figured out that he had to keep his brood busy with something, so that it wouldn't fall from idleness into debauchery and other deadly sins. Therefore, he organized a choir, the rosary group and a catechetical society, which was already mentioned.

The most interesting thing is that the vast majority of the crew were persuaded to participate in the activities of one of these clubs, even those whose great-grandfathers had been atheists. Three-quarters of the choir, devoutly singing "Hallelujah!" and other traditional songs consisted of unbelievers, plus two Muslims, one of whom had an excellent baritone and the other a contralto.

"All is good, as long as there is some variety," said Charles Mikhalov, who also joined the choir, admittedly because Malvinka Krencik belonged in it. At the same time, he took malicious satisfaction from the fact that his deputy and at the same time rival didn't have even an ounce of musical hearing and sense of rhythm, and as such couldn't belong to a choir.

"After all, nothing is happening yet, so why won't you let me finish my classes?" the chaplain roared, running after Lilianna.

"Father, don't embitter my life, okay? Now is not the time to prattle prayer," the captain finally got angry and opened the door to the catechetical room with a flourish. " Hey, mohair ladies! Enough for today, everyone to the positions. Didn't you hear the alarm?"

"And that was an alarm?" Sister Ophelia was surprised. "I thought it was the signal of the watch change."

Only now did Lilianna realize that the watch change bell and the yellow alert sounded in fact quite similar, but she was irritated anyway.

"Is the yellow lamp on the wall lit during the watch change?!" she exclaimed. "Sister, you don't have to know about it, but this whole company, damn it, should! They sat like painted dolls and didn't even move!"

"Because Sister Ophelia talks so interestingly, we listened with attention," squeaked Dr. Lemowa. The captain spoke very succinctly what she would have done if they hadn't immediately found themselves in their positions (she wasn't worse at this than the Queen of Hearts), and the catechetical society scattered like scared ants.

Only then did Lilianna turn to the completely undeterred nun:

"Do you, sister realize that most of this group are atheists?"

"Of course."

"And it doesn't bother you, sister?"

Of course not. Do all audiences of "Hamlet" have to be avid fans of Shakespeare? Nobody will throw them out of the theater just because they came to have fun."

The captain was speechless, so she just waved her hand hopelessly and turned on her heel. She had to go back to the bridge.

LXVIII.

The signals of all three hijacked ships were clear, and once you caught them, you could try to get some specific information. Inga and Malvinka immediately set to work, while 'Hermash', having his own will, spontaneously tried to establish contact with the on-board computers. He was so passionate about it that he paid no attention to anything else, and as each of his activities was usually accompanied by an acoustic effect, this one was no exception. Due to his forgetfulness, 'Hermash' didn't turn off the interconnection node, so all the speakers on the ship made sounds very similar to, as Mattias von Braun said intellectually, 'gas-peristaltic activity after oral administration of a bigger portion of peas with fried cabbage.' The other crew members called the sounds more bluntly, and they sniffed around themselves very distrustfully until someone made them realize where the suspicious noises were coming from.

"This really could happen only to us: the farting computer," said Charles Mikhalov sadly when he entered the bridge to report that, contrary to pessimistic forecasts, the warp engines withstood the crazy pace and the hull of the ship showed no major damage.

"Well, well. And it was said that such a joyful work as our repmobile, wouldn't travel even a stupid million kilometers," said Arek with such pride, as if he had personally riveted the incompatible military surplus elements.

"And that it would lose parts in the collision with the first gas and dust cloud," added Joe Stelmach, who had just taken over the duty at the engine room console and noticed with horror that Cezary Monkey had changed all the parameters.

"I remember myself when it was told to me in the shipyard. And people asked if I was not afraid to fly such a monster.

"At least no one can say that our 'Hermash' is asexual mass production," replied captain Zakrzevska. "We have a ship of undeniable individuality. Girls, are you picking up anything already?"

"We are, Captain," Malvinka reported. "Ships are at a triangulation blind spot between a planet of the class M4 and its two moons. There are no traces of life on boards, but they are detectable on the planet's surface. Quite a lot."

"Human?"

"Human and not human. Different, so to speak."

Lilianna scratched the top of her head. That the lost crews of 'Hubble' and 'Tsiolkovsky' were on this unknown planet and were in all probability in good health, she took for granted, and rejoiced at finding them, but why did they abandon their ships, and all ends up? Her instinct told her that before she sent someone to the surface it would be a good idea to investigate the matter, because after all, Star Armada personnel didn't abandon their ships just like that. She got up from the command chair and began pacing the bridge. She always thought better 'on foot'.

"Are there any signs of violence on boards?" she asked to gain time.

"Our readings don't show it. There is law and order on boards, all the systems work, but ..." Inga hesitated for a moment but urged by Lilianna, she finished:

"...the transporter circuits are open."

"It's logical," said ArCer. "If all crew members moved to the planet, the last of them had to set up automatic transport. It will also be logical to assume that they were transferred voluntarily and that they voluntarily decided to desert. From these results another logical conclusion that we must go down there and arrest them."

The captain, however, noticed that such logic wasn't worth shit and ordered to check the conditions on the planet, as well as the profile of living beings, down to the last detail. The mortally injured Uoltan bent over the scanner with such an expression that it was surprising that the delicate device didn't freeze from the aura emanating from him, as if submerged in liquid nitrogen. However, after a few minutes, ArCer's face clearly went dumb and he forgot about the image.

"Captain, I'm detecting something unusual in the spectrum of radiation," he said. "These people on the planet are alive, but they should be as thoroughly dead as possible."

There was consternation on the bridge. How's that, they should have been dead?

"You wish them death?" Aśka Kubica asked uncertainly.

"Of course not. I just detected the life-threatening factor on this planet."

"And whose ass is it about?" Stelmach was interested, but he chose badly, because Captain Zakrzevska hit him in the neck so strongly that he pecked the console with his humped nose.

"Commander ArCer, please clarify your statement," she ordered sternly.

"I'm detecting Bartolini's radiation," said the Uoltan. "Nothing should survive there for more than a week, well, maybe two. It doesn't make sense. The only planet where such a concentration of radiation has been detected so far is Omicron in the constellation of the Eagle. And this planet ... is not officially registered."

The first mate looked at his captain expectantly.

"We can send a reconnaissance group in anti-radiation suits," he suggested.

"So far, no suit material has been invented that would protect against Bartolini's radiation. However, short-term exposure is not harmful, only a few days would result in serious damage."

"And they've been there for at least six months," Inga said, having carefully checked all the readings.

Jürgen muttered something in German that implied a deep conviction that someone must have been crazy here, and Lilianna fell into deep reverie.

"Keep the synchronous orbit," she said finally. "I want a thorough surface scan, including the number of living objects found. I'm going to the library."

After the captain left, a lively discussion broke out on the bridge, during which a total of fifteen hypotheses were formulated, overwhelmingly mutually exclusive. While the senior officers discussed the mystery of the migration of crews from ships, Joe Stelmach secretly connected to the engine room and 'sold' the latest news to the local team.

The effect was that by the time the captain had dug into the library files in search for the news she needed, the entire ship was roaring with the most incredible rumors. Lilianna decided to find the priest and ask him to give a sermon about the harmfulness of all gossip, but she got sorely disappointed. Not only did Father Toadstool not intend to curb these stories, but he also himself became the author of one of the theories: the enlightenment was to come to the crews of both ships and, having experienced religious inspiration, they were to decide to abandon their mundane passions, devoting themselves to asceticism and meditation.

"Rather, they nurture these passions, it's obvious!" the captain shouted, losing all patience with her chaplain. "They hook up there nicely and make moonshine no worse than what my beloved Janicek offers everyone here! They behave like the hippies of old, the only difference is that they started to grow some plants, but I won't bet dollars to doughnuts if it's not weed!"

While in the library, Captain Zakrzevska not only used the generous database of Star Armada, but also strong observation devices. She managed to find the name of the planet, although for this she had to break into encrypted files. So she knew much more than the others, but not everything. After giving the priest such a reprimand that the walls trembled, she went to the bridge.

"I already know what to do, my gold guys," she announced. "Inga, call out Superprice right now. If you can't get the 'ship to ship' communication, send them a notice telling them they are to come here as soon as possible ... but it would be better if you were able to."

"It's as clear as crystal," Inga replied servantly, and leaned over the console.

The rest of them began to question their commander what he had discovered, but Lilianna, driving them away as if they had been intrusive flies, took refuge in the captain's chair.

"Back off, dammit, let me gather my thoughts, you'll understand everything in a moment. I won't hurt my throat in vain for your pleasure."

Soon Inga Laush was able to find the correct frequency, and Captain Kerk's face appeared on the screen.

"What's going on, do you need help?" asked the commander of the USS Superprice famous in the whole quadrant.

"I don't. The crews of 'Tsiolkovsky' and 'Hubble' need it," Lilianna replied. "The problem is that I won't give them this help, because there is no relevant information in the database. Why is it not allowed to land on Phalloos IV?"

"What?! That's where it carried you?! Woman, you are soft in your head! You face the death penalty! Please run away immediately and erase from the logbooks the information that you flew there!!! I repeat, you will not help them anyway, please escape!"

"What?!"

Kerk took the receiver out of his ear and turned to his first mate. He looked completely stunned.

She asks if, I'm quoting, anyone has ever given me a kick in the ass before," he said. "I don't know what the woman means."

"She seems to have a negative attitude towards your speech for some reason," replied Mr. Spox. "I'd risk saying she wouldn't leave until she figured out how to save those people. Which may not be easy."

Kerk shook his head and put the receiver back in his ear.

"Lilianna, you are putting your entire crew at risk," he said. "Escape from the Phalloos system as soon as possible."

"To escape is not in Polish style. We are not the French with their four-speed tanks!"

"What? What four-speed tanks?"

"You don't know that saying? A French tank has four gears: three reverse and one forward, in case the enemy attacks from the rear."

"I don't understand what you are saying to me!"

"Then move the bowels or something ... If you don't want to help, speak straightforwardly, I don't need your charity. I can do it myself. Seemingly, every guy is the same, plays a hero, and when he should set out his stall, he turns out to be a slob and he doesn't want to help a weak woman ..."

"Captain, you've already exaggerated with this playing," a distant voice interrupted. " Captain Kerk is not like that ..."

"It's not my business, First, I don't get under his bed. But I had never imagined that such a daredevil would chicken out on any occasion."

Kerk took a breath, mentally counted to ten, and replied:

"I don't chicken out; I'm just saying what you should do."

"And I warn you that at the next meeting I will punch you in the face for refusing to help."

"Don't warn me! Follow the rules!"

"Shit, dialogue like from 'Szpicbródka'," someone on the line chuckled and Kerk realized that probably half of the 'Hermash' crew were listening to this conversation.

Captain Zakrzevska didn't want to be silent at all.

"I bugger the rules when it comes to human life, understood?" here the commander of Superprice thought that he himself had acted very often in accordance with this principle and in fact he couldn't blame the little Polish woman for not wanting to sacrifice anyone for nothing.

"It's not like that, woman," he groaned. "Extremely powerful beings live there. I have dealt with them before. They can send telepathic messages over great distances, causing very realistic delusions. I have encountered them personally, and I'm telling you, there is no way to defend yourself against them. No way."

"Are they aggressive?" Zakrzevska asked.

"Probably not, but nobody wants to take chances. We had only one contact with them, which was followed by General Order number seven. It states that any officer who brings a ship into the Phalloos system will be put to death. You did it, I understand that, because of your ignorance ... and if you don't leave immediately, a firing squad will await you."

"Ooh, what a great parade! Well, would you like to live forever? It won't work anyway. Listen: I want to get these people out of here and I'll do it, with or without your help, and then they can even take me by the butt and hang me on a flagpole."

Kerk looked helplessly at his first mate. The man shook his head slowly.

"She won't budge, Jeeves."

Kerk thought for a moment, then resumed the connection.

"Lilianna, I can't join you," he said. "If I did, it would only be to arrest you and put you on trial, so I'd rather stay away. Just for talking to you now, I might lose command of the ship. However, I will send you all the materials you need."

"It's something. Also, please send me a detailed description of the incident on the Eagle's Omicron, because it seems we have a similar situation here ... or at least, we may have it."

'The incident on the Eagle's Omicron' was known throughout Armada as an example of what could have happened if the entire crew had been under the influence of a potent drug, but the details were kept secret. Apparently, it was required by reason of state.

"Agreed, but be careful, it's probably just an illusion," Kerk sighed resignedly.

"Maybe, but I'd rather be prepared and know what to watch out for when I go down there."

"The death penalty."

"And you are like that parrot which repeats what it wants ... They won't hang me twice, what's to be afraid of?"

"This one time is not enough for you?"

"I'm turning off the communicator and waiting for the file transfer."

Soon 'Hermash' began receiving the data stream from Superprice, and Lilianna leaped at them happily, to her relief finding in them exactly what she was looking for. The time came to act.

LXIX.

"Excuse me, what should I prepare?" Colorado Kviek asked in amazement, thinking he misheard.

"Do I speak Clingorgian? I repeat the order: Dust masks, five pieces! The filters are to be absolutely operational, otherwise I will personally tear your legs off of your ass. Then I will need an itch powder ... an infrasound emitter would be better, but we don't have any parts for it, I've already asked Mikhalov. You also have to find protective suits that the powder can't penetrate. I don't feel like scratching myself. Plus a solid stereo with disco polo music, the most crap stuff you can find."

"That's an order for me, Captain, it will be done ... but I must admit that I have never heard such a strange order in my life," Colorado turned off the comlink and looked helplessly at his wife.

Azalia Kviek shrugged.

"Let's settle the demand, then I'll read the coffee grounds and see what we got into again," she said.

"We haven't had any coffee for a couple of months, apart from what pours out of the synthesizer."

"Relax, I'm not that stupid. I hid a package for a special occasion."

While the supply workers were looking for the ordered materials in the hold, Lilianna ran to Vasyl Zaychik. She found him only in the kitchen, where he was discussing with von Braun the recipe for sweet blini with herring glaze.

"Vashka, drive your best shooters to the turret," she commanded, struggling to suppress nausea at the thought of the exotic dish discussed so lively. "If a ship approaches us, fire the first warning series, and then have Arek talk to them. Poniatno[40]?"

"Poniatno, captain baryshnia!"

Christopher Mayher, who was ordered to form a detachment, chose the two best soldiers, in his opinion, and SiWok as the "medical guard". It is true that Captain Zakrzevska didn't expect a fight, but it was always worth having such someone in a reconnaissance team in an unknown area. Especially since Lilianna didn't hide from him what they would come into contact with.

"These people are happy where they are," she said. "They won't want to come back as long as they feel so. It's all the fault

---

[40] *(Rus)* Understood.

of some parasites that feed on emotions and settle in the bodies of the humanoids. They also neutralize the action of Bartolini's rays. Admittedly, there is no mention in the notes of Jeeves Kerk that such rays were detected on Phalloos IV, but the situation was unusual at the time."

"What about the ban on approaching this planet?" Mayher, as always, was the best informed about the regulations.

"The creatures living here are said to be extremely dangerous, but it's just bullshit. You can get along with them. Star Armada Command is shaking in its shoes because it knows they are invincible, and a being that cannot be dominated by any means is a threat to these weenies. And here something smells wrong, because if these creatures still inhabited Phalloos IV, there would be no need for any worms or other pinworms, they themselves could neutralize the rays. The first guests of this planet didn't get sick."

"You think they're not there anymore?"

"We'll see."

While waiting for the completion of the equipment, Captain Zakrzevska made an attempt to get along with the crews on the surface of the planet, using for this purpose a 'wasp', that is, a small, self-steering transmitting and receiving device launched from the ship. Unfortunately, this attempt failed. The forced settlers answered, talking nonsense, or refused to talk at all and drove the 'wasp' away with whatever they could.

"And how do you know that they were sent there by force?" asked Arek, assisting his commander on an equal footing with other officers (there were so many of them on the bridge now that it was suspected that at least half of them were ordinary crewmen who interloped, driven by curiosity.) "Maybe they flew voluntarily?"

"Are you crazy?" the helmsman Veronika tapped her forehead meaningfully. "The whole crew couldn't go crazy at the same time, much less two."

"Bla, bla, bla," Johnnie Caterpillar supported her. "You can stick such a speech; I won't say where."

"Maybe it's some sort of settlement action?" Joe Watery spoke out of turn.

And if I'm put in the colonization
I will take a daughter of a Tatar;
And maybe in my generation
There will be a Palen[41] for the Tsar.[42]

...recited broodily Mstislav Deadskull.

---

[41] Peter von der Palen (1178-1864) was a general of the Imperial Russian Army also an organizer of the assassination of Tsar Alexander I.

[42] Fragment of the prison song from the drama *Forefathers' Eve part III* by Adam Mickiewicz, Polish bard of the Romantic era.

"Slavek, don't tire the prophetess and take care of the helm. If I'm not here, you are to listen to Arek and monitor everything," the captain commanded, tossing the headphones on the console in discouragement, as the message had just arrived from the transmission hall that everything was ready. "Yellow alert until my return. The defense is managed autonomously by Vasyl Zaychik, the bridge is taken over by the first officer. And God forbid you mess up something! You only act on orders."

Everyone, except ArCer, made offended faces that were supposed to mean that they were the most disciplined team in the Union, as while still in cradles they had acted only on orders, and this remark was absolutely unnecessary. Lilianna, who knew well what to think of her crew, paid no attention to it. She sat Gizia on Johnnie's shoulder, stroked the trubblat, with which her orderly never parted, and ran to the transport hall.

The protective suits were neat and colorful, but stiff as hell. The masks, however, fit well and you hardly felt them on your face. Despite this protection, the reconnaissance group felt very insecure as it materialized in the middle of what appeared to be a primitive agricultural settlement inhabited by humans in Star Armada uniforms. There was something fictional about it, especially since the intruders caused almost no reaction. Only the captains of both crews, guided probably by a rudimentary sense of duty, approached the newcomers with a broad smile.

"Welcome to Phalhoos IV, my friends," said one of them. "I'm Amin Robau..."

"I know, Captain of USS Hubble," Lilianna interrupted him. "And the other gentleman is, saving your reverence, Captain Le Gia Hui[43], and you better not introduce yourself to my crew ... Please stay where you are and don't come any closer. I'm Captain Lilianna Zakrzevska, the commander of PSS 'Hermash', and I'm here to take you all home."

"But this is our home," interrupted her a captain with the awkward surname[44], a short, plump Chinese with a sparse mustache on his flat face. "We are not moving anywhere from here, and when you get rid of prejudices, you will understand that this is a wonderful place. Take off these masks, they are unnecessary."

"Bullshit. We'll see. Where are the Phalloosians? Native people, I mean?"

"There is no one like this. We heard that they have been dead for a long time."

"And Captain Mikesh and a woman named Vena?" The captain listed the main characters from the classified report on the events of the First Contact. She didn't know their exact history, she had only read that Captain Mikesh had deserted from his ship in order to stay on the alien planet with Vena, who couldn't fly away with him. It had something to do with the

---

[43] In Polish, this word is a vulgar term for a male sexual organ.

[44] Wordplay. An ordinary Korean name in Polish means an insult to a popular soccer club.

indigenous people of this planet, in front of which, as you can see, the entire military power of the Union was shaking in the boots of its parade uniforms.

These people are also gone. That persons were found dead and buried. Anyway, THEY will explain it to you better," said Amin Robeau.

"Who are THEY? Where are?"

"THEY don't like the sun, so they don't go out during the day. Come with us, we will lead you to them."

"Drop your sticks, come with us," murmured Chris Mayher and nervously adjusted the mask. He had the impression that a moment more and the soft plastic would slide off his skin, leaving him vulnerable to the mysterious parasites.

Lilianna shrugged and allowed herself to be led to a rocky hill that had openings of apparently man-made caves. Strange flowers resembling dyed rhodanthes grew around. They vibrated in the wind, making melodic, barely audible sounds. SiWok held one of them. The sound stopped and the flower trembled like a living creature in his hand. When he released it, the plant rejoined the quiet choir.

"Fascinating. I wish I could investigate it ..." the boy muttered and quickened his pace so as not to be far behind the rest of the squad.

Inside, the caves were arranged like modern and even futuristic apartments with all rounded surfaces. However, this was not surprising, nor was it that the items there were completely unknown to them. They did grow into the ground, but only when they saw the inhabitants of the caves. These were not people, but also not Phaloosians whom Captain Zakrzevska had seen in the figures from the files of Captain Kerk. They were skinny, short and had disproportionately large heads, sad eyes devoid of whites, and tiny lips, as well as weak hands that gave the impression of some extremely precise manipulators. Their gender was a mystery, though neither of them wore a scrap of cloth.

"Azgartes ..." Mayher sighed with wonder and devotion at the same time.

"That's true. That's what you've always called us," one of the cave dwellers said gently, in his voice sounding distant. He tilted his head a little, staring at the newcomers with his huge eyes.

"I'm Seti," he said after a moment. "And these are Neferu and Osir. Have you come in peace?"

"No, in a spaceship," Captain Zakrzevska replied thoughtlessly, trying to somehow swallow it all and not go crazy. She had the impression that she had been hit on the head with something heavy and only a solid nudge under her rib, applied by Chris, roused her from the 'clumsy oaf' state.

"Excuse me," she said. "I'm confused. We have been told that the Azgartes became extinct sometime in the late twenty-first century."

"We haven't become extinct," Seti assured her. "All the gates leading from the Milky Way to the Pegasus galaxy have simply been destroyed or sealed for the safety of both sides. It was considered for the best. Your galaxy was threatened by Govalds and others such, and with your level of development at that time, you wouldn't have been able to deal with them."

"Right, if humanity had found out then about what was the most closely guarded military secret, such a panic would have broken out that there would have been nothing left intact," said Ensign Dysentery, who, despite difficult experiences with the ZONK collective, remained the best soldier on the ship and as such was included in the reconnaissance group.

"It was then, but what now?" SiWok asked, continuing to scan all three Azgartes.

"You see for yourself," Neferu replied. "We decided to check how our former allies were and we fell into the hands of the beings who took our technology and sent us to this planet."

"Why did you trust them? Caution has not killed anyone yet."

"They looked like you. Only later did we find out that they can change shapes. What worries us most is that without the tools they stole from us, we won't be able to get the Gate open and return to our land."

"We should be glad, anyway, that they didn't manage to figure out most of the devices," added Seti.

"It didn't stop them from selling them," muttered Mayher. "And the Gate?"

"They took it for an ornament of the ship. They don't even know what they could get if they launched it. They left it to us as an object redundant and worthless."

"Dardanelles' donkeys ... well, we'll take you from here too, together with your stuff," decided Captain Zakrzevska, adjusting the mask, which got tilted from her excitement.

"I told you, we're not leaving this place," Captain Le Gia protested.

"Someone asked you, Hui?" Lilianna muttered in a voice far from polite and touched the communicator, sending a signal to Arek sitting like on pushpins to start the action.

LXX.

It was a long time before the chaos in the arbitrary colony was tackled, the systems of both ships were examined, as well as both crews and the inhabitants of the Pegasus galaxy were brought. It turned out that the itch powder and disco polo music were way better than the infrasound emitter when it comes to inducing a state of rage. After the fourth listening to the great hit "Over Your Green Eyes", which opened a compilation created by the Kviek couple, the crew of 'Hermash' was also ready to bite and scratch, although it wasn't itchy.

Roused from the state of universal bliss, the crews took possession of their ships again, repaired minor damage and restored everything to a working condition - of course, after taking a thorough bath to remove the nasty preparation from the skin. It even caused indiscriminate jokes in the crew of 'Hermash', which, moreover, primarily wondered about how the powder had gotten into the supplies taken from Earth. Only the main supplier, i.e. Second Lieutenant Kviek, could know that.

Finally called to the mess hall to settle the matter, he calmly explained that someone with a great sense of humor had stuffed the contents of the entire "prankster shop" into the eighth hold, so he could at any time serve not only with itching or sneezing powders, but also with rubber cockroaches, artificial poops and other valuables. However, he made the reservation that he didn't know who was so smart, and he couldn't say anything about who equipped their ship with disco polo music. Whoever it was, accidentally hit the jackpot, because clinical trials conducted by SiWok proved that you didn't have to release negative emotions to get rid of spores - 'White bear' and 'Love in Zakopane' were enough - and when the unfortunate parasites heard 'Jozin z bazin' (although it is rather a Czecho-polo), they themselves escaped from the host through all the openings. It made everyone very intrigued.

The three Azgartes caused much less sensation than the plants SiWok collected. Only Father Toadstool, when he saw them, crossed himself piously, spat in disgust and declared that "these scandalizers of the little people are to clothe their pathetic limbs immediately!"

"Naked ballet?! End of the world!

He should be surpliced and chasubled!"[45] Mstislav Deadskull sang innocently and was hit with a rosary in the back.

---

[45] The quote comes from Cabaret by Olga Lipińska, a long series of TV shows popular in Poland.

"Aua!" he screamed and, just in case, escaped beyond the reach of the priest. Everyone knew Father Thaddeus' rosary, it was heavy as hell, made of carved mahogany and thick silver, and the Toadstool's hands operated it with amazing dexterity, not only in purely prayer matters.

"Calm down, both of you, now," commanded Captain Zakrzevska. "What will our guests think?"

"And what will we think about them doesn't matter?" Sister Ophelia unexpectedly supported the priest, which happened very rarely. "Who walks among people completely naked ..."

"Let's dance hoola and streap on ..." hummed Deadskull, who apparently felt like singing, but this time he was hit in his side by the commander and finally fell silent for good.

The Azgartes watched this scene with sympathy and understanding. Their huge, bulging eyes surveyed the ship and its crew with curiosity and, at the same time, the tolerance of beings at a tenfold level of development. Even the indignation of both clergymen, they didn't take as something offensive, but rather glozed over it with some mild superiority. People clearly interested them like some living ethnographic specimens, not like creatures equal to them.

However, they viewed the ship with some appreciation, especially the engine room and the infirmary, where at their sight doctor Zmiyevski widened his eyes and dropped the test tube with someone's pee.

"What can I do for you?" he muttered, trying to collect his thoughts. "Maybe give you bathrobes?"

"No, there is no such need," the captain replied politely. "It seems to me that wearing clothes is against the religion of our visitors. Be so good and show them your wonders, okay? I have a meeting with the captains. Just in case, I'll be in the conference room."

Leaving terrified Jacob in the company of the Azgartes, Lilianna went to the conference room with Bear, which, delighted, was jumping around her, panting with his wide smiling muzzle.

In the room, at a table decorated with two enormous platters (one with sandwiches and the other with cookies) as well as several bottles of various contents, sat Robau and Hui. They were both already wearing clean uniforms, neatly shaved and combed, and their expressions were very serious, despite the amber content of the glasses in front of them. At the sight of Lilianna, they both left their snacks and stood up.

"Sit down, gentlemen," she anticipated their words. "Let's not make unnecessary ceremonies. Eat and drink as much as you want. How are your boats?"

"Nice, not badly damaged. But now it's about your skin," said Amin Robau sadly.

"Exactly," Captain Hui backed him up. "We are safe, we were brought to the Phalhoos system by force and sent to this planet, but you flew into the forbidden area voluntarily. I'm afraid you will be executed, though that seems unbelievable these days. When they brought us into the system, we received a message from the headquarters that there was a penalty for breaking general order number, I don't remember which.

"Seven. Did headquarters know where you were?"

"I think so ... I don't really know, but it looks like it."

Lilianna casually stroked Bear, who rested his huge head on her knees, and stuffed one of the sandwiches into his mouth.

"Well, I already have an argument for the lawyer," she said calmly. "Don't worry about anything, it was my decision. Just tell me, who actually attacked you and the Azgartes? This is some unknown breed, right?"

"Well, completely unknown. We had asked the Azgartes about them before we got infected with the parasites, because then we didn't care about everything," Captain Robau replied. "They come from the planet Psykon, we don't even know where it is. They can take any shape, but only for an hour. This is called molecular transposition, if I remember the name correctly. They're not even particularly dangerous, they're just trying to save their planet."

"And you got in their way," finished Lilianna.

"Exactly. If they had wanted to kill us, we would be dead, but they only sent us to Phalloos so that we wouldn't be able to follow them. They probably haven't even heard of order number seven ..."

"To tell you the truth, I hadn't heard about it either until Jeeves Kerk made me aware of it," muttered Captain Zakrzevska. She somehow got it all straight in her head, and decided it would be best to accompany both crews to Earth. There was no point in escaping from justice, it was better to face what awaited her and hope for a stroke of luck. And that's what she chose to do.

LXXI.

The journey to Earth took quite a long time. The Star Armada command was silent for the first days, only on the fourth day Inga Lausch, who ouf of boredom was doing a crossword at the console, received a signal from the headquarters and almost fell off her seat.

"Captain, they are calling!" she cried so fearfully as if a centipede had come out of the loudspeaker.

"Such is their work," replied Captain Zakrzevska calmly. "Get them on the screen, lady."

There was a humming noise on the bridge, as if someone had put a stick into a hive, as everyone was aware that their commander's head was very unsteadily clinging to the graceful neck and in this situation the message from the headquarters couldn't be particularly positive.

Admiral Cormack appeared on the home screen.

"Please summon all the senior officers," he said dryly, not indulging in welcome courtesies. Inga, prompted by Lilianna's gaze, conveyed the call through the intercom. After a while, everyone who had a rank higher than an ensign appeared on the bridge, and it got impossibly crowded.

"As you all know, your captain broke General Order number seven," the admiral began. "She is therefore dismissed from service and arrested. She is to spend the rest of the journey in the cell. Command of the ship will be taken by the first officer."

"No way, forget it," Arek was offended.

"What? I'm giving you the official order!"

"Kiss my ass, Admiral, I won't be a pig for your frigging pleasure."

The admiral flushed with indignation, but restrained himself, not wanting to make a spectacle of himself in front of everyone.

"Then you will join Captain Zak in the arrest, and the second officer, Mr. Jürgen von Ravensbruck, takes command."

"Dreck,"[46] Jürgen replied firmly. "To make others tear me apart? Please don't hold a grudge against me, Admiral, but I really like to live."

---

[46] *(Ger)* Shit.

"You can spare yourself unnecessary talk, we are not scums, no one here will tear our Lilka's stool from under her beautiful buns," Christopher Mayher supported him, accidentally with the rhyming. "Captain Zakrzevska launched this pile of remains and only she will bring it to Earth."

"Is this a rebellion, Lieutenant?!"

"I can order a referendum on this matter, but it seems to me that it is a rebellion."

Admiral Cormack's jaw dropped. His gaze moved from the screen and wandered along the audience, then stopped on ArCer. The Uoltan stood motionless with his hands behind his back and showed no emotion.

"Mr. ArCer, will you take command of the ship?"

"Of each ship, but not this," replied the commander. "Mr. Admiral, 'Hermash' is not an ordinary ship, and most of all it is not an ordinary crew. Only a Pole can command the Poles, they will not listen to anyone else. If I may, I would advise a non-standard solution: let Captain Zakrzevska lead the ship to Earth and only then can a legal arrest be made."

The calm and measured words of the science officer clearly convinced the admiral. He pondered them for a moment, then said:

"Okay. Go straight to Earth. The arrest and the demobilization of the entire crew will take place immediately in the dock to avoid any surprises. End of communication."

The screen went blank.

"What do we do?" Arek asked, looking at Lilianna yawning.

She shrugged.

"What do you mean? We're simply going to Earth and that's it. I don't want to be late for my own funeral. Scatter, gang."

Then she sat down in the command chair as if nothing had happened. The officers dispersed as ordered, and word of what was happening spread through the ship with them. First, lamentation broke out everywhere. Then the crew members got angry and quietly, secretly from their own command section, decided to "close ranks, put scythes upright and not even give a uniform button". The fact that the entire crew of 'Hermash' didn't have a single button in the assets (uniforms and private clothes were fastened with magnetic locks), and no one saw the scythe on the ship (only Vasyl Zaychik held a hammer and sickle on the wall as an artistic installation) was a meaningless detail for them.

Captains Amin Robau and Le Gia Hui, who received the unpleasant news, congratulated each other silently that they hadn't been ordered to take over replacement command of 'Hermash' because something like this could end badly for them. Regardless of one another, they prepared a speech in defense of the Polish captain, which they intended to deliver before the court. Both of them, there's no denying, were impressed by this little woman who didn't hesitate to put everything she had, including her life, on the line, just to do the right thing.

What the three Azgartes were thinking about it would be hard to say, since they shared their thoughts with no one, all the time busy trying to reconstruct their strange devices. The team of Charles Mikhalov was happy to help them by providing what they wanted, but nothing could compensate for the loss of the most important elements taken by the Psykonians. The Spatial Gate, an enormous metal ring with a control console, which barely fit into the lower hold, without proper power supply, remained only an interesting ornament, and there was nothing to be done about it.

So, the return to Earth was not as triumphant as the crew would have liked. It is true that Father Toadstool delivered a fiery and very long sermon, the meaning and summary of which could be included in the lapidary slogan "... but WE won morally", but the mood among the crew members can be described as not very cheerful. It wasn't even about the fact that the flight was over, there would be no second one, and people got used to each other and this crazy ship. Suddenly everyone decided that they damnably liked their captain, who always roared at everyone, so they formed what they called 'Hermash dietine' and at the first meeting unanimously passed a resolution about defending her 'to the last drop of blood'.

ArCer soon found out about it and, uninvited, came to the next meeting to briefly make the brawlers realize that at best they would end up in one of the other colonies, but they would certainly not save anyone from criminal liability. At first, he was shouted down, but later it became clear that the Uoltan was right - they could do nothing. This caused that on all decks prevailed the mood of grim hopelessness and everyone lost their will to live.

***

In the dock where they were sent, the crew was first ordered to leave all their weapons on the ship. This order caused protests and confusion which was only contained by the captain. She appeared in front of the crew in a gala uniform, with a braid neatly combed and tied at the back of her head, and with one threatening look she silenced the murmuring crew.

"Sioy!"[47] she said sharply. "No such things here, understood? Nobody can say that Poles behave like preschoolers in a storm. With dignity, we go out and scatter in discipline and order.

Her eyesight softened a little as she ran it over the people that had become so close to her.

"Thank you," she finished. "You were a great crew and never let anyone tell you something else. Always be proud that you served on board Hermash. It's a great ship.

---

[47] *(Yiddish)* Silence.

"Thank you, princess," sobbed the on-board computer. "I will never forget you and I will not serve another crew. Even when I was to be scrapped, I won't."

The helmsman Deadskull had already started reciting one of the Polish elegiac poems, but stopped when someone behind him punched him under the shoulder blade.

"This is not the time for a poetry evening," said Captain Zakrzevska sternly. "I also know classic poems, Mr. Deadskull, but we shouldn't fall into such tones here. It didn't work and that's it. You have to live on and be content with the beautiful memories. Now, enough complaining, please form up in threes, in ancient Roman style, and let's go."

Dutifully, the crew members formed up as ordered and followed their captain up the automatic gangway to the hangar. A detachment of gendarmes was waiting there, as well as admiral Cormack, who was breathing triumph. Apparently, he couldn't deny himself the pleasure of detaining the rebellious Polish woman personally.

"Captain Zak, you are under arrest on the orders of Star Armada HQ," he said formally as the trinary column stopped in front of him, in discipline and order. "I hereby revoke you all the privileges and rights associated with belonging to the Star Armada. I advise you to think carefully about what you will say, because every word you say can be used as an aggravating argument. Anyway, at best, you're going to be demoted and sent to a penal colony."

The crew of 'Hermash' buzzed and boiled. The trinary array broke. Suddenly angry faces surrounded the gendarmerie, and curses poured out such that even Admiral Cormack lost his confidence.

"What a meanness!"

"What an ingratitude!

"The office rats' conspiracy!"

"Hey, who's a Pole, we will not give our captain!"

"That's right! The guns were taken from us, but don't we have fists?!" people cried out to one another. 'The court is the court, the law is the law, but justice must be on our side!"

"T'enga, call the Pandorian Guard to attack these scrubs!" Mayher shouted, brandishing a fruit switchblade for the lack of any other weapon.

"You will burn in hell, Satan's minions!" screamed Father Toadstool and, to add to his dignity, he waved his solid rosary around, like a bicycle chain.

"Hey, Night-heron, give me the mazer, right away they'll be madder!" Mstislav Deadskull rhymed offhand, threatening the admiral's escort with the rudder lever removed from the console.

"Wait, when I cuff with the pickaxe ...!" this voice clearly belonged to Johnnie Caterpillar, held by each of his mighty fist by two volunteers, lest he would get the admiral against all reason.

TiAllia, who didn't like this whole mess, suddenly started crying excruciatingly, which only added to the overall size of the brothel.

"The child can't even look at you, savages! I wish you had scab on your heads and too short hands!" Ensign Rozenfeld got angry, took the girl from TiShan and started rocking her to calm her down.

"Allah sees everything and writes it down in the books!" one of the Muslim crewmen yelled piously. "He will punish you on the doomsday! He will skin you and then make it grow back to skin you again! He will rip out your livers and intestines! You will be burning on hot coals for all eternity!"

The pictorial description of the torments of hell, combined with the scream of the pointy-eared baby, which no reports mentioned, completely deprived the admiral of his confidence. In addition, the huge, shaggy shepherd dog, which, it is not known how found himself besides, bit silently and painfully his defenseless seat. Cormack jumped up and hurriedly moved out of reach of the imposing ensemble of fangs.

"Bear, heel!" Captain Zakrzevska scolded the quadruped. "Don't bite the admiral, you may get poisoned. And all of you, calm down!!! What did I tell you? To form up! Mr. ArCer, Dr. TiShan, SiWok, come to me."

She moved aside, followed by confused Uoltans.

"Look after the Asgartes," Lilianna said softly. "I don't want them to get hurt somehow. It's best to take them to the planet Uoltan. Perhaps your scientists will find a way to activate the Gate and send them home."

"We'll do it," SiWok promised on behalf of all three. "But what about you, Lilka?"

"It's none of your business anymore, folks. This is a battle that I have to fight on my own."

She stroked SiWok's cheek.

"Take care, pointy-eared hotshots," she said kindly. "Live in harmony and peace, or something like that."

And she walked away towards the gendarmes waiting for her.

LXXII.

"So, what did the defendant say when you explained to her the prohibition related to Phalloos IV?" asked the prosecutor, beautiful and austere Sheree J. Wilson, eyeing Captain Kerk. He was on pins and needles, and it was evident that he wished with all his soul to be a thousand light-years away. Every now and then he looked at Spox accompanying him, at those of the 'Hermash' crew, who were allowed to enter the room, as well as guiltily looked at the bench of the accused, where this unbearable Polish woman sat, looking twice as vulnerable and innocent as she probably had ever been.

"Well, this ..." he was confused.

"So? Please reply."

"Well, she gave me some autoerotic suggestions," Kerk finally stuttered out. "Most of them would be impossible for a man built according to standard parameters."

"In a word, she refused to obey the order?"

"Objection!" called Daniel Crane, Lilianna's assigned public defender. "The prosecutor has suggested the answer."

"I have no more questions," Miss Wilson returned to her seat with a victorious expression.

"The witness is yours," Commodore Chandrol, a military judge and chairman of the court session, said to the attorney.

Daniel Crane got up and walked over to Kerk. He looked harmless to the eye - a very obese man in his sixties, in an expensive suit and somehow green tie - but Kerk knew he was the best military and civil criminal lawyer in the hemisphere. Who had brought him for this trial was hard to guess.

"You know, of course, General Order number seven," he began. "You also know why it was placed in the code. Would you please inform the court of the reasons for this step?"

It was about the extraordinary powers of the Phalloosians. They were too dangerous and it was impossible to defend against them," the captain replied. "My first mate was present during the first contact with these creatures, and the next, when he turned to them for help for the former commander, breaking the aforementioned General Order number seven. It was necessary to bring him to a military court, which only later turned out to be a real farce, because, apart from the two of us, only delusions were involved in it."

"Exactly. So, is it true that in the notorious Star Armada vs. Mr. Spox case, none of the higher military was involved, but only their phantoms invoked by the Phalloosians?"

"That's true."

"Did these illusions accompany you from the very base where the first officer rebelled?"

"Your honor, the defense is playing for time," the prosecutor couldn't stand it. "It doesn't regard the case."

"On the contrary, it does, and I'm going to prove it."

"Captain Kerk, please answer," said Commodore Chandrol.

"Yes, it's true. Commodore Gomez, for example, was neither on the shuttle nor later on Superprice. He hadn't left the base and he had had no idea what was going on until we told him about it," Kerk replied.

"Thus, the Phalloosian powers reached far beyond their system."

"It looks. In fact, they reached the devil knows how far."

"So, from then on, we know that Order number seven is useless if these creatures want to reach someone, no matter where their target is?"

"I think so."

"I have no more questions."

"The witness is free. Does the prosecution have any other witnesses?" The Commodore looked at Attorney Wilson.

"No, your honor."

"So, I'm ordering a recess and then both sides will make their final statements."

Captain Zakrzevska's face showed that she was very pleased with it. Sitting in a jury and hearing testimony about past events was poor entertainment at best, and in addition, the gala uniform pinched her mercilessly. Through the room where the trial was taking place, passed a colorful crowd: Admiral Cormack, as calm as ever ArCer, delegate Sheolian in a special suit, Commodore Gibbs, who praised the crew of 'Hermash' to the heavens, SiWok, talking about his release and observations, Captain Robau, the two Clingorgians ... The final court of the Star Armada wanted to know absolutely everything, so the trial dragged on for a cruelly long time.

Attorney Daniel Crane made no effort to shorten it, he presented only his own prosecution witnesses, and Lilianna stood hopelessly in the prisoner's dock, trying to look dignified and impeccable. Admittedly, there were quite funny moments, such as the one when the Clingorgians brought in as witnesses refused to testify, but expressed a wish to hold an honorable duel and were terribly offended when refused. Or when Malvinka, who was called to testify, replied calmly that she had forgotten her name overnight. However, in general, Captain Zakrzevska was terribly bored in the courtroom, and in her cell, she slept for the most part, because there was nothing to do there either.

That they can't be optimistic about their case, the lawyer informed her already at the first visit, adding that she wouldn't be released on her own recognizance until the end of the trial. Admiral Cormack made a firm veto in this case, and the judge acceded to his doubts and ordered the defendant to be locked. Lilianna did not care about it, but her crew members organized cat music in front of the courthouse, singing in unison:

"I'll put a screw on your radio

Oooo, Leokadiooo!"

and making very meaningful gestures at the address known in advance. The authorities didn't like this thin allusion, but unfortunately, within the limits permitted by law, unruly Poles could only be fined for disturbing the peace. Now the process was nearing its end, and it could be hoped that something would finally be settled either way.

***

"The prosecutor and defense attorney will now give their closing speeches," Commodore Chandrol said when the recess was over and the courtroom was full again. "The prosecutor will speak first. Just keep it short. I know you lawyers, one gives you the floor, and then there is no help."

"Your Honor," the prosecutor began solemnly. "Please kindly look at the defendant. Here is standing a woman who the Star Armada honored with the title of captain, even though she hadn't even crossed the threshold of the Academy. She received all the help she could get, and all the trust Armada could show her, and how did she pay it back? From the beginning of her journey, she showed a clear disregard for authority and regulations. She tolerated the crew's indiscipline and turned a blind eye to the illegal production of alcohol in the engine room. She turned the Armada ship into a real circus, allowing the crew to set up a kind of Zoo. Her behavior exposed the Union to conflict with the Sheolians and threatened the truce with the Clingorg Empire.

As if that were not enough, this woman broke the most important provision of the Armada Star Code, the prohibition of any contact with the planet Phalloos IV. She didn't pay attention to the threat, nor did she want to listen to the older and more experienced captain, she just did as she wanted to. This best illustrates the character of the defendant. Please don't be fooled by her gentle and honest appearance. She is willful, arrogant and mindless. She doesn't qualify even for steering a barge while rafting. Without any qualms, she endangered her own crew and, worse, the peace that is of paramount importance to all of us. There is no place for people like her in Star Armada. The prosecutor's office asks for the highest sentence and I believe that, given all the circumstances, the high court cannot, simply cannot, pass a lighter sentence."

"Thank you for the caution," Chandrol said wryly. "Now the defender can take the floor."

Daniel Crane stood up and buttoned up the suit on his dignified belly. Looking at his kind smile, one could expect him to agree with Miss Wilson out of mere courtesy towards the fair sex, but he had other plans.

"Your Honor," he began. "I have listened to the speech of my esteemed colleague with real admiration. Until now, I haven't imagined that she could so skillfully manipulate facts, ignoring all that was inconvenient about them, because they are in favor of my client.

It is true that Captain Zak can't boast an Academy degree. The more she should be admired for the fact that, having at her disposal the untypical ship and the poorly assembled crew, she was able to turn both into the efficient tool. The presence of the living mascots on board undoubtedly helped, as it created a homely atmosphere and prevented cosmic neurosis in people who, let us not forget, hadn't undergone any adaptation training.

Further, the prosecutor, for whom I have deep respect, mentioned the conflict with the Sheolians. Why she overlooked the fact that Captain Zak had been attacked and that the first volley came from the Sheolian side is hard for me to understand. Perhaps she doesn't know all the facts. Also, the Clingorgians' accusation, as we know, has been verified. It turned out that my client's actions were fully justified, and what is more, they resulted in the rescue of the missing cadet and the remnants of a hitherto unfamiliar nonhumanoid intelligent race. So, let's move on to the main objection: breach of General Order number seven. Well, according to all data, it is a dead regulation of no practical value. The inhabitants of Phalloos IV are dead, and when they were still alive, they could act at such distances that it was hard to say which actions of a hypothetical officer breaking this order would have been fully autonomous. It can be said that it has nothing to do with it, as the relevant provision in the code still exists. However, the mere existence of a record does not prove anything. If we took at face value everything that is written in the codes of the whole world, people would still be burned at a stake for witchcraft, because the absurd regulation was not removed from a book.

Let's not forget about something else: Captain Zak's deed was dictated by the care of two crews, and to the Phalloos system, she was driven by ... an official order from the command. It read, I'm quoting: "Find and bring to the Union space the lost ships 'Hubble' and 'Tsiolkovsky'. My client carried out this order flawlessly, at the same time taking from Phalloos IV imprisoned visitors from another galaxy. The question arises: can the good officer be condemned on the basis of the dead rule that she broke by following the official order of the command? Is it possible to punish with death for saving a life? No, Your Honor, the administration of justice cannot be unfair. This would destroy the very meaning of its existence. The defense is asking for the acquittal and unconditional reinstatement of the defendant.

Commodore Chandrol looked at Captain Zakrzevska, who was sitting in the dock with an air of innocence and hands folded on her lap.

"Before the presidium goes to the conference, does the defendant want to ask for something in the last word?"

Lilianna stood up, gracefully tossed the braid over her back and delivered a short but blunt speech:

"Your Honor, I was taken to my function from a round-up, literally overnight I was sent hundreds of light years from home. I was given the ship on which half of the instruments were out of order, and the crew, of which majority had no clue about long-range service. I myself had served on such only as part of a short internship. We all had to learn everything from scratch, and it was a hard graft. We were sent to places where Sheolians, Clingorgians and our own artillery shot at us. Our reports were treated as the product of a sick fantasy. I was beyond the galaxy, I was kidnapped by the Pornions, I was struggling with the lack of drive, strange creatures and a million objective difficulties. I reliably carried out all the orders I received. As a reward on Earth, they put me in a jail, as the saying goes, without suspenders and views. For a month now, I have only had contact with my lawyer, I'm present in this room every day, listening to various things about me and being bored stiff. So what should I ask for in the last word? Maybe for a harsh sentence?"

This conclusion caused in the room so maddened merritment that Chandrol had to hit the lectern several times with a hammer.

"The court is going to the conference," he declared.

The entire presidium rose from the seats and went to the back room, while a great chatter collapsed in the room.

LXXIII.

The meeting of the judges' presidium lasted over an hour. At last Commodore Chandrol left and took his seat behind the lectern.

"Defendant, please stand up," he said. "After reviewing the evidence, the military court has no doubt that Captain Zak is not a typical Star Armada officer. There is also no question that she treats the regulations of the service very freely. However, any accusations made against her seem exaggerated, given the unusual circumstances of all the events. It should be emphasized that all the Star Armada captains who had contact with the defendant emphasized her efficiency and commitment. In the opinion of the court, none of the allegations, except the most serious one, was sufficiently justified. As for the breach of Order number seven, the court decides not to impose the sentence, taking into account the following mitigating circumstances:

1. Captain Zak received the official order from headquarters to organize the rescue operation,

2. There was grave concern for the lives of the crews of the two ships, three hundred and eighty-six people in all, and the three beings known as Asgartes,

3. The defendant didn't receive information from the headquarters about General Order number seven, she had never heard of it before, she only knew it from the verbal message of the officer equal to her rank. She didn't have to take his words at face value.

Releasing the defendant Lilianna Zak from guilt and punishment, the court also resolves the following:

if the defendant wants to maintain her rank, she must complete a yearly course for commanders organized by the Armada Star Academy and successfully pass all exams. Only after passing these exams will, she receives the next mission.

"May I ask you something, Your Honor?" Lilianna blurted out.

"Yes, go on."

"What about my crew?"

"It also needs to undergo a training course. However, I see no reason why those who choose to do so can't serve again under your command. The court is closing the hearing," said Chandrol and banged the hammer on the lectern.

There was an uproar in the room. In front of the building, where the crew members of 'Hermash' gathered, shouts and cheers could be heard, and the exiting captain was greeted by a real roar of joy. In the evening of the same day, the crew of 'Hermash' organized a great barbecue in honor of the good ending of the very unpleasant matter. They were all in an euphoric state. Even Arkadiush Liljew indifferently accepted the degradation to the rank of second lieutenant for, as stated in the report, 'inappropriate behavior towards a senior officer'. Jürgen faced a similar punishment. Admiral Cormack didn't remit their refusal to obey, but they both, as they ananimously agreed, "didn't give a damn."

At the barbecue an ad hoc decision was made to set off on another journey together, only Dr. TiShan and Joe Stelmach firmly stated that they were staying on Earth. The doctor stated that she wanted to devote herself to raising her daughter, and young Stelmach decided to return to the bosom of his well-connected family and pursue a career in politics. ArCer and SiWok hadn't decided yet. For now, they were both on their home planet, talking to the Asgartes and trying to get their equipment started, but both considered returning to active duty.

The rest's good mood was overshadowed only by the need to undergo a year of training, which no one wanted to do.

"What the hell, a year is not a sentence, and two years are as for a brother," Father Toadstool kindly consoled his brood. "I will also write to the episcopal curia to get permission to participate in the next flight."

"Aren't you fed up with us yet?" was surprised Matias von Braun, who, having put on an apron, was voluntarily acting as a grill man. "After all, a crew like ours is a God's punishment, you, father repeated it yourself."

"Someone must take care of your souls. It seems that it's my turn to be a specialist in spiritual matters for you," sighed the priest piously and strapped himself to the extremely material sausage with mustard, as if he hadn't eaten in a week.

"And you, Dr. Nbeba?" Sister Ophelia asked the black doctor who was busy with another portion of roast.

"You can go back to Superprice now. It is such a prestigious ship," Lolita Icant accompanied her. But Nbeba just waved his hand.

"Aah," he muttered with his mouth full. "I'm used to you. I'd be bored with a different crew now."

It was only at dawn that the crew finished their celebrations and, as summoned, went to the Armada Star Academy, singing along the way:

"Army was setting out into the battlefield!

One from Płońsk, the other from Gniezno!

To make Poland

make Poland

make Poland a star, oh!"

A new chapter in life, written in white and red letters, was beginning for everyone. Also, for the lecturers of the Academy, who didn't even sense that they would atone for all sins already committed and those not committed, within the next year.

THE END